My Lord John

Georgette Heyer, author of over fifty novels, was seventeen
when she started writing her first book, *The Black Moth*,
to amuse her convalescing brother. It was published in 1921
and is still selling. Although she is known primarily for her
historical novels set in Regency London, she also wrote eleven
detective stories, relying on her husband, a barrister, for the
plots. She died in July 1974, at the age of seventy-one.

Previously published
by Georgette Heyer in Pan Books

Georgette Heyer

My Lord John

'*A vous entiere*' Motto of John, Duke of Bedford

Pan Books London and Sydney

First published 1975 by The Bodley Head Ltd
This edition published 1976 by Pan Books Ltd,
Cavaye Place, London SW10 9PG
2nd printing 1977
© Georgette Heyer 1975
ISBN 0 330 25014 0
Printed and bound in Great Britain by
Hazell Watson & Viney Ltd
Aylesbury, Bucks

Contents

Preface

The fame of my wife, Georgette Heyer, rests largely upon her historical novels, particularly those of the Regency period. But this was not her own favourite: she preferred what she called 'armour', the Middle Ages. She was especially attracted to that period of English history when the House of Lancaster was at its peak, from about 1393 to 1435.

Some years ago she planned a work, a trilogy, to illustrate this period, taking John, Duke of Bedford, the younger and most trusted brother of Henry V, as its central character, for his life-span covered the whole period, and because he was a great man though not today a well-known character. With his death the decay of the Lancastrian line set in.

Her research was enormous and meticulous. She was a perfectionist. She studied every aspect of the period – history, wars, social conditions, manners and customs, costume, armour, heraldry, falconry and the chase. She drew genealogies of all the noble families of England (with their own armorial bearings painted on each) for she believed that the clues to events were to be found in their relationships. She had indexed files for every day of the year for the forty years she was covering with all noteworthy events duly entered on their dates. She learnt to read medieval English almost as easily as modern and amassed a large vocabulary. One summer we toured the Scottish – English borderlands, learning the country and visiting seventy-five castles and twenty-three abbeys (or their ruins). Her notes fill volumes.

For the work, as she planned it, she needed a period of about five years' single-minded concentration. But this was not granted to her. The penal burden of British taxation, coupled with the clamour of her readers for a new book, made her break off to write another Regency story. After such a break it was hard to recapture the spirit of her main work and a good deal of labour to refresh her knowledge. After this had happened a second time, she laid her manuscript aside, foreseeing that at least two more such interruptions would inevitably recur before she could complete the work. So a great historical novel was never finished.

She had, however, completed nearly a third of the whole work, which is now reproduced in this book. The period covered is from 1393 to 1413, almost identical with the period of Shakespeare's *Richard II* and the two parts of *Henry IV*. The first three parts here were finalised by her. The fourth, unfinished, is from her rough draft: this has necessitated some editing.

The historian, A. J. Froude, in his famous purple passage declared that it was not possible for us to grasp the medieval mind. This is probably true. But it may be that, in this work, Georgette Heyer has come closer to bridging the gap than anyone else has done.

G. R. Rougier

The Characters

Richard II, King of England 1377–1399 (Cousin Richard). Son of Edward, the Black Prince (d. 1376), eldest son of King Edward III, and Joan, the Fair Maid of Kent

Anne of Bohemia, his first wife

Isabelle of France, his second wife

Lancaster
John of Gaunt, Duke of Lancaster, Duke of Aquitaine (Bel sire, M. d'Espagne, M. de Guyenne), the King's uncle, third son of King Edward III

Constanza of Castile (Spanish Grandmother), his second wife

Katherine Swynford, his mistress, later his third wife

Henry of Bolingbroke, Earl of Derby, later Duke of Hereford, later King Henry IV, his eldest son

Mary Bohun, Henry of Bolingbroke's first wife

Henry (Harry), their eldest son

Thomas, their second son

John, their third son

Humfrey, their fourth son

Blanche, their eldest daughter

Philippa, their youngest daughter

Joanna of Brittany, Henry of Bolingbroke's second wife

York
Edmund of Langley, Duke of York, the King's uncle, fourth son of King Edward III

Edward, Earl of Rutland, later Duke of Aumâle, later Duke of York, his eldest son

Richard of Coningsburgh, his younger son

Constance, his daughter, wife of Thomas Despenser

Gloucester
Thomas of Woodstock, Duke of Gloucester, the King's uncle, fifth son
of King Edward III
Eleanor Bohun, his wife
Humfrey, his son

Mortimer
Roger Mortimer, Earl of March, grandson of Lionel, Duke of
Clarence, second son of King Edward III
Edmund, later Earl of March, his eldest son
Roger, his younger son
Sir Edmund, his brother, later married Owen Glendower's
daughter in Wales

Beaufort
John Beaufort, later Earl of Somerset, later Marquis of Dorset, eldest
son of John of Gaunt and Katherine Swynford
Margaret Holland, his wife
Henry, later Bishop of Lincoln, later Bishop of Winchester, his brother
Thomas, his brother
Joan, his sister, later married Ralph Neville, Earl of Westmoreland

Holland
John Holland, Earl of Huntingdon, later Duke of Exeter, son of the
King's mother, Joan of Kent, by her third marriage
Bess, his wife, daughter of John of Gaunt
Thomas, Earl of Kent, later Duke of Surrey, his nephew
Margaret, Thomas's sister, later married John Beaufort
Edmund, Thomas's son

Arundel
Richard Fitzalan, Earl of Arundel
Thomas Fitzalan, later Earl of Arundel, his son
*Thomas (Archbishop Arundel), Archbishop of York, later Archbishop
of Canterbury*, his brother
Joan, Dowager Countess of Hereford, his sister, Mary and Eleanor
Bohun's mother, Henry of Bolingbroke's mother-in-law

Warwick
Thomas Beauchamp, Earl of Warwick
Richard, later Earl of Warwick, his son

Neville

Ralph Neville of Raby, later Earl of Westmoreland
Joan Beaufort, his second wife
Sir John Neville, his eldest son by his first marriage
Thomas, Lord Furnivall, his brother

Percy

Henry Percy, Earl of Northumberland (the Fox)
Henry (Hotspur), his son
Thomas, Earl of Worcester, his brother

Mowbray

Thomas Mowbray, Earl of Nottingham, later Duke of Norfolk
Thomas, later Earl of Nottingham, his eldest son
John, his younger son

The Countess of Norfolk a remote cousin of Henry of Bolingbroke,
grandmother of Thomas Mowbray
Sir Hugh Waterton, governor of Henry of Bolingbroke's children
Sir Robert Waterton, his cousin, constable of Pontefract Castle
Thomas Swynford, Katherine Swynford's son by her first marriage
Sir Robert Umfraville, a friend of Ralph Neville
Gilbert, his nephew
John Talbot, a friend of Harry's
John Oldcastle, later Lord Cobham, a friend of Harry's
Henry Scrope of Masham, a friend of Harry's
Richard (Archbishop Scrope), Archbishop of York, his uncle
Reginald Grey of Ruthin, a friend of Henry of Bolingbroke
Master Chaucer, a scrivener
Messire de Froissart, a canon of Chimay

In France

Charles VI, King of France
Isabeau, his wife
Louis, Duke of Orleans, his brother
Charles, later Duke of Orleans, Louis of Orleans' son
Philip, Duke of Burgundy, the King's uncle
John (the Fearless), later Duke of Burgundy, Philip of Burgundy's son
John of Montfort, Duke of Brittany
Joanna, his third wife

In Scotland

Robert III, King of Scotland

James, later James I of Scotland, his son

Robert, Duke of Albany, his brother, *later Regent after Robert's death in 1406*

In Wales

Owen Glendower (Prince of Wales), leader of the Welsh forces

Part One
Richard the Redeless
1393–1399

Ther is no hye estate so saddle and stable,
  Remember wele, lat it not be forgete,
But he to falle in perile is ful able.

Hoccleve: Regement of Princes

1 M. de Guyenne

1

The children had been sent to play in the herber with Kate
Puncherdown. The damsel hired to serve the youngest of four
nobly born imps was glad to escape from indoor tasks on a bright
June day, but she thought it due to her dignity to tell Agnes
Rokster that it did not lie within her duty to wait upon the
Lord John. Agnes said: 'I am sure it is never my lording who
makes unease in the nursery! You may take him to oblige me.'

'You may take him because you are bid!' said Johanna
Waring.

'Oh, well, to oblige *you*, Agnes—!' said Kate.

Johanna resented this, and took an unthinking revenge. 'And
if I were you,' she said disastrously, 'I would not let my lord
Humfrey go a step without you hold his leading-strings, for he
looks so baggingly, poor sweeting, that I dread to see him walk
into a wall and break his sely nose!'

This was importable provocation. My lord Humfrey had an
irregularity in his left eye, but to say that he squinted was a piece
of wicked despite. My lord Humfrey – he was not two years old
– was a child of singular promise: intelligent, well-grown, and
(Kate said significantly) so lusty that he had never caused his
mother to feel an hour's anxiety.

The rush of colour to Johanna's cheeks should have told Kate
that it was needless for her to add: 'What a pity that my lord
Harry should be so sickly, and he the eldest!'

It was fortunate that the nursery-tower lay at some distance
from the Countess of Derby's chamber, for the jangle of strife
would not have pleased her. But the Lady Blanche's nurse,
swaddling the infant in fresh bands; and Johanna Donnesmere,
who had charge of my lord Thomas, listened to the quarrel with

unshadowed enjoyment, for each knew herself to be unassailable. No one could find fault with the fair babe in Isobel Staines's lap; and no one could deny that of all the Lancaster brood my lord Thomas was the stoutest as he was the most well-visaged. From the day that he had come fighting into the world (so unlike the Lord Harry, who had had to be slapped before he would draw breath!) he had not suffered a day's illness. My lord Thomas's nurse had never been obliged to sit through a distressful night because a fond grandparent had stuffed her charge with marchpane. While my lord Harry retched and retched, my lord Thomas, more than a year his junior, slept soundly beside him, no more disturbed by a surfeit of doucets than by a tumble from his pony. The worst anyone could say of my lord Thomas was that his was not an influence for peace in the nurseries; and not the most jealous nurse could pretend that a hot temper and a determination to have his own way were characteristics to be regarded with anything but pride.

When everything that could possibly be said in disparagement of one boy of seven and one infant who had just learnt to walk out of leading-strings had been uttered, the quarrel ended, and Kate took the children into the garden, carrying Humfrey down the newel-stair, and giving John her hand to hold.

The inner court was flooded with sunshine, and seemed oven-hot after the cool of the castle. It was almost surrounded by buildings, so that there was not enough stir in the air even to ruffle Kate's coif. Most of these buildings were new, including those on the south side of the court, which housed the family. Indeed, neither the Chapel, situated towards the base-court to the east, nor the Great Hall, occupying most of the western side, were quite finished. Masons and dauberers were always at work; and the nintey-foot front of the Hall was still masked by a scaffolding. Behind this, the walls, like the rest of the castle, glowed pink in the sunlight. The old Hall had looked much like the Keep, which towered at the north-east angle of the court, and had been built hundreds of years before, when even kings' palaces were lit only by slit windows; but the new Hall was quite a different style of building, with an oriel, and four other windows with pointed arches and many lights. They were richly

16

ornamented; and ever since the family had removed from Peter-
borough to Kenilworth the Countess's ladies had not ceased to
complain that they could hear the 'chip-chip' of the masons'
hammers even in their dreams. The nurses were not behindhand
with their grutchings. It was predicted that while the Lady
Blanche lost her sleep the lordings would break their necks,
clambering over the scaffolding, and losing their footholds. But
the Lady Blanche slept through the worst of the hammering;
and although the lordings fulfilled the expectations of those who
knew them best by swarming all over the scaffolding, and
driving every honest craftsman out of his five wits by the per-
tinacity of their questions, not one of them had yet been picked
up lifeless in the court.

The lordings loved Kenilworth: loved it so much that
throughout their lives it remained in their hearts a place of
happiness, rosy-hued, and soaked in sunshine.

2

To reach the herber, which lay beyond the inner curtain wall,
the little party had to pass the base of the Grand Staircase, which
led up to the door into the Great Hall, traverse the kitchen
courtyard, and go through a postern. It took time to accomplish
the journey, since Kate allowed herself to be detained in the
kitchen-court by a man-at-arms in the blue-and-white livery of
the family; but the herber was reached at last, and my lord Humfrey set upon his feet. Too young to be interested in the disports
of his brothers, he toddled off on some ploy of his own, and was
soon happily engaged fast by the Swan Tower, a look-out built
in the angle of the barbican. John paid no heed to his away-
going, but squatted down with the toy he had found in the
depths of a hutch in the nursery.

It was a fascinating toy, originally one of a pair, given to
Thomas by Cousin Richard, the King: two puppets, clad in
armour, each holding in one hand a sword and in the other a
buckler. The limbs were jointed, and there were strings attached
to them, so that if you learned to manipulate them cunningly the
puppets could be made to fight, like real knights. Only God and
the devil knew what Cousin Richard had paid for them, had

17

said Bel sire, their grandfather, when he saw them. Fool-largesse, he called the gift; but perhaps that was because it had been bestowed on Thomas, rather than on Harry, or on John, who was his namesake, and his favourite grandson. Only one of the mammets had survived Thomas's rough handling, and that one had long outworn its novelty, and had been tossed into the hutch, to lie forgotten there until John discovered it.

It was hard for the fingers of a four-year-old to manipulate the mammet, but impatience was not one of John's failings. He set himself to master the toy; and Kate, seeing him thus absorbed, presently yielded to the becks of the man-at-arms, and left the curtilage. The children were quite safe: neither was old enough to climb the wall, and so tumble into the mere which lay at the foot of the castle mound; and if John took it into his head to explore the scaffolding round the Great Hall he would be obliged to pass through the kitchen-court on his way to it, and must so come under her eye again.

No such ambition crossed John's mind; he was engrossed with the puppet, and would have continued to struggle with the wayward movements of its limbs had he not been interrupted. Thomas, released from his lessons, came bounding across the greensward, pulled up short beside his brother, stared for a moment, and then exclaimed: 'That's mine!'

A mulish look came into John's face. He clutched the mammet to his chest, but said nothing.

'Give it to me!' ordered Thomas, stretching out his hand.

'No!' said John.

This seemed to Thomas a monstrous thing. 'Why, you buzzard, you – you hell-puck!' he cried, borrowing from the vocabulary of those worshipful craftsmen at work on the Great Hall. 'Give it to me at once!'

Abusion left John unmoved; but as Thomas snatched at the mannikin he quickly laid it down behind him on the grass. Unlike Thomas, who would have torn it asunder in the struggle to get possession of it, he was determined that it should not be broken in the inevitable fight. The next instant both the noble lordings were locked in what bore all the appearance of a death-grip. Thomas was a year older than John, but John was the

18

more powerfully built, able to hold his own for several minutes. In the end, Thomas would overpower him, but he had once succeeded in tripping Thomas, and although he had been too much surprised to take advantage of this triumph he hoped one day to do it again, and to follow it up in a suitable fashion.

Neither combatant was destined on this occasion to bring the other to the ground; they were wrenched suddenly apart, and found that their eldest brother, Harry, was between them. 'Fliting again!' said Harry, in mimicry of Johanna Waring. 'What's amiss?'

Thomas, always jealous of Harry, said, 'Nothing to do with you!' and tried to close with John again.

Harry held him off. He was a slim boy, but surprisingly strong. 'Stint!' he ordered. 'I said, what's amiss?'

Thomas might resent Harry's assumption of authority, but he knew better than to provoke his anger. He said: 'He stole my mannikin!'

Harry turned his eyes towards John. 'I did not!' John declared, going very red in the face at such a knavish accusation.

'What mannikin? Whose is it?' demanded Harry.

'Mine!' shouted Thomas.

'John?' said Harry, keeping his eyes on him.

Harry had very bright eyes, the colour of hazel-nuts. When he was pleased they were as soft as a dove's, but when anything angered him their expression would suddenly change, and then they more nearly resembled the eyes of the lions painted on Bel sire's shield. The smallest feeling of guilt made it impossible to meet their challenge. John did not attempt the feat. He began to dig a hole in the greensward with the toe of one foot, and kept his gaze lowered. 'Well,' he said. '*Well* . . .'

He was almost felled to the ground by the buffet Harry dealt him. 'Give it to Thomas!' Harry commanded.

He picked it up, and held it out rather blindly, since his eyes were watering. By the time he had blinked away this moisture Harry had gone, and Thomas, the mammet lying disregarded at his feet, was staring in astonishment towards the postern.

John eyed him, but without much fear of reprisals. Thomas fell out of his rages as quickly as he fell into them, and never bore malice. He turned to look at John, exclaiming, 'He took my part!'

John sniffed. 'You knew he would!'

'No, I never thought it! Why did he?'

'He knew it was your mannikin,' said John, manfully owning the truth.

'But he likes you best!' said Thomas.

This put all thought of the puppet out of John's head. There was no one whom John loved as he loved Harry, but it had not occurred to him that a brother removed from him by such a span of time as three years could prefer him to Thomas. He said: 'No, d-*does* he?'

'No force! I was sure he would give the mammet to you!'

'No,' said John. 'It was yours.'

'Well, if I liked anyone best I would take his part!' declared Thomas.

'Harry wouldn't.'

'He ought to!'

'Not if it is wrong. Not Harry.'

'Oh, wrong!' said Thomas. Tired of the discussion, he added: 'Here, you may have the mammet! I don't want it!'

But when they looked for the mannikin it had vanished, because Humfrey, who had deserted his play to watch the fight between his brothers, had borne it off while they argued. By the time it occurred to them that he must have taken it, he had grown tired of a toy too intricate for him to manage, and had abandoned it in a bed of gillyflowers. When Thomas demanded to be shown where he had dropped it, his lip trembled, and he said piteously, '*Kate*!' which was one of the few words he knew.

'I daresay he doesn't understand,' observed John.

'Yes, he does,' said Thomas, giving Humfrey a shake. 'Show me, Humfrey!'

Whether or not Humfrey understood what it was that Thomas wanted, he perfectly understood that Thomas was displeased with him, and he broke into lamentation. His cries brought Kate Puncherdown to his rescue, her kirtle caught up in both hands, and her coif askew. She snatched him up, calling him her pig's eye, her cinnamon, her honey-hive, and scolding Thomas for having hurt him.

'What a little swineshead he is!' remarked Thomas. 'I didn't hurt him!'

Kate wiped Humfrey's blubbered cheeks with the palm of her hand. He stopped crying, and suddenly chuckled. 'Thomas!' he uttered.

Thomas knew that it was cunning, not fear, which had prompted Humfrey to set up a yell, but he was unresentful. No one could be angry with Humfrey for long. He said: 'Oh, well! Make him show where he put the mammet, Kate!'

After some persuasion Humfrey pointed to the gillyflowers, but before his brothers had found the toy Kate said sharply: 'Listen!'

They stood still, their heads jerked up.

'In the base-court! Someone has arrived!' said Kate.

3

When my lord Derby was from home his castles were so quiet that the visits of such everyday folk as a pardoner, selling indulgences; a chapman, with knacks to tempt the maids; or a wainsman, with a load of merchandize sent from London, were events of interest. The children made for the postern as fast as their legs would carry them. Thomas reached it first, and darted through it to the kitchen-court. Kate, hampered by Humfrey on her arm, brought up the rear. Her ears had not deceived her: someone had certainly arrived at Kenilworth, and someone of more importance than a chapman or a pardoner. The castle, which had before drowsed in the sunshine, now seemed to be alive with expectancy. Kate saw Thomas, and, shifting Humfrey to sit astride her hip, called out to him, 'Who is it, lording?'

'A herald!' shouted Thomas.

'Whose?' panted John.

Thomas was not sure. It was an important part of any young bachelor's education to learn to recognize at a glance the shield, the colours, and the badges of a gentle family, but it was not an easily-mastered lesson, and he was not six years old, after all. He said: 'Well, I only saw him a hand-while. They have taken him in to Mother.'

'Perhaps he has brought a letter from my lord,' said Kate, in the voice of one resigned to disappointment.

The lordings discarded this suggestion as unworthy. A herald would certainly be employed on such an errand, but it was more likely that this one had been sent to warn the Countess of the arrival of some distinguished visitor. A dizzy thought entered John's head, perhaps because Thomas's mannikin had brought Cousin Richard to his remembrance. 'Do you think it is the King?'

Thomas stood spellbound for a moment. It was impossible that children of quick in-wit, living in a large household, should not have grasped from the clapping of servants that Cousin Richard was not universally held in high esteem, but in their eyes he was a magnificent personage, distributing largesse with a lavish hand, and indulging small cousins in a manner as gratifying to them as it was displeasant to their preceptors. He was said to hold exalted ideas of his state; but whenever the children had been in his company it had been with a conscience-stricken effort that they had remembered to say 'Sire,' and 'Pleaseth it your Majesty,' as they had been taught. Even Harry forgot the deference due to Cousin Richard when Cousin Richard called him his little nuthead, and played at kyle-pins with him, and pretended to hold him in awe, because (he said) he thought he must be the Henry of whom it was long ago prophesied that he would achieve such greatness that the world would be lit by the rays of his glory. It seemed strange that anyone so full of merry japes could have so many enemies.

The children suspected that even Father was not overly fond of Cousin Richard, although he always spoke of him with reverence. Yet there had been a time when Father had actually taken up arms, not, indeed, against Cousin Richard himself, but against the Earl of Oxford, who had been the King's dearest friend. He and the Earl of Nottingham had joined forces with the older Lords Appellant, the King's uncle of Gloucester, and the Earls of Warwick and Arundel, had led an army to the gates of London, and had been admitted, and had thrust their way into

22

the royal palace of the Tower. Old Wilkin, who had been in the service of the family for longer than anyone could remember, said that their leader, Great-uncle Thomas of Gloucester, had soothed the King's mind by showing him the army drawn up on Tower Hill. The lordings knew what such ambages as that meant, and none of them wanted to hear more of a story that was so discomfortable. It was splendid to hear how Father had routed the steerless Earl of Oxford at Radcot Bridge; but when it came to hearing that Great-uncle Gloucester had threatened the King with deposition it was no longer splendid. None of them liked Gloucester, who was an overbearing person, nearer to Father in age than to Grandfather, whose brother he was, and generally on bad terms with both of them. He had ruled the country for a year; but he had demeaned himself so intemperately that moderate men were driven off from their allegiance to him, and hardly anyone was sorry when Cousin Richard took the government back into his own hands.

That was another of Cousin Richard's japes: the children never wearied of that tale. They could picture Cousin Richard, playing with one of his jewels, perhaps swinging to and fro the sapphire which he sometimes wore round his neck, and suddenly unsensing his Council by asking them how old he was. When they told him that he was two-and-twenty, he thanked them, and said that he thought he was now old enough to govern for himself. Then he had taken the Great Seal away from my lord of Arundel, and had given it to the Bishop of Winchester, and nobody had dared to withsay him.

That had all happened in the year of John's birth, and no one had tried since than to wrest the government from Cousin Richard's hands. There was a good deal of grutching at his rule, but he had never brought back the favourites the Lords Appellant had made him banish, so the chief grievance they had held against him had disappeared. He had new favourites now: contemptible foppets, according to Bel sire, but a source of entertainment to the lordings. Some of them wore piked shoes so long and pointed that the toes had to be attached by silver chains to their garters; some had short pourpoints with dagged sleeves trailing on the ground; some affected hoods twisted to look like

23

coxcombs or rabbits' ears; others preferred tall hats, with peacocks' feathers stuck up beside the crowns; and not one of
them would dream of having a mantle lined with any less costly
material than taffeta.

'Oh, I do hope it may be Cousin Richard!' exclaimed Thomas.

'Not when my lord is from home!' said Kate.

'Grandmother?' suggested John, not hopefully.

Thomas's face fell. A sister of my lord of Arundel and a
Bohun by marriage, Grandmother was a very great lady, and
one who set store by manners and learning. When she came to
stay at Kenilworth the children went about on tiptoe; and if they
so far forgot themselves as to fall into one of their hurlings the
sight of her tall figure in its widow's weeds was enough to make
them spring apart, smoothing tumbled raiment, and trying to
look as if they had not been fighting at all.

'No, no!' said Kate. 'It is only a month since my lady of
Hereford left us!'

They brightened. Grandmother spent much of her time with
Mother, her younger daughter, when Father was away, but she
would hardly return to Kenilworth so soon, particularly when
she had left it for Pleshy to visit her elder daughter, Great-uncle
Gloucester's wife.

At that moment Harry came strolling up. When his brothers
shouted to him that someone had arrived, he said: 'I know. Who
is it?'

'A herald,' answered Thomas. 'Well – a messenger, anyway!'
Harry cocked an eye at him; he reddened, and added: 'I only
saw him a pasternoster-while!'

Harry grinned. Kate, seeing the Steward, ran to intercept him.
'It is not my lady of Hereford, is it, good Master Greene? Is it
a message from my lord?'

'A'God's half, woman, don't spill my time with asking questions!' he replied testily. 'My lady of Hereford, indeed! It is
M. de Guyenne, coming with a great company, no later than
tomorrow!'

His words carried across the court to the ears of the children.
Harry let a shout, and flung his cap in the air; Thomas began to
caper. 'Bel sire!' shrieked the noble lordings.

4

A visit from Cousin Richard would not have seemed to them an event of so much importance. Cousin Richard was the King, but he could not govern his realm without Bel sire's support. He had thought, once, that he could, and had been glad to see Bel sire set sail to fight in Spain, for he was jealous of him, and ever and again suspected him of plotting to seize his power, though why he should do so was obscure. Perhaps it was because his favourites never ceased to drop poison in his ears; and perhaps he knew, at his heart-root, that he had nothing to fear from Bel sire; for although he had several times fallen into one of his fits of rage merely because some brew-bale had hinted that Grand-father was imagining treason, these never endured for long; and when he found himself beset by the Lords Appellant he had not hesitated to recall Bel sire from Spain. Bel sire had been in favour with him ever since: he even wore Bel sire's collar of SS; and he had created him Duke of Aquitaine for life.

Many people supposed that it was these distinctions which were the cause of the enmity between Bel sire and my lord of Arundel, but old Wilkin knew better. 'Nay, nay!' he said. 'M. d'Espagne could not forgive the Earl the death of his friend Sir Simon Burley: that was what began the garboil! Yea, I warrant you! For when the Lords took arms against the Earl of Oxford and the other rush-bucklers about the King, my lord of Arundel would have Sir Simon's head with all the rest, no force!'

So many of Bel sire's old servitors still called him M. d'Espagne that the lordings knew quite well whom Wilkin meant, and merely corrected him, saying: 'M. de Guyenne,' to which he paid no heed, because he was too old to master new-fangled titles. He had first followed Grandfather to Spain ferne-ago, with Great-uncle Edward, the Black Prince, who was Cousin Richard's father, and had parted his life so long ago that he was no more real to the lordings than Sir Theseus of Athens. It was sleeveless to remind Wilkin that Bel sire had relinquished his claim to Spain to his daughter, their aunt Katherine, when he had married her to the King of Castile's son, because the only thing Wilkin ever found to say of the Queen of Castile was that he remembered her as a puking infant.

'Yes, it was my lord of Arundel that would have Sir Simon's head off, mark me!' Wilkin said. 'My lord of Derby, your noble father, would have spared him, and the blessed Queen was three hours upon her knees, begging that he might not be headed. And my lord of Arundel said to her: "M'amie, look to yourself and your husband: you had much better!" Ah, he is an orgulous man!'

The lordings nodded. They knew that my lord of Arundel had grown so orgulous that he had lately dared to marry the Earl of March's sister, without license. He had had to pay a large fine for his presumption, and no one had been more indignant at his conduct than Bel sire. To make matters between them worse, the new Countess of Arundel had behaved rudely to Dame Katherine Swynford, Bel sire's mistress, and that was an affront Bel sire would not readily forgive. It was true that the Countess was of the blood-royal; but, as Mother told Harry, when he ventured to enquire into these matters, so were other ladies, notably Aunts Philippa and Elizabeth, whose governess Dame Katherine had been, and who always conducted themselves buxomly towards her.

And to crown the rest there had been a rising in Cheshire only a month or two ago, which Cousin Richard had sent Bel sire to quell; and Bel sire was making no secret of his belief that my lord of Arundel was behind the insurrection.

'Let the Fitzalans look to themselves!' said Wilkin. 'Out of dread, M. d'Espagne will take order to them!'

The lordings thought that it must go ill with Arundel if Wilkin were right, for they could not conceive of anyone more powerful than Bel sire. The chain of his castles stretched across the land, from remote Kidwelly, in the Welsh Marches, up and up to Dunstanburgh, which was so far north as to be almost in Scotland. Bel sire himself could not recite the full tale of them; and the children, coached by his retainers, who knew them all so much better than he did, could never carry more than a bare dozen in their heads. There was Grosmont; Kenilworth, which they considered their own; Hertford, Bel sire's favourite; Leicester, Bolingbroke, where Father had been born; Tutbury; High Peak; Chester; Halton; Liverpool; Clitheroe; Pontefract;

Knaresborough: all these, and many more besides, garrisoned by the men in Lancaster blue-and-white; to say nothing of the manors, the franchises, and the advowsons which were dotted all over England.

People called him M. d'Espagne before he relinquished his claim to the throne of Castile; they called him M. de Guyenne now that he was Duke of Aquitaine; but when his herald announced his coming in full state he named him John, by the grace of God, Duke of Lancaster, Duke of Aquitaine, Earl of Lincoln and Leicester, Baron of Hinckley, Lord of Beaufort and Nogent, of Bergerac and Roche-sur-Tonne, Lord High Steward of England, and Constable of Chester.

And some spoke of him familiarly, by the name of his birth-place, Ghent, or their English version of it, and called him John of Gaunt.

5

In all that great household only Mother remained undisturbed by the news of Bel sire's coming: everyone else, from the Marshal down to the meanest kitchen scullion, was thrown into such a state of agitation that one might have supposed that the visit was as unwelcome as it was unexpected. It was not, of course. The Marshal might wring his hands over the state of the Great Hall; the head cook inform the Clerk of the Kitchens that no mortal man could devise and execute subtleties for the high table in one day; the Yeoman of the Cellar declare by the faith of his body that if my lord Duke should call for a cup of mus-cadelle he would be totally undone; and the Gentleman Usher demand where he must find lodgings for the ladies, if my lord Duke, as was all too probable, brought a bevy of them in his train; but no one acquainted with these persons doubted that they were all of them a-charmed by the prospect of several days of unremitting toil and contrivance.

The only thing which caused the Countess anxiety was the demeanour of her sons. She gathered the three elder ones about her, and reminded them of the things they must and must not do. M. de Guyenne was a haughty prince, but he showed another face to his grandsons, and could be trusted to encourage them

27

to take all manner of liberties with him. But, like many other indulgent grandparents, he would be more than likely to censure their parents for malapert behaviour which he had himself invited. So the Countess warned her sons that they must not speak until spoken to; and must then stand still, not allowing their eyes to wander, not forgetting to bow to their grandfather, and not forgetting to call him Bel sire. M. de Guyenne belonged to the generation that clung to the Norman–French which was falling into disuse, and this would please him.

'And at table,' pursued the Countess, 'take heed that you lay the bones on the voider, and wipe your mouths before you drink! Don't leave your spoons in the dish, or dip your meat in the salt, or lean on the table!'

'Shall we dine in the Hall, madam?' asked Thomas eagerly.

'Yes, you and Harry,' replied the Countess.

A lump rose in John's throat. He said nothing, but stared woodenly before him.

'And John, madam!' said Harry.

The lump swelled to uncomfortable proportions. There was no service John would not have performed for Harry at this moment, but he did not look at him; he turned his eyes upon his mother.

She hesitated; and then, reflecting that her woman, Mary Hervey, could share a mess with Thomas and John, and might be trusted to keep them in good order, nodded. 'Yes, if he will mind his manners.'

'I will!' John said.

'And Harry must not eat of the boar's head, or the viand royal,' added the Countess, remembering a fell day when a messenger had been sent foot-hot to London to summon a physician, Master John Malvern, to Harry's sick-bed.

His colour rose; he said quickly: 'No, madam, no!'

'But I may eat of both, for I am never sick!' boasted Thomas.

'Madam, madam, Doucet is tangling your skein!' John interrupted.

All three boys dived for the little spaniel at the Countess's feet. It darted away, the skein of silk between its teeth, and the children in pursuit. The popinjay in its cage nearby began to

screech; and in the confusion Harry's queasy stomach was forgotten. He said nothing to John; but later in the day, when it was
learnt that Bel sire's Yeoman-at-horse had arrived at the castle,
with two fewterers in charge of greyhounds, a ymerer, and
several grooms and chacechiens, he allowed John to go with
him and Thomas to visit these interesting officials. They were
lodged with the parker, by the Chase, but there were more ways
out of the castle than by the great gate at the end of the cause-
way. There was a postern on the southern side of the base-court
which opened on to the slope above the mere: trust my lords
Harry and Thomas to know where the key to it was to be found!

When it was discovered in the nurseries that the lordings were
missing, consternation reigned, all the nurses rushing about the
castle precincts like so many flustered hens. Happily for the
Countess's peace of mind, none of them dared tell her that her
sons were lost. It was Johanna Waring who had the wit to run
to the lordings' tutor. Father Joseph was a cheerful person, with
plenty of kind-wit, and he did not for a moment suppose that
the lordings had been drowned, or stolen by robbers. He bade
the nurses stint their clapping, and himself sallied forth to bring
home the truants. They were in the kennels, of course, the
hounds all over them, and their raiment smutched out of recognition. Father Joseph's eyes twinkled, but he pointed awfully
towards the castle. The lordings went meekly up the steep slope
to the postern, and Father Joseph came after, his long robe
brushing the nettles beside the path. He whipped them all, and
for several hours they lived in dread lest he should have disclosed
their villainy to Mother. It seemed probable that none of them
would be permitted to dine in the Hall while Bel sire was at
Kenilworth. Only Harry maintained that Father Joseph was no
carry-tale, and he was right: Father Joseph held his peace; and
when M. de Guyenne's meiny was reported to be at the gate
next day, the Countess waited in the inner court to receive him
with her three elder sons grouped touchingly round her, all
dressed in their best gowns of scarlet tartarin, with silver-gilt
girdles of Father's forget-me-not badge round their waists; all
redolent of the rose-water with which they had been scrubbed;
and all looking as sely as saints.

6

It had not occurred to M. de Guyenne that his daughter-in-law
might like to know the number and the degrees of the persons he
was bringing to visit her in her seclusion, so the lordings were
not the only members of the household to scan with anxiety the
cavalcade that swept presently into the court. There was a
horse-litter: that might mean that the Duchess had come with
her lord, but more probably it carried Dame Katherine, his
mistress, decided the Countess's ladies. The Duchess – she was
not the children's grandmother, but the Duke's second wife, a
Castilian princess – rarely accompanied her lord on his pro-
gresses. She lived mostly at Leicester, and was very pious: quite
unlike her younger sister, who was married to the Duke of
York, and of whom some merry tales were told. No one could
feel surprise that M. de Guyenne had looked beyond the
marriage-bed, for he was one who liked a lady to be witty and
well-visaged, and the Duchess, poor soul, was as dull as she was
dish-faced. His first wife, the heiress of Lancaster, had been one
of the loveliest of the Court dames: my lord Harry was said to
resemble her.

Riding beside M. de Guyenne, on one of the strange ladies'
saddles brought into England by King Richard's good Bohem-
ian Queen, was a lady of great beauty, at sight of whom the
Countess's heart sank. One would never wish to speak despitously of one's lord's own sister, but it was impossible to
forbear the thought that if Bess had not been M. de Guyenne's
daughter she must have hidden her head in a nunnery, seven
years ago, instead of marrying the King's half-brother, and
riding about the country in a mantle lined with ermine, and a
wired coif of such preposterous dimensions that her hood would
not cover it, and was allowed to hang carelessly down her back.
Handfast to the Earl of Pembroke she had been, and had played
him false with Sir John Holland, half-brother of the King. She
had been found to be with child by Sir John, and M. de
Guyenne had had to delay his departure for Spain to settle the
affair. So well had he done it that although everyone knew she
was divorced from Pembroke very few people knew just what
had happened to bring about this sad state of affairs. The infant

had not survived; and the marriage to Sir John was celebrated with as much pomp as if it had been a decently arranged contract instead of the hasty union which it really was. King Richard had created his half-brother Earl of Huntingdon, so that it seemed as though it was true that the wicked flourished like bay trees.

There was no doubt that the Earl of Huntingdon was a wicked man. Besides being a spouse-breaker, he had certainly one murder to his discredit, and probably two; and no one could doubt that it was her desperate attempt to induce King Richard to pardon him the death of young Stafford which had killed their mother, the Dowager Princess of Wales. To make matters worse, he claimed kinship to my lady of Derby, his elder brother having married one of her Fitzalan aunts. This gentleman, the Earl of Kent, although not, as far as anyone knew, a murderer, was generally held to be as great a cumberworld as Huntingdon. A bad, upsprung family, the Hollands: the Countess hoped that Bess had not brought her husband with her to Kenilworth.

She would have been startled had she guessed that her sons' eyes were just as swiftly searching the cavalcade for signs of Huntingdon as her own; and shocked to have known that he figured in their minds as an ogre whom it was a terror and a delight to see. They knew quite as much as she did about his plunging his sword into Hugh Stafford's heart, and riding off with the echo of his own fiercely uttered name still quivering on the night air; for they had had it all from Wilkin.

'Yes, yes,' said old Wilkin, 'that was what slew the Princess of Wales, dead as a stone, for she was a corpulent dame, look you, and all that running about to save Sir John from having his head took off was what killed her, poor soul! Ay, I remember her when they named her the Fair Maid of Kent, so lovesome she was, and her middle no thicker than two hands might span! But so it goes! Three ells of cloth it took to make her a gown at the latter end! Ah, well! God assoil her! She lies in her grave now, and King Richard for very grief gave Sir John his life, more's the pity, for mark me if he does not work a greater mischief yet!'

The lordings knew not whether to be glad or sorry that the Earl had not accompanied Aunt Bess to Kenilworth. They accepted their aunt's arrival with indifference, and craned their necks to see who else was following Bel sire. A fleshy young man, with a look of sleepy good humour, rode immediately behind him: Cousin Edward of Rutland, Great-uncle York's elder son. If he could be coaxed to talk he had enthralling stories of the chase to recount, for he was a great hunter, and already knew more of the ways of harts, hounds, and horses than men twice his age. Beside him rode Uncle John Beaufort, about whom there hung a mystery the lordings had not yet unravelled. There were three Beaufort uncles, and also Aunt Joan Beaufort, who had lately married the Lord Ferrers of Wem; but why they should be called Beaufort instead of Lancaster was a problem no one had satisfactorily explained to the lordings. Johanna Waring said that it was because they had been born at Beaufort, and that children who asked questions would go supperless to bed; Agnes Rokster said that it was because Dame Katherine was their mother, but that answer was no better than Johanna's, because Dame Katherine's son was Thomas Swynford, as everyone knew. He was one of Bel sire's retinue, but certainly not his son, which the Beauforts as certainly were.

Of the three Beauforts it was Henry whom the children liked the best. In spite of the fact that he was not a knight, but an oblate priest, he was better company than Sir John. Sir John was a disappointing uncle. He was very handsome, and so notable a jouster that when he was only fifteen years old he had been Father's and Sir Harry Percy's only rival at the great jousts held at St Ingelvert. He had been on a crusade to Barbary, too, and had helped to take Tunis; but he was taciturn, and could never be lured into divulging his adventures. The children were shy of him, finding his grave smile more awesome than his youngest brother Thomas's horse-play.

7

M. de Guyenne, alighting from his hackney, raised his daughter-in-law from her curtsy, and embraced her. He approved of the Countess: she was pretty, and shamefast; she had borne her lord four sons; and she was heiress, with her sister of Gloucester, to the possessions of the great house of Bohun. It was not a small thing to have married the Earl of Hereford's daughter. Henry of Bolingbroke was first cousin to the King, but he did not disdain to add the Bohun Swan to his badges. Indeed, he taught his children to be as proud of the Swan as of his own Antelope, or the single Ostrich Feather of Lancaster.

'Well, and so I find you in good heart, ma mie!' said the Duke, holding Mother at arm's length, and looking her up and down. 'You will not lack a husband many weeks now, let me tell you!' He laughed to see the glow in her cheeks, and added: 'Yes, I have had letters from my son! You shall see them presently.'

'He is in Venice,' disclosed Lady Huntingdon, who had been lifted from her palfrey by her cousin Rutland. She offered her cheek to her sister-in-law, saying: 'I hope he may remember to buy some gold fringe there, but I daresay he won't: men never think of anything! Edward, why don't you help Dame Katherine down from that stuffy litter, instead of standing awhape? Is there a freckle on my nose that you stare so?'

Rutland assured her that there was not, and turned to do her bidding. The fact that he stood high in the King's favour had led him to embrace all the extravagances of fashion, but it could not have been said that a pourpoint scarcely reaching to mid-thigh, with sleeves padded high at the shoulders and their dagged ends brushing against his ankles, flattered his burly figure. Bess Holland gave a giggle, and exchanged a mischievous look with my lady of Derby.

M. de Guyenne had turned to survey his grandsons. The three elder boys louted till their noses nearly touched their knees; and Kate Puncherdown, who was holding Humfrey in her arms, curtsied to the ground. 'Well, my mannikins, you have grown!' said M. de Guyenne, seeing this as a praiseworthy thing. 'What have you all learnt since I saw you last, eh? Are you scholars yet? Can Harry play another air on the gitern?'

Harry, like Mother, was musical. He said: 'Not the gitern, sir, but the harp!'

'And I can ride my pony, Bel sire!' said Thomas, forgetting Mother's precepts.

'Thomas, not so hardy!' Mother said.

But Bel sire was in a benign humour, and he only laughed, and said that before he went away he would see all their accomplishments. After that the noble company trooped into the Great Chamber; the Countess's ladies begged those who attended Dame Katherine and my lady of Huntingdon to accompany them to the bower; the Steward and the Yeoman took the gentlemen of the Duke's household in charge; horses were led off to the barmekin; chests and coffers were carried into the several buildings of the castle; but just as the nurses were trying to remove the children out of the bustle they caught sight of an elderly man, rather thickset, and dressed in sober raiment, who was watching them with a smile in his eyes; and they broke from restraining hands, and ran across the court, shouting: 'Master Chaucer! Master Chaucer!'

8

Only Father could have been more welcome, and not even Father could tell such stories, much less have them transcribed in bound volumes. Bel sire, who possessed these, said that one day they should be allowed to read them, a promise which they received with more civility than enthusiasm. None of them wished to struggle with the written word when they could listen to the stories from Master Chaucer's own lips. Sometimes he would tell them as their nurses might, only much better; and sometimes his expressive voice would drift into poetry, reciting lines that made the lordings' ears tingle, even though they might not always understand them.

He was not one of Bel sire's household, but Bel sire was his patron; and at one time his wife had been in attendance on Spanish Grandmother. He did not seem to have liked his wife very much, but he was on good terms with Dame Katherine, who was her sister. His purse was a farthing-sheath, yet he had held several good appointments in his time. Bel sire, who had given him one of the pensions he had sold in a moment of stress, said that he was unthrifty; but he said it indulgently, because Master Chaucer had thought no lady the peer of Grandfather's first wife, and had written a long poem about her death, and

Grandfather's grief for it. There were some good bits in the poem about hunting; but far too much of it was taken up with the moan of a Man in Black, who appeared to be Bel sire, bewailing the death of Grandmother Blanche of Lancaster. It did not sound at all like Bel sire, and the lordings disliked it. Master Chaucer quite understood their feelings, and he never inflicted the poem on them, unless commanded to do so by Bel sire, when he naturally obeyed, but with such a twinkle in his eye that the lordings forgave him.

The nurses knew that there would be no hope of wresting their charges away from Master Chaucer without a brawl, so although they knew the poet to be a mere scrivener, and (if report did not lie) at one time guilty of a scandalous fetching, they raised no objections to his taking care of the lordings for an hour. The lordings dragged him off to see all the wonders of the Great Hall; and here Bel sire, who had himself come to cast an eye over the stonemasons' work, found them. 'Ah!' said Bel sire. 'So you have met a friend, have you? Well, Master Chaucer? Do you see something of my lady in this knave?'

He dropped his hand on to Harry's head, and Master Chaucer, pulling off his hood, said: 'Verily, monseigneur.' He added, in a soft voice: ' "So steadfast countenance, So noble port and maintenance!" '

'Well, well, we shall see!' Bel sire said. 'What was it that you wrote? "Ruddy, fresh, and lively-hued," eh?'

The lordings resigned themselves. Bel sire was going to recite the lines which described Grandmother's golden hair. He would falter for a word, and call upon Master Chaucer to take up the tale; and after that they would be lucky if they escaped hearing the whole of the poem.

9

M. de Guyenne supped in the Great Chamber, with only his kinsfolk and the more important members of his household to bear him company. When the roasted apples were set upon the table, the blanch-powder, and the cheese, the ladies withdrew. Bess, who had exchanged waitings of eyes with Rutland throughout the meal, grew weary of him, and went away to her bedchamber, regretting the whim that had prompted her to accompany her father on this journey.

Dame Katherine was left with her hostess in the bower, eating dragés from a silver bowl. She was able to give the Countess good rede on the cure of infantile complaints, for before he had raised her to be his mistress she had had the care of the Duke's daughters by his first marriage; but in-wit told her that it was not of her children that the Countess wanted to talk; and she was not surprised when Mary of Derby dismissed the ladies who attended on them. She said: 'Well, and now we can be cosy! Out of dread, madam, you will be blithe to have your lord home again!'

'Yes,' Mary said. She paused, and then said, almost inaudibly: 'Oh, yes! If I were not so much afraid!'

This did surprise Dame Katherine, for although my lord of Derby's wooing had been hasty, she had always supposed Mary to have tumbled headlong into love with him. 'Afraid?' she repeated.

'Of the King!' said Mary, staring at her.

'Oh, come, come!' said Dame Katherine. 'The King is well disposed towards your lord!'

'No,' said Mary. 'He does not love my lord.'

'Well,' said Dame Katherine, 'I daresay he is jealous of him, for they are exactly of an age, and your lord has won so much worship that it is no wonder the King should have envy at his heart.'

'The King will never forgive my lord for Radcot Bridge,' said Mary.

'Oh, now, what a foolish gaingiving! They say the King has never spoken Oxford's name since the day he broke in on him, crying that he had been betrayed, and his army scattered. Oh, dear, what a miserable creature Oxford was found to be, wasn't he? No, no, I warrant you the King never spares him a thought!'

'But my lord joined the Lords Appellant, and the King doesn't forget that. My lords of Arundel, and Gloucester, and Warwick stand out of his grace, and sometimes, madam, I cannot help but wonder – and fear!'

'Oh, I am sure you are wrong! I should not say it, but you

may take it for truth that no one was ever yet able to 'scape quarrelling with Gloucester! Handsome is as handsome does – people used to say he was the fairest of all the old King's sons: well, those golden curls *do* take the eye, don't they? – but whenever I hear of the borel-folk raising a cheer for him as he rides past, I can't forbear thinking to myself, Yes, it's very well to smile, and look so debonairly, but if ever there was a man with a sturdier temper may I never meet him! No, no, you can't wonder at the King's setting him from his grace! And as for Arundel, it's time someone took order to him, or he will grow so large there won't be room for another in the realm. Content you, the King looks on your lord with quite another eye. He and Nottingham were never in so deep!'

'Madam, I wish he had not joined Thomas Mowbray of Nottingham! I don't trust the Mowbrays!'

That gave Dame Katherine a moment's pause. 'Well, no, there I don't say you are wrong, and a strange alliance I always thought it, for there has never been any love lost between Lancaster and the Mowbrays. You can't explain these things! I've seen it happen oft and lome: one family will just naturally mislike another, and if they were all holy saints it wouldn't make any difference, for no force but that one of them would chew his meat in a fashion that gave offence to another, or some such witless thing! But as for these thoughts of yours about the King, my dear, put them from your head! Why, there's no one stands higher in his grace than Monseigneur, and would he do his son scathe, think you?'

'Richard,' said Mary, 'never forgets, and he never forgives. He waits.'

Dame Katherine reflected that Mary must have been thinking of the way in which Richard had brought down the Lords Apellant four years ago. It was true that Richard had waited: rather surprisingly, for he was a man of impetuous temper. But he had been younger then and the poor boy had had a fright. Dame Katherine knew what perhaps Mary had never been told, that his uncle Gloucester had threatened him with the death of Edward II. No wonder he had stayed quiet for a whole year! The only wonder was that he had dared to raise his head again.

But he had dared, choosing his moment. Dame Katherine, about to pop another dragé into her mouth, but it back in the bowl. Mary was rousing discomfortable thoughts. She said uneasily: 'Well, he is a strange man, but there is always the Queen, and she is one for peace, give her her due!'

'I have heard Monseigneur say that the Queen is too easy, will not do what she might.'

'Oh, now, that is not just! I daresay she has her troubles, like the rest of us, and does as she may!'

'He is asotted of her,' said Mary.

That was true, and oddly true, thought Dame Katherine, for you would be hard put to it to find a plainer woman. Such a shock as it had given them all when they had first clapped eyes on her! She was a German, sister of the Emperor Wenzel, and of Sigismund, King of Hungary, and platter-faced, like so many of her race. She did what she could to distract attention from her lack of beauty, but neither the dimensions nor the magnificence of the coifs she had made so fashionable had deceived critical eyes. Everybody had expected the young King to turn from her in disgust, but he had seemed to love her from the start. Dame Katherine was heartened by this reflection, and said: 'Yes, so he is, and so you may be easy! She may not steer him always as she should – well, good soul, she has no more notion of strait-keeping than he! – but she is not one to bosom up malice. Mark me if she does not lead the King to her own kind way!'

She saw that Mary was pensive still, and leaned forward to pat her hand. 'You have been husbandless overlong: there is nothing makes a lass so mumpish!' she said, in her warm voice. 'All this roiling about the world! If I have said once I have said a dozen times that a married man would do better to mind his affairs at home. Let your lord leave crusading to greenheads like my son John, and you will soon be amended of your cares, my lady! There, then, he will not keep you waiting long, please God!'

2 Beau Chevalier

1

He did not keep them waiting long. Before the household had settled down after M. de Guyenne's visit, it was known that my lord Derby had reached Calais. Ships were being chartered for his passage; he had applied for a licence to bring certain foreign goods through the Customs; and Derby Herald had ridden to Kenilworth with letters for my lady.

The children were wild with excitement, their chief concern being to discover what Father was bringing home from his travels. Only Harry and Thomas were of an age to remember it, but even Humfrey knew that Father had brought them a bear from Pruce, when he had gone there to fight for the Teutonic Knights. It had found its way into Cousin Richard's collection of wild beasts in the Tower, but it was still their very own bear: Cousin Richard said so. They tried to find out from Derby Herald what Father had for them this time, but he would only grin, which made them certain that it was something of more than ordinary splendour. Then they forgot about this in the bustle of removing from Kenilworth to London. Father owned a great inn, called Cold Harbour, in Dowgate. It was part of Mother's inheritance, a stately stone mansion of many storeys and countless rooms, occupying all the ground between All Hallows Lane and Hay Wharf Lane. It had been built by a rich merchant, and sold by him to the Earl of Hereford for the payment of a rose at midsummer. It was situated on Upper Thames Street, but it was set back from the street, behind the Church of All Hallows the Less, under whose steeple and choir its arched gateway was curiously placed. It could be reached as easily, however, by water, for its gardens and tenements ran down to the river to a private strand. It was one of the largest of the

39

London inns, and so secluded that it was possible to sojourn there even in July, when the heat made much of the city noisome, and the dread of pestilence haunted the minds of anxious parents.

For a little while the lordings found enough to interest them on the river. Despising the spaceful inner court, with its lawns and flowers, they made the quay their favourite playground. Here, within flight-shot of the Steelyard, with its high, embattled walls enclosing the Hanse merchants, they would watch the tilt-boats drifting past, and learn to recognise the galleys of Gascony and Genoa, the woad-ships from Picardy, the Flanders scuts, the common whelk-boats from Essex, and the laden lighters coming down river from Oxford, all putting in to Billingsgate and Queenhythe. Once they saw, jump-eyed, the Lord Mayor's gilded barge making its stately way towards Westminster; but although they could obtain a distant view of London Bridge they were not close enough to see the traitors' blackened heads that embellished it, or to watch the barges and the wherries shooting the arches – not always, as their valet delightfully informed them, without dire mishap. They soon became clamorous to be taken to see these sights, and many more besides.

Across the river, east of the orchards and the meadows on the Surrey bank, a huddle of buildings with spires and towers rising amongst them had been pointed out to the lordings by a well-meaning but daffish servitor. That, he said, was Southwark, little recking what visions he conjured up in their minds. At Southwark, they knew, could be seen the Tabard Inn, familiar to them from Master Chaucer's tales, the Clink, an awesome prison, where such men as babbled and frayed on the streets were clapped up; and the Marshalsea, a high court where matters of chivalry were decided by the Lord High Constable, and the Lord High Steward. Who, demanded the lordings of their harassed attendants, had a better right than they to visit these places? Was not Bel sire the Lord High Steward, and had they not heard Master Chaucer's tales from his very own lips? The nurses, and Father Joseph, thinking of the naughty stews, of which the lordings were as yet unaware, said repressively that Southwark was no fit place for nobly born imps, not foreseeing the time when the lordings would be known and welcome guests at every tavern on the south bank. But Southwark was only a part of what the lordings wished to see. They wanted to visit the ruins of Bel sire's old palace of the Savoy, burned before their time by an angry mob; they wanted to see the Great Conduit in West Cheap, with the bakers' carts from Stratford gathered round it; the Tun, in Cornhill, where night-walkers were imprisoned; the menagerie at the Tower; the great ships in the wharves east of the bridge; the horse-fair at Smithfield, without the walls; and all the teeming life in the narrow streets, where, between the limewashed houses, sleds were drawn noisily over the cobbles, and one might see guildsmen in their liveries, apprentices ripe for mischief, a jack-raker, a water-bearer, trundling his tankard along on wheels, a town-crier: all humdrum sights to town-bred persons, but to the lordings invested with the magic of novelry.

But Mother feared that one whiff of the air blown from the meaner streets would infect them with sickness; they were not allowed to go beyond the wall of the inn; and the gatekeeper was a pebblehearted person who refused to open the gates as much as a crack to let them peep at the busy world. They had hoped that at the least they would be taken to High Mass in St Paul's Cathedral, for Father Joseph had told them that there was a clock there, with an angel whose arms pointed to the hours. Not even this was permitted; they attended Mass in their own chapel, for although it was now forbidden to the citizens to cast household refuse on to middens at their gates, and pigs no longer rootled in the kennels, Mother suspected that in the poorer parts of the town these abuses still continued, just as she suspected that the rules for the clean disposal in the markets of offal were too often broken. The nurses, with the exception of Johanna Waring, were as disappointed as their charges; but Johanna had no opinion of London, and said that it was bad enough to bring the sely children into a city where the bells made more din than the masons at Kenilworth, so that they would all become diswitted, without exposing their precious persons to the evil infections that were well known to lurk in crowded streets.

The sely children, of course, showed no signs of becoming diswitted: it was Johanna's head which ached. The bells rang all day, and (Johanna said) all night too, for not only was the Gabriel bell rung at dawn in every church, but bells rang earlier still for the morrow-mass. After that they rang incessantly until the hour of Prime from all the larger churches, where Masses were said at short intervals. Warning bells, sacring bells, passing bells, bells controlling the markets, and handbells sounded in a confused jangle until curfew bell was rung from four churches within the walls. The city grew quieter then, for after curfew only persons of good repute might walk abroad. Many, of course, who were of extremely bad repute did walk abroad, and several times Johanna was awakened by the hubbub of a hue and cry. The only thing that roused the sely children was a fire, which broke out close to Cold Harbour one night. The bells rang in every neighbouring church, the beadle's horn blared, and shouts and screams, and the crash of falling timbers, as men pulled down the blazing walls with iron hooks, rendered the night hideous. It was enough, Johanna said, to make the sely children forstraught. In fact, their enjoyment of the episode was only marred by the refusal of their attendants to allow them to run out to see all the excitement. They knew that during the summer months every household was compelled by law to set a leathern bucket of water outside its gates at curfew-time, and nothing would convince them that they were not old enough to form links in the chain of men handing these from the river to the doomed house. 'We might as well have stayed at Kenilworth!' said Thomas, furious at this prohibition.

Then that grievance was forgotten with all the others, because Father was with them at last; and the inn throbbed with as much life as could be found without its walls. As soon as he came home there was movement in the house, and sudden laughter; the comings and goings of strangers; clatter of unknown voices; the ring of hooves in the outer court; and the echo of minstrelsy creeping through an unshuttered window to drift into the children's dreams.

They had thought they had been able all the time to picture him clearly, but when he stood before them they knew that they had forgotten much that came flooding back to their memories: the upward jerk of his chin when he laughed; the quick turn of his head; the russet lights in his hair; the arrested smile in eyes as bright as Harry's; and the searching gleam that flashed for an instant and then was gone, like a blade half-drawn from its sheath.

He was of no more than middle height, but so well-made that it was easy to see why he was the most famous jouster of his day. His movements were decisive; and for all his look of strength he was rarely ungraceful, and never, even when arrayed in his harness, clumsy.

The Londoners loved him as they had never loved his haughty father. No angry mob would ever burn Henry of Bolingbroke's house to the ground. When he rode into the lists at Smithfield the apprentices stamped and cheered their approval, and sober citizens did not disdain to join in the roar of applause that burst forth when he unhorsed his adversary, neatly, as only the best jousters could, the blunted point of his lance striking his rival on the helm, and tumbling him out of the saddle. The Londoners knew all his tricks, and they used to wait for them, and nudge one another when they saw him take his lance and balance it for a moment in his hand, like a jongleur, before setting it in the rest, and grasping it with the cuddling gesture that never failed to delight them. That was the kind of lord they liked: a handsome, jolly knight, richly caparisoned, splendidly horsed, riding forth with a noble meiny at his back, but not so high that he had not a wave of his cap for a cheering crowd, a jesting word to toss to a maid hanging out of an upper window, and a 'God thank you!' for a common fellow who ran to pick up the glove he had dropped.

He was brought to the gates of his inn by a rout of apprentices who ran beside his horse, shouting 'Noël' to him. 'I thank you, I thank you!' he called, jostling a way through them. 'But let me pass, good friends, a' God's half!'

He had sent one of his squires forward from Southwark, and the youth had arrived just long enough before him to give the Countess time to reach the outer court, her children gathered about her, before his company clattered into it. He sprang from his saddle, caught her up in his arms, and held her, and kissed her, laughing at her protests, saying in his quick way: 'Who has a better right, madam? Tell me, then!'

But when he had kissed her again he set her down, and turned to his children. They were shy, but he was delighted with them, exclaiming: 'By the faith of my body, ma mie, we have done well by each other, you and I! This young squire my Harry? This Thomas? And is this great creature little John?'

They were all three kneeling, but he had them on their feet in an instant. It was he who knelt, so that he was on a level with them, the better to scan their faces, holding John within his arm, stretching out his hand for Harry and Thomas to kiss, asking if they had forgotten him, and if they had been tendable to Mother while he had been away. Then there was Humfrey to be greeted, and Blanche to be admired, and he was calling out to one of his company: 'Will you match me this brood of mine, Hugh?'

Then, embracing them all in his bright, smiling glance, he said: 'What do you think I have brought you, my sons? Well? Well?'

'Oh, what, sir?' cried Thomas.

But he would not tell them; he would only say things like, 'A birch-rod,' which made them dance with impatience; and he swept Mother into the house while they were still pelting him with questions.

They had been right in guessing that he had brought them something of more than ordinary splendour: he had brought them a leopard and a tame Turk. The Turk was rather too tame for their tastes, but the leopard was all that could have been desired. Father had chartered a special ship for its voyage; and for a week it was housed in the garden, pacing up and down behind the bars of its cage, and snarling in fiendly wise. For a week Mother endured sleepless nights; for a week the nurses prophesied disaster; and then Thomas, to his lasting shame, woke in the small hours yelling that the leopard was eating him up; and the leopard, like the bear, went to the menagerie in the Tower.

Hardly had Father's bales of baggage been untrussed than he went to visit the King, as his duty was. Cousin Richard was summering at Sheen, and Father took Harry with him, so that the other lordings heard all about it. Sheen was the Queen's favourite palace. It was built beside the river, in a great garden, and it was so crammed with treasures that Harry could not remember the half of them to describe to his brothers. The King was always spending fortunes on the adornment of his person or his palaces. One of the first things he did, on the arrival of his cousin of Derby, was to take him to see a set of hallings, executed by Michel Bernard, and sent over from Arras. Father admired them much, which pleased the King. In fact, nothing could have gone off better than this visit. The King was at his most gracious. He made Father tell of his adventures, while he lounged on a carved seat under an elm tree, and ate cherries out of a gilded bowl. He wore a short pourpoint, one half of it pink and the other white, the trailing sleeves being lined with bawdekin, which shimmered in the sunlight. His hose were white, too; and the toes of his shoes curled upwards in stiff points. His eyes were so blue, and his scented curls so fair, that Harry thought that the princes in Johanna's fables must have looked just like him. Cousin Richard made Harry sit at his feet, and from time to time he dangled a cherry above him, dropping it as soon as Harry opened his mouth.

He was not much interested in Father's sleeveless errand to Pruce. He said: 'And so you disbanded your followers, and went to visit the Holy Sepulchre! How you do troll about the world, fair cousin! Did they make you good cheer in Venice?'

They had made Father royal cheer in Venice, feasting him for days on end; and many foreign knights had challenged him to combat.

'And you unhorsed them all!' said Cousin Richard, letting fall another cherry into Harry's mouth.

'Oh, not all, sire!' Father replied, laughing.

'Shivered their lances, then. We can't believe you were not the victor, can we, my little nuthead?'

'Well, perhaps I had the advantage,' Father admitted.

'No force! And then you sailed for the Holy Land?'

Father had sailed for the Holy Land in a galley equipped for him by the Venetians. He had landed at Jaffa, but the hospitality he had received during his journey had made it only possible for him to pay a flying visit to the Holy City. Sir Thomas Erpingham, alone of his company, went with him; they were led by a guide called Jakob; and their baggage was carried on a donkey. But on his way home Father stayed for some weeks in Milan, the guest of Gian Galeazzo Visconti, whose daughter Great-uncle Clarence had taken to be his second wife. Cousin Richard was much more interested in that, because Gian Galeazzo was a patron of the arts, as he was himself, and collected even costlier treasures. Harry had not paid much heed to this part of the conversation; he had a more impressive piece of news to divulge. He said carelessly: 'And I am to enter Cousin Richard's household.'

'You are not!' said Thomas.

'No?'

'When?' growled Thomas.

'Oh, well – as soon as I am old enough!' replied Harry. 'I am to be one of his pages: he said so!'

3

At the Cold Harbour the Great Hall teemed with guests, not only at the dinner-hour, but often at supper-time, when the Steward would frequently find himself with so many unexpected mouths to feed that he had to send varlets running to the cook-shops for messes and cooked meats to eke out the provisions. The children took no part in these entertainments, but they could hear the minstrels; and they had seen the female tumblers

46

who walked on their hands; and the joculator who had an ape and a cock trained to walk upon stilts; and the troupe of dancers who capered about to the tinkling of the bells sewed to their motley.

Then the household removed again to Kenilworth, and remained there through the autumn months. Father seemed to be content to stay at home. He played at handball with his gentlemen; he hunted buck in the Chase, or went hawking; he began to teach Harry and Thomas their knightly exercises; and he played chess with Mother. Whenever in after years the lordings looked back to that golden time, the sounds that echoed in their ears were the far-off notes of the forlogne; and the picture that rose in their memories was of Father and Mother playing at chess, the sunlight slanting into the chamber, and one of Mother's little dogs lying curled up in the pool of warmth it cast on the floor.

The lordings made a new friend this autumn, for the Earl of Warwick was sojourning at his great castle nearby, and he used to ride over to Kenilworth, bringing his son with him. Richard Beauchamp was eleven years old, which at first made the lordings stand in awe of him. He had beautiful manners, and he was already expert in arms. Father said he wished his own sons showed such knightly promise; and Mother said that they should take heed how demurely he behaved; but in spite of this unpromising beginning the lordings liked him. He was not tall, but well-made, like Father. He had curly brown hair, a long upper lip, and a delicate nose that turned up slightly at the tip. It was not long before the lordings discovered that he was not as quick-witted as they were: sometimes it would be a full minute before he was able to perceive a jest they had all seen in a flash; and when they asked him what thing was most like a horse, or why men set cocks instead of hens on church steeples, which were quite easy riddles propounded by their domestic fool, he could never guess the answers, but stood with an anxiously knitted brow until one or other of them shrieked the answers at him between gusts of rude laughter. He was a proud boy, often quite unbending, but he never minded being laughed at by Harry and Thomas; and when they fell into

47

hurling he was far too chivalrous really to exert his superior strength against them. His father was almost as old as Bel sire, and, like him, he was engaged in large building plans. He used to prowl about the Great Hall at Kenilworth, shaking his head over the expense of such an erection. He was adding a new tower to his own castle at Warwick, besides building a church there; and if you had not known that he was swimming in riches you would have supposed that the costage was ruining him. The lordings thought him as troublous as Great-uncle York. He pretended that he came to Kenilworth to watch the progress of the building; but what he seemed to want to do was to be private with Father: talking, talking, and always with his lips close to Father's ear, as though he were afraid of being overheard. The lordings often saw them pacing about the herber together, my lord of Warwick's hand on Father's shoulder, and a look in Father's face that told his sons he was holding his temper on a tight rein.

Father set a guard on his temper, but he was not a patient man, and nothing exasperated him more than folly or clumsiness. He would fold his lips, but sometimes his irritation got the better of him. The lordings quaked when they saw a certain flash in his eye. He was a fond father, but they knew better than to presume on his indulgence. John and Humfrey could take liberties with him, for he dearly loved the babies of his family; but Harry and Thomas frequently fell into disgrace, and smarted for hours because of some piece of recalcitrance. Thomas erred through a love of mischief; but Harry was too much inclined to pit his will against Father's.

'That whelp,' my lord of Derby more than once told his lady, 'will live to be a thorn in our flesh!'

Then he would catch sight of Harry, running like a hare in a game of Bars, easily outstripping Richard Beauchamp, and he would exclaim, softening: 'God's love, the boy runs as fast as a hart!'

He was proud of Harry's musical talent, too, and of his quickness at his lessons. Harry, leaving Thomas labouring behind him, had mastered his hornbook, and was at work on a Latin primer. Father had no liking for unlettered gentlemen.

Not until the leaves dropped from the trees, and the mists, rising from the mere, stole into the castle, did they leave Kenilworth. A November day saw my lord of Derby's household setting forward upon the road to Leicester. The lordings were disconsolate, foreseeing winter days ahead, when they would be kept between the walls of Bel sire's castle, and made to mind their books. 'I wish we might live at Kenilworth for ever!' said Thomas.

'When the summer comes again we shall return,' Mother answered.

'I don't suppose it ever will!' muttered Thomas.

John said nothing. Curled up in the litter at Mother's feet, he looked beyond Thomas's pony to Kenilworth, still pink, but fading fast into the fog. Summer would come again, but it would not be the same. Harry might be a page in the King's household; Father might have gone overseas again; Richard Beauchamp would certainly be a squire, with no longer leisure to play with them.

Harry, riding on the other side of the litter, said: 'One couldn't stay always in one place! I want to go on!'

'Where will you go, my son?' Mother asked, tenderly watching him. 'What will you do?'

He coloured, but he did not speak. It was Thomas who supplied the answer. 'France, like Bel sire, and he will make a grande chevauchée! I know what Harry means to do!'

'But Bel sire is making a peace with France,' Mother reminded them.

'A sickly peace!' Harry said quickly. 'That's what Wilkin says!'

'Oh, Wilkin!' Mother said, laughing.

3 Parting Hence

1

It seemed afterwards as though Kenilworth, which held the summer, held also the happiness of the lordings' childhood; as though when it slipped into the mist tranquillity vanished with it. If there was happiness at Leicester they could never remember it, yet there must, they supposed, have been happy days in Bel sire's castle. There had been Christmas-tide, with mumming in the Great Hall, sweet music provided by Spanish Grandmother's foreign musicians, and a joculator who created illusions so astonishing that Johanna Waring signed herself, and muttered that it was sorcery. Father had visited the castle then; probably he had brought gifts for his sons, but they were forgotten too. They saw little of Father that winter; he stayed in London, with Bel sire. He was keeping his sword loose in the scabbard, if Wilkin were to be believed, for my lord of Arundel's enmity was growing apace. He was one of many who disliked M. de Guyenne's peace policy, seeing it as shameful that the conquests of the King's father and grandfather in France should slip away, the Treaty of Brétigny become meaningless, England, year upon year, be threatened with a French invasion. But his enmity had its root in something that struck nearer to the bone than that. A scandal was whispered through the chambers of Leicester Castle. Bel sire's son, Messire Henry of Beaufort, had got my lord of Arundel's daughter, Alice Fitzalan, with child. Oh, yes! She had been his mistress since he had returned from his studies abroad. No question of marriage, of course; he was a priest dedicate, already held two prebendaries. Well, well, he was not the only man in Holy Orders with a bastard or two to his discredit; and, to do him justice, he was rearing the child at his own costage. A personable youth, Messire Henry: one could not wonder at the Lady Alice's wanton conduct; one could only be surprised that my lord Arundel should not have caged this dove of his more securely, instead of scheming, when the mischief was done, to pull down the whole house of Lancaster.

In late November, when draughts crept up the stairs and whistled under doors, stirring the rushes, and making all the ladies tuck their robes round their feet, news came to Leicester that Great-aunt York was dead. She was Spanish Grandmother's sister, so the lordings were put into mourning clothes, and scolded if they dared to play a game. There were endless services held in St Mary's Church, fast-by the castle, and reached through a private doorway; nothing might be sung, said Thomas sulkily, but *placebo* and *dirige*. Thomas had had to endure a homily for humming *Dieu sauve dame Emme* within Father Joseph's hearing. Agnes Rokster said it was well for him that the Father was too holy a man to know the words of that song. They were certainly rather rusty: Thomas had picked them up from the men-at-arms.

It was an uneasy winter. The Countess was childing again. She seemed nervous, starting at sudden noises, her eyes too large for her face. The nurses put their heads together, nipped their talk off in mid-sentence when the lordings came within earshot. My lady had borne her lord six children, four of them easily enough, God be praised! But her first two sons had nearly cost her her life. The eldest had never drawn breath: she had been too young for childbearing, as one person at least had known. Her mother, my lady of Hereford, had removed her daughter from her lord's side after that disaster. Later had come my lord Harry. Jesu defend! Would any of the ladies forget that summer's night at Monmouth? The child born out of time, my lord from home, my lady so forspent that they had all thought the soul parted from her body; and the infant so puling that no one had expected him to live an hour: ah, what a night that had been! But Thomas, John, Humfrey, and Blanche she had carried proudly, and dropped as easily as any Nance or Moll. She had not waxed thin, or lost her colour; she had not jumped almost out of her skin at the lifting of a door-latch, as now she did.

Wisps of rumour filled the castle: it was a relief when some part at least of the truth was known to the lordings. In the New Year Bel sire accused the Earl of Arundel apertly of having fostered that Cheshire rising. My lord let his spleen carry him too far: his counter-accusations came near to touching the King. Cousin Richard had himself upheld his uncle of Lancaster; and the end of it was that my lord was forced to utter a humiliating apology, while Bel sire stood higher than ever within the King's grace. Only Mother and Great-uncle York seemed still to see a wolf at every turn. Great-uncle York came on a visit to Leicester, with his younger son, Richard. The lordings, who liked good-natured Edward of Rutland, were not fond of Richard of Coningsburgh. He had fewer than twenty years in his dish, but a sneer had already worn clefts that ran down from his nose to the corners of his mouth. Unlike Edward, he was slenderly built, took little interest in the chase, and had womanish habits, such as wearing his hair in overlong ringlets, loading his person with jewels, and being much inclined to fancy himself slighted on small provocation.

Great-uncle York seemed to be more concerned with his brother Bel sire's affairs than with the death of his own wife. He was one who hated to be caught up in the toils of warring factions, for he could never see clearly what was best to be done, and was always worrying about it. When M. de Guyenne was in Spain seven years ago, Edmund of York had allowed his forceful brother Thomas of Gloucester to drag him at the heels of his own policy. It had frightened him; and he had been relieved to welcome M. de Guyenne home again, because he had believed there was safety to be found in his shadow. And now, just as he was thinking how wise he had been to abandon Gloucester for Lancaster, what must Lancaster do but quarrel with Arundel? It was all very well for Lancaster to think himself secure because he had driven Arundel from Court, but no one could think that Arundel was not even now planning his revenge. And since Thomas of Gloucester was Arundel's friend, and only God and His Saints knew which way the redeless King would jump, the future was so dangerful that Edmund of York could neither relish his meat nor sleep sound at nightertale.

M. de Guyenne, however, thought himself safe enough to

leave England in the late spring. Not many weeks after the Countess of Derby was brought to bed of a second daughter, he set out for France at the head of an embassade. He left my lord of Derby to manage his affairs: another circumstance which threw poor Edmund de Langley into a fever of foreboding. What, he demanded of his Spanish sister-in-law, did Harry of Bolingbroke know of plots and stratagems? A splendid man in the jousting-field, and possibly a good leader of crusades, but a rashhead if ever his uncle saw one!

The Duchess of Lancaster said piously that the Trinity would have them all in keeping: an observation which made Edmund remember his dead wife with quite a pang. Not by any means the most shamefast of wives, poor Isabella – in fact, much too gamesome a lady – but worth a score of women like this sister of hers. With all her faults (and he shuddered to recall them) she would never have met his fears with so unhelpful a truism.

2

The new baby was christened Philippa. She was a lusty infant, and my lord, with four sons to stand between his name and oblivion, was delighted to have fathered a second maid-child. He came to Leicester to carry her to church; he would have taken the Countess back to London with him had she been in stouter health. But she had barely enough strength to drag herself from her couch to be churched; and my lord rode away without her. Letters arrived from him presently, commanding my lady to remain in Leicester until he came himself to fetch her: an outbreak of pestilence had driven the Court away from London, and my lord would not for his life bring his wife into the infective area.

The Countess's women had a tale to tell of night-sweats and tossings from side to side on an uneasy pillow: the Countess could not rid her mind of its dread that one day Derby Herald would come riding up to the castle on a foundered horse, crying to the gateward to open, so that he might lose not a moment in flinging himself at my lady's feet with the news that my lord was stricken with the pestilence, and she must make all speed to London if she desired to see him alive.

But it was not at my lord of Derby that Plague pointed a bony finger. In June the servants whispered to my lady that death was stalking abroad in Leicester town: no honest death of kind, but a terror that gripped men overnight, and released them only at their forth-bringing. The gates of the castle were shut; the lordings told that they must forgo their hopes of watching the pageant on the Feast of St John the Baptist. Almost at once they were caught up in a fate over which they had no control. At the break of a summer's day, at the hour of Lauds, the nurses woke their charges, shaking the sleep out of them, bundling them into their raiment, thrusting bowls of brose into their hands, and telling them to eat, and to spill no time in asking questions: they were going on a journey. Where were they going, demanded Harry: was it to Kenilworth?

'Kenilworth? No! Deliverly, now, and eat your brose!' Johanna said. When he pressed her to say more she answered that they were going to my lady of Hereford's castle at Bytham.

That was all she would tell them; but before they left Leicester Mother came to the nursery to bid them farewell; and she explained to them that Spanish Grandmother was sick. When she was amended they should return, and perhaps set out for Kenilworth again. She blessed them all, and seemed as though she could not bear to let them go. Her maid, Mary Hervey, said to her: 'Madam, go yourself, for God's love!'

Mother was holding Humfrey's face between her hands, tilting it up so that she could gaze into his eyes. She pressed a kiss on to his mouth, startling him. Then she rose from her knees, saying; 'No, I must remain, as my duty is.'

Bytham Castle was one of my lady of Hereford's dower houses. It was not very large, and it was situated in the undulating country between Stamford and Grantham. With Kenilworth it could not compare, and the lordings disliked it on sight. Grandmother Hereford was not there; they were welcomed only by a harassed steward, who seemed to have scant notice of their visit. Nothing was in readiness for guests, and there were not many servants at the castle to wait on them. However, the lordings brought so many nurses, valets, pages, and chamberers that this was not a felt want. Some of the nurses grumbled that the castle was old-fashioned, the chambers too small, and ill-lit; not a shot-window in the whole building! But Johanna bade them stint their grutching, and be thankful to have escaped from pestilence-stricken Leicester.

It was dull at Bytham, with no Wilkin to regale them with rambling stories; no companies of jongleurs; scarcely a chapman to break the tedium of empty days. Kyle-pins, closh, quoits, and even Dun-is-in-the-mire (which was popular with the lordings largely because the nurses frowned on it as a lewd, rustic game) palled; and when Harry and Thomas tried to practise their knightly exercises Thomas all but put Harry's eye out with the withy-wand which served him for a lance, so that that sport was forbidden.

A feeling of expectancy dwelled in every corner of the castle. The nurses were always on the watch from turret windows; and the sight of a horseman in the distance was enough to make them clutch their bosoms, and utter such disturbing exclamations as 'Christ it me forbid!' or 'God have us in His keeping!' The lordings paid little heed, for no traveller seen from afar ever proved to be anyone more interesting than a reeve trotting home from market, or a friar mounted on a donkey. When a servant with the badge of the Ostrich Feather of Lancaster on his sleeve did at last arrive at the castle he took them by surprise, for they had begun to think themselves forgotten.

The man brought ill tidings: Spanish Grandmother was dead of the plague.

The nurses said Wellaway! They had known from the start how it would be: had not the children's thirdfather, Henry, the first Duke of Lancaster, come to his last end at Leicester, and of the plague too? The lordings felt more awe than sorrow. What disquieted them more than the knowledge that they would not see Spanish Grandmother again was the discovery that the Foul Death could touch their lives so nearly. They knew how dread a disease it was: Wilkin had told them stories of the great plague that had swept over England when he was a boy; how one hundred thousand persons perished in London alone, and Sir Walter Manny, that was a worshipful knight, of his charity bought a plot of ground outside the walls and in it buried fifty thousand poor souls whose bodies were carried out of the city piled like turves upon dung-carts. Men called it the Black Death, but although the lordings knew that it had claimed one of Great-grandfather King Edward's daughters, it had never occurred to them that it could come so much closer to them. Year upon year the servants spoke of the pestilence, telling how it had visited this district or that, and slaying serfs flock-meal; but it had not seemed as though it could enter the castles of the nobly-born.

All the mourning clothes were pulled out of the hutches again, but the children were not taken back to Leicester to attend the requiem services for Spanish Grandmother. Thomas thought this the only piece of good-hap in the whole affair, but Harry was uneasy. Now that Spanish Grandmother had come to her last end they might have expected to go back to Leicester, but nothing was said of a return.

Another messenger arrived at Bytham: even Humfrey recognized the badge of the Bohun Swan on his sleeve, and knew that not Mother but Grandmother Hereford was coming to Bytham.

She was with them an hour after her harbinger had ridden in; and scarcely had she been handed out of her litter than she sent to command all the lordings to her presence. Two of the nurses conducted them to the solar leading from the Hall. Grandmother was seated in the window-embrasure, gazing out, her hands folded in her lap. She sat as still as a statue, and for a moment she did not turn her head. The lordings stood in a row before her, Harry holding Humfrey's hand, his eyes fixed on my lady's profile, the ruddy colour draining from his cheeks. Humfrey felt his hand gripped more tightly, and glanced enquiringly up into his brother's face.

Grandmother moved at last, turning her head to look at the children; she seemed remote, like a figure moulded in alabaster.

'Madam!' Harry said, in a strange voice. 'Madam!'

3

They had stood stockishly, staring at her. What she said meant nothing, or so much that it could not immediately penetrate to their minds. Not until Father came to Bytham did they know that the words, 'Mother is dead,' had meaning. Then it was that they knew that nothing would be the same again, for not only did Father appear altered, but the security of their lives was shattered. Father left the four younger children at Bytham, with Mary Hervey; but Harry and Thomas he took away with him to London. For three nights running Agnes Rokster found the Lord John sobbing into the chalons that covered his bed.

The Foul Death took a heavier toll yet. Barely a month after the gaunt finger had pointed at Leicester the news came to Bytham that the Queen had been stricken, and was clay-cold in a matter of hours. The servants said that the King was rage-mute with grief; he had torn down the palace of Sheen in his despair: yes, rased it to the ground that none might ever live and laugh there again. The only comfort he could find was in planning the Queen's obsequies. These were to be so magnificent that although the Queen was coffined she was not interred for a full month. Every noble in the kingdom was to attend the ceremony. There was an awesome love for you, said the nurses.

But the end of it was that good Queen Anne, who loved peace, was in her death the cause of a bitter garboil. They carried her to Westminster, and all the great lords were gathered there to do her honour save one. My lord of Arundel came late to the ceremony, excused himself to the King on the score of ill-health, and begged leave to depart incontinent. The servants said that the King, snatching his baton from a herald felled my lord of Arundel to the ground, and spilled his blood – yea, in the very Abbey, the Archbishop standing rooted, unable for a full minute to collect his wits enough to decree what should be done. The ceremony had gone on; but men had signed themselves, averting their eyes from that sacrilegious stain on the pavement, wondering what bane would now befall the realm.

The lordings thought that they would never forget Mother, but memory cheated them. So swiftly did her image fade that when her name was spoken it conjured up only the echo of a gitern; the picture of a tabler with chessmen set out on its squares, and a dimly remembered face bent over it; or a glimpse of little dogs in blue-and-white collars playing in the sunshine.

The younger children remained at Bytham for a year, and saw their brothers again only at Leicester, on the yearday of Mother's death. Here, dressed in sable gowns, so much oppressed they dared not exchange glances, they endured an age-long requiem service. Rigorously tutored, they demeaned themselves so well that tears coursed down the cheeks of many who saw them. Four noble imps, all so handsome and so pale, and two fair maid-children, drooping in the arms of their nurses, provided a spectacle to move the hardest heart: only their attendants, silently praying that no untimely swoon should mar the propriety of the ceremony, knew that the pallor was born of exhaustion.

When the service was over, the black raiment was cast aside for the fripperer to take away; the children were attired in scarlet; a shapster measured them for state robes of bawdekin; and it seemed that mourning was ended.

They had dreaded a return to Leicester, but they found when they saw the castle again that they scarcely remembered it. Bitter memory held no place beside present happiness: the lordings were together once more, often fliting, but held by such strong ties of affection that it was many hours after their reunion before they troubled themselves even to discover what other guests were staying at Leicester.

It was a disappointment to find that Bel sire was absent. He had set sail for Aquitaine some months earlier, and had not yet returned. It was his first visit to the Duchy since it had been bestowed on him, and he could think himself fortunate if it proved a peaceable one. His new subjects were showing every sign of recalcitrance: they said that they did not choose to be sequestered from the Crown. It had to be remembered, of course, that they had a particular kindness for King Richard, who had been born at Bordeaux; but those who knew Guyenne best said that the people were curst, liking no foreigner above the average, but preferring the English to the French, whom they detested.

Bel sire had taken Sir Harry Percy with him as his Lieutenant, and Sir Harry, sent home on a mission, was at Leicester, and could often be seen strolling about the courts, with his hand tucked in Father's arm. He and Father were old friends. They had received knighthood together; Sir Harry had gone to St Ingelvert in Father's train, and shared the honours of the lists there with him; and although their ways had fallen lately apart they were glad to meet again, and seemed to find plenty to talk about. The lordings were a little disappointed in Sir Harry. Every English child knew the history of his battle against the Scots at Otterburn; no English child could be brought to believe that a man whom his enemies had nicknamed Hotspur was not worthy of worship; but the Lancaster boys were taken aback to discover that the hero of a score of Border fights was a man older than their own father; rather rough-mannered; not, judged by their standards, quickwitted; and speaking with a northern burr.

This accent sounded on all sides at Leicester, spoken by the tongue of a Percy, a Neville, a Beaumont, a Scrope, or a Greystoke; for a number of persons, bound to the house of Lancaster by blood or by allegiance, had come to attend the memorial service. Prominent amongst them was the Lord Neville of Raby, a tall man who was hip-halt, and spent most of his time staring at Aunt Joan Beaufort. Like Father, he was lately a widower. He had a numerous progeny, and was said to show considerable talent in the making of advantageous matches for his sons and daughters.

All the Beauforts were at Leicester: Sir John; Henry, with his swift mind, and his keen eyes lively under their tilted lids; Thomas, the least well-visaged of the family; Joan, as intelligent as Henry, whom she much resembled.

Both the great-uncles, Gloucester and York, were at Leicester, too; and my lord of Gloucester had brought his lady with him, and his son Humfrey. Humfrey of Gloucester was older than his cousins, but they held him in poor esteem. He was a nervous boy, quiet unlike his overbearing father. But my lord of Gloucester was in his sunniest humour. He had spent a year trying to regain his influence with the King, and he seemed to have succeeded. Wagging tongues said that my lady of Derby's death had raised his spirits wonderfully, for her sister, his own lady, was now sole heiress of Hereford. If he could do it he would outscheme his nephew in the attempt to succeed to all the Bohun dignities; meanwhile he demeaned himself right lovingly towards my lord of Derby.

Great-uncle York came alone to Leicester. He had lately fallen into unwit, and at the age of fifty-four had taken his second wife out of leading-strings. The Lady Joan Holland, offspring of Thomas, Earl of Kent, was his choice; and whether he was snared by her dowry or her roving eye none could tell. My lord of Derby said that he was a lickerish old fool, an overheard observation which made his interested sons recall occasions when they had seen pretty chamberers slapping Great-uncle York, and running away from him with shrieks of pretended dismay.

The children remained at Leicester for some time after the noble guests had dispersed. Some rather disquieting rumours reached them: they were to be separated again, but when, or where they were going they neither knew nor dared to ask.

They met my Lord of Warwick's son, Richard Beauchamp, again while they were still at Leicester. He and Harry were made to joust under Father's eye. They were quite unfairly matched, but Father wanted to see his son pitted against one who promised to become a master. Harry, whose life was blackened by Father's determination that he should excel in his knightly exercise, entered the lists with a sinking heart. Set Harry to wrestle, and you would see what strength and cunning there was in his slim body; but when he entered the jousting-field almost any aspirant to knighthood could beat him at all points.

'I hate jousting!' Harry said. 'You will have the field!'

'No, I shan't,' said Richard.

The lion-look leaped to Harry's eyes. 'No, and indeed? Richard, dare – only *dare* to let me score one point!'

Richard's upper lip lengthened as it always did when a smile was coming. 'I'll knock you out of the saddle at the first wallop!' he promised.

'Do so! The sooner over!' said Harry.

Richard did not, of course, but he did not insult Harry by allowing him to score against him. My lord of Warwick sat puffing out his cheeks, and saying things like: 'Well, well, my whelp is four years older than the Lord Harry, after all!' Father frowned, tapping an impatient foot.

Before Father left Leicester, John knew his fate. While Humfrey and his sisters were to be placed in the care of Sir Hugh Waterton, who was one of Father's gentlemen, he was to live with the Hereditary Countess Marshal. He could only stare at Father, going red, but bosoming his emotions. Children did not demand explanations of their parents, and since none was volunteered John never knew why he was handed over to the Countess Marshal. She was a kinswoman, but of the half-blood only, and so remote a cousin that he did not think that could be the reason. Indeed, he had only the vaguest idea who she was, and sought enlightenment of Harry. Harry said that she was an ancestress.

'She can't be!' objected Thomas. 'Our fore-elders are all dead!'

'Not this one!'

'Harry!' exploded John.

'Well, I'll tell you,' offered Harry. 'She is King Edward I's granddaughter! And *he* begat Edward II, and *he* begat our thirdfather Edward III, and *he* begat Bel sire – so if she is not a fore-elder I should like to know what else she can be!'

Thomas and John fell upon him, incensed at such leasings. When they had him flat on his back they demanded that he should retract, but as well as he could for laughing he held to the truth of his story.

'Harry, you losel, Edward I was hundreds of years ago!' said Thomas.

'No, he was not. Besides, he had two wives. Get off my chest, John!'

'I will not get off your chest. Two wives don't make any difference – *if* he had two wives!'

'He had, and the second one had a son called Thomas of Brotherton, and he was Earl Marshal and Earl of Norfolk, and the Countess Marshal is his daughter. And *she* had two husbands and I forget who the first was, but the second was Sir Walter Manny, so now!'

'Where did you learn all this stuff?' demanded Thomas.

Harry sat up, rolling John over. 'Wilkin!' he said, clinching the matter.

4

Father left the children at Leicester when he went south to attend the King's Council. From scraps of gossip the lordings understood that Cousin Richard was taking a new wife. It was to be expected that a childless King should marry again, but why he should set his fancy on a maid no older than Harry, and a princess of France to boot, was another unexplained mystery.

Hard upon the heels of Father's departure Sir Hugh Waterton came to Leicester to take the younger children into his charge. He and his cousin, Sir Robert, were both knights in Bel sire's retinue; he had a young son of his own, and was a good, plain man, devoted to Lancaster. Mary Hervey remained with the little girls as lady-mistress, and the whole party left Leicester within twenty-four hours of Sir Hugh's arrival.

The lordings were fond of their sisters, but it was Humfrey's away-going which they felt the most. He was only four years old, but so forward that not even Thomas despised his company. He had a ready tongue, and so much charm that no matter what he did he was always forgiven. 'Soon ripe, soon rotten!' said Bel sire, who did not like him.

It was quiet at Leicester after that; but the tedium was enlivened by a visit from Master Chaucer, who was travelling north on one of the state errands with which he was sometimes entrusted. He stayed only for a night, but left behind him a legacy in the form of a poem about one Sir Thopas. The lordings drank in Sir Thopas, and clamoured for more. Their confessor said that if they would con their catechisms as readily as they committed a lewd poem to memory he would be the better pleased. Father Joseph did not share the lordings' enthusiasm for giants or elf-queens, and after having had his chaste ears assailed for days with snatches of Master Chaucer's knavish rhymes he said that it would be the worse for anyone who was again heard to utter 'He had a seemly nose,' or 'the giant shall be dead, Betide what will betide!'

In the autumn M. de Guyenne was in England again. Hardly

had they heard the tidings than he arrived at Leicester, bringing in his train a scrivenish-looking foreigner whom he had found disconsolately following the Court from place to place. He told his grandsons that this was an old friend, a notable scholar, and a Canon of Chimay: one who could tell them better tales than Master Chaucer had ever imagined. They were not at first hopeful. A notable scholar, with white hair and a grey gown did not promise much in the way of entertainment, besides, he spoke English as one long unaccustomed; and although they could all of them speak the language of Oil they much preferred their birth-tongue.

But Bel sire was right: the Canon of Chimay, whom Bel sire called Messire de Froissart, had such tales to tell as held them spellbound, seated on the floor at his feet, hugging their knees, and holding their breath for fear Bel sire should suddenly say that they should all of them be in bed.

He was a Hainaulter, and many years ago he had been Great-grandmother Philippa's secretary. He had known Great-uncle Edward, the Black Prince of glorious memory; and he had visited the French hero, Gaston de Foix, at Orthez. The lordings nodded wisely, for Edward of Rutland had told them that Gaston Phoebus had been the greatest hunter in Christendom. All the stories that old Wilkin told Messire de Froissart could tell better; and their transcendent merit was that they were true.

M. de Guyenne leaned back in his chair, looking down the years, sometimes smiling at the light in Harry's eyes, sometimes interpolating a word that conjured up new memories.

Messire de Froissart had not visited England for seven-and-twenty years. He said: 'I thought if I could but see this land again I should live the longer.' He paused, and then added: 'The faces are all new to me. My heart has been filled with a great sadness and longing.'

Bel sire said nothing. After a silence Messire de Froissart sighed, and said: 'I remember that I journeyed to Guyenne in the train of your brother the Lord Edward, whose soul God pardon! I remember when you, monseigneur, set forth on a great riding through France.'

'Ah, the old days!' Bel sire said.

'Of those who fought at Poitiers, how many remain? It seems to me that I find only their sons today. And Crécy—'

'Crécy! Why, I myself was not out of the nursery then!' Bel sire interrupted. 'There were ten years between Edward and me. As for Poitiers – well, that was a long time ago, too. I had the French King whom we captured there lodged in the Savoy for years. A good man: the best of the Frenchmen I have known. They have never paid his ransom to this day, you know.'

'A chivalrous knight,' Froissart said.

'Oh, yes! He came back to us when he found that that son of his wanted him so little he would not pay his ransom! Very proper, though I always thought he liked it better here than in his own land. God assoil him! We had been feasting together in the Savoy a day or so only before he died! It was a merry evening – a very merry evening!'

'And now the French raid our coasts!' muttered Harry.

Neither of the elderly gentlemen heard him. They forgot the lordings as their memories flitted backwards and forwards across the past. At one moment they were laughing over a sea-fight with the Spaniards, which Queen Philippa, Bel sire's mother, had watched in anguish from the shore; at the next they were recalling fighting at Najera in 1367, and it was Bel sire who took up the tale, for Messire de Froissart had not gone to Spain with Great-uncle Edward. He seemed to know a great deal about the campaign, however, and he put quick questions to Bel sire, as though he wanted to know the truth behind some story he had been told. Bel sire had led the vaward of the English army across the Pyrenees, in the middle of winter; and never, he said, would he forget the frozen mountain-tops as they came to the Pass of Roncesvalles, the cold that bit into their bones, the flaming scarlet on the pennons of Sir John Chandos's retinue, seen against the snow.

The lordings had heard the story before; they were eager to reach the battle. Harry interjected: 'Du Guesclin!'

Bel sire glanced down at him. 'Yes, Du Guesclin led the Bastard of Navarre's vaward against us. He was Sir John's prisoner: we held him for many months. He told Edward he was proud to think he dared not release him. But Edward was the prouder: he let him go. A hundred thousand francs his ransom cost Du Guesclin! A good fighter, but not Edward's equal. Well, well, we had our differences, Edward and I, but I shall never see his match on the field of battle.'

'But it was you who went to his aid at Najera, Bel sire!' John reminded him.

'So you remember that, do you, mon tresâme? Yes, it was I.' He was shaken by laughter. 'He told me that all the time the Spaniards were hurling stones with slings upon our men – they found it anoyous! – Don Pedro, the rightful King of Castile, rode up and down shouting that he would see the whore's son dead who called himself King in his place! When the battle was done, he would have had the heads of every prisoner we took but for Edward. I expect he had them as soon as we were over the passes after putting him on his throne again: he was not called the Cruel for no cause. I married his first daughter, God rest her soul!'

Then memory led Bel sire home to England, to Hainault, back again to Guyenne, and all at once the talk died, withering at the mention of a name. 'Limoges,' Bel sire said, and fell suddenly silent.

The lordings sat mouse-still. They wanted to know more, but in-wit told them it would be unwise to ask for more. Something had happened at Limoges of which Bel sire never spoke.

Messire de Froissart broke the silence. 'My lord Edward was then a sick man,' he said. 'They tell me he was carried into the city on a horse-litter.'

'True,' Bel sire said curtly.

'And also that it was you, monseigneur, who begged the life of the false De Cros when your brother would have headed him.'

Bel sire gave a short laugh. 'Yea, and saw him safely on the road to Avignon! I take no credit: a traitor, but he was a bishop. What else could I do? Edward was a sick man.'

It seemed for a moment as though there would be no more talk; but Messire de Froissart put a question that led Bel sire's thoughts away from Limoges, forward across the years to his Grande Chevauchée. He had led three thousand men from

Calais to Bordeaux in 1373 in a great semi-circle through France, and very few Frenchmen had dared to oppose him. 'Let them go!' had said the French King – ignobly, Harry thought. What men Bel sire had lost – and he had lost the better part of his force – perished from sickness. It was a splendid hosting, and the story never failed to kindle a light in Harry's eyes. Thomas liked it too; it was only John who said that he did not see what had been gained by it.

'Can't you understand?' Harry said. 'Bel sire led his men almost to the walls of Paris, and the French dared not sally forth against him! He cut a great path through France! One day I shall do the same!'

'Well, I hope you will get some good by it, and not lose half your army, that's all!' said John.

4 Herod's Feast

1

Framlingham Castle, the home of the Countess Marshal, to which the Lord John was conducted towards the end of the year, was situated near the mouth of the River Ore, and had a large park attached to it, which made it at once of better liking to a boy than Leicester. It was of considerable antiquity, but little was left of the original structure, the Bigods, the Montacutes, and the Uffords, who had held it each in turn, having embellished and greatly enlarged it. Its walls were built to a height of over forty feet, and above them rose no fewer than thirteen square towers. It was the principal residence of the Lord John's guardian, my lady of Norfolk, but it belonged to her grandson, Thomas Mowbray, Earl of Nottingham and Earl Marshal, whom John knew as Father's uneasy ally.

It was with a bursting heart that John parted from his brothers, and in a mood of black misery that he arrived at Framlingham; but a measure of comfort met him in his guardian's welcome. At first glance she seemed an awesome figure; but within an hour of making her acquaintance he had discovered that although she might be an ancestress she was livelier than many a younger lady. She lived in great state, but set little store by it; and instead of consigning her charge to the care of the officers of her household she took him immediately under her own wing. New faces, added to his importable sense of loss, had brought the Lord John so close to tears that he could scarcely utter a word beyond the formal phrases he had committed to memory. Astonishment drove his tears back: the Countess Marshal then and thereafter treated him as though he had been a man grown.

He partook of supper in her company; and when the lump in his throat made it difficult for him to swallow the mortrews set before him, the old lady said cheerfully: 'Don't fancy dish-meats, eh? You shall have a broiled herring. Now, that's something you *will* relish, for I'll warrant it as fresh as a rose in June, not like the stinking fish you get inland. Here, you! Take away this pap, and set a herring before my lord, and a dollop of sober sauce atop! There you are! And if it don't lie as soft as silk on the belly, which I warrant you it will, you shall have a roasted apple after, to ease it, or a bit of hard cheese. And a drop of ozey to warm your heart: nothing like it! And how did you leave your elderfather? Lord, I don't know how many years it is since I met John of Ghent! I sold him a set of drapes once. A fine young man I always thought him! God glad me, what hurlings there used to be between him and his brother the Lord Edward! They could never agree, but, meself, I always held to it that your elderfather was right to let the old King get a bit of comfort in his dotage, when his wife had died. Mind, I never went next or nigh the Court while that doxy reigned!— what was her name? Ferrers, or Perrers: what a Felice she was! But if an old man can't have his leman to warm his bed for him without his sons turning pope-holy, God amend all, is what I say!'

The sweet, fiery ozey was making John feel dizzy, but much happier. He was sorry that Harry was not present to enjoy this incredible old lady's conversation, but Harry's absence no longer caused him to feel such acute sorrow. He smiled vaguely upon his hostess, and she smiled back at him, her face rimpling into a thousand furrows, and nodded, and said: 'That's better! Take a bit of paindemain to mop up your sauce, and you shall have your apple!'

2

On the whole John was not unhappy at Framlingham, though he was often lonely. Humfrey and his sisters he saw not at all during the following few years: they were living many miles away on the Welsh Border; Harry and Thomas he met from time to time, whenever it pleased Father to bring him to London for a few weeks, or whenever all three boys sojourned with Bel sire.

For his guardian he developed an easy affection; and as soon as he had discovered her foibles he rarely fell foul of her. The greatest of these was her dread of uncovered wells, or, indeed, of any water: John was bewildered for days by her fury when she found him hopefully fishing in the moat. Later it was explained to him that her only son had been drowned while of tender age. Her other children were daughters and all but one, who was an Abbess, long since deceased. She had lost one grandson under tragic circumstances, too, and never came to watch John being instructed in his knightly exercises. Sir John Hastings, the Earl of Pembroke, who had once been handfast to Aunt Bess Holland, had been accidentally killed in a tournament; which led my lady to expect disaster every time her charge so much as tilted at the quintain.

Framlingham was a long way from the busy world, but the Countess Marshal had an old lady's knack of gathering news. Very little happened that she was not speedily aware of; within a few weeks of his arrival at Framlingham John learned from her that Cousin Richard was behaving rather oddly. Queen Anne's death seemed to have unsettled his mind. What, demanded the old lady, must get into his head but a witless thought to canonize King Edward II? He was pestering the Pope about this within a year of the Queen's death, citing all sorts of miracles which were said to have been performed at that unhappy monarch's tomb. Well, well! My lady was never one to search for the motes in other people's eyes, but to be turning poor Edward of Carnarvon into a Holy Saint – well, God amend the Pope!

Cousin Richard had also had his old friend the Earl of Oxford's embalmed body brought home from Louvain, to be interred in the family vault at Earl's Colne. The Earl had met his end at a boar hunt; and sober persons were taken aback when King Richard not only had the corpse conveyed to England, but caused the coffin to be opened, and sat mournfully fondling the dead Earl's hand.

The King's French marriage was not popular either. Many men considered that he would have done better to have espoused the daughter of the King of Aragon, who was of marriageable age. Madame Isabelle was the eldest daughter of the French

King: an infant of eight years old. Cousin Richard, always at his best with children, so captivated her that she became a sotted of him after being only an hour in his presence. He went to Calais in the autumn of 1396, and in November – the bride's father being amended of his annual fit of summer madness – married her. My lady of Norfolk had it on good authority that he wore a new suit of clothes every day throughout the festivities; the Commons, grutchingly furnishing the money for all this costage, could have supplied her with further details. It was to be hoped that the French lords were impressed by the display: it was unlikely that King Charles noticed it. He was always a trifle vague upon his emergence from his summer malady.

Bel sire still stood within the King's grace, but he was growing old, and the men who were the highest in favour were the Hollands, Edward of Rutland, and Thomas Mowbray, my lord of Nottingham. There was even a rumour current that Cousin Richard meant to name Edward of Rutland his heir. This made Bel sire's hackles rise. Some years earlier, when Richard had named as his heir his handsome cousin, Roger Mortimer, the Earl of March, Bel sire had paid little heed. It had been expected then that Richard would beget heirs of his own body; moreover, Roger certainly stood next in the line of the succession, for he was the grandson of Bel sire's elder brother, Lionel of Clarence, through his daughter and only child, Philippa, Countess of March. The King had at first delighted in him; but of late years he had seemed to like him less. Just as the redeless Commons cheered Father's badge of the Antelope, so did they cheer the White Lions of Mortimer: a displeasant sound to Cousin Richard's ears. But no mob ever raised a shout at the Falcon and Fetterlock of York: a good sort of a man, Edmund of Langley, and no one knew any ill of his son, Rutland; but neither of them was of the mettle to take the fancy of a crowd, which may have been why Cousin Richard preferred that one of his cousins.

Towards the end of the year, my lord of Arundel's younger brother, Thomas Fitzalan, was promoted from York to Canterbury. He was known to his generation as Archbishop Arundel; and when the Countess Marshal told John of his translation she spoke of him as: 'Your grand-uncle, the Archbishop.' It was true, of course; but John, passionately embracing the enmities of his father and grandfather, repudiated the relationship with violence. The Archbishop had been foisted on to Cousin Richard as Chancellor at the time of the Lords Appellant's triumph. But he was a man of such address that although he had been compelled to resign the Great Seal to William of Wykeham, three years later he had won it back again after the retirement of the aged Bishop of Winchester, and always seemed to stand on good terms with the King. John, who had spent Christmas-tide at Hertford with Bel sire, knew with what hostile eyes his grandfather regarded his translation to Canterbury: the Fitzalan star was once more in the ascendant. The new Archbishop resigned the Chancellorship, but no one could doubt that his influence would be the greater for his elevation to the See of Canterbury. Lancaster partisans hoped that his zeal would be directed against Lollardy, a nuisance that was daily becoming more anoyous in the realm. Oddly enough, Bel sire, who had been one of John Wycliffe's chief supporters, regarded this possibility with equanimity. The truth was that Bel sire, seeing in Wycliffe a weapon to be used against the power of the princely churchmen, had befriended him rather unwarely. It had been one thing to support one who inveighed against the abuses of the Church; quite another to be the patron of one whose intellect seduced him to utter blasphemies about Transubstantiation. No prince of the house of Lancaster, orthodox to its bones, could be found to befriend an arrant heretic.

It was not until the beginning of the following year that Archbishop Arundel received the pall, and this ceremony was cast into the shade for the lordings by events which touched them more nearly. Aunt Joan Beaufort's husband died, leaving her with two infant daughters; and the Lord Neville of Raby lost no time in petitioning for her hand. It was granted him, and he bore her off to his northern fastness before the spring broke. And Bel sire, whose connection with Dame Katherine Swynford had been a thing accepted from time out of mind, set the world abob by marrying her.

Some of the repercussions were surprising: the Countess

Marshal chuckled for days over the indignation of those ladies who, having lived for years on the best of terms with M. de Guyenne's leman, behaved very unbuxomly to his wife. They were schooled by their lords; but in the same year many of these same lords were roused to a like indignation by the legitimation at one blow of all the Beauforts. Within a few days, Uncle John Beaufort was created Earl of Somerset; and my lord of Warwick, hitherto one of Bel sire's friends, discovered that he was expected to yield precedence to the new Earl, and promptly veered again to the side of Gloucester.

The one person who remained unmoved was John Beaufort himself. He had lately returned from foreign parts, unruffled by hair-raising adventures. He had joined King Sigismund of Hungary's unlucky crusade against the Turk Bajazet, had fought beside Sigismund at Nicopolis, and had escaped with him, leaping aboard the last boat to push off from the shores of the Danube. He was more fortunate than men better born than he. The Duke of Burgundy's son was taken prisoner, and had to be ransomed at enormous costage; and less affluent persons were massacred on the stricken field. Sir John returned to England; and when he was begged to tell the story of his adventures he merely said that Nicopolis had been ill-fought; and that he did not think Sigismund a match for Bajazet. When his Earldom was bestowed on him he accepted it unemotionally, so that all who were waiting for him to show the signs of an upspring were disappointed.

3

In the summer of '97 the three elder brothers met again, at Hertford. Harry was eleven years old; and Father was talking of sending him to Oxford, to be under the tutelage of Uncle Henry Beaufort, the new Chancellor of the University. But it was John who had changed the most. Holding his hands, Harry cried out: 'Holy Rood, Thomas, look at little John! Why, you losel, will you learn to know your place, or must I show you which of us is the eldest?'

'I challenge you!' John said.

After that, they were obliged to wrestle, and of course Harry won the bout. But John, both shoulders pinned to the ground, grinned up into Harry's face, and murmured: 'Are you still sick when you eat of the viand royal, Harry?'

'For that you shall die unshriven!' Harry said, making pretence to strangle him where he lay.

John chuckled, and grabbed at his wrists. Thomas would have had to fight in earnest had he uttered that particular taunt. Thomas swung ever between admiration and jealousy of Harry. He stood aloof now, hating both his brothers, until John called on him for aid, when he launched himself into the struggle, and all ended in laughter, and a tangle of legs and arms.

'Tell us about our ancestress!' Thomas commanded, when breath failed, and the combatants sprawled panting on the ground.

'No, tell me about Father, and Bel sire, and everything!' said John.

'Oh, there's nothing to tell!' said Thomas, plucking a blade of grass, and chewing it. 'Except that Thomas of Kent is dead, which Wilkin says would be a good riddance if *young* Thomas were not just such another as his father; and Uncle John Holland is grown so great with Cousin Richard that everyone hates him more than ever; and Edward of Rutland, and that beast, Nottingham, are his other chiefest councillors: just think of Edward giving anyone counsel! How to know a great hart, I suppose!'

'Well, it is something to know that,' remarked Harry, lying at full stretch, with his hands linked across his eyes.

'And Cousin Richard,' pursued Thomas, 'grows more wood every day, since he came home from Ireland. I daresay he lost his senses there: Wilkin says the wild Irish are all of them wood.'

'The King is not wood. It is treason to say so!' Harry said.

'Who cares? If he headed all who do say so there wouldn't be many people left!' retorted Thomas. 'Everyone knows you are one of his lovelings, but you can't deny that he does the strangest things! And Father said, because I heard him, that if he doesn't take heed those Cheshire archers of his will be his bane, so insolent and oppressive as they are!'

Harry sat up. 'Father said that?'

'Well, something like it!'

'Oh!' said Harry, lying down again.

'What archers?' asked John.

'His bodyguard,' replied Thomas. 'Lusty rogues, full of bobance, swaggering about with the King's badge of the White Hart on their jacks, and doing as they list. Cousin Richard goes nowhere without them.' He rolled over on to his stomach, and grinned at John. 'Have you heard about Humfrey? He's going to be a scholar! Does *your* tutor tell Father you are the aptest pupil he ever had? Ours doesn't, and I'll swear Richard Beauchamp's never told my lord of Warwick so, either!'

'Oh, how is Richard?' John asked. 'Do you see him still?'

'Sometimes.' Harry's voice sounded as though he did not wish to say more.

'I heard that my lord of Warwick took it ill when Uncle John Beaufort was made Earl of Somerset. True?'

'Yes, I think. He doesn't hold by Lancaster now, at all events. Ask Thomas! He knows all the scullions' janglery!'

'Scullions' janglery! You know as well as I do that the old Lords Appellant are got together again!'

'Not Father?' John exclaimed.

'No, not him, and not Nottingham either. But Uncle Gloucester, and Arundel, and old Warwick are imagining mischief, because they can't stomach the Hollands and Edward of Rutland ordering all as they list. Uncle York was wringing his hands over it the other day – you know his way!'

'Enough!' Harry jumped up, and held out his hands for John to grasp. 'On your feet, little John! I can still throw you: can you outpace me yet? I'll give you fifty paces scope-law, and reach the postern before you!'

4

Within the month events proved that Thomas had been right. Piecing it together as well as they could, the lordings gathered that the three original Lords Appellant, Gloucester, Arundel and Warwick, had been meeting in secret to imagine treason. There were those who would have told the lordings that treason there

74

was none, but only the long bosomed-up rancour of the King against those who had once humiliated him.

He bade his uncle of Gloucester and my lords of Arundel and Warwick to a feast at Westminster: Herod's feast it was afterwards called. Only my lord of Warwick obeyed that summons and he was put speedily under arrest. My lord of Gloucester sent a message from Pleshy, begging to be excused because he was unhale. My lord of Arundel sent no excuse, but shut himself up in his castle at Reigate, where he would have remained had not his brother, the Archbishop, persuaded him to render himself up. The King swore to the Archbishop, by St John the Baptist, that no ill should befall my lord; but how little store the Earl set by this oath was seen in the contemptuous smile with which he greeted those who arrested him. He was hurried away to Carisbrooke; and hardly was it done than Master Whittington, the Mayor of London, received orders to call out the trainbands. Placing himself at their head, the King rode into Essex that same evening, to the royal palace of Havering Bower. With him went the Steward of his Household, Sir Thomas Percy; Thomas Mowbray, my lord of Nottingham, the Captain of Calais; and the King's half-brother, the Earl of Huntingdon. They rested the night at Havering Bower, and set out for Pleshy early next morning. It was a lovely summer's day, with a haze promising later heat. The castle stood on a mound, overlooking the Essex countryside, with a great moat surrounding it. Swans glided on the water; and every now and then widening circles betrayed where a fish had risen. My lord of Gloucester received his nephew in the inner bailey, and made obeisance, while his lady, his daughters, his young son Humfrey, and all his household stood uneasily behind him. The hour was Prime, and the chapel bell was ringing: my lord was about to hear Mass.

'Bel oncle, we will go to church together, for you are my prisoner,' the King said. Then, as my lord stood rooted, and my lady's breath rattled in her throat, he said, as though he found the incident amusing: 'I think this will be the better for both of us.'

My lord's eyes searched amongst the King's retinue, but met

only the eyes of his enemies. Dry-lipped, he said: 'Very dread sire, I am unhale!'

The King smiled.

'Grace!' my lord said, the word wrenched out of him. 'Give me grace, my liege!'

'Yea, such grace as was given to my tutor Sir Simon Burley, Bel oncle!' the King said, still smiling.

Then he went into the chapel, all following him; and when he had heard Mass he rode away to London, with his uncle in his train. But at Stratford he parted from him, with never a word or a backward look. My lord was surrounded by men in blue-and-tawny, with the White Lion of Mowbray on their sleeves; and he saw beyond them only the Crescent of the Percy badge embroidered on russet liveries. My lord of Nottingham had ridden on with the King, but Sir Thomas Percy's hand was on Gloucester's bridle. 'Come, my lord!' he said, the burr in his speech making his voice sound harsh. 'We are for Calais!'

5

Within an hour of the King's return to Westminster, M. de Guyenne swept into his presence. He was attended by an ominously large company: the King's servants found Lancaster blue-and-white jostling royal scarlet, no man's hand far from his basilard. But presently M. de Guyenne came out of the King's closet with his nephew, and it was seen that the King's arm was linked in his, and that the King was laughing.

Edmund of York, arriving from King's Langley, made, not for Westminster, but for the inn in quiet Holborn which M. de Guyenne rented from my lord Bishop of Ely. He found his brother in the herber, pacing under the trees with my lord of Derby, and broke in on their discourse, demanding to know what fate had befallen Thomas of Woodstock, their brother of Gloucester.

'He is in ward, in Calais,' M. de Guyenne answered.

'I told you! I told you!' Edmund cried, wringing his hands. 'Christ have him in keeping! What does Richard mean to do with him?'

'He says, no harm. He will bring him to trial when an end has been made of Arundel.'

'He will have his head!'

'He dare not.'

'You will see.' Edmund rounded on my lord of Derby. 'Was this your doing, rashhead? Dog eats not dog, Harry of Bolingbroke!'

'As God sees me, it was not done with my knowledge or by my counsel!'

'I have seen the King,' M. de Guyenne interposed.

'What said he?'

M. de Guyenne shrugged. 'Fair words!'

'God's love, will you trust to them?'

'No, but to my own power! Let Thomas repent him awhile that he dabbled in treason!'

'He is steeped in treason!' Edmund exclaimed. 'Will you head Arundel, and spare Thomas? Will Richard?'

'Richard will do as he must. I am Steward of England, and so he will find when Thomas is brought to his assize!'

But Edmund shuddered, and said over and over again: 'He is shent, I tell you! He is shent!'

Before my lords of Arundel and Warwick were brought to trial, John was at Framlingham again, with his sisters to bear him company. Blanche, at five, reminded all who saw her of her mother. She was pretty, and had a gentle disposition, with none of the self-will that characterized Philippa, still tottering in leading-strings. The Countess Marshal took only a cursory interest in either, but she was glad to see John again. She shook her head over Gloucester's arrest, but she refused to take it seriously. 'Mark me if this windmill dwindles not into a nutcrack!' she said. 'Kings' sons have nothing to do with doom's carts; and as for Arundel, God shield you, my grandson of Nottingham is wedded to his daughter! Let it sleep! Wind blows chaff away, my child!'

But in September, when my lord of Arundel was brought to his assize, the news that reached Framlingham was disturbing. John's nights were witch-ridden, not because he cared whether

Arundel lived or died, but because Father, and Bel sire, and Cousin Richard were all demeaning themselves in a way that made them seem like kindless strangers. Arundel was well liked by the citizens of London, and when he was hailed before his judges the King's Cheshiremen had to draw their bows on an angry mob. Bel sire, presiding at the trial, and Father, amongst my lord's peers, had each of them flung fierce words at Arundel, who stood proudly arrayed in scarlet before them, and threw back word for word. He relied for his defence on the pardon granted him years before; and when Bel sire said: 'The faithful Commons have revoked it, villain!' he answered, swift as the thrust of his dagger: 'The faithful Commons are not here!'

There was never any hope for him. He was condemned to die a traitor's death – commuted, of course, to plain heading – and was led out at once. He was executed on Tower Hill, and he made a good end. Some said that his son-in-law, Nottingham, bound his eyes, but that was untrue: the Earl Marshal raised no hand to save him, but he was not present at his passing. Delicacy may have kept him away; it did not stop him snatching at the dead Arundel's possessions as soon as the breath was out of his body. He and the Hollands picked over the bones between them, the Earl of Huntingdon obtaining the wardship of Arundel's children, young Thomas Fitzalan and his sister Margaret.

Hard upon the heels of Arundel's death came the arraignment of my lords of Warwick and Cobham. This, thought John, was the worst of all, for although my lord Cobham, eighty years old and as brisk as a bee, cheerfully defied his judges, Warwick cast himself at the King's feet, weeping, and imploring mercy. The King banished him and old Cobham to the Isle of Man, and confiscated their estates. Never had John been so glad to be at Framlingham, where no chance could bring him face to face with Richard Beauchamp! It was importable to picture Richard's humiliation: had it been Father who had so abased himself could he, or Harry, or Thomas have met the eyes of any man again?

On the day of Arundel's heading, my lord of Nottingham, Captain of Calais, was ordered to bring the Duke of Gloucester before the Parliament. He answered that my lord Duke had died at Calais, of an accesse; but he was able to present to the King my lord's confession of his guilt, made by him to Sir William Rickhill, a justice of the Common Pleas, who had been transported to Calais to receive it. The confession was read in Parliament, but Sir William was not called upon to give his evidence. My lord Duke was pronounced to have been guilty of treason; his estates were confiscated; his lady fled to sanctuary with her daughters; and the King took young Humfrey of Gloucester into his household.

Archbishop Arundel was also impeached; and when he would have replied to the charges brought against him, the King hushed him. The King told him privately that it would be well for him to leave the country for a space; and when the Archbishop replied that where he had been born he would also die Richard soothed him, promising that while he lived no other prelate should sit on the archiepiscopal throne. Arundel, knowing that sentence of banishment was being prepared, allowed his haughty temper to guide him; and on the eve of his departure for Rome sought an interview with his liege-lord, and set him upon the hone. It was whispered behind the hand at Westminster that my lord Archbishop addressed the King for half an hour without once checking for a word. He swept out of the chamber without giving the King time to make an answer. He betook himself to Pope Boniface, but the Holy Father had his own troubles, and however much he might sympathize with his austere son he was not in a position to make an enemy of any Christian monarch. King Richard supported Rome, but he seemed to be a wayward man, quite likely to transfer his allegiance to the rival Pope at Avignon on small provocation. The Holy Father translated Arundel to St Andrews, and obligingly appointed King Richard's own choice to Canterbury.

Before September was out, the King gave the world something fresh to gape at. He said that those who were of his own blood ought to be elevated above their peers, and in one swoop created what his lieges soon derisively dubbed his Duketti. Edward of Rutland became Duke of Aumâle; my lord of Derby was Duke of Hereford, in his dead wife's right; the Hollands, Huntingdon and his nephew of Kent, were Dukes of Exeter and Surrey; and the Countess Marshal was made Duchess of Norfolk for life. At the same time, her grandson, my lord of Nottingham, who had served the King so well, became Duke of Norfolk. Uncle John Beaufort was raised to the degree of a Marquis, a title strange to English ears; Lord Neville of Raby was made Earl of Westmoreland; my lord of Northumberland's brother, Sir Thomas Percy, was rewarded for his services with the Earldom of Worcester; and the King's friends, Thomas Despenser and William Scrope of Bolton, were elevated, to most men's disgust, to be earls of Gloucester and of Wiltshire.

Notwithstanding these marks of the King's favour, two of the Duketti sought instant measures of self-protection. Before the new titles had been announced, the faithful Commons were begging the King to declare that my lords of Derby and Nottingham had been innocent of malice in their association with Gloucester, Arundel and Warwick of ten years ago. The King, still enjoying his private jest, smiled upon them both, and said that he would himself vouch for their loyalty.

6

At Ely House, M. de Guyenne sat gripping the arms of his chair. His robe fell in folds about his spare frame, and lay in a pool of velvet round his feet. He was beginning to look a little frail, parchment-skinned, but his eyes were as bright as a hawk's under his gathered brows. 'How did Thomas die?' he asked harshly.

The chamber was close, sun-baked all day. My lord of Hereford had thrust open one of the shot-windows, and was standing by it. He answered without turning his head: 'I think he was smothered.'

M. de Guyenne's grip tightened on the chair-arms. 'Do you know this, Harry?'

'No one knows, sir, except those who slew him.'

'Mowbray!' said M. de Guyenne.

'Oh, affirmably! But also Richard!'

'Edmund is right! Richard is wood! Again and again he has broken his pledges, but I did not believe he would stain his honour with murder of his uncle. Look to yourself, my son!'

'Be sure! But Mowbray?'

'May he hang in hell!'

My lord turned his head at that. 'No force! But he might be hastened hellward, sir. Shall I look to it?'

'Look to yourself!'

'Oh, yes!' my lord said, with an impatient movement. 'Richard will find it hard to revoke *this* pardon, and harder still to have me murdered!'

'Leave that! He is the King.'

My lord shrugged. 'For how long, his present gait?'

'For as long as I hold power in this land, Harry!'

My lord looked over his shoulder, a smile lifting the corners of his mouth. 'He has had a faithful protector in you, my father. Have you never thought—?'

'Christ it me forbid!'

Again my lord shrugged, and turned his head again to stare out into the leafy herber. He was silent for a while, and then said lightly: 'Old Froissart told me that seven years before my birth he heard it had been prophesied in the Book of Brut that neither Edward of Wales nor Lionel of Clarence should wear the Crown, but that it should fall to the house of Lancaster. True?'

'I have heard the tale. There are many old tales, most of them leasings!'

My lord laughed. 'Why, yes! But there is another tale, which I once heard you tell, monseigneur, that Edmund Crouchback, that was the founder of our house, was King Henry III's first-born son, but laid aside in favour of King Edward I because he was misshapen. More leasings?'

M. de Guyenne glared at him.

'Or,' continued my lord, smiling, 'was he in sooth the second-born, and called Crouchback only because he wore the Cross upon his back, in token of his worshipful crusade?'

M. de Guyenne put up a hand to hide his quivering lip. 'He was a proper man, I think,' he admitted. 'But when Richard names Mortimer his heir, and then that mooncalf Rutland – God pardon me! *Aumâle!* What is the word the Commons have for this foison of new Dukes?'

'Duketti,' responded my lord Duke of Hereford affably.

'When my royal father, whose soul God pardon, created Dukes in England, I was the fourth to be so elevated,' M. de Guyenne remarked disinterestedly. 'A great honour, I counted it.'

'I,' said his son meekly, 'would have been content to have received the Earldom of Hereford – not esteeming myself a man of larger worth than was Humfrey de Bohun!'

M. de Guyenne's hooded eyes lifted, and a glance, sharp and searching as steel, caught and held his son's. 'No?'

My lord wore about his neck the collar of SS, a golden Antelope dangling from it on his breast. His fingers, idly playing with the links, tightened so suddenly that a worn thread of gold snapped, and his badge lay in his hand. He closed his fist over it. 'No!' he said. Then he said: 'Give me leave, sir!' and strode out of the stuffy chamber.

5 Another Absalom

Dame Katherine, who was now Duchess of Lancaster, was troubled by wan dreams. It seemed to her that my lord of Hereford's dead wife visited her in the still of the night, and whispered in her ear: 'I am afraid!' Dame Katherine knew this to be an impious fancy, but she remembered that '*I am afraid*' was what Mary de Bohun had once said to her at Kenilworth, and she signed herself, and bought a Trental for Mary's soul. She thought it was well for Mary to be laid in earth, for all that Mary had dreaded was coming to pass. Harry of Bolingbroke might wrest pardons from the smiling King, but what had a pardon availed Arundel? A visit to Bess, her stepdaughter and the new Duchess of Exeter, at her lord's inn by Paul's Wharf, made her drop pregnant words in Harry of Bolingbroke's ear.

She had found Bess half-exultant at new dignities, half-frightened by her lord's mounting power. John Holland, who had so much captivated her youthful fancy, was a violent man: Bess said that she dare not for her life remonstrate with him.

'But I tell you, Harry,' said Dame Katherine, 'he is laying up trouble for himself, and for all of us! Dear knows I have no cause to pity a Fitzalan, but to use young Arundel as Huntingdon— oh, I shall never remember these new titles! What is he, then? Exeter!— to use a sely lad, I say, as that man uses his ward young Thomas Fitzalan is to behave worse than any Paynim! He treats him as though he were a scullion, Harry!'

'What folly! – if it be true!'

'I had it from Bess herself. Now, I have endured this world some few years, and I have seen a-many men attainted, and their children given in wardship to good men and bad, but never till now did I hear of a man so hardy that he would misuse his ward! Well, Holy Virgin, what profit is there in it? Late or soon the boy will have livery of his lands, and a pretty garboil there must be if he have cause to hate his guardian!'

'What has this to do with me?' my lord asked. 'Let Bess look to it!'

'Bess!' exclaimed Dame Katherine. 'It has this to do with you, Harry! Give the Hollands and Mowbray full rein, and they will bring us all to ruin! If you have forgot the burning of the Savoy, I have not! God send I see no more revolts in this land! Once let the borel-folk taste blood, and you know not where it will end. Ay, smile, if you choose, but I tell you the times are ugly!'

'The Commons hate not me,' my lord said.

'They had little cause to hate your father, but they burned his palace to the ground, and would have had his head, could they have caught him!' retorted Dame Katherine. 'Oh, they shout "God bless Harry of Bolingbroke!" when you ride abroad: do you think that makes Richard love you the more? God rest her soul, your lady knew!'

'Neither Exeter nor Surrey is worth a leek,' interrupted my lord. 'What, madam, do the Commons shout when Norfolk rides through the streets?'

She stared at him. 'They are silent. Beshrew your heart, what should sely folk care for that sour visage? But Gloucester they loved, Harry, and what did that avail him in the end?'

'My uncle of Gloucester ran on his death. I shall not run upon mine.'

'Harry, Thomas of Gloucester threatened Richard once with the death of Edward II! I don't say that you – But if he were pulled down, which of us would remain?' She saw his eyes, and gasped. 'Holy Mother of God! Harry, tide him life, betide him death, your father will stand for the King!'

'So must we all, madam,' said my lord, honey-smooth. 'As for my brother of Exeter, I mell me not in his affairs!'

2

John spent Christmas-tide with his grandmother, my lady of Hereford, at Pleshy, a change from Framlingham which he did not welcome. Pleshy was a castle of mourning, for Mother's sister, my lady of Gloucester, had emerged from sanctuary, and moved silently about the castle, trailing black weeds, and looking as though she had wept the night through. Even her voice was tear-drenched; and she had grown so thin that it seemed as if her bones must pierce her skin. Two only of her daughters were at Pleshy: Anne, who was handfast to the Earl of Stafford; and Joanna, never out of her mother's shadow. Isabella was serving her novitiate at the Friars Minories; and Humfrey was at Court, happier than ever before in his life.

John, at eight years and a half, was as tall as Thomas, and bigger boned. When they wrestled now he could throw Thomas, but they were good friends. M. de Guyenne said that John had the best temper of all his family, and the greatest talent for peacemaking. In his old age, M. de Guyenne too was a peacemaker.

Since his mother's death, John had seen little of my lady of Hereford; and because his memory was of an austere dame, it was with misgiving that he journeyed into Essex. But whether because he had grown accustomed to dealing with elderly ladies, or because she was not as formidable as his infant fancy had supposed, he soon found himself standing on comfortable terms with her. She did not regale him with anecdotes unsuited to his young ears, but she raised no objection to his launching a boat on the broad, tree-hung moat, and fishing from it. She let him ride out with his eyas-musket on his wrist, too, and questioned him intelligently about this hawk of his own manning, not calling it a bird fit only for a holy-water clerk, as Thomas did.

Of her brother Arundel's death, she never spoke; and the only time she mentioned M. de Guyenne it was coldly. But towards Henry of Bolingbroke she seemed to feel no resentment. Her rancour was stored up against Mowbray and the Hollands; and when the news reached Pleshy, at the end of the year, that my lord of Hereford had accused Norfolk of treasonable talk, such a light sprang to her eyes as betrayed the hatred that lay beneath her calm.

It was a tangled affair. John, gleaning accounts from every source available, was left bewildered at the end. Some said that

Norfolk, riding one day with my lord of Hereford, confided to him that no man durst trust the King, and they would do well to look to themselves; and that Hereford had carried this straight to the King, appealing Norfolk of treason. Others asserted that it had been Norfolk who had appealed Hereford. To the end of his life John never discovered the truth, though somewhere, at the root of the quarrel, he thought, lay the death of Gloucester.

Parliament met at Hereford in the New Year. My lord of Norfolk was absent when Henry of Bolingbroke publicly repeated his appeal; but he was ordered to appear within fifteen days at Oswestry, to answer the charge. He did so, and an ugly scene was the result, which ended in the King's decreeing that the case should be tried by a Court of Chivalry, to be held in April at Windsor. When he heard this, John was jubilant. A trial by this court would almost certainly mean that the issue would be decided by personal combat, and was there a knight alive who could worst Harry of Bolingbroke in the jousting field? If such a knight existed, he was not named Mowbray.

Lancaster spirits soared when it became known that although Hereford went free Norfolk was lodged in the Tower, pending his trial. As John had expected, the Court of Chivalry decided that the quarrel was one to be settled by combat. Coventry was to be the scene of the encounter, which would take place in September. Meanwhile the King continued to smile upon his cousin of Hereford, and my lord of Norfolk was confined within the Wardrobe Tower.

3

Before the combat took place, John was at the Cold Harbour, with Thomas, and his sisters. He had spent the first two months of the year at Framlingham, and had found the meeting with his guardian less difficult than he had feared it must be. Unlike my lady of Hereford, the Countess Marshal did not embrace with passion any cause. She was so old, and had seen so much, that she had become a little withdrawn from the world. She only shook her head, and said that no good would come of the garboil. 'Mind this, John!' she said. 'If ever you are so elvish as to pursue a quarrel as your father now does it will be your bane!

86

Whitherward do they travel, your father and my grandson? They will be shent, mark me well!'

These words John scarcely heeded; but when he reached London he found his grandfather in a sombre mood. Father, however, was in high fettle. He had sent Derby Herald to Milan, and its Duke, Gian Galeazzo Visconti, had straightway caused the best Milanese craftsmen to fashion a suit of armour for him. Several of these armourers would bring the harness to England, to make such adjustments as might be necessary. The costage would be enormous, but Gian Galeazzo begged his cousin to accept the whole as a gift. The camail and the hauberk would be made of the finest steel links; coudières and genouillières were to be enriched with chasing; and gussets of mail inserted behind each joint in all the plate-armour. A magnificent hip-belt was also promised; and the bascinet was to be fitted with an orle, for the better support of the great tilting-helm: rather an innovation, this, but one of which my lord of Hereford approved. The crest and the mantling were being made in London; the one a royal lion, moulded in boiled leather and painted; the other of gules and ermine, dagged at the edges, and falling about my lord's shoulders. Over his hauberk my lord would wear a jupon, a sleeveless garment reaching from neck to mid-thigh, and blazoned with his arms. This, too, was being made in London. Layer was stitched to layer of some coarse material until the whole might almost stand without support; and when this was done it was covered with red and blue velvet, embroidered with three lions passant or, with a label of France, impaling the arms of Edward the Confessor: a cross flory between five gold mart-lets, which the King had granted his cousins the right to wear. Let Mowbray match that if he could! said Thomas and John, full of bobance. My lord of Hereford, amused, reminded them that Mowbray also bore these arms.

'But not a label of France, sir!' said Thomas. 'His label is of three points argent only!'

'And he has sent into Almaine for his armour!' interpolated John. 'Everyone knows that there are no craftsmen to equal the Italians!'

'Who told you that?' asked my lord, smiling.

'Wilkin. But it is common talk!'

'I see. And you believe that I shall prevail?'

'It is sure!' Thomas said, staring at him.

At that my lord flung back his head, and laughed out. Then he bowed to them, and said: 'I shall try not to disappoint you, my sons!'

They had no fear of that; and neither had more than one regret: Thomas's that he was not old enough to act as his father's squire; John's that Harry was absent from their counsels. Harry was at Oxford, under the tutelage of their uncle Henry Beaufort. 'Rather he than I!' said Thomas. 'Harry says he likes him!'

'Why not?'

'Oh, I don't know! He's too cautelous, I think. People say he would have made a better merchant than a Churchman. Myself, I don't like any of the Beauforts much. I know they have been legitimated, but—'

'People say,' remarked John.

Thomas grinned. 'Well, so they do! Oh, John, I wish you were not returning to your ancestress!'

But John never did return to his ancestress. In May, the Countess Marshal, whom everyone had begun to believe to be immortal, parted her life. John attended her obsequies. He was sad, but he shed no tears, which earned him a rebuke. He said: 'She told me not to mourn when she came to her last end, for she had lived overlong, and cared not how soon God called her. She said that times had changed, and in no wise for the better. And she said also that she marvelled that a son of the Lord Edward, the Black Prince—'

'Stint, stint, my lord!' begged his shocked tutor.

'Well, that is what she said,' insisted John.

4

The children spent the summer months at Bel sire's castle at Hertford. In July, Harry was with them again; and Uncle Henry Beaufort became Bishop of Lincoln, by papal provision. As this elevation had been made at King Richard's request, it seemed as though the house of Lancaster stood higher than ever within his grace. Only the new Bishop, glancing at his half-brother out of his lively, tilted eyes, knew better. 'Policy – Bordeaux fashion!' he said. 'Affirmably, brother, this is to drive a wedge between us. You have grown too large for Richard's peace. It must be thought that I shall cleave to the King: a makeweight!'

'Yea – nurseling?' my lord of Hereford said, smiling.

The Bishop – he had not yet attained his twenty-third birthday – acknowledged the jibe with an answering smile. 'Yea! And if you think I could not be such a makeweight, Richard knows me better than you do, brother! Enough of that! Has young Harry come to the end of his holiday? Send him back to Oxford! Don't waste him at Court: there is greatness in that boy, or I am much mistaken!' He saw my lord's brow crease, and said: 'Ah, yes! You wish he would show more skill at jousting, but I will tell you, saving your presence, that jousting makes not the man! Give him to me!'

So the Bishop swept Harry off in his train, and his brothers saw him no more that summer-tide. Humfrey remained in Sir Hugh Waterton's charge; but my lord would not part with his little maids. They were being taught to read and to write; and sometimes Blanche was sent for when my lord had guests. He liked to see her decked out in cloth of gold, queening it at his board. Mary Hervey pulled down the corners of her mouth, and was glad that the Lady Philippa was not of an age to share these treats with her sister.

When September came, none of the children could talk of anything but the trial at Coventry. If the lordings were more interested in the Milanese harness and the seven horses Father was taking with him, the girls knew every detail of the bardings, and every stitch set in his great banner.

The lists were being prepared outside the town, and Bel sire, lately returned from the Scottish border, was to have a special pavilion, like the King. Edward of Rutland, whom the lordings had not yet learnt to call Edward of Aumâle, had been made Constable of England; and Thomas Holland of Surrey was Marshal for the occasion, in Norfolk's room; and all the arrangements were in their hands. The children discovered that they would be attended by men dressed in silk sendal, and armed with silver-tipped staves. There would also be heralds and pursuivants; and, if gossip did not lie, a contingent of men-at-arms and archers. Everyone who could do so was going to Coventry to watch the encounter, and Cousin Richard was afraid of large gatherings. The lordings were puzzled to know why he should in this instance dread an outbreak amongst the borel-folk: they supported Hereford almost to a man, and would only start to hurl if Norfolk won the combat. And as not even Norfolk's friends would have wagered a groat on his chance of success against Henry of Bolingbroke the presence of ten thousand armed men seemed ridiculous.

The day appointed for the trial was the 16th September. The lordings' hopes that a miracle would cause them to be taken to Coventry in Father's train had remained unanswered, and Thomas was in a black rage because someone had disclosed to him that Harry was going, as page to Father. 'Harry cares nothing for jousts!' he said. 'Everyone knows I can unhorse him! It is unjust, unjust!'

'No, it isn't,' replied John. 'He is the eldest of us, and it is his right.'

'You always take his part!'

'Wherein? If you were the eldest, I should deem it your right to go. How far away is Coventry? Do you think the same weather holds there?'

It was a cloudless day, so hot that the lordings lay sprawling in the shade of a tree, with their doublets cast off. Thomas glanced at the sky. 'Seventeen-eighteen leagues: I don't know! I should think it would. It may be too hot.'

'Better than rain.'

'Yes, only that one sweats so in harness! *You* know what it is when your armour gets sun-baked! And the surcingles stretch.'

'True, but it was cooler at Prime. Father thought that by Sexte it would be ended.'

'Sooner!'

'If the ceremonies were not overlong. When shall we know?'

'I'll lay you a wager Father unhorses goky Norfolk at the first wallop!' offered Thomas.

'You'll wager what?'

'Your sorrel mare against— oh, what you will!'

'All thanks, brother! I'm not such a lurdan! Of course he will! Will he send us tidings, think you?'

'Yes, for I asked him,' Thomas said.

5

Tidings came, but not in such guise as had been expected. Sir Thomas Dymoke, who was a knight in Bel sire's retinue, came to Hertford, informing the children's guardians that he was sent to escort my lord's family to London. The lordings besieged him with questions. He replied only: 'The King threw down his warder before my lord had advanced seven paces. He is banished the realm within fifteen days!'

'Banished!'

'Both! My lord for ten years; Norfolk for an hundred winters!'

'But – but *why*?'

'The King said that since treason was the issue it was not meet that royal blood should be spilt. My lord of Norfolk confessed at Windsor certain matters which show him to be one likely to trouble the realm.'

'Witterly! But *Father*?' demanded Thomas.

Dymoke shrugged up his shoulders. 'Ask that of those who may know the cause, lording! I am not one of them!'

While the valets trussed up their baggage, they sought a known face amongst Sir Thomas's following, and, finding it, straitly demanded the full tale. A grizzled man-at-arms told them what he knew.

'Hot? I warrant you! When his squires were busy with his arming-points, my lord said – you know his merry way! – "God send the bridle slip not in my hand!" Sweating? A full hour before Prime, as the Lord is my judge, it was running off him in a river! Folks swooned by plumps in the crowd, smitten by the sun: yea, yea, as God's my witness! They set up traverses above the sieges at either end of the lists, above my lord's chair and Mowbray's, to shield them a little. My lord's was green and blue; Mowbray's white and red, and his siege hot as the sun, crimson velvet. And all the Marshal's men coursing hither and yon with their fine sendal dark with their sweat! Enough to make a man laugh himself into an accesse, you would say, but list! list! My lord horsed him on his white horse of deeds—'

'Blanchemains!' interjected Thomas. 'Barbed in green and blue velvet, with Swans and Antelopes!'

'So it was, lording, so it was! He came riding up to the entrance to the lists at the hour of Prime, with his visor up and his sword naked in his hand, and cried aloud that he was Henry of Lancaster, come thither to do his devoir against a traitor. When they heard him, the redeless folk set up such a shout that it was like the crack of thunder. The heralds opened to him straight, and in he rode, the noble destrier beneath him spurning the ground, and throwing up his head for very disdain. There was a great panache of plumes set on it, and I saw all the feathers tossing. My lord swore upon the Holy Evangelists that his quarrel was just, and another shout went up that set his horse fretting and jouncing, foaming at the bit. Then my lord voided his horse – nay, nay, you know his usance! he needs no aid! He voided him featly, and signed himself, and went to his siege, his sword sheathed, and his spear held in his hand.'

'And Mowbray?' demanded John.

'Late and light, lording! Mowbray came not yet! First entered the King into his pavilion, with the lords about him, and the little Queen in his hand. She was jump-eyed to see the sport, decked out like a mawmet, and her mantle lying a full ell behind her on the ground. Well, well, she is a fair maid enough, but to take such a nurseling for his bride, and himself three-and-thirty years old, come Epiphany, is against nature, no force!'

The lordings cared nothing for Madame Isabelle, and demanded matters more germane to the issue.

'Well,' proceeded their informant, 'the King took his warder in his hand, and on the one side he had the little Queen, and on t'other him they call the Count of Saint-Pool, come over to watch the combat, though there is some as holds it was him caused the King to stop it.'

They nodded, their brows lowering. The Count of St Pol had married the King's half-sister, Maud Holland, and, according to Bel sire, he was far too fond of meddling in English affairs.

'Then there was the Lollard Earl of Salisbury, and a frape of Percies, and Nevilles; and Despenser, and Sir John Bussy, and —'

'Oh, leave that! Bagot, and Green, and Wiltshire, and all the other cumberworlds!' Thomas exclaimed impatiently. 'Where was our father the while?'

'Why, seated on his siege, for sure! I compassioned him, I warrant you, for the sun was riding high, and the traverse over him small comfort. One of the Kings-at-Arms read out a proclamation, but what it was I know not. Then another herald sounded his trumpet, and we knew my lord of Norfolk was come, and they opened to him, and he rode in, shouting, "God aid him who hath the right!" Well, he was brave to see, but it was a pitiful small cheer he got from the people. He voided his horse, but clumsily: you could see his harness weighed heavy on him! His horse was barbed in crimson velvet, bespent with silver lions and mulberry trees; and his squire carried his banner before him, but not wind enough to flutter it. Then my lord of Surrey, which was Marshal, took both the spears, and viewed them fairly, and my lord's he rendered up to him again with his own hand, but Norfolk's he sent back to him by one of his knights. Then the heralds ordered the sieges and the traverses to be removed, and it was done, and the lords mounted again, but my lord first, so it would have gladded your hearts to have seen him, so strong and nimble, and he caparisoned at all points! He shut down his visor, and took his spear in his hand, balancing it in the palm before he set it in the rest, which made the redeless folk set up another great shouting and roaring. When the trumpets sounded, he set forward on the echo. Six – maybe seven paces he took before my lord of Norfolk was fairly started. You could not then hear a sound in all that rout of people, but they say the French lord was whispering all the time in the King's ear. Then there was a commotion, the heralds shouting Ho! Ho! and my lord reining his horse in so hard that he reared up, and fell to snorting, like he was araged to be held from his foe. I saw my lord knock up his visor with the back of his gauntlet, and look towards the King's siege. I knew no more than the next man why the heralds shouted, but they say the King threw down his warder. The word ran through the press of people, and well it was for the King he had his Cheshiremen there! Yea, by my head! The heralds took the spears from the two lords, and said they should go back to their sieges. Holy Rood, if ever I saw men sweat like them that had to bring back the sieges and the traverses foot-hot!'

'But what happened?' John asked.

'That's more than I know, lording. Two full hours the lords sat waiting. The King went to his pavilion, and they do say that he held a council there. No one saw him again, but a knight came out at last, and read a great proclamation. Well, it was all long words, and so many of them I heard but the half, but certes it was the King's sentence that both the lords should be banished the realm. The sely folk began to hurl, but the Cheshiremen had their shafts fitted in their bows, and all ended only in grutching.'

'But, for God's love, *why*?' cried Thomas.

6

He had the answer from Wilkin, in London. 'Why? Because the King fears Lancaster, lording! Christ give him sorrow, for he has dealt M. d'Espagne his death-stroke! May my own ending-day not come till I have seen Lancaster avenged!'

'But if he fears Lancaster—Rood of Chester, is the world arsy-versy? When did Lancaster cleave to Mowbray? Why, then, is Norfolk banished too?'

Wilkin stabbed a gnarled finger at him. 'Who sent Thomas of Woodstock to the deathward, lording?'

'Out of dread, Norfolk!'

'Yea, but at whose word? At whose word, lording?'

Thomas stood staring at him; John said: 'I see. The King fears to be betrayed by Norfolk, and dare not slay him. Thus he thinks to be rid of him.'

'But this is unwit!' Thomas exclaimed. 'Will banishment silence Mowbray? It will unleash his tongue!'

'Nay, who lends ear to a banished man?'

Thomas flung away, biting his nails. He ran straight into Humfrey, arrived that moment at the Cold Harbour from Monmouthshire. He halted in his tracks, blinking. When last he had seen Humfrey, Humfrey had been a chubby five-year-old. He beheld now a tall, slender boy, and only by the oddity in his left eye did he recognize him. 'God amend the Pope! Humfrey!' he ejaculated.

There was something fawn-like about Humfrey. He looked at Thomas out of his great brown eyes, and said softly: 'I think you are Thomas. God have you in His keeping, brother! What do we all do here?'

'We bid farewell to Father!' Thomas said.

'Not you, I think,' murmured Humfrey, glinting a smile at him under his long lashes.

He was right: his brothers had yet to learn how often Humfrey could be right in small matters. Father told Thomas that he was to go with him into exile.

'N-not Harry, sir?' Thomas stammered.

'Harry stays with the King,' my lord answered.

Even a nine-year-old knew that the King, taking Harry into his household, would hold him as hostage. John was troubled, knowing that it was Thomas, not Harry, whom Father best loved.

My lord had sent for his children so that they might be with him to the last, but he had little time to spare for them. The preparations for his exile occupied his every moment. He was under oath never to meet or to communicate with my lord of Norfolk, or with the exiled Archbishop Arundel, and since the second was in Rome, and the other bound for Almaine, he was going to Paris, where he had good friends.

M. de Guyenne also had preparations to make. The Beauforts, sons of his middle years, gathered behind him, yet stood aloof, knowing that not in them were his hopes centred. His pre-occupation was with my lord of Hereford's vast inheritance. He did not expect to outlive the period of my lord's exile, and as matters now stood his possessions would pass at his death into the hands of King Richard. All his remaining energy – and only his wife and his quiet son John Beaufort knew how little was left in him – would be devoted to the fight to secure Henry's inheritance to him.

The younger Henry was permitted to remain with my lord until his departure. It was hard to discover what he thought of it all. His brothers found him withdrawn, guarding his counsel. The months he had spent at Oxford seemed to have set a gulf between them. He no longer fought with Thomas, and no longer engaged in hot argument with any of them. The only time that Thomas tried to grapple with him his body stiffened, and he held Thomas off, his hands like steel about his wrists, and in his eyes a look so blazing yet so austere that Thomas was startled.

'You should know that Harry doesn't like to be mauled,' said John.

'What daffish talk is this?' said Thomas. 'Harry has always been a wrestler!'

'Yes, for the sport, and when he lists. He will not be touched if he doesn't so choose.'

Only to John did Harry reveal a glimpse of the thoughts at war in his head. 'There is no justice in Father's banishment,' he said. 'The reason for it lies in what you've heard: half London is gathered outside our gates, to cheer him whenever he rides out! Do you know what the Commons say? They call him the only shield, defence, and comfort of the commonwealth! No King will stomach that! I would not!'

'It seems to me,' said John, 'that King Richard would do better to give the Commons cause to say that of him!'

'Yes,' agreed Harry, with the flash of a smile, 'but he would not then be Cousin Richard!'

John looked curiously at him. 'Do you love him so much, Harry?'

'Yes, I love him so much,' Harry said. 'He piles wrong on wrong. From the day in his boyhood that he promised the villeins they should be free, he has broken all the oaths he has taken. Nothing that he has done would I do, if I stood in his shoes! But I love him, still or loud!'

'Is it true that he has grown so asotted of himself that if his glance falls on anyone that man must kneel?'

'No! No! Leasings!'

' "As fair among men as another Absalom," ' said John.

'Who said that?'

'Some clerk, I think. One of Mortimer's men. I have heard it repeated. Bel sire thinks him wood. Is he?'

'I don't know,' Harry said. 'I – oh, enough, John! I tell you I don't know!'

7

My lord delivered Harry up to the King at Eltham on the eve of his departure, when he rode there with M. de Guyenne to take his leave. King Richard was at his most charming. He embraced his cousin, saying: 'Forgive me, Harry! Indeed, I am unglad to part with you!'

'All your life, Richard, you have spoken fair words,' M. de Guyenne said.

The King turned his head. Still clasping one of my lord's hands, he held out his own left one to his uncle. 'Then let me speak some few more, bel oncle! I will remit four years of my cousin's exile. When six years have passed, let me see you again, Harry!'

My lord dropped on his knee, and formally kissed his hand.

'I shall not live to see that promise redeemed,' the Duke said. 'Of your grace, fair nephew, grant me one boon!'

'Why, what is this?' the King said, drawing him towards a chair. 'Be seated, bel oncle! You and I shall welcome Harry home together!'

'One boon!' the Duke repeated.

'It is yours, if it lies within my power to grant it to you.'

'Give my son leave, sire, to appoint attorneys who shall receive on his behalf his inheritance when I unbody me.'

'Why, faithly!' the King said. 'Letters shall be issued. And for your needs, cousin, while you sojourn overseas, you shall not find me ungenerous.' He glanced at Harry, silent at his father's elbow, and smiled at him. 'I will take good care of your son,' he said. 'As good care as if he were mine own.' Harry knelt; and the King laid a hand on his head, repeating mournfully: 'As if he were mine own! Don't repine, cousin! Though I am forced to banish you for a space, you are more fortunate than I.'

6 Sa, sa, cy avaunt!

1

My lord of Hereford left London on the third day of October, but so large was his retinue that he found it hard to charter the necessary ships for his conveyance to Calais, and was obliged to beg the King's permission to remain for six weeks at Sandgate Castle. It was granted. Not even the news that the Mayor and the leading citizens of London had escorted my lord as far as Deptford on his departure made the King abate any of his kindness. He was allowing his cousin two thousand pounds a year for his maintenance in France; and he raised no demur at his remaining a whole month in Calais. All my lord's friends augured well from these signs; only M. de Guyenne had his fading eagle's gaze fixed on something beyond other men's sight, and paid no heed to these tokens of the King's favour. He seemed always to be waiting for something; and he was perhaps the only man to show no surprise when it became known in England that my lord, courting the French King's cousin, Marie de Berry, found his suit rejected at the eleventh hour. King Richard had told his father-in-law, King Charles, that such a marriage would be displeasant to him. Later, my lord was begged by the embarrassed French King to remove himself from his dominions: his presence in Paris was as displeasant to King Richard as had been his proposed marriage.

My lord found a champion in King Charles's brother, Louis of Orleans, who said that if he returned to England with force of arms he would be acting like a wise man. My lord cocked a sardonic eye at him, and said nothing. The Duke of Orleans was not the man to inspire Henry of Bolingbroke with confidence. He removed to Blois; and from that city sent a messenger into

Brittany, desiring to know if his good uncle, the Duke, was willing to receive him in his dominions.

John the Valiant opened wide his aged eyes, and enquired of the messenger what had caused his nephew to halt on the road to Brittany. 'Let him come!' he said. 'He will find a hearty welcome! No one could more glad my heart, for although I never clapped eyes on him his father, by my reckoning, was the best of all the old King of England's sons! They tell me your master is a proper man. Let him come!' He nodded to his fair Duchess, and said: 'You will like him, ma mie! He is the nephew of my first wife, whose soul God pardon!'

His third wife, a Navarrese princess who might well have passed for his daughter, said meekly that if her dear lord liked him, without guess she would like him too.

In England, young Thomas Fitzalan, the dead Arundel's son, unable to bear the indignities heaped on him by his guardian, my lord of Exeter, and his guardian's Steward, who had him in ward, escaped from Reigate Castle one night, and made his way in disguise to the coast. Try as he would my lord of Exeter could discover no trace of him; but after many weeks Fitzalan retainers were gladdened by the tidings that he had reached Utrecht, and was safe there in the care of his uncle, the Archbishop.

At Ely House, John was sojourning with Bel sire. He was not unhappy, because the Court remained at Westminster or at Eltham, and Harry was often at Ely House. Harry was happy too. He was the King's favourite page, ousting his cousin Humfrey of Gloucester from that position. He always insisted that despitous tongues maligned the King, but some strange stories reached Ely House. Uncle Thomas Beaufort recounted them to his mother, Dame Katherine, often within John's hearing. He said that the King had shocked all but the glosers who fawned upon him by declaring that the laws of England were in his mouth or in his breast, and that he alone could change them. 'Then there are his ragmans,' Thomas said.

'For God's love, what are they?' asked Dame Katherine.

'Well, he calls them La Pleasaunce,' replied her son, 'and all I can tell you is that men are obliged for very dread to sign them, owning themselves to be misdoers. He drags fines from them then. He said the other day that soothsayers foretold he should be an Emperor; and the latest abusion is that any man heard to speak ill of him shall not be tried by jury. Yes, and those curryfavours he keeps about him sing *placebo* to him until he thinks himself the wittiest conqueror that ever was, so to have rid himself of his enemies!'

'Hereford?' gasped Dame Katherine. 'Jesu defend! Mary was right! My son, not a word of this to your father! Poor soul, he has enough to cumber him!'

'Bel sire knows,' John said.

'Ho, so you are there, are you, malapert?' said his uncle, pulling his ear. 'And who told Bel sire?'

'Great-uncle York,' replied John. 'And more besides! You need not regard it, madam: Bel sire doesn't! He only smiled.' He was surprised to see her shedding tears, and added, 'It is true: I was there!'

'Alas, Thomas!' Dame Katherine said, wiping her eyes with her long sleeve. 'He cares for nothing, my dear lord! He went away with Harry.'

These words meant little to a ten-year-old, but M. de Guyenne had become divorced from the cares of the world since my lord of Hereford's banishment. His mind wandered backwards over the glorious past, and he would recount forgotten triumphs to John; or fall into reminiscence with Master Chaucer, who was old, like himself, and remembered Bel sire's first wife, the Lady Blanche, and Thirdfather Edward, and others who had been dust for years. Nothing that happened in the inglorious present seemed to touch M. de Guyenne nearly: even the news that Sir John Beaufort was contracted to the Lady Margaret Holland drew no more from him than a lift of the brows, and some rather daunting recollections of the rise of that family. 'Varlets,' said M. de Guyenne. 'Surrey's sister, is she? I misliked it very much when I was forced to bestow Bess upon a Holland. The first of them I ever heard of was Steward to Thomas of Lancaster. He did very well for himself: stewards always feather their nests! *His* son was Steward to Salisbury: that was how he came to marry Joan of Kent. She was handfast to Salisbury, but

Holland's leman for all that. A lovely woman, but gamesome! I never thought that any good would come of my brother Edward's marrying her. A widow, too! But he was asotted of her, and she paid for all in the end, poor wretch! So you mean to espouse her granddaughter, do you? Well, she should be a warm maid!'

She was indeed heavily dowered, and pretty besides, with a merry eye, and a gurgling laugh; but so young that Dame Katherine advised her son to wait awhile before he bedded her.

2

By the end of January John knew that Bel sire was drawing to his last end. His physicians never left Ely House, but when Dame Katherine's eyes besought comfort of them they shook their heads: leechcraft could not mend grief.

He had been busy making his Will for many weeks, taking pleasure in bequeathing two golden cups to Harry and to John, and striving to recall who had given him the arras he wished Dame Katherine to have. In his last days he added a codicil. Sir Robert Whitby, his Attorney-General, drafted and redrafted it, and still he could not be satisfied. He added my lord of Wiltshire's name to the long list of his executors, smiling disdainfully as he did it. Wiltshire was a lickspittle lord, but Treasurer of England. M. de Guyenne's old friend and follower, Sir Thomas Percy, who was now Earl of Worcester, was another of his executors. Sir Thomas came to visit him, and stayed for a long time, remembering for his pleasance old campaigns. At parting, he dropped tears on a hand that lay feather-light on his, but M. de Guyenne, looking down on his grizzled head as from a remote peak, said only: 'Do my son right, Sir Thomas!'

'As God sees me!' Worcester said.

King Richard also came to visit his uncle, attended by certain members of his Court. It pleased my lord of Lancaster to receive the King in his Great Chamber, clad in his parti-coloured robe of blue-and-white, and seated in his chair of state, his Beaufort sons, and the officers of the Duchy of Lancaster gathered behind him. He said: 'Very dread sovereign, I cry your pardon that I am not able to rise to greet you!'

'Dearest uncle, what need of such ceremonies between you and me?' King Richard said, taking his hand and holding it.

M. de Guyenne's eagle-look swept over the gentlemen who had entered the Chamber with the King. He lifted his left hand, and his Controller stepped forward. 'The King's servants,' said the Duke. 'See them entertained, Master Haytfield!' He saw his grandson amongst the King's servants, and added: 'Come here, Harry!'

The courtiers who had so lately commiserated their master on the need to visit a dotard tottering to the vault, discovered that experience had not taught them how to counter so comprehensive a dismissal. They looked towards the King, but he shrugged, and waved them away.

M. de Guyenne, permitting his nephew to hold his hand for as long as it should please him to do so, looked Harry over, and nodded. 'You will make a proper man!' he said. He turned his head. 'I pray you, fair nephew, be seated!'

Someone set a siege for the King; he took it, saying, 'I would I might ease your heart, Bel oncle! It touches me as near as my shirt to find you in such case!'

'Richard,' said the Duke, 'I have stood your friend this many a day, and while my life holds I am your man. Turn the leaf, and take a better lesson! I speak to you with a dying breath. Set aside your false and favel flatterers: they will lead you to your doom! I tell you, my liege, as you have done, so shall you feel!'

The colour rose to the King's cheeks; he answered hotly, stammering, as he did when he was moved: 'Bel oncle, you presume too much upon my love!'

He recoiled before the flash in the Duke's eyes. 'I? I presume too much, Richard of Bordeaux? You speak to Lancaster, boy! A King's son, and one that has spared you again and yet again! Light as linden have you been, all the days of your life, wasting your livelihood, taking to your bosom men not worth a straw! I had done better to have brought in the Scots against you! As I might have! Yea, Richard, as I might have!'

Sir John Beaufort dropped on his knee. 'Monseigneur! Father!'

The King had sprung up. He plunged over to the window,

and stood there, breathing hard. M. de Guyenne had fallen back in his chair. They restored him with a cordial, but although he opened his eyes, he did not speak. My lord Bishop of Lincoln murmured in his brother's ear, and John Beaufort moved towards the King. 'Of your grace, sire! My father is forspent!'

'My lord of Dorset!' the King said angrily. He turned, and his gaze fell upon his uncle. His face softened; he passed a hand across his eyes, and said in an altered tone: 'I did not know how ill he was. I will go.' He stepped to the Duke's chair, and bent over him, kissing his brow. 'Christ have his soul!' he said. 'Harry, come with me!'

3

M. de Guyenne died upon the third day of February. Only the children of his last marriage were gathered about his bed, for his daughter Bess, the Duchess of Exeter, was so much affected that she was obliged to withdraw. She brought her two sons to receive their grandfather's blessing: Richard, her eldest-born, and stolid little Jack, who was not quite four years old; but the sight of her father's wasted hand on their heads proved to be too much for her fortitude. 'Which,' said her half-sister, the Lady Westmoreland, 'is just what one would have expected of Bess! All of us have known for months that Father was at his last end, but would she heed? No! Nothing but the latest jets of fashion!'

Within an hour of M. de Guyenne's passing, Sir Thomas Dymoke was riding for the coast, where a ship waited to convey him to Brittany; and Henry Bowet, Archdeacon of Lincoln, who was my lord of Hereford's proxy, was closeted with M. de Guyenne's Attorney-General, his Receiver, his faithful Clerk, and his clever son, the Bishop of Lincoln.

M. de Guyenne had left minute instructions for his interment, and they were fulfilled. He was laid to rest beside his first wife, in the choir of St Paul's, and nothing could have exceeded the magnificence of his obsequies. The King was present, and was seen to shed tears: a circumstance that lulled into brief oblivion the fears of even so anxious a man as Edmund of York. But within a month the letters patent granted to my lord of Hereford had been revoked, and Master Bowet arrested for his share in having procured them. The King said that he had granted them inadvertently, and without proper advice; and declared the vast Lancaster estates to be forfeit to the Crown. My lord's six-year exile was changed to banishment for life; and the Lord John's confessor, hearing these tidings, snatched his charge away to sanctuary in his own Abbey of Waltham. Acting with equal promptitude, and more worldly wisdom, Sir Hugh Waterton conveyed the three younger children to London, and installed them in the Cold Harbour, no Lancaster possession, but part of the Bohun inheritance. The inn bristled with men in blue-and-white; but Sir Hugh was placing his trust rather in the citizens of London. When they gathered outside the gates, shouting 'Noël' to welcome the children, he allowed them a heartrending glimpse of Humfrey and the two angelic little maids. The citizens wept to see such fair children so tragically orphaned, and swore it should go ill with any who sought to do them scathe.

King Richard showed no disposition to harm them, nor was he less kind to Harry. He was preparing for his second expedition to Ireland, which he meant to undertake as soon as summer made the sea-passage less hazardous. His cousin, the Earl of March, had been slain by the wild Irish, and it was needful to undertake an expedition to the troublesome island. But even those most familiar with his irresponsible moods had expected him to postpone this when he seized the Lancaster inheritance, and were aghast to discover that he had no such intention. All the preparations were going forward; he was taking with him the most redoubtable of his knights, the wisest of his counsellors; and leaving the realm to the governance of his uncle of York, and his rushbuckling favourites.

'Now we know he is wood!' said Thomas Beaufort. 'Rob Harry of his own, and not look to see him come to claim it at the sword-point? What kind of a stockfish does he deem him to be?'

'Rather,' said the Bishop, playing with the tassel that hung from the left sleeve of his dalmatic, 'he has been glosed into thinking himself divine. A strange creature, all the time at odds with himself!'

'At odds with himself?' repeated Thomas, staring. 'I never heard of such a thing!'

'Possibly not. It is a malady of the soul.'

'It sounds elvish to me! And for what reason does he bring Bowet to trial?'

'My dear brother,' retorted the Bishop, 'no man who believes that the laws of the realm are locked in his breast need search for reasons for what he may list to do!'

'But they say Bowet will be condemned to die a traitor's death!'

'Very likely,' agreed the Bishop. 'His sentence will then be commuted to banishment, and our brother will have another strong man beside him.'

'Another?' said Ralph Neville of Westmoreland, who had been listening with knit brows to this interchange.

'Archbishop Arundel has gone to Rennes, under coverture, taking young Fitzalan with him,' said the Bishop.

My lord of Westmoreland thought this over for a full minute. 'I am for the North!' he pronounced at last. 'I must look to my meiny!'

4

As Bishop Beaufort had prophesied, so it came to pass: Henry Bowet was condemned to be executed for having advised Henry of Bolingbroke, but the sentence was commuted to one of life banishment. His archdeaconry was taken from him; but then the King, who had shown such ferocity, dropped into one of his fits of accidie. They were not strange to him, and they usually followed an outbreak of passion, but never had such a fit been worse-timed. His favourites, who had pandered for years to his every whim, could not rouse him from a deep melancholy. He would sit for hours, still as a statue, propping his chin in his hand, so mournful a look in his eyes that no man durst intrude upon his hidden thoughts. Only his uncle of York, knowing that since M. de Guyenne's death all the dignity of an earlier generation was invested in his shrinking person, spoke roundly to him. Tears coursed down my lord of York's cheeks, but he spoke out like a man, and a true son of King Edward.

'Look you, my liege!' he said. 'You have slain two of us who were your great father's brothers and his comrades in arms, for as surely as you did to death Thomas of Woodstock you slew John of Lancaster, who was the best friend ever you had! Let that sleep! We of King Edward's blood stand by the King, and so will I, who am the last of his sons in life! You have stolen from my nephew of Hereford what is his by right of inheritance, and now – now, with all this realm astir! – you will go to Ireland, taking no order to what may befall when you are gone! Harry of Bolingbroke is no man of straw! If I speak to you with my last breath, so be it! Take heed, Richard! Take heed what you do now!'

Those who stood about the King thought that he attended to these words, for he kept his eyes fixed on his uncle's face throughout. Yet when Edmund of York ceased, he said nothing but only moved his hand, in a gesture hard to read. Something he waved aside; but whether it was his uncle, or the cumbersome world, no man knew.

He sailed for Ireland on the 29th day of May, leaving Edmund of York Lieutenant of the realm. He gave the Queen into the care of the widowed Countess of March; and his dear friends, Sir John Bussy, who had so often told him he was the greatest monarch that had ever been in Christendom, Sir Henry Greene, Sir William Bagot, and my lord of Wiltshire, he bade succour her, and lend their aid to my lord of York. He took with him young Harry of Monmouth and Humfrey of Gloucester. My lady of Gloucester wore her knees out, praying for her son's safety; and Lancaster adherents exchanged glances, and said: 'Well – my lord has other sons, after all!'

Uneasy stillness brooded over England that June-tide. The leaves were seen to wither on the trees, and as suddenly to bud again. No man knew what this strange sign portended, but each man looked to his basilard. Chapmen carried the news from town to village that in the north the great lords were mustering their meinies.

Sir Hugh Waterton sent to Friar Peter, at Waltham Abbey, to bring back the Lord John to London. Sir Hugh could not be at ease until he had gathered all the Lancaster brood under his wing; and no one could have been more thankful to be brought to the Cold Harbour than John. Sir Hugh was startled when he came striding in, flinging his hood one way, and his mantle another, and demanding fiercely: 'Harry, Sir Hugh? Harry? Where is he, a'God's half?'

Sir Hugh thought that he had never known a boy to grow so fast as the Lord John. He had not seen him for nine months, and here he was, only ten years old, and looking every day of fourteen. He ejaculated: 'God glad me, I scarcely knew you, my lord!' He added severely: 'What manners are these you show me, stamping in with no greeting, and nothing but questions in your mouth?'

'I cry your pardon! Where is Harry?'

'He is with the King,' answered Sir Hugh. He watched John whiten, and said, turning his eyes away: 'The King loves him: he will not harm him!'

John went to the window, and thrust it open, breathing deep. 'It is hot in here – stifling! What tidings of my father? Where is he?'

'No tidings, lording.'

'He cannot do it!' John said, as though to himself. 'No, no, he won't risk Harry's life!' He stood leaning against the window-frame for a moment or two, but turned presently, and said in a quieter voice: 'I've been so mewed-up I know nothing! How stand our affairs? Where is Dame Katherine? My uncles?'

'All that belonged to Lancaster the King has seized. The Bohun heritage he cannot touch – cannot? *Has* not touched, for God knows justice is dead in England! The Duchess has her dower, and has gone to Lincoln. Your uncles you will see soon enough. And it is to be hoped,' said Sir Hugh, 'that you will greet them in more seemly wise than you greeted me, my lord!'

'Again I cry your pardon, sir!' John said, and went off to find Humfrey.

Humfrey was delighted to welcome him, but he could give him little news. Smiling at him, slipping a hand in his arm, he said: 'All one hears is from the lips of varlets: leasings, I daresay! Some say Father is in Paris, some that he abides in Brittany. Myself, I don't see what he *can* do, with Harry held as hostage. Of course, it is true that Cousin Richard loves Harry, but he is said to be quite wood, and we all know the things he can do

108

when he is araged. He even tried to stab Bel sire once, didn't he?'

John nodded. 'Yes, and Father knows as surely as any man, but— oh, Rood of Chester, I would that Harry were here!'

'Oh, so do I!' agreed Humfrey. 'But don't let wantrust take hold of you, John! I expect that Father will set the lawyers to work.'

'The King has done him importable injury!' John said. 'He will not suffer it! Not Father!'

'No, but what *can* he do?' Humfrey repeated.

He had to wait three weeks for the answer. It came then, tumbling from the tongue of a messenger who rode into the court of the inn, dropping with fatigue, stained with sweat and dust, and flecked with foam. He was so parched with thirst they had to give him to drink before he could do more than open and shut his mouth soundlessly. When he did speak he told his tidings in a hoarse croak: Father had landed at Ravenspur, in Yorkshire, and had unfurled the banner of Lancaster.

'Breton ships brought him,' the messenger said, staggering on his feet. 'He has come to claim his own, and they are flocking to his banner, my lords: Percies, Nevilles, Beaumonts, with their meinies! The North is up, lordings, and I am sent to bid you be of good cheer, for my lord will be with you presently!'

Part Two
The Unquiet Time
1399–1403

The blood is schad, which no man mai restore.

Gower

1 Which no Man then Repugned

Richard, who had been a King, was watching Henry, who
would be crowned King on the morrow, dub more than forty-
six young bachelors. He was creating a new Order of Knighthood. Richard, achieving a mood of detachment after an eternity
of rage and anguish, looked critically at the acolytes, and
thought that Henry would have done better to have consulted
him before deciding on the robes of these new knights. He
could have told him that green was an unsatisfactory colour;
but Henry always thought he knew best. No doubt he thought
he knew how to be a King, too: well, he would learn some few
lessons before he came to his last end.

Flushed with success you are, fair cousin, but if you think that
a hundred thousand men who flocked to your banner – O God,
a hundred thousand of *my* subjects! Stint, stint! Discontented
barons or redeless serfs: what should I, Richard Plantagenet,
care for any such? If you think, Harry of Bolingbroke, that
these will not be the first to grutch at your rule, I, who have
owned myself to be unfit to govern this realm, can still teach you
something! The Londoners shouted 'Noël' to you when you
entered this my city, with me beside you, mounted on that sorry
hackney, but I know them as you do not! Ungenerous of you to
have so mounted me, Henry! I spared your son; you might have
remembered that! You had your revenge when you executed
my oldest friends. You had it when Thomas Percy, Earl of
Worcester, broke his rod of office before my face. You had it
when Math, my hound, fawned on you! Strange that that should
have hurt me more than all the rest! Yea, more than the deaths
of my friends Wiltshire, and Green, and poor Bussy! More, far
more, than my uncle of York's joining you without one blow

struck in my name! Bel oncle, you need not bear yourself so wretchedly! I did not think you would stand for me, if Harry dared to come, or that your false son Rutland would not betray me before you! That is something you will none of you understand. Only Anne would have understood, and perhaps Robert of Oxford. Dead, both of them, and my heart too. Fools! Not one of you had the wit to guess why I took Isabelle for my wife, and not a woman grown! Not even you, Harry, knew that I would set no other woman in Anne's place, and yet I believe you loved your Mary, after your fashion.

What do you mean to do with Isabelle? What do you mean to do with me? I must keep my hands quiet, for a man's hands will betray him though he keep the smile on his lips, as I do, as I will do, God helping me! They are watching me now, this frape of Lancaster lickspittles, hungry to see how I demean myself while Henry of Bolingbroke dubs his Knights of the Bath. Well, they will say that I bore myself debonairly; and only Henry, perhaps, knows something of what I do not choose to show. Henry is not a fool: I should not have hated him if I could have despised him. If he had been just another armipotent man he might have won all the honours in Christendom, and I should not have grudged him one of his triumphs. But he is subtle as well, and he can bear his part in argument with the schoolmen. Only he does not laugh when I laugh. He is serious now: in his place I should have known how japeworthy was this ceremony. Anne would have known too, and Robert, and Michael de la Pole, and Bussy: that is why I liked my favel flatterers, Henry! They laughed when I laughed! None of these dullards you have gathered about you will laugh, but I suppose you won't care for that. And although you may know that I suffer, you will never know that I wished at this moment that you had left just one of my friends to enjoy this jest with me. They tell me that Bagot is still on life. I wonder if he knows what is happening in my palace of the Tower this day? Do laugh with me, Bagot! Even though you lie in chains, laugh! You cannot see the faces of Henry's friends, but you surely know who they must be, and how they will look! Old Northumberland, like a cat at a cream-pot; his son, Harry Hotspur, no more than a shakebuckler; Berkeley, with his hound's face; the Cliffords; the Beaumonts; the Nevilles; the Greys – how much I dislike your dear friend Grey of Ruthin, Henry! Do you mean to find a place in your Council for Warwick, who grovelled at my feet, and wept like an old woman, and has not forgotten it, for all you have enlarged him, and do him honour today? His son is more of a man: Richard, my godson, whom you are knighting!

But you will not knight your own son, Henry! Not your first-born! At my hands young Harry received the accolade, and he is remembering that, so pale and still at your elbow. If I had been the miscreature you forced me to declare myself I should have slain Harry for your treachery. Did you guess that I loved him too well to hurt him, or are you without ruth, cousin? They tell me that he will carry Curtana at your coronation tomorrow: will you recall that it was you who carried it at mine? Had he been my son, had Anne borne me children, there would have been another tale to tell today! Look at me, Harry of Monmouth! Though I would send your father hellward I wish you God-speed, my child: perhaps you are in sooth that Henry for whom the old prophecy foretold a glorious destiny! If Harry is to succeed to Harry, you will not mount the steps of your throne as I did, a redeless child, the tool of every man who seeks to rise by your favour! Ill fares the land that a child rules! Yea, and ill fares that child! He must mislike those who are set over him, as I misliked Warwick, my tutor; he must be at the mercy of those who flatter him, as I was. Had my father lived, how different my life would have been! I knew him not, and I have hated the mention of his name. How often have those words dinned in my ears! *Your great father!* Can you wonder that I turned to those who never spoke them?

Too late to think of that! Who comes now to receive your accolade? Where is young Humfrey of Gloucester in all this bachelry? No, I recall that I was told he had died upon his journey homeward: bog-fever, I suppose. That is one death you cannot lay at my door! He was well when I sent him and Harry to Trim Castle. It is being said that I imprisoned the children there, but you know better! I set them under guard to keep them safe: would you have wished me to have carried your son to

Wales with me, and to have kept him at my side all those weeks when I, a King anointed, travelled in a mean disguise, only to end my journey at accursed Flint? How much I wish that Anne were alive today, that I might tell her how wrong we were to think we could have been happy without that heavy weight of the Crown upon our brows! It was not true, Anne: I, who was a King in leading-strings, and thought to be well rid of my royalty, know now that it was not true. When my foolish uncle of York tried to warn me, I cared not a rush what might befall. Yet when they brought me the tidings that Harry of Boling-broke had dared to raise his standard in my realm, then, Anne, I knew that kingship cannot be so lightly cast off. Even now, when I have borne so many indignities, and schooled myself to betray nothing of what lies in my breast to these mine enemies, there is such rage burning in my veins that I know not how to sit quietly in my siege. Strange that with so much anguish at my heart I can still find pleasure there! I have out-played Henry of Bolingbroke, and well he knows it! From the moment that we met at Flint, I have borne myself more kingly than he. He hoped I should let my rage master me, while he crushed me with civility. I am sure that he is wishing now that he had not com-manded me to sit in this hall, watching him dub his new knights. I would they had haled me to Westminster when he challenged my throne and my realm! They say he spoke out boldly: not so boldly had you known that I was watching you, Henry! And laughing at you, as I am laughing now!

How fortune has favoured you! Even Norfolk, who might have troubled your peace, lies dead in Venice! But fortune is my Lady Changeable, as you will yet discover. It is the Fox, Northumberland, who has set you on your throne, and be sure he will not let you forget it! It may even be that my faithless brother John Holland of Exeter will not run doucely in your bridle, for all that you are knighting his sons today. If little Jack Holland kept his vigil, I know nothing of babes! What folly! He cannot be a day older than four years! Bess's doing, of course. If you would but look at me, Henry, you would find there is one jest we can both enjoy. I know your sister Bess!

Well-visaged bachelors, all these sprigs, but none so fair as your own sons. You keep your countenance graven, but you cannot conceal the pride that swells your bosom when you look upon your children. I hear you have made Thomas Steward of England. They are much alike, he, and Harry, and Humfrey: Lancasters all! John is the only one who has not that straight nose: he is going to be hawk-faced, and makes me remember old John of Gaunt. They are taking care not to look towards me: how discomfortable I am making them! Richard Beauchamp keeps his eyes lowered too. I have had a sturdy look only from that lad with the close eyes, who, from his tight mouth, should be young Fitzalan. You will do well to look to yourself, brother Exeter, now that that boy is loose. His is not a forgiving face, and you used him shamefully when you had him in ward.

What do you mean to do with me, Henry? My desire is for peace; when I placed my ring upon your finger that was the thought in my head. It is there still; yet under it, under this accidie which holds me in its thrall, I can feel the old rage stirring. Only it is nothing worth: Anne is dead; and I have no son.

2

The new King rode in procession from the Tower to Westminster Palace that evening. His Knights of the Bath rode with him, and all the citizens gathered to watch him go past. The rain fell steadily, damping the ardour of those who, with sunlight to encourage them, would have shouted themselves hoarse. The standards and the garlands hung limp and sodden; once or twice a horse's hooves slipped on the shining cobblestones. Pageantry had been arranged in West Cheap, but a hurried conference had decided the Mayor and the aldermen to send the mummers to shelter. No one cared if the nymphs and the heroes of antiquity perished from rheums caught in the downpour, but Master Barantine knew better than to make his new monarch pause on his journey to Westminster to watch a pageant, while his raiment became saturated with rain. It was bad enough for the royal party to have to ride all the way along the Strand to Westminster, for the road was not paved beyond the Savoy Palace, and the mud that was kicked up quite ruined the green tartarin mantles of the King's new knights.

Westminster Palace was very large, a jumble of towers and halls which were to bewilder the young princes for days. It seemed strange to them not to be at the Cold Harbour, which Uncle John Beaufort of Dorset was now to inhabit. They did not think that they would like it as well, for much of it would be forbidden ground to them. There was to be no running in and out of the various buildings, Sir Hugh Waterton, their governor, said. The likelihood was that they would find themselves in the Exchequer, or the Council Chamber, and fall into the blackest disworship.

They rode in by the north gate, past the Clock House and the Star Chamber. There was a fountain in the middle of the court; and the Great Hall, flanked by towers, dominated the whole enclosure. Beyond this, and the Chapel of St Stephen, the second court was reached. Here were the royal apartments. They were magnificently furnished, and hung with tapestries bright with the gold thread of Cyprus; and when the princes were escorted to their bedchambers they found beds as grand as Bel sire's, with dorsers of velvet, or bawdekin, or even cloth of gold. There were chairs covered with stamped Cordovan leather, and cushions of silk tossed carelessly into them; and the candle-sconces were of gilded silver. Men in the Lancaster livery ran to divest the princes of their dripping mantles; but for every man in blue-and-white there seemed to be two in royal scarlet.

The princes were tired; and when they had stripped off their sodden finery they shrugged themselves into houpelandes: comfortable, loose tunics, slit up the sides, and reaching to below the knee.

They found Harry in a solar overlooking the river, seated in the window-embrasure. He had changed his robes for a pourpoint, with long hose, and a jewelled belt clipped round his waist. He was dragging a melody from the strings of his harp, and his face wore a closed look. He had been in this mood ever since his return from Trim Castle. John knew that when he chose to do so Harry could shut himself away from the world; but Thomas was puzzled. He cast an enquiring look at Harry, but did not venture to address him. He threw himself on a cushioned banker, with his arms flung wide, so that his fingers touched the rushes on the floor on either side of the banker, and said: 'God's dignity, what a day! I envied Jack Holland, curled up in his cloak last night, in the Chapel!'

'Why didn't Father knight the Mortimers?' asked Humfrey. 'Where are they?'

'Oh, too dangerful!' said Thomas. 'There are bound to be many who will say the Mortimers stand nearer to the throne than we do. Father will keep them out of sight: that was all talked over in Brittany!'

'But does anyone want Edmund Mortimer for King? How old is he? Younger than any of us, isn't he? What was it like in Brittany, Thomas?'

'Oh, well enough, though *I* liked Paris better! You never know what may happen there! The hurlings that go on! It made me laugh to think what would be the end of it if one started brawling in London after that fashion! The sheriff's men would throw one in the Clink before one could say a paternoster! Father was too ware to mell himself with the Burgundians or the Orleanists, but he was friendly with Louis of Orleans. I don't think he likes him much, though. They all say that Louis has been Queen Isabeau's lover for years, and is the father of at least three of her children. Fancy cuckolding your own brother! All the same, I liked him better than Burgundy's son: the ugliest man you ever saw! He has a nose as long as your arm, and a great loose mouth with wet lips. His people call him the Fearless, because he fought at Nicopolis.'

'Did he perform some worshipful feat of arms?' asked John.

'No more than any other. But that's just like the French! If Uncle John Beaufort had taken to calling himself the Fearless everyone in England would have thought it a jape.'

'But the Burgundians aren't French, are they?' said Humfrey.

'No, but the Duke is. He is the King's uncle, one of the sons of the old French King Great-uncle Edward took prisoner at Poitiers. He and Orleans are always fighting over which of them is to rule France when the King is wood. It's not like that in Brittany, of course, because the old Duke isn't mad. Did you know that our thirdfather Edward made him Earl of Richmond?

I didn't, but it is so. I think he married one of our grand-aunts, but she parted her life years ago, and I'm not sure about that.'

Humfrey, the precocious, was more interested in the Duke's third wife. 'Tell us!' he invited. '*Is* Father asotted of the Duchess?'

'Now, who told you that?' demanded Thomas, sitting up.

'Oh, it is noised!' Humfrey said vaguely. 'We learn that she is very fair.'

'Yes, she is, but if you are thinking that Father has been cuckolding the Duke you are out! He lives very chaste. All his French friends wondered at him!'

'Forget-me-not!' murmured Humfrey.

Thomas burst out laughing. 'What a crumb-fox you are! Yes, Father did give her a jewel with the forget-me-not badge on it, but I daresay it might as well have been the Antelope, or the Greyhound. I am going to take the Greyhound for *my* badge. You will take the Bohun Swan, of course, because you are named Humfrey. Is it still raining? It won't be thought a good omen if it rains tomorrow.

'No, and if we are to be soaked to the skin again—' Humfrey broke off, turning his head as the rings rattled along the rod across the doorway, and the traverse was thrust aside. 'Supper at last!'

But it was their father who entered the chamber, not looking like a King, as he had looked all day, in his grand robes, and with his face stiffened and aloof, but as they had always known him, in his pourpoint and hose, the collar of SS about his neck, and his eyes bright and smiling. He said, as all four boys leaped to their feet: 'No, no, you cannot eat me! Are you so keen-bitten? Send for your supper, then! But not too many doucets! My new knights must be in good point tomorrow.' His quick glance ran over them. 'You are tired, but you enjoyed it? You liked to be the first of my new knights?'

Thomas answered for all: 'Certes, sir!'

'And you, Harry? You are well, my son?'

'I am well, sir.'

'I would I might have knighted you too, but since you have already received that honour – well, sleeveless to repine!'

'Sir, what will you do with the King?' asked Harry, as though he had not heard his father.

The smile was arrested in Henry's eyes, but he answered quite gently: 'I am the King, Harry.'

'With King Richard!' Harry corrected himself, flushing.

'Why, what do you think I shall do with Richard my cousin? He shall live retired in one of my castles. I shall do him no scathe.' He saw Harry's mouth quiver, and turned with one of his swift movements, and said: 'Away with you, my children! I must be private with your brother!' He waited until the three younger boys had left the chamber, and then sat down, and said: 'Come here, Harry!'

Harry came to him, and, at a sign from him, sat down on a stool, holding his clasped hands between his knees. His father said: 'Have you gall at your heart because I risked your life upon this throw?'

'No!'

'The thoughts are upsy-down in your head, eh?' Harry looked up, surprised. 'Yes, yes, I know!' the King said. 'You love Richard, and I do not blame you for that. But you are my eldest son, and I shall need you.'

'My duty is to you sir,' Harry replied formally.

'After my coronation,' said the King, 'Parliament will meet again, and I shall create you Prince of Wales.' He watched Harry's eyes fly to his, and a laugh sprang to his own. 'You have not had time yet to think what all I have done will mean to you, have you? Think now! Do you too wish to rule this realm, Harry?'

'Yes!' Harry said, looking beyond him, 'I wish to rule this realm!' He brought his gaze back to his father's face, and added: 'I have always wished that – the King – King Richard – aside.'

King Henry stretched out his hand. 'Richard placed that ring on my finger.'

'Enforced!'

'Enforced. Few men have ruled so ill, my son.'

'I know.'

'A little you know. Not all – nor I, yet! He has so wasted his livelihood that if I have taken from him his sceptre I have also taken on me his troubles. Perhaps nothing but trouble lies before me: that I know not, though some of it I can already perceive. There are many who will seek to undo us. How old are you, Harry? Past thirteen, by my reckoning. In a year you will be a man. I must be sure of my son!'

'Yes, certes, yes!' Harry said. 'But tell me what you will do with King Richard, sir!'

The King fingered the links of his collar. 'Archbishop Arundel would house him for me at Leeds Castle in Kent. If that does not serve – and it is overly near to London – I might send him to Pontefract. Robert Waterton would guard him straitly. Using him with all courtesy, of course.'

Harry had risen from the stool, and was pacing about the solar. He said, over his shoulder: 'The Hollands will make you trouble sir! They are his own kin!'

'Dreadless! Others too. There will be a vengeance demanded on all who gained by Gloucester's death.'

Harry checked in his stride. 'Gloucester's death! But—!'

'Awkward,' agreed King Henry. '*I* gained by that death, and your uncle John Beaufort was one of those who appealed Gloucester. Mariners tell of whirlpools in the sea: there is a whirlpool of blood at our feet at this hour, Harry! If I can steer our vessel wide of it I shall do so. Fortunately,' he added thoughtfully, 'there is a sop I may well throw to the hounds. Yes, they have arrested one Hall, who seems to have had a hand in Gloucester's murder. He can die, and shall; and since Norfolk is gone to his last end there is no need to spill more blood. But it will be difficult sailing, my son!'

3

The coronation took place on the following day, and nothing occurred to mar the propriety of the ceremony except the unfortunate incident of the phial of sacred oil, which Archbishop Arundel, restored to his dignities, was to have poured over his master's head.

The phial, which had been discovered amongst King Richard's treasures, contained the oil miraculously bestowed on St Thomas by the Virgin Mary, and was originally a Lancastrian possession, having been won by Henry, John of Gaunt's great father-in-law, and given by him to the Lord Edward. Malicious persons said that when the Archbishop broke the seal lice fell out of the phial, and swarmed over the King's head: the truth was that nothing issued from the phial. The Archbishop was much too astute to betray that anything had gone awry; but a good deal of capital was made out of the incident; and many men said that it was an ill-omen.

Two days later the King created his eldest son Prince of Wales, Earl of Cornwall and Chester, Duke of Lancaster, and Aquitaine; and two days later still he granted Master Chaucer a new pension. Master Chaucer was in straits again, but no discomfort could dim his wit. He sent the new King a ballad, calling it his Complaint to his Purse. He wrote in it that he was shaved bare as any friar; and when they read it the lordings rocked with mirth, knowing that he had meant them to laugh. The King granted the pension willingly, glad that one of his first acts should be charitable, for well he knew that less agreeable duties lay before him.

Hardly had the rejoicings at his accession died than the trouble he had foreseen broke out. Every man who had a grudge to avenge or an ambition to realize rushed into the lists; and above the clamour of voices shouting for the arraignment of the abdicated King arose the cries of those who demanded that Bagot, the only one of Richard's friends on life, should be impeached. King Henry allowed him to be brought before Parliament. Edward of Aumâle was his accuser, but Bagot brought so many counter-charges against him that Edward lost his temper, and flung down his gage, demanding that the issue should be tried by combat. This witless action caused the cauldron to boil over. More than forty gages were cast on the floor of the Chamber at Westminster, each rashhead accusing the next of treason, and the hubbub so great that it was many minutes before the King could make his own voice heard. He rode the storm, but only by promising that enquiry should be made into the death of his uncle of Gloucester. He met his Council with a firm front. He would not wade through blood to the throne, he said; and any man so hardy as to demand King Richard's death should be set out of his grace.

He quelled his barons, but amongst his own friends there was scarcely a man who did not urge him to violence; amongst King Richard's there was not one who was not ripe for mischief. He had restored young Thomas Fitzalan to his dignities, but nothing short of vengeance on his one-time guardian, John Holland of Exeter, was going to satisfy the new Earl of Arundel. His uncle, the Archbishop, preached Christian doctrine to him, but to the King he said: 'My nephew, sire, is a yellowbeak, but he is one of many. Too much kindness shown now may lead you to bloodshed later. I dare not guess how many men are watching to see how strong your hand is on the bridle.'

'Or how sharp my spurs?' said the King, snapping out one of his quick retorts. 'I never rowel the flanks of my horses, Father, nor is it the custom of my house to spill blood wantonly!'

'God knows, my son, that I desire bloodshed as little as you, yet while Richard lives, and his friends go unpunished, I fear for the peace of this realm.'

'I will not have Richard touched!'

'The Commons are demanding his arraignment. If he were to be tried—'

'No!' Even the King's tawny beard seemed to jut belligerently. 'He shall be privily removed from the Tower, and carried to a safe hold! As for those who appealed my uncle of Gloucester, we will do justice on them, but wallow in blood I will not!'

The Archbishop frowningly regarded his bony hands. 'Very dread lord, there is a time for unguents, and a time for more desperate remedies,' he said significantly.

Nearly all who stood for Lancaster agreed with him; the Percies; Clifford, whom the King had made his Privy Seal; dry Scarle, his Chancellor; Sir Thomas Erpingham, his Chamberlain; Reginald Grey of Ruthin, his close friend. Only Ralph Neville of Westmoreland, his Marshal, said: 'We have a shorter way on the Border, but I am not one to be teaching my King his

124

trade, and I have known bloodshed to lead to worse gall.'

'And too strict enquiry into loss of title, my lord of West-moreland!' Grey flung at him, in his rough way.

The King laughed. 'Thriftily, Reginald, thriftily! There were some others who came by new titles when Neville of Raby was made Earl of Westmoreland! Duketti, they called us!'

'My liege!' Grey stood aghast. 'You had no hand in Glouc-ester's death!'

'No, nor Ralph, so let that sleep!' said the King.

'Ay, let all sleep!' growled the Lord of Ruthin. 'I warrant you Richard's friends are wakeful!'

2 King Richard's Nurselings

1

King Henry's first Parliament was not distinguished for seemliness. Day followed upon day of acrimonious debate, sometimes culminating in such scenes of violence that the hardiest of the King's friends wavered. Only the King stood firm. He handled his Council and the turbulent Commons skilfully; and when the clamour for King Richard's arraignment reached its height he removed his cousin secretly from the Tower, and sent him no man knew whither. Choosing what he saw to be the lesser of two evils, he diverted attention from Richard by giving his consent to an enquiry into the death of Gloucester. Norfolk's old servant, Hall, was brought before the Commission, and deposed that Gloucester had been smothered in a house in Calais by one Serle, sometime valet-de-chambre to King Richard.

King Henry threw his sop to the hounds, not greatly caring whether Hall was guilty or innocent of any share in his uncle's murder. He seemed a nasty little man, worthy of the nasty death which befell him. Sir William Rickhill, standing primly before the Commission, wonderfully clouded the issue in precise, legal terms; so that the only fact to emerge from his evidence was that when he would have visited Gloucester a second time, in Calais, Norfolk, then Earl of Nottingham, had prevented him. Yes, he said, he had found my lord Duke in unease of spirit, greatly fearing his fate at Nottingham's hands. This was enough to set men thirsting for Mowbray blood. The King thought it a pity his old enemy had died in exile. He had left no heir of an age to stand as scapegoat for him, not the most ruthless of the barons wishing to be revenged on two lads no older than Prince Harry and Prince John. The dukedom was not revived for young

Thomas Mowbray, but he succeeded his father as Earl of Nottingham, and hereditary Earl Marshal. The King placed him and his brother Edmund in the care of their aunt, the Countess of Hereford, who was his own mother-in-law; and sought for fresh sops to throw to his loving lieges.

He told his half-brother, the Marquis of Dorset, that he must be prepared to lose his outlandish title. 'Is that all?' said John Beaufort. 'I was amongst those who appealed Thomas of Gloucester and have thought my head sat loosely on my shoulders ever since your accession, brother!'

'For God's love, let me hear no unwit in my privy chamber!' said the King irritably. 'When all this hurling has abated, I want you for my Chamberlain!'

'You might be wiser to stick my head on the bridge with the rest,' said John Beaufort.

'*No* heads shall be stuck on the bridge in this cause!' swore the King.

He kept his word, but got small thanks for his clemency. Titles, not heads, came tumbling down. Three of the Duketti, Aumâle, Exeter, and Surrey, became again the Earls of Rutland, Huntingdon, and Kent; and Dorset, deprived of his unvalued marquisate, was once more the Earl of Somerset.

2

In the middle of all this turmoil, news was brought from Brittany that the aged John of Montfort was dead, leaving his eleven-year-old heir in the wardship of his mother, the lovely Duchess. King Henry gave no sign that these tidings were of more than formal interest to him; but turned his attention to the safe bestowal of the young Earl of March and his brother. Edmund Mortimer, directly descended through his granddam, the only offspring of M. de Guyenne's elder brother, Lionel of Clarence, from King Edward III, seemed to be a healthy child, but rather dull-witted. Roger Mortimer was undersized, and looked sickly. The King sent them off to Windsor, suitably attended. Their mother, who was a Holland, and King Richard's half-niece, at once raised a shriek of protest; but as no objection was made to her visiting her sons, who were not more strictly guarded than any other noble imps, nobody paid any heed to her.

In the meantime, the three degraded Duketti, and the Lord Despenser, were placed in the nominal custody of the Abbot of Westminster: an act of clemency that caused dissatisfaction to rage amongst the King's friends. His youngest half-brother, Thomas Beaufort, told him that such weakness would bring all to ruin. 'You should have had the heads of Rutland, and the Hollands!' he said. 'All this mercy—! Men wear the badge of King Richard's White Hart openly since the judgments, and say they are his nurselings! With respect, I say—'

'When you sit upon my Council, Thomas, you may say what you list, and until that day you may hold your peace!' interrupted the King.

But Thomas Beaufort was the mouthpiece of men more worshipful than he; and the grutchings were gathering volume when the Scots provided King Henry with a diversion. With both the great Border lords, Percy and Neville, absent from the North, it seemed good to King Robert of Scotland's subjects to seize the Castle of Wark, and to bear off the Constable's two sons to Scotland. As King Henry was at the time engaged in prolonging the truce between the two countries this provided him with a pretext for losing his temper in a public and awesome manner, and announcing his intention of marching in person against his perfidious neighbours. Percies, Nevilles, Beaumonts, Cliffords, and even the Greys of Heaton, nearly concerned in the loss of Wark, at once set aside the question of the treatment of King Richard's advisers to dissuade the King from so rash a venture. It was plain to them that he had no understanding of Border politics. While they were still trying to convince him that truces counted for little, and that small noyances were to be expected when the Wardens of the Marches were known to be absent from their posts, he wrung a fairly generous grant out of Parliament, and adjourned it until after Christmas-tide.

He was going to spend the festival at Windsor, with all his children, and several days were to be devoted to a tournament. Heralds were already proclaiming this in public places, and the attendance was expected to be enormous. The King was not going to adventure his person in the lists, so that it was probable that unless Richard Beauchamp's brilliance outmatched their greater experience John Beaufort and Harry Hotspur would have the field.

All the royal children but Harry were sent down to Windsor at the beginning of December. None of them had ever visited the castle before, and they were overawed when they passed over the Great Bridge and through a heavily embattled Gate Tower into the Lower Bailey, only to discover that there were two more bridges and gates to pass, and a Middle Ward to circumvent before they reached the Upper Bailey, where the royal lodgings were situated. Westminster Palace had not filled them with this awe; and not even Father's coronation had so forcibly brought it home to them that they really were a King's children as their first sight of this huge nursery of their race, with its massive Keep, high on the mound which occupied almost the whole of the Middle Ward; its countless towers, some round, some square, some so menacingly old that they made one think of dark and bloodstained times, some so new that they were still unweathered; the courts, and the hidden curtilages; and the mass of buildings which furnished lodgings for canons, and knights, stables, brewhouses, bakehouses, spiceries, pantries, and larders. For several days their awe persisted; and when they ventured out of the royal lodging they walked with sobriety through the wards, looking about them with unaccustomed timidity. Mannerly and shamefast, the new King's children! That was what the canons and the chaplains said. Mary Hervey and Hugh Waterton accepted compliments on the royal family, and wondered how long humility would endure.

Not for many days, of course. Long before the King arrived to join his offspring, the princely children had driven everyone in the vast castle distracted. If the whole brood were not playing Hunt the Hare in and out of the cloisters, with the Mortimer boys to add to the clamour, they were swarming up the mound to the Keep, asking innumerable questions of the men-at-arms.

Whatever the churchmen might think of the Lancaster children, the men-at-arms took them to their hearts; and great was the scandal when the two noble ladies were discovered in the guard-room by nurses who had only taken their eyes off them, they vowed, for five minutes. The Lady Blanche, attired in a furred robe only very slightly mired round the hem, sat enthroned upon a table; the Lady Philippa, a stout five-year-old, occupied the knee of a man in a leathern jerkin; and their brothers were grouped with casual grace about them: one with a rent in his pourpoint; one with his hose muddied to the knees; and the third with a clout bound round a cut hand. All five of them were munching fat bacon and pease-bread, and refreshing themselves with draughts of some liquid their attendants preferred not to identify.

Dame Hervey represented to Sir Hugh the impropriety of such conduct; but although Sir Hugh agreed that the Keep was no place for the Ladies Blanche and Philippa, he said that there was no better place for the lordings. The only thing he deplored was the accident that had discovered the bowes to his charges; but even of this he said, with a long-suffering sigh, that if a frape of lads were brought to live where subterranean passages ran beneath the castle buildings to posterns opening into the dry ditch any man knew what to expect. He was roused to wrath, however, when he found that the lordings were well-known figures in Windsor town. The gatewards swore that never had they permitted the royal children to pass out of the precincts; and Sir Hugh knew better than to ask his charges how they had contrived to slip out unnoticed. He merely growled that he would be glad when their royal father came to school them.

But when the King came to Windsor he was in holiday mood, and he only laughed at the tale of their iniquities, saying that now that he had loosed Harry amongst them he supposed they would never be out of mischief. This was probably true, because Harry had a fertile mind; but before he could lead his brothers into any exploit disaster overtook the family. The King and his sons, Sir Harry Percy, and others of the officers of his household were all smitten by a strange malady. Thomas and John, sick for two days, soon recovered; but Humfrey went on vomiting for some time; and Harry was so ill that the King dragged himself from his own sickbed to hang tenderly over his heir's. Nobody died of the visitation; but when the physicians informed the King that the Prince would live they waited only for him to return thanks to God before telling him that it was the opinion of them all that an attempt had been made to poison him and his heirs. The King listened with an inscrutable countenance, and waved them away.

It was Dame Katherine who exclaimed: 'Harry, it was that Frenchman Richard was used to have about him! Jean Poulle, he calls himself, and I saw him here the very day I came! I knew how it would be!' She saw a smile touch the King's lips, and added tartly: 'Fleer, if you choose, but ask my son John if I did not tell him, when you seized Richard's throne, that it would be your bane! Well, you have made my son your Chamberlain, and be sure I am grateful to you, but let me live in peace hereafter, I beg of you! And let me tell you, Harry, which I would allow no one to do while you were stricken, that my lady of Gloucester has parted her life – broken-hearted, they say, and no wonder! – and you must all of you put on mourning-weeds!'

'No, I don't think I shall do that,' said the King.

'Which,' said Humfrey later, pale and languid on a banker, 'is fortunate, because we might have been expected to have been condemned to wear weeds to eternity, mourning, as we do, an aunt and a great-aunt in one person!'

3

The news of the illnesses at Windsor leaked out, and before the dawn of the new year a deputation of his chief barons waited on the King to beg him to dispose of his cousin Richard. He said hastily: 'Stint! No more of this!' but they showed him how the realm must be troubled while Richard lived; and wrung from him at last a promise that if an uprising were to take place Richard should die. 'I would he *were* dead, but not by my hand!' Henry said, sore-goaded.

No man who had been borne to his throne on the enthusiasm of a hundred thousand men much feared a general uprising, but the King was already finding Richard an embarrassment. He had sent him to the Lancastrian hold of Pontefract, where he lived in the custody of Sir Robert Waterton, and Dame Katherine's son, Sir Thomas Swynford. They reported of their charge that he swung between moods of accidie and rage, sometimes refusing to partake of the choicest viands for days together. The King could not forbear the wish that his cousin would prolong these fits to the point of real starvation. Apart from the precarious nature of his position while the deposed King lived, the French Court was now brewing trouble for him. The news of his son-in-law's abdication had so much affected King Charles that his madness had come on him, and with such violence that he had had to be confined in a barred chamber in the Castle of Creil. Orleans, who had so often urged his dear cousin Henry to descend in force upon England, was loudly condemning his actions. There was also the little Queen Isabelle; and what to do with her was a pressing problem. Henry had set ladies about her whom he could trust, and had sent her to live at Sonning, but this was only a temporary expedient. If Richard were dead he could make a push to marry her to Harry, for although it had been reported to him that she was inconsolable for the loss of her husband he did not take this very seriously. She was only a child, and had never been more than a wife in name. The match would be a good one, and might lead to a lasting truce with France, which was regrettably necessary: a war could only be conducted at huge costage, and King Richard had left his cousin empty coffers.

Henry, who loved jousting, was not fond of war, but he could see that an expedition against France would have provided his malcontents with a diversion. He did not doubt his ability to command such an expedition, because one of the accepted axioms of his upbringing had been that whenever an English army sallied forth to do battle against the French it trounced them soundly. Or anyone else, he reflected, remembering the hardy warriors who had fought under his banner in Pruce. Not that he wished to see that form of warfare in Western Europe: it was uncivilized, and there was too much slaughter, which made it disgusting to Englishmen, because it was wasteful. There was no profit in slaughter: you could not hold dead men to ransom; and profit was what the borel-men sought when they enlisted under their liege-lords' banners.

But a King of England ought to show his people that he could win battles. If he did that he might afterwards do as it pleased him: until he had done it he would win no worship.

At once the King's mind took a turn: in another year young Harry would be a man. He would hand him over to his old friend Hotspur to be taught his trade. A taste of Border warfare would blood him nicely. He had been a little too much under the influence of his uncle, Bishop Henry Beaufort, but that could be amended. The King liked the Bishop of Lincoln the least of his half-brothers. Henry was already at loggerheads with Arch-bishop Arundel, fast becoming the King's dearest friend, and he had made himself the head of a Court party opposing Arundel. He would have to be watched. John Beaufort was not as clever as Henry, but far more dependable. Alone amongst the degraded nobles he had made no outcry at the loss of his marquisate: so unlike that moon-calf, Edward of Rutland, who had been sulking ever since he had ceased to be Duke of Aumâle!

Thoughts of his cousin Edward led the King's mind to the other lords whom he had deprived of their titles, and who were not in the least grateful to him for having saved them from the axe. Huntingdon! Well, he was married to Bess, and might perhaps believe that he had only to bide his time before she won for him a place on her brother's Council. Then there was Despenser, whom Richard had had the effrontery to make Earl of Glouces-ter. After Norfolk, he was the one man who could probably tell at first hand how Thomas of Woodstock had met his end. There had been little love lost between Henry and his uncle, but they were Plantagenets both, and it made Henry long to get his hands round Despenser's throat when he thought of his share in that ugly business. He would have no compunction in dealing with Despenser after his deserts, if he gave him an excuse to do it. But would he? He was wedded to York's daughter, the Lady Constance, and York desired peace. However, one never knew: Constance was an intriguer. She and her brother Richard of Coningsburgh favoured their Castilian mother. With all his faults, thought Henry, Edward of Rutland was more a Plantagenet than a grandson of Pedro the Cruel.

But it was Edward, not Richard, who was concerned in a new plot to murder the King and his four sons.

4

The younger princes made no bones about it: they enjoyed the affair from start to finish. Harry's enjoyment was overcast by his fears for Cousin Richard's safety, but the news certainly had an invigorating effect upon him. At one moment he lay wan upon a sickbed; at the next he was on his feet, tottering on his legs, but driving the physicians from his chamber, and declaring himself to be ready to do whatever might be required of him.

It all began with the arrival of the new Mayor of London at Windsor, upon a blown hackney. Master Knollys demanded audience of the King; and when he was brought to the King's chamber he straightway disclosed a plot against the life of his royal master.

It had come from the lips of a common file, one who had lain with a man wearing Huntingdon's livery, and had learnt from him enough to send her running to the sheriff. Huntingdon was one of the conspirators, his nephew of Kent another; and probably, since the treasonable meetings were said to have been held at the Abbey House, the Abbot of Westminster as well. The wench had not been able to remember all the names which had tripped off her lover's tongue, but what she had recounted was matter enough for the King's ear. Windsor Castle was to be taken by surprise, the men who were to achieve this being smuggled through the gate in the carts which carried the barrels of harness for the coming tournament.

It sounded rather improbable, but by dusk the story had received confirmation. Edward of Rutland arrived from King's Langley on a rowelled horse, flung himself at his cousin's feet, and poured out a tearful confession.

He had been up to the hilt in the plot. He said that he had been cozened by his sister, the Lady Despenser, and if the Abbot of Westminster thought it right to set his name to the bond, who was he to think he knew better? The Bishop of Carlisle was concerned in it too, and several lesser churchmen. Huntingdon, Kent, Salisbury, Despenser, and others had all signed the bond; and as many as six thousand of their men were mustering at Kingston at this very hour. They had with them a priest whom Richard had favoured, and who bore a remarkable resemblance to his old master; and they meant to show him to the common people, pretending that he was the King.

King Henry listened calmly to the story. His eyes scanned the blubbered face at his knee; he said: 'And why, fair cousin, have you brought this tale to me?'

'I repented me!' Edward groaned. 'I had not understood what it was that I had set my name to!'

'You had better tell me the truth,' said the King. 'There may be six thousand men who have sworn to take my life, but I still have the power to take yours!'

'Grace!' cried Edward. 'Very dread lord – Harry, we have hunted the hart together!'

'The truth!' said the King.

Out it came, Edward hanging his guilty head. My lord of York was coming hard upon his son's heels, the traitorous bond safe in his clutch. It was he who had discovered the existence of the plot, and had dragged the details of it out of Edward; and he was riding to Windsor, not to beg for his son's life, but to urge the King to head a cumberworld who kept faith with no man. Never had Edward seen his mild father roused to such fury! He had stood stockishly staring while my lord stamped out, calling for his horse; and he might still have been so standing but for the advice of his quicker-witted brother and stepmother. They had counselled him to fling himself astride his fleetest courser, and to ride to Windsor ahead of his father. He had done it. He added sadly that he feared he had killed that noble animal.

It was too ridiculous. The King heard Sir Thomas Erpingham choke behind his chair, and put up his own hand to hide his mouth. 'Well, now you will come to London with me, and help me to disperse these rebels,' he said.

Several of the King's friends exclaimed at this, but Edward was kissing his hand, and swearing to bring the heads of his fellow-conspirators to him on pikes.

'It would be folly to head such a stot as Rutland!' the King said. 'He has no more wit than a sparrow.'

'Witless he may be,' said Sir Peter Buckton grimly, 'but we'll have him under guard, my liege, or likely he'll be off to warn his friends they are betrayed.'

'Keep him under guard until we reach London,' said the King. 'After that he may warn his friends with my goodwill.' He saw Buckton gaping at him, and added acidly: 'If you think I mean to risk a battle against my own subjects you are as wan-witted as Rutland! Let the redeless men be dispersed! Their leaders I will take order to, content you!'

5

The royal party left Windsor at nightfall, and were met outside Ludgate by the Mayor, attended by the sheriffs and aldermen, and a company of the train-bands. The children were lodged in the Tower; and the King swept off to set on foot a number of brisk measures. He took Rutland with him as his lieutenant, an arrangement which araged no one more than my lord of York, who was so full of bitterness against the son who had done his possible to destroy his peace that he passionately urged his nephew to make an end of Edward.

The princes hoped to hear that Father had won a notable battle, but the tidings that came to them were of something quite different. Hearing that the rebels, having sacked Windsor Castle, had drawn off to Colnbrook, the King had marched to Oxford. It was said that Thomas Holland of Kent, finding Father flown from Windsor, had called him a rat who dared not face him. The princes bristled at this, but the sequel was all that could have been desired. Warned by Rutland of the failure of their plot, Kent, Salisbury, Lumley, and the Lord Despenser drew off to Cirencester, where, however, the inhabitants were so much dismayed by the arrival of a rebel force in their midst that they saw nothing for it but to take up arms against them. They barricaded the ways out of the town, and waged such a brisk war that by the small hours of the morning the lords were forced to surrender. Only the Lord Despenser managed to escape; Sir Thomas Berkeley took the other three into custody, and lodged them in the Abbey, pending the King's pleasure. Unfortunately, a priest in their meiny fired a number of houses in the town, hoping that in the rush to put out the flames the lords might make good their escape. But the citizens, instead of running to rescue their chattels wrested the lords out of Sir Thomas's hands, and headed them without more ado. After that, they packed the three heads in a pannier, and sent these trophies to Oxford, with their humble duty to the King. The deputation found him at breakfast in the Carmelite monastery where he was lodging; and after louting low they unpacked the pannier, and showed him its contents.

The Mayor of London delivered these tidings to Harry, as his duty was, and even Sir Hugh admitted that Harry behaved very well, considering . . .

It was Humfrey who was responsible for what happened. After a stunned moment, he said: 'What – what a splendid morning-gift for Father!'

Thomas and John exploded into peals of mirth; Harry got up, and strode to the window, his shoulders shaking. The Mayor stood looking from one to the other of them, not understanding why they laughed. But the Mayor did not know Father, and probably he thought that any man would be blithe to be given the heads of his worst enemies. The princes knew their father too well to suppose that he would have felt anything but disgust. At his breakfast too, when he would have been at his most testy! 'And what said the King's majesty when he was given this Hanguvelle?' grinned John.

'My lord, his majesty was right glad, and spoke comfortable words to the men of Cirencester!'

So Father had risen beautifully to the occasion! Harry pulled himself together, and came back to his chair. He thanked the Mayor graciously, and only when the puzzled man had bowed himself out did he let go the laughter that was consuming him.

A week later Father was back in London, with the news that Despenser had been captured and headed at Bristol. The only leader of importance who had escaped was the Earl of Huntingdon; but hard on the heels of the King's return to the City came news out of Essex. The Earl, breaking back to London, had dropped down the river in a small boat, but, being driven ashore by storms, he had landed on the Essex coast, near Hadleigh Castle; and had sought shelter with an old acquaintance, the valetudinarian Earl of Oxford, who was its Constable. Sir Aubrey de Vere was the uncle of King Richard's dead favourite, and the guiding principle of his life was to keep away from factions and intrigues. When he beheld Huntingdon within his gates, his emotions threatened to prostrate him. Happily for him, Huntingdon had been seen near the castle. It was with relief that Oxford handed him over to the citizens who demanded him. It seemed likely that Huntingdon, like his nephew of Kent, would be headed by the mob; but before the men of Essex had reached agreement a company of men-at-arms arrived from Pleshy, announcing that my lady of Hereford had sent them to take the Earl into custody. They conducted him to Pleshy, and imprisoned him in the gatehouse. My lady of Hereford, who was born a Fitzalan, sat down to write a letter to her son-in-law, King Henry. She was as calm as ever, but her women thought that she looked happier than at any time since her brother of Arundel had met a shames-death.

6

Everyone wondered what the King would do; and even those who most condemned his clemency acknowledged that his position was awkward. Huntingdon deserved no mercy, but he was wedded to the King's own sister, and the Lady Bess was not one to spare either effort or eloquence in her determination to save her husband from the block.

The King was rescued from his difficulty. He told his sons that he had sent a trusted officer to bring Huntingdon to London, but that before this could be done the men of Essex had taken matters into their own hands, and executed the Earl.

This statement was amplified by the princes' cronies amongst the men-at-arms. The Earl, they said, had made a good end. If they were to be believed, he had done so under trying circumstances, for he had been disembowelled before being headed. According to one veteran, he had sat in a chair with his guts burning before his eyes, and had maintained an affable conversation with his executioner. 'He was offered to drink,' said the man-at-arms, 'but, "Nay," quotha, "I have no place, friend, to put it." And then he forgave his enemies, and commended his soul to God, and his head was taken from him at one stroke.'

Harry, kindling to a tale of high courage, said that Huntingdon's end atoned for all his crimes; but when Sir Hugh Waterton heard the story he said the same had been told of at least two other traitors who had suffered this particular penalty. He had seen a-many men drawn and headed, and it was his opinion that if they were not dead by the time the drawing was done they were certainly in no case to bandy words with their executioners. 'Courage?' said Sir Hugh. 'Ay, no charge! A man has need of hardihood who mells himself in treason!'

Sir Hugh's verdict was disappointing, but was presently forgotten in a fresh disclosure. Harry discovered that the trusted officer sent to bring Huntingdon to London had been none other than Thomas Fitzalan, the young Earl of Arundel, my lord's vengeable ward. He went white when he heard the truth, and for days he could scarely bring himself to look at his father. He said that Father had demeaned himself unknightly; and that was the worst thing Harry could say of anyone.

'I daresay you will find yourself that knightliness and kingship can't always be practised together,' remarked Humfrey lightly.

Harry's eyes flashed. 'As God sees me, I will never tread a crooked path to achieve my ends! A King should be fearless and just, or forfeit his kingdom!'

'As Cousin Richard did,' said Thomas, not kindly.

Harry's fists clenched, but he did not fly at Thomas. He turned away, saying: 'Yes. As Cousin Richard did!'

3 After Wind Cometh Rain

I

It might have been expected that after nipping rebellion in the bud the King would have lost his frown, but it seemed to bite deeper into his brow as the days passed. None of his sons had more than a vague knowledge of what the cares were which pressed so hard upon him, but they all knew that he was besieged with demands and petitions; and they could all see that the first flush of his popularity had waned. The great lords who had placed him on the throne had ambitions which they looked to him to gratify; and the redeless Commons, hailing him as their preserver, expected him to right every grievance which was brought to his notice. Lords, Church, and Commons were at one in ignoring the unpleasant truth that without money little could be done; and if all the three estates had united in condemning King Richard's unthrift they were equally united in the belief that in placing King Henry on the throne they had filled the royal coffers. They thought that the demesne lands should provide him with money for his personal needs; but his predecessor had granted so many of these as rewards that they were much diminished.

Of the four princes, only John took a real interest in the country's revenue. Harry studied it as a duty; Thomas was bored by it; and Humfrey preferred the Humanities. John was fascinated by it; and soon discovered that it was derived from direct taxation and from Customs, of which the King's levy on wool was the most important. This, 'the sovereign merchandize and jewel of the realm', was the most valuable of the exports, the best Cotswold wool fetching as much as twelve marks the sack, of which the King claimed half a mark. Next to wool came corn, cloth and honey; and, some way behind these, lead, tin, salt, fish, hides, and other such commodities. There were also tallages on the counties, boroughs, and cities; and a special duty on all wine imported into the country.

More lucrative than the duties were the land-charges. Forfeits and escheats brought in a respectable sum; but although the deaths under attainder of several rich lords had brought their estates into the hands of the Crown the money thus accruing was speedily swallowed up by the barons who had lent the King their aid, and demanded reward for their services.

It was one of the chief complaints of John Wycliffe's disciples that the richest body of men in the land paid relatively the least towards its maintenance. Both the Southern and the Northern Convocations met every year to vote a fraction of the Church's wealth to the Crown: it never seemed to amount to more than a tenth, yet all men could see the opulence of bishoprics and abbeys; and all men knew what large gifts poured into the coffers of the great mendicant orders of Friars.

One of the easiest, and, on the whole, the most satisfactory ways of rewarding a man to whom the King stood in debt was to grant him a valuable wardship. It was seldom that this arrangement was abused, for a man who held in ward a minor of substance found it to his advantage to administer the estates wisely. He enjoyed the revenues until the last year of his ward's minority; if possible he married the ward to one of his own daughters; and if he were a kind guardian he found himself at the end of his guardianship not only wealthier, but linked by marriage-ties to a powerful ally. From time to time, of course, the custom did suffer abuse, as when my lord of Huntingdon misused Thomas Fitzalan, but these exceptions to the rule were rare, the most threadbare of cunning amongst the barons being well able to perceive the result of such misusage.

There were some, however, notably my lord of Northumberland, who would not be content with this form of reward. Northumberland was Warden of the Eastern Marches, and he said that for years he had been obliged to maintain his own charges. He had been the most lavishly rewarded of all the King's supporters, even having bestowed on him the office of Lord High Constable of England, but never was he satisfied.

John ventured to observe to his father that, in contrast, my lord of Westmoreland was making no such extortionate demands upon him.

'Ah, Ralph Neville must stand or fall by Lancaster!' said the King.

'Percy too, for he would not go with King Richard to Ireland,' said John.

The King looked at him sideways, and arranged a fold of his gown over his knees. 'The Percies are very powerful, my son. Moreover, Thomas Percy of Worcester, Northumberland's brother, was Bel sire's Admiral when he sailed for Spain; and Hotspur and I were lads together.' He saw the dissatisfied look on John's face, and added, with a sigh: 'That counts, John, as one day you will discover for yourself. Eh, the times we have seen, Harry Percy and I! The jests we have laughed at together!'

John said: 'Yea, but I spoke of Northumberland, not of his son Sir Harry, sir. I know he calls himself your Mattathias, but Bel sire said he was a crafty old fox!'

The King laughed, and pulled his ear. 'Master Jackanapes, it is time and high time that you returned to your books!' he said.

2

To John's disgust the King sent his four younger children to Berkhampsted Castle, in Sir Hugh Waterton's charge. Humfrey, who was going to Balliol College, asked nothing better than to be chained to his studies; but not even the acquisition of a new tutor, who was a close friend of Master Chaucer, could reconcile John to what he thought a waste of time. Master Scogan was a stimulating teacher; and when he saw how methodically and accurately John worked, and compared his exquisitely neat writing with Humfrey's often careless scrawl, he entertained hopes of making a scholar of him. He failed, because John was more interested in the problems of the world he knew than in the writings of the Romans; but Master Scogan's wit and his understanding at least made John's last year of pupildom less irksome than Father Joseph could ever have done.

It was not until the end of February that the princes removed to Berkhampsted; and before they left Westminster the rumour that King Richard was dead had received confirmation.

King Richard had died of pure displeasure: that was what the Commons were told. He had decreed in his Will that he would be buried in the Abbey at Westminster, which he had done so much to embellish, but his interment took place, very quietly, at King's Langley.

It was not to be expected that Harry would accept King Richard's death without question. In a manner unbecoming a son he demanded how King Richard had met his end. Perhaps King Henry had been prepared for this question, for he answered readily: 'In one of his fits of woodhead Richard would not eat, though the richest viands were set before him. He died forhungered.'

The King had been signing some documents when Harry had thrust past those who guarded the door. A draught fluttered the topmost – it was the petition of Master Chaucer for a fresh warrant for his pension, he having negligently lost the original – and the King sought for a weight to set upon the papers, and so did not meet the beam of Harry's lion-look.

'There have been many messengers sent to Pontefract in these last weeks!' Harry said, breathing hard through distended nostrils.

'Affirmably,' said the King, setting the ink-standage on his papers. He lifted his eyes, and said in an indifferent tone: 'He lies in an open coffin: there is no mark on him.'

Harry shuddered. 'Forhungered?'

'As I have told you. By his own will, and for despite, belike. He would commit any deed of folly when he was araged.'

Harry remembered the destruction of Sheen Palace; the scenes of fury when Richard would destroy whatever came within reach of his hands; the long spells of accidie when he could scarcely be coaxed to eat or drink. It was possible, it was even dreadfully probable, that one of these fits had visited him in prison. No one would have coaxed him to swallow food at Pontefract. 'Did he slay himself?' he asked, horror in his boy's breaking voice.

'Well, he was not possessed of his wits,' said the King soothingly. He was himself a man of orthodox beliefs, and he had taken care that his children should be reared in these; but he found himself wishing that his heir were not quite so devout. Sometimes he felt that Harry would be more at home in a cloister than on the throne; then he would recall Harry's headstrong pranks, and be reassured. A strange lad, Harry: half the time with his confessor, half the time chin-deep in devilry. He saw the haggard look in Harry's face, and tried to find something to say to comfort his distress, for however noyously Harry might demean himself he was his son and his first-born, and he loved him. 'I have bought a thousand masses for his soul,' he said.

3

After the requiem service at St Paul's for King Richard the younger children went away to Berkhampsted. Some instinct prevented Thomas from discussing Cousin Richard's death within Harry's hearing. He told John that he did not care a rush how Richard had died, because he had heard enough to show him that there would never be peace while he lived. Harry himself repeated to John what Father had said to him, and John replied: 'Very like.'

Harry said, a challenge in his eyes: 'I believe it to be true!'

'Yea, no force!' John said, not because he thought it, but because he knew it was what Harry desperately wished to believe.

Berkhampsted Castle, which lay some ten leagues from London, was surrounded by low hills. It was a spacious home for the King's children, but except for the keep, which was built on a mound, no prospect could be obtained from any of the buildings. King's Langley, which lay at no great distance from Berkhampsted, was more openly placed: the children thought it a pity they could not exchange residences with Great-uncle York, who hardly seemed to care where he lived.

He had aged rapidly since the accession of Lancaster to the throne, and nothing seemed to afford him pleasure. He lived retired from the world, refusing for some time even to receive his elder son, and hanging fondly instead on Richard of

Coningsburgh. Richard was still unmarried, but his father had arranged an alliance for him with the Lady Anne Mortimer. She was an infant, but it was hoped that when she became of marriageable age she would prove a more satisfactory wife than Rutland's lady, whose childlessness was a source of grief to her, and of reproach from her father-in-law. Only Rutland remained cheerful under a series of yearly disappointments. He patted his wife in the kindly fashion he used towards his hounds, and bade her be of good cheer. 'We do very well as we are, ma mie! A man's children will often grow up to be a bane to him,' said good-natured Rutland, accurately stating the relationship he stood in towards his father.

The spring passed uneventfully at Berkhampsted, with nothing to break the tedium but a visit to Windsor, in April, for the Feast of St George. All four princes were invested with the Order of the Garter, Harry succeeding to his grandfather's stall at the head of what had been known, since the Lord Edward's day, as the Prince's Table. The King gave them jewelled Garters; and the two youngest lordings saw their shields for the first time. They looked very bright: John's with a label of five points, ermine and France; Humfrey's with a border of argent and azure. Humfrey said how fortunate it was that the late troubles had emptied so many stalls: a remark which made Harry flush, so vividly did it conjure up the picture of King Richard in what had become Father's stall.

The younger princes enjoyed the subsequent feast; Harry demeaned himself manfully, and spent the next two days recovering from it.

'Harry, why *does* this happen to you?' John said, looking down at him in concern.

'God knows!' replied Harry, prostrate on his bed. 'If I could school my belly to hold rich meats I would, but since I can't I shall forbid all feasts when I am King! And another thing I shall do,' he added, smiling at John, and stretching out his hand, 'will be to make you my Chancellor, or my Lieutenant, or some such thing! Which will you be?'

John took his hand, and held it. It was slender, but very strong. It did not seem possible that anyone with so vital a hand could be sickly, however often his belly might betray him. He was comforted, and replied: 'I don't mind. I'll be anything you like!'

4

In June, the King announced his intention of going against the Scots. The existing truce would expire in September, and King Robert was withholding homage. King Henry reached Leith, but his army was not strong enough to enable him to proceed farther; so after wringing some vague assurances from King Robert and his brother the Duke of Albany he retired again. As far as the princes could discover, the only results of his expedition were the renunciation of homage to King Robert by the Earl of Dunbar and the Scottish Earl of March (by no means to be confused, Sir Hugh warned his charges, with young Edmund Mortimer), and the marriage of Aunt Bess Holland to Sir John Cornwall.

The King had found time to preside over a tournament in York where Sir John had distinguished himself so worshipfully that Henry had rewarded him with the hand of his dear sister. Old-fashioned persons considered the match to be beneath the lady, for although Sir John claimed King Henry III's brother, the Earl of Cornwall, as his progenitor, his descent from this royal personage was, at the best, lefthanded. King Henry IV cared nothing for that if he could but silence his dear sister's reproaches for the death of her first husband. She was quite unreasonable about Huntingdon's taking-off; and when her brother told her that he was well aware that she had had several lovers during Huntingdon's lifetime she said that this was nothing to the point, and no excuse at all for making her the widow of an attainted man. There were those who said that Sir John already knew her better than was seemly. The King thought this extremely probable, and counted the match as one of his most successful strokes of domestic policy.

His foreign policy resulted only in the prolongation of the truce between England and Scotland; and if this was a tame ending to the affair it was at least preferable to a state of open hostility, for by the time the truce was concluded the King's attention was called to his other Border.

For this he was largely indebted to his old friend, Reginald Grey, Lord of Ruthin, in whose person loyalty was combined with some less amiable attributes. He was not much older than his royal master, but in temperament he belonged to an earlier and more predatory generation. In the belief that might was right he had appropriated lands which were alleged to belong to one of his neighbours, a Welsh gentleman of startling lineage, who, failing to obtain redress by such methods as he had learnt during three years' study of the law in London, resorted to a course more in accordance with the tastes of his tenants, and embarked on a systematic harrying of the Lord of Ruthin's lands. Neither his legal studies nor his exalted birth – he claimed to be a descendant of Cadwallader – were enough to subjugate more primitive instincts: the veneer of London was lost in his first taste of Border warfare, and he imprudently sanctioned the murder, under rather nasty circumstances, of a number of men of the Lord of Ruthin's household. Reginald Grey was not the best kind of Marcher baron, but such savagery as this roused him to just, if implacable, wrath. Matters went from bad to worse in North Wales. On the eve of his departure for Scotland, King Henry, uneasy at the bickering in that part of his dominions most well affected towards the late King, wrote to urge better government in Wales, and an appeasing of riots. The Lord of Ruthin's answer, directed during the King's absence in Scotland to the Prince of Wales, showed how far from appeasement his thoughts ran. One of his foe's supporters, whom the Lord of Ruthin apostrophized as the strongest thief in Wales, had swooped upon the park at Ruthin Castle, slain several men, and borne off a number of my lord's horses. My lord promised him 'a rope, a ladder, and a ring, high on gallows for to hang,' and wrote to the Prince demanding 'a plainer commission.' He made no mention of his arch-enemy, perhaps because the theft of his horses at that time loomed largest in his mind; perhaps, as was suggested by the Court fool, because he could not spell his name. Cadwallader's descendant was one Owain ab Gruffyd,

Lord of Glyndyfrdwy, but he was not destined to be widely known by this title. Englishmen had their own ways of dealing with outlandish names; and in much the same spirit as they had altered the Eschevinage at Calais to the Scunnage, and the Rue des Béguines to Bigging Street, they changed the Lord of Glyndyfrdwy to Owen Glendower.

When King Henry returned from his Scottish expedition, he was in no mood to listen with a believing ear to Owen's excuses for not having responded to the summons to follow his King to war. Owen said that Reginald Grey had of malice withheld the summons from him until it was too late for him to join the King's muster. But the Lord of Ruthin swore that the Welsh robber lied; and King Henry issued new writs; and in the autumn marched for Shrewsbury, taking the Prince of Wales and Sir Harry Percy with him.

King Henry was not destined to be lucky in war. Inclement weather made the progress of his force difficult; Owen had been declared a rebel, and as a rebel he sought the protection of his mountains, sallying forth only on harassing raids. The King penetrated some way into Wales, but except for the confiscation of Owen's estates on the English side of the Border the expedition achieved less than the Scottish one. All over England Welshmen were deserting town, university, and Inns of Court to rally to the side of one who declared himself to be the true Prince of Wales. The other Prince of Wales the King left on the Marches, in the charge of Sir Harry Percy.

5

In October, the princes were saddened by the news of the death of Master Chaucer. It was something to know that he had ended his days comfortably, often visited by a new poet, Thomas Hoccleve, who wrote a touching verse in his praise, and, it was to be hoped, brought the companionship to his old age which was denied him by his son. Thomas Chaucer, the King's Butler, was a flint-faced person, bent on self-aggrandizement, and desiring nothing less than to be known as the son of a disreputable poet who had deserted his wife, figured in a scandalous law-suit, and

148

had been forced to eke out a bare existence on a series of pensions.

All the King's children were at Eltham Palace that Christmas-tide, and there were tournaments held in honour of a distinguished visitor to England. This was none other than Manuel Paleologus, Emperor of Constantinople, who was making a tour of Western Europe in the endeavour to interest even-Christians in the fate of his capital. It was closely beleagured by the Turk Bajazet, whom Sigismund of Hungary had failed to crush at Nicopolis. Marshal Boucicault, with twelve hundred lances, had undertaken the defence of the city; but he was forced to retire; and the Emperor, accompanied by a large retinue, composed of priests, nobles, and his Varangian guard, went with him to Paris. In December, he crossed the Channel, and journeyed in a stately fashion to Eltham Palace.

After one look at his guest, the King, acting with great presence of mind, told Sir Hugh Waterton that he should hold him responsible for the demeanour of his hopeful family during the Emperor's stay. To this Sir Hugh replied that he preferred to be relieved of his high duties, since no man alive, in his opinion, could vouch for the behaviour of the noble lordings in the face of such a collection of oddities as the Emperor and his Court.

'Well, what's to be done, Hugh?' demanded the King, abandoning the regal manner. 'Once those whelps of mine clap eyes on them – ! You may beat them, of course.'

'Well, and so I do,' said Sir Hugh. 'Much they will care for that!'

However, he promised to do his best to preserve decorum amongst his charges, and went back to the princes' apartments, arriving there in time to witness a spirited pageant, in which Prince Henry figured as the Emperor; Thomas, with a silver charger reversed upon his head, as that worshipful scholar, Manuel Chrysoloras; and John and Humfrey, draped in napery stolen from the Buttery, and wearing beards made from the stuffings of several cushions, impersonating two of the priests in the Emperor's train.

The year 1401 passed uneventfully for John at Berkhampsted. Blanche, whose hand in marriage was being sought by the Emperor Rupert, titular Duke of Bavaria, and Elector Palatine of the Rhine, for his eldest son, remained at Windsor throughout the year. This match was progressing more smoothly for King Henry than his proposal to his cousin of France that Harry should espouse the widowed Queen Isabelle. All the previous year the French had evaded giving him a direct answer; but in the New Year a demand had been received for her restoration to her own country, together with one for her dower, her jewels, and the revenue due to a Queen Dowager of England.

King Henry, who had maintained the little Queen in state at Havering Bower, was so much exasperated by this that he made no attempt to recover her plate and her jewellery from his children, amongst whom he had distributed it, and told the envoys that her dower should be subtracted from the sum owing to him for King John's unpaid ransom of so many years ago. As for her revenue as Queen Dowager, his Council were unanimous in declaring that she was not entitled to it.

Since Madame Isabelle's heart remained faithful to King Richard, only a Paynim could have kept her in England. King Henry made arrangements for her return to her loving father, and told his heir snappishly that if he had shown more address in wooing her things might have gone otherwise.

But Harry, in his fifteenth year, was not interested in brides; he was learning his trade under Sir Harry Percy, and learning it well, Hotspur reported. When Madame Isabelle was brought to London to take leave of the King he was recapturing Conway Castle, which had been snatched from the English on the day that the old Earl of Warwick died. The new Earl, Richard Beauchamp, was with Harry on the Welsh Marches: Harry said that he had not altered a whit, though he was twenty now, and had been two years married.

When Madame Isabelle stood before the King she would not unclose her pouting lips. The King was so kind that even her

French attendants rebuked her for discourtesy. But Isabelle had been betrayed by her childhood: she had not meant the expression of her mourning heart to appear as the sulkiness of a little girl.

In the spring Archbishop Arundel's zeal resulted in the passing of a statute against Lollardy, and the burning of a priest tainted with heresy. John knew that Lollardy was serving as a cloak for much treasonable activity, but he was less interested in it than in the reports that came from Wales; Harry had a place on his father's Council, but no official title, the reins of government in North Wales being held by Hotspur. It was estimated by the grutching Commons that he and his father Northumberland between them had received more than forty thousand pounds from the Exchequer since King Henry's accession, but neither of them let a week pass without petitioning the King for further monies.

There was no end to the calls on the King's purse, or to the troubles gathering about him. Hardly had the Earl of Worcester delivered Madame Isabelle into the hands of the Count of St Pol than the Council was obliged to accept open war with both France and Scotland; while the unrest in Ireland was such that in August the King sent Thomas there, as his representative. Thomas would not be thirteen until September but he was a well-grown, handsome boy, with the easy manners of all his family, and a rueful grin that endeared him to his fellows. He was the least witty of King Henry's sons, and he was inclined to let his impetuosity rule him. King Henry, preparing for yet another Welsh campaign, hoped that the Irish, also impetuous, might take Thomas to their hearts.

The King journeyed west again with yet another care upon his shoulders. He had contrived to send Hotspur more money, but Hotspur complained that it was only half what was needed for his costage, and had begged leave to relinquish his command. His uncle, Thomas of Worcester, took his place as Harry's guardian; and Edward of Rutland was installed as Warden. Hotspur himself accepted a commission to negotiate a peace with the Scots, so that on the surface at least amenities were preserved. Only the Percies and King Henry knew how delicately balanced was an old friendship. The King had let his biting tongue hint to Hotspur that with better government less gold would have been required in Wales, and Hotspur had too proud a stomach to digest rebuke.

4 The Red Rigs

1

Christmas-tide was spent at Windsor that year, not so gay a Christmas as the last. The autumn campaign against Glendower had been ruined by bad weather; there had been an attempt to murder the King in September; and when he rode through the streets to attend the christening of John Beaufort's first-born, to whom he stood sponsor, he rode through silent crowds. Only a man who had been used all his life to wave his cap in acknowledgement of cheers could understand the meaning of the bitter smile that curled the King's lips.

He missed Thomas, who was in Ireland, and none too comfortably placed. Everyone missed Thomas, even Harry, who so often quarrelled with him. Thomas might exasperate his brothers by his elvishness, but the royal residences seemed empty without him; and when they no longer heard his whistle, or could see his grin, the princes remembered only his warm heart, and forgot his temper, and his fits of jealousy.

Blanche was also in a pensive mood, inclined to shed tears when she recalled that this must be the last Christmas-tide she would spend with her family. It was not, in fact, very likely that she would behold any of them again. It was the common fate of royal ladies to be sent to be wedded to strangers in a strange land; but the thought of the coming separation kept Blanche wakeful at night. 'They say he is handsome,' she confided to Harry. 'If only he will be kind!'

Harry tried to console her with tender jesting. 'Send me word if he is not!' he said. 'I will come at the head of an army to rescue you!'

She smiled, but said: 'Oh, Harry, I shall miss you so much!'

'Nay, Louis will bring you to visit us! You won't care a leek,

I daresay! Don't you remember what the envoys told us? Louis is so handsome that you will love him more than all of us together!'

Harry, in his sixteenth year, was a man grown. He was tall, not as large-limbed as John, but well-proportioned as his father. Months of campaigning had hardened his muscles, and tanned him berry-brown. The life seemed to suit him; he had never looked so well, and his energy was inexhaustible. He and John spent much time together, hawking in the Park; and once Harry started a buck, and ran it down on foot for sport. His chest was heaving when John caught him up, but as soon as he had got his breath he was ready to mount his horse again, not in the least exhausted by a race that would have made another man burst his lungs.

John had so often heard his father speak in the most despitous terms of the Welsh that he was surprised to find that Harry liked them. He chastised them rigorously, but bore them no ill-will. Harry, who was merciless to traitors, did not see the Welsh as traitors; and was urgent with the King to pardon penitents. He said that the King mishandled the Welsh, and he said it impatiently, his beautifully curved lips hardening.

'You can't blame Father for having rancour at his heart,' said John. 'Wasn't Glendower one of his own people?'

'One of Arundel's men, and three parts wood!' Harry exclaimed. 'Must all Welshman suffer for his sins? They are a wild, sely people: conciliation would serve us better than this policy of Father's! As for these raids of his—! Owen boasts that the Severn fights for him. I could make it fight for me – had I the means!'

'What of Hotspur? Did you like him?' John asked.

'Well, he knows how to handle Borderers. He taught me much I'll take heed I don't forget. And some things he taught me which he never knew I marked!' Harry said, with a choke of laughter. 'Do you remember what a lurdan we thought him, when we first met him?'

'Yes – but I don't love any Percy!'

'A grasping race,' Harry agreed. 'I liked Sir Harry more than I like his uncle Worcester, though I know Worcester better, because when I was – when I was page to Cousin Richard, he was his Chamberlain. And holding that office of trust – Well, let that sleep! I like Rutland best of all who are set over me.'

'Edward!' John said. 'What a dodipoll! Unfaithful, too!'

Harry laughed, but shook his head. 'No, no! He may be cozened into setting his name to another bond, but he won't mean us any harm! You can't help liking him, you know! He understands nothing but war and the chase, but he's no dodipoll in war, and I never knew anyone more skilled at the chase. The man I mistrust is young March's uncle, Sir Edmund Mortimer. If he is not on better terms with Glendower than he'd have me think, believe me never!'

'Is he the man who is said to have played with swords in his cradle?'

'Oh, a greater ferly than that!' Harry said. 'At his birth, the horses in the stable stood up to their hocks in blood! He is very proud of it, too!'

'Is it true?' John asked, blinking.

'I don't know. The Welsh are full of such tales. I think he's dangerful, for if he trafficks with Glendower he might draw Hotspur in. Hotspur is married to his sister, and they are close friends.'

'What, Hotspur throw in his lot with a Welsh rebel?' exclaimed John incredulously. 'What profit lies in that?'

'None, but Hotspur is just the man to do it.'

'Holy Virgin! *Why* does Father like him?'

'Oh, because they have been comrades in arms!' Harry answered unhesitatingly.

'Harry, you can't like everyone with whom you've been a comrade in arms!' objected John.

'No, but when you've camped with a man, and ridden knee to knee with him, and fought at his side, as I have done with Richard Beauchamp, and Gilbert Talbot, and Jack Oldcastle—'

'Hotspur and Father have never fought side by side,' interrupted John. 'Unless you mean at those jousts, and jousting is not real fighting. Harry, *was* Otterburn the great victory we always thought it?'

'I don't believe it was a victory at all!' Harry said, his voice trembling on the edge of laughter. 'Scrope of Masham told me that the Scots count it as a victory to them! Hotspur has described it to me, and I may be unlearned in war, but Christ it me forbid that I should so order a battle! *But* he knows better than Father how to handle Marchers!'

2

Hardly were the Christmas revels done than a celestial wonder burst on men's sight. A new star, with flames ascending from it, appeared in the west. The redeless folk called it the Blazing Star, and signed themselves when they saw it; scholars named it *Stella Comata*, and asserted that the like had been seen before, but few persons paid any heed to them, because it was well known that learned men loved nothing so much as saying that what any man with the least mother-wit could perceive to be a heavenly sign arose from natural causes.

'A portent of prosperity,' King Henry said, but confided to his unimpressionable son John that he wished the Blazing Star otherwhere.

He confided another matter both to John and to Harry. He was going to take a second wife.

Yes, the lady was Joanna the Dowager Duchess of Brittany, a dame of thirty-three summers, and surpassing beauty. He had been asotted of her since first he had seen her, but until her son had attained his twelfth year she would in no wise entertain his suit. But in March of the old year young John of Montfort had been invested with the ducal habit, and his mother considered herself free to follow the counsel of her heart.

'*March*, sir!' interpolated Harry.

He had not mis-heard his father: March it was, the delay in announcing the alliance having been due to the circumstance of the Duchess's belonging to the Communion of the rival Pope, at Avignon. Nothing was more unlikely than that Benedict XIII would grant a dispensation for the marriage of Dame Joanna to an adherent of Boniface IX in Rome, whom he had frequently stigmatized as Anti-Christ. But the Dowager Duchess was none of your hen-witted women: without allowing the Holy Father at Avignon to suspect the identity of her suitor she had contrived so cleverly that at any moment now she expected to receive a general dispensation to marry anyone within the fourth degree of consanguinity.

King Henry told his sons that their new mother would be found to be as virtuous as she was beautiful. She was a daughter of King Charles the Bad of Navarre; and she seemed to have had a trying life. When scarcely more than a child she had been wedded to the aged Duke of Brittany, who had already been the death of two wives. She had borne him eight fair children; and never, said King Henry, had she given him the least cause for a display of his lamentable jealousy. It was her fate to be so lovely that men made the most unseemly advances to her. It would be the privilege of himself and his sons, said King Henry, to treat her with the consideration she had never yet known.

They were married by proxy in April; but if the King expected his bride to arrive in England hard on the heels of this ceremony, he was doomed to be disappointed. The French Court, alarmed by the marriage of one who, besides being King of England, was brother and half-brother to the Queens of Portugal and Castile, to a Navarrese Duchess of Brittany, hurriedly begged her royal uncles of France to represent to Dame Joanna the unwisdom of her choice. They found her meek, but (she said) helpless to rectify matters. Since she was only a female, with no understanding of problems of state, it was sleeveless to point out to her how useful a close alliance with Brittany would be to a grandson of Edward III; but when it became known that the Duchess proposed to transport all her children with her to England her most astute uncle, Philip of Burgundy, announced his intention of paying a state visit to his beloved niece. The Duchess thought it would ill beseem her to sail for England before she had entertained her uncle with all the honour due to him; and as affairs of state demanding Burgundy's presence in Paris continually intervened to oblige him to postpone his visit the year wore on without bringing any immediate prospect of the arrival of the King's new wife.

Meanwhile, King Henry, not long after his proxy wedding, received unwelcome tidings from Harry, in Wales. His old friend, Grey of Ruthin, had been captured by Glendower, who was holding him to an enormous ransom. This news more than counterbalanced any pleasure the King may have felt in the proposals he had received for the hands of Harry and Philippa.

These came from the far north, where the old Queen of Norway was planning to marry her adopted heir and his sister Catharine to their best advantages. Eric, King of united Denmark, Sweden, and Norway would be no bad match for King Henry's younger daughter; King Henry was not so well pleased with the alliance planned for Harry; but he received the ambassadors with courtesy; and, in May, took them to Berkhampsted, where, with more aplomb than Dame Hervey could approve, the eight-year-old Philippa announced that the proposals for her hand pleased her well. She was much too young, of course, to be sent to her marriage-bed; and before King Henry would set his hand to any contract he sent ambassadors to King Eric's Court, and charged them to take note of all they saw there. As for the offer of Catharine to be the Prince of Wales's consort, King Henry, whom the Emperor Manuel Paleologus had declared to be the wiliest and wittiest of men, uttered a number of fair words which committed him to nothing.

Junc brought King Henry a grandiloquent challenge from the Duke of Orleans. He treated it with dignity; but after a further exchange of missives Orleans launched an attack on Guyenne, which, while it achieved little, was another anxiety added to King Henry's burden. Reports of riots were brought to Westminster; there was a rumour that a pretender, resembling the late King, was being fostered by the Franciscans; and on the seventeenth of the month Sir Edmund Mortimer was taken prisoner by Glendower. Harry, who came to Windsor to bid farewell to Blanche before she departed for Almaine, told his father that there was reason to suspect that the ambush into which Sir Edmund had fallen had previously been concerted between him and his captor. Harry brought no cheering tidings from Wales: he needed money, and had already spent most of his personal grant in paying to his soldiers a moiety of their long overdue wages.

'Christ's Wounds, can no one enter my presence without demanding money of me?' exclaimed the King, letting his sorely tried temper ride him. Harry stood stiff and silent. 'Well, well, I will do what I can!' the King said, waving him away.

He was much affected by the parting with Blanche, and shed tears when he gave her into the care of John Beaufort, who was the chief of the Councillors appointed to escort her to Cologne. He had contrived to scrape together the first instalment of her dowry, but he was sending her to her bridegroom with fewer jewels and less costly plate than befitted the wardrobe of the King of England's daughter.

Harry went back to Shrewsbury as soon as the Lady Blanche left Windsor; and it occurred to the King, in the midst of his own bale, that his son John was also out of spirits. Humfrey was at Oxford, and Sir Hugh Waterton's son was entered as a page in a noble household. It was thought that perhaps the Lord John was lonely; so the King, bethinking him of two other lonely lads, decreed that the young Earl of March and his brother should join him at Berkhampsted. March was only two years younger than John, but since he was backward for his age they were not well suited to one another. However, John was kind to both the Mortimers, good-naturedly allowing them even to handle his hawks. John, whose first hawk had been an eyas-musket of his own manning, had acquired more hawks and falcons (said Sir Hugh) than he knew what to do with. Nor did his passion for birds stop at falcons. He had a raven, which he had taught to speak; several small birds kept in an enclosure built for them in the curtilage; a pair of peacocks; and a flight of doves, which would take corn from between his lips. His favourite bird, a fierce-eyed gyrfalcon, went everywhere with him. He had a pair of silver bells from Milan for her; and when he took her upon the fist he scarcely troubled to hold the jesses between his fingers. She would allow him to handle her as he pleased, but she was capricious, and if Sir Hugh attempted to touch her she would bate instantly. The King had promised to make John the Master of his Falcons; he was already well known to the astringers at the Royal Mews by Charing Cross, and had picked up from them an astonishing amount of knowledge of the characteristics, needs, and ailments of the various species of hawks in their charge.

At the end of July, when the King was preparing for another expedition to Wales, and the beacons in the north were laid ready for kindling, the Lady Blanche's escort returned to England, and the King's heart was gladdened by the tidings they brought. Prince Louis had looked and loved. He was eleven years older than his bride, a fine young man, with the most winning manners, and he had treated Blanche with such kindness that her heart had been won, and her homesick tears dried. He took her to Heidelberg, and from there both he and his father wrote to King Henry in the most gratifying terms. She was Prince Louis's 'sweetest wife'; he knew not how to thank King Henry for so rich and rare a gift.

These were the only cheerful tidings the King received for many months. In Ireland, the Lord Thomas was beleagured in Naas; at the beginning of August the Court was plunged into mourning by the death of the Duke of York; and in Wales the war bickered on.

By September the King had crossed the Border, but the slippery Welsh evaded him, and bad weather compelled him to withdraw. Men said that such gales had never before been experienced at that season; and many considered that the fury of the weather must be due to sorcery: a large body of opinion maintaining that the Franciscans had wrought the storms by their spells; and a not inconsiderable minority suspecting that God was araged with King Henry for usurping his cousin's throne. During one tempest his pavilion was blown down, and his lance fell upon him, an omen that could only be regarded as barful. Three weeks later he was back in Westminster; but before he reached his capital glorious tidings were brought him from the North: the Scots, crossing the Border in force, under the Duke of Albany's son, Murdoch Stewart of Fife, and Archibald, Earl of Douglas, had been met by Hotspur and his father, near Wooler, and utterly put to rout. Five Scottish earls were Percy's prisoners, scores of Scots had perished under the English arrows; and hundreds, trying to retreat into Scotland, had been drowned in the hungry Tweed.

4

They called it the Red Rigs, because it was fought on the ploughed slopes of Homildon Hill, and rig was the northern word for such ground; and in the rejoicings at so notable a victory the King's own ill-success in Wales was forgotten. The Earl of Northumberland brought the Scottish prisoners to Westminster, and paraded them before him, with the notable exception of the Earl of Douglas, whom Hotspur did not produce. Besides Murdoch of Fife there were also the Earls of Angus, Orkney, and Moray; five lesser lords; and knights past counting. Murdoch of Fife, the most important prisoner of all, had been captured by Sir John Skelton, to whom the King at once made a grant of an hundred marks, mentally consigning the Earl of Fife to honourable imprisonment in England for the rest of his life. The prisoners knelt before the King, and he addressed the usual homily to them. This they endured stolidly, knowing that when it was over he would invite them to dine with him. The feast was spread in the Painted Chamber; and under the influence of the wines of Bordeaux several facts emerged, the most interesting being that it had been George Dunbar, the Scottish Earl of March, who had lately renounced homage to King Robert, to whom the King owed the victory, rather than to his friend Hotspur. It had been he who had prevented the battle from becoming a second Otterburn, because he had persuaded Hotspur to let his longbowmen decimate the Scottish lines before launching his knights into the mêlée.

It might have been expected that this triumph would have brought nothing but thanksgiving in its wake, but the sequel proved far otherwise. The Percies maintained that the prisoners were all theirs to dispose of as they pleased. The King was forced to point out to them that political prisoners belonged by custom to the Crown. His refusal to permit them to hold to ransom such persons as the Earls of Fife and Douglas they took in bad part; and matters were not improved by his subsequent refusal to allow Hotspur to raise the ransom set by Glendower of Sir Edmund Mortimer. Sir Harry almost forced his way into the King's presence to argue the matter; and the word was passed

from mouth to mouth at Westminster Palace that an ugly garboil had been the outcome. Hotspur addressed such words to
the King as no man might stomach; and the King, starting up
from his siege, snatched his dagger from its sheath, exclaiming:
'Traitor, unsay that!'

Sir Harry's hand flew to his own weapon, but he checked it.
'Not here, but in the field!' he said fiercely, and swinging round
upon his heel, strode from the presence.

5 The Witch Queen

No one cared to mention his quarrel with Hotspur to the King. When he seized the estates of Sir Edmund Mortimer only his own half-brother, the Bishop of Lincoln, raised questioning eyebrows. The King said angrily: 'It is Harry who tells me that Mortimer has played fast and loose with me!'

'I have a great regard for Harry,' replied the Bishop, 'but if it was he who advised you in this pass to snatch at Mortimer's possessions I think the less of him.'

'Holy Sepulchre, do you think I ask rede of Harry?' demanded the King.

'No,' said the Bishop. 'I think not that, brother!'

In the late autumn the news reached London that Sir Edmund had married Glendower's daughter. 'Now see!' said the King. 'I do see,' replied the Bishop. When, a little later, Sir Edmund published a manifesto declaring that he stood for King Richard (of whose death he was by no means convinced), or, failing him, for his nephew the young Earl of March, the Bishop said: 'What now, very dread sovereign?'

'Would you have me play King Herod, and murder a child?' said the King.

'Certainly not,' replied the Bishop. 'But which way will the Percies jump?'

This was a question which troubled many minds; but in the North Hotspur and his father made no sign; and in the south another Percy, the Earl of Worcester, recalled from the Welsh Border to go with the King's half-brothers to Brittany to escort his bride to England, accepted the commission without apparend hesitation.

The Duke of Burgundy had at last found the opportunity to

visit his niece. Reaching Nantes upon the first day of October, he had remained there for a month, achieving an end as agreeable to France as it was displeasant to the English. He behaved in a very lavish way, feasting the Dowager Duchess, bestowing on her jewels of worth, and scattering amongst her Court such largesse as made it no matter for wonder that her Breton attendants should have urged her to appoint him guardian to her children. When he rode away to Paris the little Duke of Brittany, with his brothers Arthur and Gilles, rode with him. He permitted the Duchess to bring with her to England her infant daughters, Blanche and Marguérite; but consoling though this might be to her it afforded no gratification to her English subjects. If King Henry was disappointed he gave no sign of it. 'I do believe Father is making a love-match!' said Humfrey. 'She must be lovely indeed!'

Lovely she was, but her stepchildren had to wait until February before they saw her. Although the fleet which was to bring her to England sailed for Camaret in the old year, under the young Earl of Arundel, the Duchess was obliged to keep it waiting many weeks in harbour. Even the Earl of Somerset became testy as December wore into January; but when the Duchess at last arrived at Camaret she was so apologetic that she won forgiveness from all but my lord of Worcester, who told the Bishop of Lincoln that he was too old to be cozened by losengery.

The cortège embarked in the several ships provided for the Duchess's passage on the thirteenth day of January, matters being complicated by the lady's reluctance to be separated from her infant daughters, her natural brother, who was also her Chamberlain, or from any of her attendants. Nothing was farther from her thoughts than to be the least trouble to anyone, but it was impossible that a mother should allow her children to sail in another ship than her own; and the delicacy of her position made it imperative for all her ladies to remain at her side. Arundel sought aid of Worcester; and Worcester, who had been captain of a ship of war some years before Arundel's birth, knew no hesitation. He informed the Duchess's Chamberlain that since the ships would carry only a limited number of persons his mistress might take so many attendants with her, and no more. A quarrel was the outcome, but Percy won the issue. He thought poorly of base-born Navarrese princes, and he rather imprudently let this be seen.

The Duchess endured a hideous passage, tossed on stormy seas for five days and nights, and reaching harbour not at the port of Hampton, where she was expected, but many miles farther to the west, at Falmouth. She and her ladies had all to be carried ashore, so far-spent were they; and the only two persons who seemed to have thrived on the gales were her infant daughters, whose nurses were only too glad to relinquish them into the care of the Cornish dames hastily mustered to wait on the new Queen of England.

2

While King Henry was undergoing all the anxieties natural to a man who from day to day awaited tidings of his bride's arrival, my lord of Northumberland again applied to him for added livelihood. King Henry caustically granted him all the lands of the captive Earl of Douglas in Scotland. His aged Chancellor, the Bishop of Exeter, thought it his duty to point out to him that the Earl of Douglas's officers were unlikely to hand over his possessions to a Percy. 'Then let the Fox seize them!' said the King.

'Sire,' said old Stafford, 'this is not conciliatory!'

'I have come to the end of conciliation,' replied the King.

By the time all the Queen's ships had reached port, and she herself was sufficiently amended to set forward on the rest of her journey, it was several weeks later. She reached Winchester in February; and here, at Wolvesey Palace, the King, and four of his children, were awaiting her.

Humfrey had been right as usual: a love-match it clearly was. When the curtains of the Queen's litter were parted the King waved aside those who would have lifted her down, and himself performed this office. 'At last!' he said, holding her close. 'Ma mie, my heart's welcome to you!'

She was a tall woman, and their eyes were on a level. A blush mantled her cheeks; she hung her head in charming confusion, uttering the one word; 'Monseigneur!'

He was never one to stand on ceremony, and he embraced her as any goodman might his wife. A half-forgotten picture crossed John's vision: for an instant he remembered the Cold Harbour, and Father's return from the Holy Land. It faded; not the gay Earl of Derby but the King was presenting Harry to their new mother; and next it would be his turn to kneel and kiss the Queen's hand.

They were all agreed that she was the most beautiful woman they had ever beheld, quite outshining Aunt Bess, who was present, with her husband, Sir John Cornwall, to welcome her dear sister. Aunt Bess said that she was well enough, but wore clothes unsuited to a journey, and would be improved by a more modest coif. She also said that try as she would – but no one could feel that she had tried very hard – she could not trust women with large jump-eyes. Sir John made protesting noises in his throat. No one, he maintained, could call the Queen jump-eyed. Aunt Bess could, and did.

The wedding ceremony was performed by the Bishop of Lincoln, for William of Wykeham, the Bishop of Winchester was so stricken in years that for some time past others had ordained for him, while he lived in retirement. After a splendid feast, the royal party journeyed to London. The Queen was crowned on the twenty-sixth day of February; and at the subsequent tournament held in her honour Richard Beauchamp, the young Earl of Warwick, appeared as her champion, and held the lists against all comers.

Harry took John to visit Richard in his pavilion before the jousting began. They found him surrounded by his squires and pages, two of them kneeling to lace the sides of his jupon, and a third strapping a brassart round his left arm. His hair, John saw, still curled tightly over his head; he still had a deceptively slim figure, and a long-lipped grin.

'Richard, I'll wager you don't know this great fellow I have with me!' Harry challenged him.

'You lose, sir,' Richard responded, shaking off his squires, and bowing. 'Sir John!'

'Yea, but you never called me that before!' John said, grasping his hands.

'Richard is so mannerly!' quoted Harry, picking up a chased coudière, and inspecting it. 'Richard, *more* new harness? A new jupon, too! What an airling you are! Everyone will suppose it is the first time you've entered the lists.'

'But everyone must know it is not!' said Richard seriously.

This reply so vividly recalled a younger Richard whom they had all delighted in teasing that John's shyness vanished; and he was soon vying with Harry in the attempt to convince the Queen's champion that none of his new armour fitted him, and that the crest on his helm of a swan's head and neck rising out of a gilded coronet looked more like a goose. Richard bore it all with his wry grin; and his squires, deftly threading the linked camail through the slots in his bascinet, tried their best not to laugh. When he stood caparisoned before his tormentors they shook their heads, and said it was a pity to think of him rolled in the mud in all this costly harness; and Harry, taking the great tilting-helm out of the squire's hands, earnestly recommended him not to wear it, because it was so top-heavy that it would unbalance him.

'I wish you were going to ride against me, Harry!' said Richard.

'Yes, I know you do,' said Harry. 'And wish you may!'

Then they went away to take their places in the King's gallery; and when Richard presently rode into the lists he looked so splendid in his new harness, with his jupon and his horse's bardings blazoned with the six gold cross crosslets for Beauchamp, and the blue-and-white checky for Newburgh, that John said in Harry's ear: 'He wears his armour as easily as other men wear pourpoints! I wish I could!'

Harry nodded. 'He owns great livelihood, and can bear the costage of very good harness, but I never saw anyone wear armour better.'

'Except Father.'

'Yes, except Father. And neither of them has any mastery in war! That's odd. Thomas, too, is a far better jouster than I am, but not so good a soldier.'

However little mastery in war Richard had he had great mastery in the jousting field, and he carried the Queen's kerchief triumphantly through the day. The Queen clapped her hands, saying that he reminded her of her dear lord, the King, who had once jousted before her at Rennes.

The Queen had something kind to say of everyone, and never did she utter a word in anyone's dispraise. It was plain that something had happened to set a gulf between her and my lord of Worcester, but when the King enquired what this might be she would by no means tell him. She said that she had not come into England to make bad blood between him and his friends. She thought it was the greatest infortune that when she desired merely to be gracious she should so frequently be misunderstood. Whatever had gone asquint between her and my lord of Worcester was quite her own fault, and she implored the King to put it from his mind. My lord, jealously questioned by the King, was not more forthcoming; and the resultant coolness between them was regretted by no one more than by the Queen. She told Humfrey, one of the first victims to the shafts of her fine eyes, that throughout her life she had been pursued by the gallantries of men for whom she had never cared a rush. Her late husband had come near to slaying out of hand Sir Oliver de Clisson, merely because he had been informed by someone who should have known better that she nourished a guilty passion for him. When it transpired that this person was none other than the Queen's own father Harry was startled. But Humfrey said that such a piece of despite was what one would expect of a man surnamed the Bad, and no doubt he was right.

John was the only one of the King's children who did not succumb to the Queen's charms. Harry's chivalry was fired by the recital of the wrongs she had suffered at the hands of a jealous husband; Humfrey courted her caresses; and Philippa found her so sympathetic that within two days of making her acquaintance she was enlisting her support against the prohibitions of Dame Hervey.

But the redeless Commons refused to recognize the Queen's virtues. They called her the Witch Queen, behaved with the greatest rudeness towards her bastard brother, and took an instant dislike to the Breton ladies and gentlemen of her retinue. Nor was their dislike ameliorated by the enthusiasm with which her late subjects threw themselves into the French custom of harrying the southern shores of England. While King Charles VI's men ravaged the Isle of Wight, Breton sailors worried the coast of Cornwall; but even the Bishop of Lincoln, newly succeeded to his brother of Exeter's room as Chancellor, admitted that these depredations could hardly be laid at the Queen's door. While fresh envoys were sent to France to negotiate a prolongation of peace, the Chancellor renewed the periodic ancient demands for payment of King John's ransom. This was always an excellent gambit, for however indignantly the French might repudiate the debt they could never resist the temptation to argue about it.

3
At the beginning of May, the family mourned the death of Dame Katherine. She had seldom left Lincoln since the death of Bel sire, but the Lancaster children felt her passing hence almost as keenly as the Beauforts. There was little time, however, for private griefs. In the North, Hotspur, attempting to take possession of the Douglas lands, suffered a check at Cocklaw, and another at Ormiston. Rumours that King Richard was alive were rife, and had even spread to France; but the King's old friend, Henry Bowet, now Bishop of Bath and Wells, who had led the emissaries to France, managed, in spite of these, to prolong the peace. A peace with France bore a strong resemblance to a peace with Scotland: acts of violence committed by individuals were excluded from its provisions, so that each country was able to continue a system of raids on the other's coasts, disclaiming responsibility for its own depredations and loudly complaining of its neighbour's. But it did preclude an open declaration of war, and this, in King Henry's precarious position, had to be counted a gain. From Raby Castle, Ralph Neville addressed laborious letters to him, warning him to expect a fresh and more powerful invasion by the Scots; from his various headquarters in the West, Harry wrote again and again, demanding men and money. Harry had led a punitive raid into Wales in May, had ravaged a large tract of territory, and had burnt two of Glendower's strongholds; but Owen

had marched south to the Vale of Towey. Three castles had seceded to him; he had laid waste an ever larger tract of country than his foe; and had burnt Carmarthen town to ashes. Though Pembroke was up in arms against him there seemed to be little to stop his progress eastward.

But just when King Henry had decided that the Welsh danger was more pressing than the Scotch, Glendower, the self-styled Prince of Wales, sought counsel of a seer, who informed him that he would shortly be taken prisoner, under a black banner, between Carmarthen and Gower. The next news that reached the King was so good as to be almost incredible: Owen had abandoned his advance, and was retreating to the mountains. The King seized the opportunity to make one of his swift moves. Writs had already been issued to the sheriffs of the midland and northern counties; the King reached Lichfield on the thirteenth day of July, intending to march against the Scots; and while he lay at the castle word reached him that the Percies were in open revolt. Hotspur, with a counterfeit King Richard in his train, had arrived at Chester, on his way to join forces with Glendower and Sir Edmund Mortimer; and from Shrewsbury, where Prince Harry lay, the Earl of Worcester had slipped away to his nephew's camp.

4

'My lord,' said Sir Hugh Waterton, 'I am going to join the King, for in this pass he has need of his friends.'

'With my good will!' said the Lord John. 'I am for Westminster!'

Sir Hugh eyed his charge sideways. It had been reported to him that upon hearing the tidings from the West my lord had hurled his books into the stewpond, and had broken his inkstandage on the head of a protesting valet. The Lord John was the easiest tempered of Sir Hugh's royal pupils, but once or twice he had shown his governor that Plantagenet fire ran hot in his veins. Sir Hugh temporized. 'To what end, lording?' he asked, pulling his long moustache.

'I must have speech with my uncle the Chancellor!' declared the Lord John. 'I have done with books!'

Sir Hugh was not overly fond of Henry Beaufort, but he had a plain man's respect for a man of letters, and he thought that perhaps the wily Bishop of Lincoln would know better than he how to deal with rebellious youth. He said: 'Well, you may do so!'

'Witterly! Go, you, and join my father! And I pray you send me tidings, Sir Hugh!'

'As to that,' said Sir Hugh, 'I am not apt with my pen—'

'No force of that! Send me tidings!'

'Well, I will do so if I may – and if you talk to me in this malapert manner, lording, it will be the worse for you!' said Sir Hugh.

'No force of that either. Sir Hugh, set a strong guard about the Mortimers!'

'My lord, it needs not that you should teach me where my duty lies!' exploded Sir Hugh.

'Nay, but take care that no stranger comes near them! King Richard is dead, and Hotspur knows it: he will declare for March before the month is out!'

'I hope,' said Sir Hugh, with feeling, 'that my lord Bishop will take order to you, lording!'

But my lord Bishop, confronted by a large and hawk-faced nephew, who demanded that he should be released from his books and given employment befitting a man, took no order to the Lord John. He regarded him with interest, invited him to dinner, and listened to the outpourings of his chafed spirit with sympathy. When he judged that the sensibilities of youth had been sufficiently soothed by meat and wine he said: 'How old are you, my son?'

'Fourteen – past!' replied John.

The Bishop looked thoughtfully at him. Rage had coloured the Lord John's discourse, but under it the Bishop perceived kind-wit. He sipped his wine, considering the big, flushed boy, who gave him back stare for stare.

'I am as apt as Thomas for a command, Father!' John urged.

'Yes, I think you are,' said the Bishop. 'Also I think that you will have your command. Patience a while yet, John!'

'I will not go back to Berkhampsted!' said John.

'You may go to Westminster,' said the Bishop.

'I had liefer you sent me to Shrewsbury.'

'That shall not serve. Westminster!' repeated the Bishop.

At Westminster his stepmother made John welcome. She was trying to decide between two sets of hallings for the King's Great Chamber, for (little heart though she now had for the task) she was refurnishing the royal apartments.

'I would I were at your father's side,' she told John. 'Alas, he would in no wise permit it, but bade me be of good cheer! So I am busying myself with making the palace more easeful for him. For myself, I don't care how I live. I have always said I could be happy in a peasant's hovel.'

'Have you word from my father, madam?' John asked.

'Oh, my dear John, no, and I am for-pained with dread! And now they tell me that my lord of Worcester has deserted your dear brother, and I can see that everyone believes it to be my fault. I am sure I would have borne anything rather than have brought trouble on your father. Over and over again I implored him not to think there was anything amiss between that man and poor little me, but of course he could not but see that something had happened to distress me, try as I might to conceal it!'

She told him that to have him at her side was the greatest comfort to her, for she felt herself to be friendless in a strange land. John looked surprised at this, for the palace seemed hardly large enough to accommodate all her Breton attendants; but she explained that she kept these persons only because she had no other friends. She could not help shedding a tear or two, but she wiped them away, and smiled bravely, begging him not to repeat her words to the King. She added, sighing, that he did not know what trials assailed women. Two days in her company, however, enlarged his horizon; and he soon knew that the trials of women included almost every persecution, from unsolicited advances from such persons as the Earl of Worcester, to the churlish behaviour of the English Parliament, in refusing to allow her Breton ships to discharge their cargoes at the Port of London without paying duty on wares which she imported solely for her husband's benefit.

John spent the following days anywhere but at Westminster, and mostly at the Bishop of Lincoln's inn without Ludgate, by

Temple Bar. The Bishop had little time to spare for him, but he several times entertained him at supper. He learned from his secretaries that the Lord John's way of passing these anxious days was to make himself familiar with as many of the details of government as could be gleaned from them. The Bishop's interest in this scarcely-regarded nephew grew. He encouraged John to talk, and answered at least some of his questions. It did not take him long to discover the mainspring of this rather taciturn boy's hopes and fears. 'How many men has Harry with him?' John asked. 'Is Shrewsbury a defensible town? What force can Hotspur lead against Harry?'

'You are very fond of Harry, are you not, my son?'

John nodded.

'I too,' said the Bishop. 'But you will have to learn not to let your heart be so much troubled when he goes to war. If I read Harry aright, war is his trade. As for his present plight, I do not believe it to be desperate. Certes, Hotspur will find many to support him in Cheshire, for that was ever King Richard's stronghold; but chiefly he is relying on the Welsh rebel. What has Harry told you of Owen Glendower?'

'That he fights no pitched battles. But if he could join hands with Hotspur might he not venture?'

The Bishop's quizzical brows rose. 'It is not likely that your father will permit him to join hands with Hotspur, my child.'

'Father has never been fortunate in Wales,' said John bluntly.

'He has always crossed the Border at the worst time of the year,' replied the Bishop. 'It is now high summer, and there will be no storms to hold him back. If the issue lies between him and Harry Percy – why, the King, my son, is very much the better man!'

'Yea, no charge! But where is my lord of Northumberland, Father?'

'In his own country, where I trust my good friend of Westmoreland will keep him,' said the Bishop.

'I have seen one of Hotspur's manifestos,' said John. 'And I am right glad that it bears Northumberland's name, for now we may see an end to that accursed brood!'

'H'm, yes!' said the Bishop dryly. 'We may!'

5

Antelope Pursuivant, the herald who brought the tidings of the King's victory outside Shrewsbury to the Chancellor, brought also a letter from Sir Hugh Waterton to the Lord John. It told him only one new thing, and that made him look up quickly from the letter, and demand: 'How is the Prince wounded?'

'An arrow struck him in the cheek, my lord. He said it was no matter, and he would in no wise leave the field. It is given out that he will be speedily amended.'

John crushed the letter into a ball, and tossed it aside. He pushed forward a stool with one foot, and said: 'Sit! Now unbosom! I want to know the whole!' He saw that the man was shy, and added: 'I know that Hotspur was slain, but who else? What of Worcester? What of the Earl of Douglas?'

'As for the Scottish Earl, my lord, he is the King's prisoner. My lord of Worcester was taken also, but him they headed. The King's grace would have spared him, but the great lords wouldn't have it so, saying that if Hotspur had sent another than he to parley before the battle was joined the bloodshed would have been spared. As for Sir Harry Hotspur, no man can say whose was the hand that slew him. But he knew himself a dead man before ever he put on his harness.'

'How?' John interjected.

'They say, lord, that it was foretold by a soothsayer that he would meet his end at Berwick. He was in right blithesome humour, but when he learned that the village where he lay that night was so named his mirth forsook him, and he stood as still as a stone a paternoster-while. And at last he said full heavily: "Then has my plough reached its last furrow!" But he fought manfully, seeking all the time to come at the King, and slaying three that wore the King's cognizance.'

'It was not the King who slew him?'

'Nay, lord, it was not the King. The Scots Earl of March, and some others, would by no means permit the King to venture his person in that cause. And, sooth, I think he did not desire Hotspur's death, for when we brought the body to him later he wept in all men's sight. He had no joy in the victory, nor any man, for it was the worst battle that ever was fought in England, lord, and the unkindest.'

When the full tale was known few men wondered that the King had little joy in his victory. The heralds, whose bleak task it was to go forth on to a stricken field, counting and naming the dead, reported that sixteen hundred men lay stiff and stark amongst the trampled crops. Chief amongst them was the Lord Stafford, who had led the vaward of the King's army. People shook their heads, and signed themselves: no charge but Thomas of Gloucester's bale had descended upon his children. Twice had his daughter Anne married a Stafford, and twice had she been widowed, this time left to mourn the flower of knighthood, with his heir an infant in swaddling-bands.

To the last the King had striven to avoid bloodshed. Slipping through Hotspur's lines, he had reached Shrewsbury on the eighteenth day of July, and had sent immediately to parley with Hotspur. But Hotspur, some said urged thereto by his uncle of Worcester, whom the Witch Queen had driven off from his allegiance, was determined to try the issue upon the field of battle. Many of his men wore Richard's badge of the White Hart; others, as John had foretold, held by the White Lions of Mortimer; but neither his father, mustering men in the north, nor Glendower, hovering in the Welsh mountains, came to join him. My lord of Northumberland found Ralph Neville of Westmoreland blocking the way, and was forced to retreat to Newcastle; and Owen Glendower still hesitated to risk a pitched battle. The engagement was fought out between fairly matched armies, and for a long time the issue hung in the balance. But Hotspur fell; the great standard of the rampant blue lion wavered; the cries of '*Esperance, Percy!*' faltered; and the heart went out of his levies.

The King gave his body to a kinsman for decent burial, against the advice of all his officers, and it was interred at Whitchurch. But the King's advisers had been right: within a day a whisper was abroad that Hotspur lived yet, and would fight again. They were obliged to dig up the corpse, and to set it, rubbed in salt, between two posts on the highway for all to see. After several days it was taken down and dismembered, the head being sent to York, to be set above the bridge there. Worcester's head was sent to London; and for many months the crones on the Surrey side of the river earned groats from travellers by pointing out to them the grinning skull that was all that was left of M. de Guyenne's old friend, the Earl of Worcester.

6

From Shrewsbury the King marched north, trying to come to grips with the Earl of Northumberland. The Earl sought refuge in his hold of Warkworth, closely beset, but John's spirits sank when he learned that he had been induced to render himself up to the King at York, under promise that no hand should be lifted against him before he had appeared before Parliament to answer for his treachery. The Fox of the North, the very picture of benevolent old age, reminded the King of his great services, and pleaded that he was not accountable for the misdeeds of his son. The King sat like an image; and the only words he spoke in answer to his Mattathias were not comfortable. He carried him in his train to Pontefract, and compelled him there to render up all his offices. But he did not head him; he sent him instead to await impeachment at Baginton.

John was so angry when he heard this that he spent the day amongst his falcons, preferring feathered company to man's. The King had appointed him Master of the Falcons; and he was the first of the Masters for many years who treated the honour as something more than a distinguishing title. The astringers grew to like and respect a prince who was not content to ride out with a hawk on his fist, but who kept a tally of their accounts; knew when fresh turves were really needed for the Royal Mews; understood the use of orpiment and dragon's blood for sick birds; and was not above inspecting hoods, and stocks, and terrets.

The Chancellor's messenger found the Lord John and the chief falconer intent upon a gerfalcon troubled with ungladness. 'Waiting for me?' John said absently, his careful fingers feeling the falcon's swollen leg. 'I'll come anon.' Then it occurred to him that his uncle must have important tidings to disclose if he had ridden to Westminster to seek him; and he cast the falcon, and went away at once with the messenger.

The Chancellor had such tidings as drove all thought of Northumberland out of John's head. 'My son,' said Henry Beaufort, his mouth prim, but his tilted eyes laughing, 'I have come to tell you to truss up your baggage: you are for the North!'

'Reverend father!' gasped John.

'And also to hand you your commission,' continued the Bishop. 'The King has been pleased to appoint you Warden of the Eastern Marches, and Captain of Berwick, in my lord of Northumberland's room. Are you satisfied?'

The dark colour rushed up to the roots of John's hair; he said gruffly: 'I owe this to you, my uncle: God thank you!'

'Well, yes, a little you owe me,' acknowledged the Bishop. He held out his hand, and, when John knelt to kiss it, he said: 'Go north, John, and learn how to wage war! But also learn how to rule a turbulent land – and judge not your father hastily! The headsman's block is not always the answer to the troubles which beset a king.'

Part Three
The Lord Warden
1403–1405

'And this prince most discrete and sad,
... Was the first that did his entent,
By grete advys and ful hy prudence ...'

John Lydgate
Of the English Title to the Crown of France

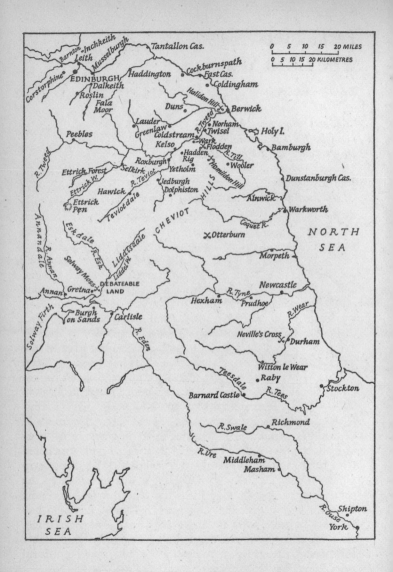

The English-Scottish Border

1 The Lord Warden

1

The Lord John reached Pontefract in the middle of August. His first sight of the great hold was not encouraging. The day was overcast, a light rain falling, like a sea-mist; and the castle, which might in sunshine have appeared golden, loomed sour yellow above the town at the foot of its rock. Originally a De Lacy hold, it had come into Lancastrian possession when Thomas of Lancaster, grandson to King Henry III, had married the heiress of the last Earl of Lincoln. He had built one of the seven towers, and had been beheaded for treason within sight of the walls. One of his escort chattily informed John of this circumstance, and was about to embellish the story when it occurred to him that the reminiscence was scarcely felicitous. It had been received in silence; glancing sidelong at the Lord John's hawk-face he saw it inscrutable, and was thrown into confusion. But the Lord John was not thinking of his great-great-great-uncle; he was staring ahead, his eyes lifted to the keep, which reared its massive bulk high above the flanking towers. Within its huge walls King Richard had died, by what means perhaps three men knew. It seemed to rise out of the sandstone knob on which it had been erected, and was plainly of ancient date, faced with weathered stonework, and lit by narrow, slit windows. An ill place in which to end one's days, John thought. He remembered the silken luxury in which King Richard had been wont to live, the treasures in which he had delighted, the favourites who had flattered and caressed him, and a shiver ran down his spine. Probably King Henry had ordered his prison to be comfortably furnished, but no hallings, no cushioned sieges, could transform grim Pontefract into another Sheen.

Three gates had to be passed, the way all the time ascending, before the inner bailey was reached. Once within the walls the castle appeared less forbidding than when seen from a distance. In the castle yard John was met by the Governor, Sir Robert Waterton, who greeted him with affection. Sir Robert was one of Father's oldest friends; it was difficult, looking into his pleasant countenance, listening to his kindly voice, to believe that he could have had any hand in King Richard's death. Like Sir Hugh, he seemed too honest a man for dark dealings. He told John that the King was awaiting him, but he warned him that he would not find his father in good point. King Henry had been scouring the North like a brisk besom: no doubt he was for-wearied. No weariness of mind or body, however, could abate his energy. His squires swore that he had killed thirty men with his own hand at Shrewsbury; and since then he had allowed neither himself nor his officers a day's rest. When John was ushered into his presence he was engaged with his secretaries, a mass of papers on his table; and he glanced up with an impatient frown. But when he saw who had entered the chamber the frown lifted, and he held out his hands, exclaiming: 'Welcome, John!'

John had not stayed to change his raiment, and he knelt before his father with the mud still clinging to his ox-leather buskins. The King kissed his brow. The laugh that was not as ready as once it had been made him jerk up his chin. 'Holy Rood! Do you mean to tower above us all, whelp?'

'No force, sir!' John said, grinning.

'Well,' said the King, 'you are grown too big for Hugh Waterton, and shall have a new governor in Ralph Neville.'

'That is a change I am blithe to make,' responded John.

'I shall make you Constable of England presently,' pursued the King.

John nodded. If he was gratified by the promised appointment he did not show it; he was certainly not surprised. This great office had belonged of old to the Bohuns. It had passed, on the death of the last Earl of Hereford, John's grandsire, to his elder son-in-law, Thomas of Gloucester. After his taking off it had been first granted, by King Richard, to Edward of Rutland; and later, by King Henry, to the Earl of Northumberland.

'While you are under age the business must be done by deputy,' added the King.

Again John nodded. His father regarded him with a mixture of amusement and exasperation. 'Well, my son, well! Is there a weight tied to your tongue?'

'I thought that when the Fox was shent the office must be mine,' said John. 'If Thomas is Lord High Steward, I must be Constable, and Humfrey, I suppose, the Lord High Chamberlain, presently.'

The King was shaken by laughter. 'True!'

Recollecting himself, John began to thank him, but the King interrupted, saying: 'No, stint! You have said sooth: the office must be yours: it belongs to our family by inheritance. Is there nothing you wish me to tell you?'

'Witterly, sir!' John answered. 'How does Harry fare? I heard he had been wounded, but it was thought not dangerful. Is he well?'

The King stared at him between narrowed eyelids. 'So! I learn that Harry is amended of his wound: perhaps it may mar his beauty – that I cannot tell!'

'He'll take no force of that,' John said. 'I heard – Antelope Pursuivant told me – that he demeaned himself right worshipfully in the battle.'

'Right worshipfully,' the King agreed.

'I expect he enjoyed it,' John said reflectively.

'I expect he did,' responded the King dryly. 'It was his first pitched battle. When he has fought in some more he will not enjoy them so much.' He saw the disbelief in John's face, and raised his brows. 'No?'

'Sir, my uncle, the Bishop, said to me that war is Harry's trade, and I think he spoke sooth. But it is not against the Welsh that he would choose to fight.'

'Let Harry rid himself of dreams of French conquests!' the King said sharply. 'There lies no profit in war with France! As for your thirdfather King Edward's large claims, I tell you without ambage, my son, I deem them folly!'

John knew that he would not himself choose to lead an army into France, but he was too much the disciple both of Bel sire and of Harry wholly to agree with his father. He maintained silence; and after a pause the King said abruptly: 'I am recalling Thomas from Ireland. He may join Harry in Wales for a space.'

Again John made no comment. He wondered how Thomas would demean himself under the command of a brother he was always ambitious to excel. He thought there would be some trials of strength between them, but this he did not say to the King. Harry could be trusted to handle Thomas without aid or advice. There might be stormy scenes, but there would be no lingering rancour, for neither ever bosomed up malice, and under his jealousy Thomas deeply respected Harry.

Two days later John left Pontefract with the Earl of Westmoreland, Ralph Neville, bound first for York, where he must pay his respects to Archbishop Scrope; and next for my lord's hold at Middleham. The King advised him privately not to stay at Middleham, but to seek a lodging at the Cistercian monastery of Jervaulx. 'Always lodge in a monastery!' said the King, who made this his own rule. 'You will have far better entertainment. Middleham! Yes, yes, I know it! I had as lief lie in Shrewsbury Castle, which Harry would have had me do!'

'Harry told me once that Shrewsbury Castle is like Kenilworth,' said John.

'What a daffish thing to say!' exclaimed the King fretfully. 'It was built of the same red stone, but to compare such a paltry, ancient hold with the palace your grandfather built at Kenilworth—! But no force, no force! It is well enough for such a youngling as Harry! *I* lodged with the Grey Friars, of course: good entertainment, and the Abbot a witty, conversable man.' He paused; and added thoughtfully: 'They are Cistercians at Jervaulx – you will find them all over the north! It is the rule of their order to abjure the company of men, but latterly they have become less strict. You will be better housed there than at Middleham.'

John was easily able to believe him. Like any other well-to-do person he had spent the first night upon the road north at the great Abbey of St Albans, where the arrangements made for noble travellers by far outshone what could be offered by any hostelry. However, he was not of an age to set much store by ease, and as he had reason to suppose that the Nevilles were preparing lavishly for his reception he returned his father an indifferent answer, and left the arrangements for his journey in his new guardian's hands.

2

The Earl of Westmoreland took him by a roundabout way to Raby, by York, and his own manor of Sheriff Hutton. 'For it will be well if you know all this land, John,' he said, 'and where my chief holds lie.' Passing over the bridge at York, he volunteered more information, jerking his chin upwards at a grisly relic set upon a pike. 'Hotspur,' he said.

John lifted his eyes to look at the head. Such sights were common enough, and the head was quite unrecognizable, stripped bare of flesh by the crows.

'Your father did not like to see it there,' remarked the Earl. 'They were boon-friends once. Well! He was my kinsman, you know, and I am sorry for his ending; but if a man choose to mell himself with treason he may count it good fortune to die upon the field of battle, and not from a doom's cart.'

He found that his charge was more interested in surveying the walls of York than in heads on pikes, and regarded him with approval. The Lord John inspected the city's defences, explored the town, heard High Mass in the Minster, and rested that night at the Archbishop's palace of Bishopsthorpe.

Here he had rather austere entertainment, Archbishop Scrope being renowned for the simplicity of his life. He was an elderly man, scholarly, but not, John thought, witty; and he was too closely connected with the Percy interests to be a favourite of the Earl of Westmoreland. He had been joined with Archbishop Arundel in enthroning King Henry – surprisingly, for he had been one of King Richard's friends, and, indeed, owed his translation to the Archbishopric of York, in defiance of the choice of the Chapter, to King Richard's influence with the Pope. It had been he who had gone to Rome, at Richard's behest, to seek the canonisation of King Edward II: John, seated at his board, glancing at his thin, aloof countenance, recalled the Countess Marshal's well-salted words, and wondered what could have possessed so seemingly-saintly a man to engage on such an embassy. The Archbishop did not enlighten him, but spoke instead of his nephew, the heir to the barony of Masham, who was with Harry on the Marches, and bidding fair to become his closest friend.

Ralph Neville took John north next day betimes, leaving York by the Bootham Bar, a strong gate which had formerly guarded the city against Scottish invaders. 'But they do not reach York now!' said the Earl, with one of his horse-laughs.

Sheriff Hutton, a small brown hold rather less than three leagues north-east of York, had little of interest to show. Ralph Neville said that a long time ago, before the memory of man, its constable had been charged with the duty of ridding the neighbourhood of the rogues who had infested the great Forest of Galtres. Forests were still the haunts of desperate men – robbers, outlaws, one-time soldiers, villeins who had deserted their masters – but of this particular forest not much remained. It was said to have harboured wolves once: John, staring at a wilder, larger country than any he had yet seen, was hopeful that wolves might yet lurk in the valleys; but Ralph Neville said there were no wolves to be found south of Northumberland, and not very many there nowadays.

Dropping into one of the valleys they came to the Abbey of Rievaulx at the hour of Sexte, and stood uncovered in the chequered sunlight while the bell tolled the Angelus. The wooded hills rose steeply on either side, and a small river burbled over the stones on its bed. No other habitation had been seen for many miles; the place seemed remote, very lonely. Ralph Neville said that Cistercians always chose such sites. This did not promise good cheer, but when they were admitted by the porter, and conducted to the guest-house, they found very seemly accommodation. The Abbot himself received the Lord John; and if it was his custom to abjure the company of men this did not appear in his manners or in the easy flow of his conversation. At first unhopeful of exchanging ideas with so young a princeling, he soon discovered that the King's third son, besides having enjoyed the advantages of a careful education, had delved deeply into mundane matters. Sheep-farming was the chief worldly business of the Cistercians, and it was not long before the Abbot found himself talking about wool with the Lord John. They talked of ewe-flocks, of wethers and hoggets; of the perils of the lambing season; of fells; of the advantages and the disadvantages of a fixed Staple; of the guile of the Lombard merchants, and the wiles of the brokers; of the circumstances which had led great families to lease their farms to tenants; and – this was a homethrust delivered by the Lord John – of the sand-blind policy that induced sheep-farmers to sell their wool for many years ahead to crafty Flemish and Italian merchants. The Abbot flung up his hands, crying, '*Peccavi!*' and Ralph Neville, whose livelihood depended on rents and coal, smothered a yawn; and the Lord John's confessor, a Black Friar, wondered when the company would be allowed to sit down to dinner. An excellent man, Father Matthew, but not one who was indifferent to his body's needs. Like most Dominicans, he was learned; he was also ambitious; shrewd rather than saintly; correct in doctrine; chaste in his life, but thinking it no sin to be fond of the pleasures of the table and of the chase. The Abbot, a man of another kidney, regarded him with austerity, for when Father Matthew rode on a journey he wore the dress of a layman, so that only when he pulled off his hood, and his tonsured crown was made visible, could he be recognized as a man in Holy Orders. This custom spared him the pain of seeing lewd fellows cross their fingers to avert the evil eye, as common folk were too prone to do when they encountered friars, but it found no favour with the stricter clerics. The Abbot could scarcely have been more shocked had he come in with a hawk on his fist. But he kept no hawks: such a practice would not have been tolerated by the King. The bare-faced falcon, mantling in the Abbot's parlour, was upon John's fist. He had flown her at a heron on the road to Rievaulx: Father Matthew's only part in the sport had been to point the heron out to John; he did not even permit himself to ride forward with John to retrieve the falcon. Ralph Neville thought it unwit to go hawking without dogs, and called out that she would carry; but the friar smiled, and said: 'Nay, she will keep her mark, and come again to the lure. I know her well!'

The Lord John had made a gift of the heron to the Abbot, and it had been borne off to the larder: birds were not accounted flesh by the Cistercians.

3

Middleham was not reached until dusk had laid shadows across the landscape, but the Lord John had seen enough to make him conscious of a vast loneliness. He had seen also that the ground over which he passed was good, arable land, saving only the lifting moors, where the little, horned, black-faced sheep grazed, and wondered to see it so sparsely populated. 'We are enough to account for the Scots!' retorted the Earl.

Middleham, one of a chain of formidable holds, lay in the Honour of Richmond, some three leagues or more south of Richmond Castle. South of it, the country belonged to the Scropes of Masham; a little to the north-west, their kinsmen of Bolton held Wensleydale; and all around lay the vast territory owing fealty to the Nevilles. It was inhabited by my lord's elder son by his first marriage, Sir John Neville, who was wedded to a Holland, sister to John Beaufort's vivacious lady. She claimed John, with a giggle, as her nephew. 'For since Meg married your uncle of Somerset I must perforce be your aunt!' she explained, with a roguish twinkle strongly reminiscent of her lively sister.

Her husband explained to John that since his father was Warden of the Western Marches the greater part of his duties lay about Carlisle. 'You will see when you reach Barnard Castle, which is my lord of Warwick's hold, where the road runs westward over the moors,' he said. 'Indeed, I think my father may take you to see the new fortress he is building at Penrith. But it is not in general by the west that the Scots come in force against us. It is an ill country for their needs, and my uncle Thomas, the Lord Furnivall, holds Lochmaben and all Annandale for the King.' He smiled, and added: 'Yours will be the harder task, my lord. They keep the beacons ready for kindling all the year round on the Eastern Marches!'

John put one or two questions to him; and afterwards John Neville said to his father: 'How old is this great lad, sir? I think him likely, very likely!'

'Yea, saving only young Harry of Monmouth, the likeliest of the brood,' replied the Earl.

Middleham was not a very large hold. Various towers had been erected round the rectangular enclosure, but it boasted no Great Hall, this being incorporated in the keep, and reached by an outer stair leading to the main entrance on the first floor. A solar lay beside the Hall, with the Chamber of Presence behind it; and it was heated by a fire kindled in the old-fashioned way in the centre of the room, with a louvre cut in the roof above it to allow the smoke to escape. The Lord John could understand why the King thought poorly of it; but for himself he was well-pleased; and guessed, from the savoury odours pervading the air, that an excellent supper would shortly be set before him.

The Lady Neville did not appear at supper, the company invited to meet the new Warden being strictly male, and including, besides many who owed fealty to Neville, my lord of Warwick's lieutenant from Barnard Castle, and the Lord Greystoke, who had ridden over the moor from beyond Penrith. Listening to the northern voices, John was carried back in memory to Leicester, where he had first heard the unfamiliar burr. It seemed a long time ago; he glanced round the chamber, trying to recognize faces, but could not. Only he remembered Sir Harry Hotspur, pacing about the curtilage, with his hand tucked in Father's arm. He wondered what these stranger lords and knights were thinking of Hotspur's successor – for the King had bestowed on him Hotspur's Cumbrian estates for his livelihood. They seemed friendly; he reflected that Ralph Neville would not have bidden any adherent of the Percies to this feast. He sat at the high table, between his hosts, a big lad with a beaky nose, penetrating eyes, and a full-lipped mouth, curling up at the corners, as Harry's did, and Thomas's. He was not shy, but he said little. He listened, and stored away what he heard in his retentive memory. None of the company who watched him yet knew the Lord John's infinite capacity for listening, and for remembering. Although his eyes were so bright, the lids were heavy, giving him sometimes a sleepy look. The upward tilt of his lips made him seem to smile, and lent an expression of good humour to his face. On the whole he was approved: a lusty lad, too young to be of much account, but giving himself no airs, and listening to his elders with deference.

Accommodation at Middleham was restricted, most of the noble guests being obliged to spend the night in the Hall and the solar; but the Nevilles conducted John, by way of a wooden bridge, to the tower at the south-western angle of the bailey which had been prepared for his use. This was a three-storey building, two rooms to a floor, and a steep newel-stair. Wooden shutters had been set up in the narrow windows, and braziers of charcoal made all snug, but John's servants thought the quarters wretched indeed, quite unlike any of the royal palaces, quite unbefitting his dignity. His valets made a great fuss over the business of bringing water for his washing, conveying to him in their own way the information that they had been obliged to fetch it from the kitchen; his attention was drawn to the absence of any fireplace; and his chief valet, who had waited on him since his childhood, expressed his conviction that not a wink of sleep would he get for the moan of the wind blowing off the moors.

'I like it,' said John, stretching himself out in his bed.

'And no garderobe to this tower, my lord!'

'I know. Take away the brazier: I don't need it.'

The moan of the wind lulled John to sleep, and he slept sound. When his servants came to him in the morning, they found him standing mother-naked by the window, gazing out at the grand sweep of the moor, rising immediately beyond the castle ditch. He had taken down the shutters, and a sharp wind was blowing into the room, for the windows were unglazed. Steed, the chief valet, exclaimed at him, and made haste to huddle a furred bedgown round his shoulders. John let it fall, and kicked it aside. 'I like this land,' he said, filling his lungs.

Ralph Neville took him to Penrith that day, by the road that led across the moors. There was little to be seen but sheep in all that windswept country, patches of yellow ragwort, and swathes of heather, in all the purple brilliance of its first flowering, but it pleased John, and he would have been glad to have journeyed farther into Cumberland. Ralph Neville dissuaded him from visiting his new possessions: he thought that Hotspur's tenants would accord no merry welcome to his successor, and said that John ought rather to visit the royal hold of Richmond. So they rode eastward again from Penrith, which was a-building in hot, red sandstone, and reached Richmond that evening. The Constable had made good preparation for John's reception, but the castle, in spite of its size, had been built for defence rather than as a dwelling, and apart from the keep, which was enormous, there were few buildings of any size within its walls. It stood perched on a precipitous cliff above the River Swale, and presided over a market-town, up whose steep streets the travellers rode on their way to the gatehouse. It possessed no drawbridge, but only a portcullis, giving access to the barbican. The north-western side of the keep abutted on to this, instead of standing, like that of Middleham, in the centre of the bailey. Within the walls there was a huge court, at one corner of which stood the building called Scolland's Hall, an ancient erection containing the Hall and a solar overlooking the cockpit. The Constable told John at supper that King Arthur and his Knights were said to be sleeping in an underground chamber beneath the castle, waiting for someone to enter, and to draw the magic sword Excalibur; but he admitted that he had never been able to find this chamber. 'Leasings,' said Ralph Neville, mopping up the sauce on his platter with a piece of bread, and stuffing it into his mouth. He sucked the ends of his moustache, and added: 'I've listened to a score of such gestes in my day, and not one of them true. Why, they'll tell you that young Warwick's thirdfather, Guy – he that was called the Black Dog of Arden – slew a dragon in Northumberland. Well, I don't say there are no dragons overseas, because for all I know there may be many of them in the Paynim countries, but I do say that there are none in these parts, nor ever have been.'

On the following day they rode north again, through wild scenery, to Barnard Castle, on the Tees, belonging to the Beauchamps. Its situation closely resembled that of Richmond, and it overlooked a thickly wooded countryside. John found it a commodious place, and wondered that Richard should never have mentioned it. But the lieutenant said that my lord had only once visited it, when he had been a child. 'My lord of Warwick owns so many holds,' murmured Father Matthew.

Ralph Neville grunted. He was a warm man himself, but he suspected that the new young Earl of Warwick was wealthier by far. It had begun to seem as if he would become a person of great consequence too, for he was sworn-brother to the Prince of Wales. Ralph regretted that he had not made a push to arrange a match between Warwick and one of his own daughters. But an alliance with the Beauchamps had not seemed to be wise policy when King Richard had banished the old Earl to the Isle of Man, and it was too late now: Warwick had been for several years wedded to Lord Berkeley's daughter.

Raby, which was no more than two leagues distant from Barnard Castle, was set in a milder scene. The travellers reached it at mid-overnoon, and John, who had begun to think that all the northern castles were grim, old-fashioned fortresses, was surprised to find it so magnificent a dwelling. Its many towers already covered more than an acre of ground, and it was still a-building, to accommodate the Earl's rapidly increasing family. It was not very defensible – indeed, the Earl confessed that when danger threatened he sent his wife and his children to the less opulent but stronger hold of Brancepeth – but its situation was pleasant, and it stood in the middle of a well-stocked deer-park.

When the cavalcade rode over the drawbridge and through the covered way to the second gate, and thus into the inner bailey, almost as many officers and varlets as M. de Guyenne had been used to keep under his roof were gathered to meet their master. Most of them wore the badge of the Dun Bull on their sleeves, but some showed the Pied Bull of Raby, and one or two the Buck of the Nevilles. John's own household, wearing his badge of the Golden Tree-root, were swamped in a tide of sanguine liveries: it was easy to see that in the North my lord of Westmoreland was a man of huge consequence.

John found his aunt, Joan Beaufort, as brisk as ever, her

spirit undismayed either by the rigorous climate or the size of her family. My lord had had ten children by his first marriage: two sons and eight daughters; his second lady had already borne him four lusty babes; and by her own first marriage she was the mother of two daughters. The elder of these was betrothed to the Lord Greystoke's heir; the younger, though still of nursery-age, was handfast to young Ralph Neville my lord's second son; and both, together with Ralph, Anne, Margaret, Anastasia, and the two sons and two daughters of his second union were living at Raby. Two of my lord's daughters had taken the veil; but the three eldest, all of whom were married to northern barons, lived within reach of the castle, and were often to be seen there.

'Honest souls, but lewd as asses, every one!' his aunt told John. 'I warn you, John, so you will find it here! My lord never opens a book – quite conceitless! But he has plenty of kind-wit: never think he has not! And no chinchery! You will often hear it said of the northern men that strait-keeping is their vice: they will have every groat accounted for. Leasings! Careful, yes! Chinchery, never! Those books you see there he bought me at great costage. You are bookish, John? *All* our family are scholars!'

'Nay, madam, Humfrey is the only true scholar amongst us,' John disclaimed.

'Is it so? But you read? Yes, yes, I know you do! In this wilderness you will find few men who will do more than scan their stewards' accounts! I except Sir Robert Umfraville! Yes, I except him. I lent him my *History of the Crusades* (I wonder if Harry would care to read that?), and he liked it very well. Perhaps he is not book-hungry, as *we* understand it, but certainly a cultured gentleman. You will meet him presently, and you will like him. My lord's daughter Anne is handfast to his nephew Gilbert – still under ward, but a likely lad, we think, and, of course, the head of his house.' She then regaled John with several stories, redounding not at all to the credit of various of my lord's neighbours. She caught herself up in the middle of a rusty anecdote, exclaiming: 'But I am putting you to the blush! You are so big a fellow, John, that I forget you have not yet fifteen years in your dish. Child, I hope that your wit may match your inches, for you have a thankless task before you! His people venerate Northumberland, and will ill stomach a successor to his power!'

2 Green Wood

I

John had four months in the North before winter closed down
on the Cheviots; and when he journeyed south again he was well
instructed in Border law; could preside at need over the Warden's Court; had taken part in at least one skirmish; knew the
Eastern Marches as well as he knew the kindlier country round
Berkhampsted; and had won for himself the grutching approval
of the dour men under his rule.

The duties of the Wardens were performed largely by deputies; but the big princeling who had succeeded to Northumberland's power soon made it plain that he did not mean to be a
puppet-warden. Raby offered a life of ease and rich entertainment; but Ralph Neville was not more anxious to school his
charge in the duties of his office than John was to learn of him.
He listened, and tucked away what he was told in his memory;
and was soon ready, in his guardian's judgment, to be taken on
a tour of his territory.

They rode to Newcastle by way of Durham, through a
country disfigured by open-cast mining, and dotted with bell-
pits. 'Coal,' said Ralph Neville. He told John that so number-
less were the diggings about Newcastle that it was hazardous to
approach the town after dark. All the mining had originally been
open-cast, but there were now many pits, generally protected
from the weather by thatched hovels with wattle walls built over
the top of them. Within these, windlasses had been erected
for raising the corves; and the corves were sent to Newcastle on
pack-horses, and wains. He talked of rokes, and buttresses,
fothers, chaldrons, and keels; and, questioned, explained to John
the mysteries of iron-working and lime-burning. He himself
owned iron-works at Bywell. He was building a fortress there,

to protect the village from the raids of the thieves of Tynedale, and promised John a sight of it. So hardy were these rogues that every night the sheep and the cattle had to be driven into the street, where a watch was kept all the year round. 'A masterless land you will find it,' he said. 'Tynedale thieves and Redesdale robbers!'

Newcastle surprised John. After Durham, he had felt himself to be penetrating farther and farther into a savage wilderness, and he expected to find nothing more than a fortress-town. It was certainly the most heavily fortified of all the towns he had seen. The walls varied in height from twelve to twenty feet, and were nowhere less than eight feet thick; and beyond them had been dug a fosse, called the King's Dykes, sixty feet broad. There were seven gates, besides posterns and water-gates; and towers innumerable. Every free burgess was a man-at-arms, and no fewer than a hundred men formed the night-watch. But within the walls the four great orders of mendicant friars had their establishments, and many of the Border lords their houses. There was a Benedictine convent; several hospitals for the aged and sick; four churches; and a maze of twisting streets lined with every sort of building, from the richly decorated houses of the ironmasters and the wool-merchants to stark storehouses, and the huddled dwellings of the humbler folk. It was not a beautiful city; its buildings were dingy with the smoke of the coal burned in and around it; it was malodorous from the acrid fumes of the coal; but it was prosperous, and it had been raised lately, by royal charter, to the dignity of a county.

It was here that the Lord John made the acquaintance of his officers and some of the principal Border families. He held informal court, and with no other help than a few words muttered by Ralph Neville in his straining ear, grappled with a foison of strange faces and unknown names. Greystokes, Dacres, and the Greys of Heaton he had encountered; but these were swamped in a tide of Swinburnes, Lilburnes, Radcliffes, Cartingtons, Erringtons, Mitfords, and Fenwicks. 'One of the Herons of Chipchase,' Ralph growled incomprehensibly. 'A Clennell, out of Coquetdale . . . Bertram of Bothal . . . Robert Ogle, lately prisoned by the Scots, but for-bought this year, out of the wool-customs of this city.' John snatched at the memory of a Scottish raid on Wark Castle, said something: enough to show knowledge, not enough to betray ignorance; and turned, with relief, to greet one who was already known to him. He saw perceivance of his difficulties in Sir Robert Umfraville's amused eyes, and grinned at him.

'You tread charily, my lord – and featly!' Sir Robert said.

'I do my power,' John replied, stammering a little. 'It is not much, but over that I can no more – wellaway!'

'It is not so little, and will be more.'

'God willing!' John said.

Sir Robert told Ralph Neville that the Lord John would win worship. Ralph was pleased, for he felt himself to be chargeable for John; but he only said: 'Yea, a likely lad, but he hasn't cut his wit-teeth yet.'

'He bears himself mannerly, and seems to be no prateapace.'

'He!' Ralph ejaculated, with a snort of mirth. 'I misdoubted me at first that he was a leatherhead, for he'll stay mumbudget while the rest of the world is clapping! But I'll tell you this, Robin: what you may impart to him, and what he may see, he won't readily forget!'

2

From Newcastle, his guardian conducted John to Berwick, following the Roman road to Alnwick. They travelled with a considerable meiny, but they left Warkworth unvisited. Warkworth was my lord of Northumberland's favourite hold; and while it was unlikely that any hand would be raised against the King's son while my lord lay in custody, with Borderers one never knew. Ralph Neville growled in Umfraville's ear that they would stretch their arms no further than their sleeves would reach; and told John that it would be unmannerly to thrust themselves into this Percy stronghold.

'Yea, witterly!' said John, his face lifted to the sky. 'What is that bird, my lord?'

Ralph, who had had ample opportunity to discover the Lord John's tastes, sighed, and said: 'It's only a curlew. You will see many of them in these parts. You should know, John, that we are now in the very heart of the Percy domains. Like enough you will get some black looks, but we shall lie at Hulne Abbey when we come to Alnwick, so—'

'Is there some fellow here who can tell me about these birds?' interrupted John. 'I have seen a-many that are strange to me!'

'For God's bane, John—!' exploded the Earl.

But Sir Robert, laughing, called up a man of his own household, and bade him tell the Lord John all that he desired to know. So the Lord John and a redeless man-at-arms rode together, and the Lord John's guardians rode side by side in their wake, one amused, the other hovering on the edge of exasperation.

'Nay, let the boy be!' Sir Robert said. 'That churl will tell his fellows the King's son is no foppet, and that will serve him well.'

'I daresay he'll understand no more than one word in a dozen that are said to him!'

But the Lord John's ear was becoming attuned to the northern speech, and he seemed to find little difficulty in understanding his companion. By the time the cavalcade reached Hulne Abbey, he knew where the sea-parrots made their burrows in the nesting-season; where the shags flocked in their thousands; where he would see the fulmars; and how the peregrines would hover above the crags of the Henhole chasm high up on the Cheviot. He learned too of the crows that stole the twigs from the roof of the blessed St Cuthbert's hut on Lindisfarne, but made him reparation, when he exhorted them, by bringing him a piece of bacon. He learned that there were wolves in Redesdale, and seals on one of the Farne Islands; that cloudberries were ripe only when they were yellow; and that a flock of sheep was called a hirsel; and he listened to strange legends, and scraps of folk-lore, all mixed up with stranger tales of chance-raids and March-days.

At supper, he questioned Sir Robert on these matters; but just as Ralph Neville had begun to think that a glimpse of a golden eagle was the sum of his ambition, John turned to him, and said: 'I want to visit Dunstanburgh, please you, and, by my reckoning, I think we are near it?'

'Sea-birds?' said Ralph sardonically.

'No. Dunstanburgh is our own – Bel sire's northernmost hold!'

'So you know that, do you?' said Ralph. 'Well, we shall lie there tomorrow. I will warrant you a warm welcome, but it's a dour place. Windswept, too. It will be well enough now, but I wouldn't choose to abide there in winter-time. The wind howls nightlong, and the sea crashes on the rocks with such a din that you must shout to be heard above it. You'll be blithe to leave it, I daresay.'

John was not at all blithe to leave it, though he did agree that it was not the sort of castle one would choose for a winter visit. It was a huge hold, built on the dark crags of the Whin Sill, jutting out to sea, and continually pounded by the waves that broke at the foot of the rocks. On the north and east the sea guarded it from approach; to the west lay treacherous swamps; and on the southern side the entrance to the great outer ward was protected by ramparts and an escarpment. So large was the outer ward that it contained, besides stables and cow-byres, a cornfield. With the accession of Henry of Bolingbroke to the throne it had become a royal hold, but many of the men who garrisoned it still wore Bel sire's badge of the Ostrich Feather; and the welcome they accorded to young John of Lancaster threw into ugly relief the reluctant civility he had met else-where. Under the aegis of the captain, John inspected the defences, and the buildings added by M. de Guyenne. The captain, looking at his hawk-nose, thought him very like his grandfather. Then he thought that perhaps he was not so very like him. The captain had not, of course, known M. de Guyenne in the days of his boyhood, but he could not picture him at any age amusing himself, when business was done, by exploring the rocky shore, or standing motionless and silent to watch a shag diving for fish in the tumbled waters; St Cuthbert's ducks bobbing on the waves; or the grace of a tern's flight. M. de Guyenne's pleasures had been of a very different order.

3

No enthusiastic welcome awaited the Lord John in the town of which he had been made Captain. The people of Berwick watched his meiny ride in over the bridge that spanned the Tweed, and they watched in silence, neither friendly nor hostile. Hostility had been slain by the rumour that my lord of Northumberland had offered Berwick to the Scots, friendliness by the sharp knocks the town had received from King Henry after Shrewsbury fight. Sir William Greystoke had held the castle against him, and King Henry's new great gun had torn a breach in its walls. A Clifford was now its captain, a middle-aged man who seemed not to relish his command. The castle he governed had been battered, and the town itself was in no very defensible condition. The walls, though strengthened by towers, were in bad repair, and there was no money forthcoming to set them in order. In moments of depression, Clifford could fancy that even the links of the chain that stretched across the river had worn thin. Berwick was the gateway into Scotland, and no one seemed to care in what case the defences stood.

Ralph Neville let John inspect the town, himself not uttering a word. Only he watched John out of the corners of his eyes, and chewed the ends of his moustache. John was similarly silent, until that gash made by King Henry's gun in the castle wall jerked an exclamation out of him. 'Jesu, mercy! This is worse than all!'

'My lord of Northumberland has often said that his wardenship cost him twenty thousand pounds – unpaid,' remarked the Earl.

'He spent little of that sum here!' retorted John. 'This must be repaired!'

'Certes it should be repaired, but at whose costage?'

'The King's – my own!' John stammered. 'If I am Warden I will be so in deed!'

The Earl grunted. 'You must needs own great livelihood, nephew! Take care how you loosen the strings of your purse on this charge!'

'Have you kept the strings of yours tied?' demanded John.

'Oh, I have great interest here!' replied the Earl, with one of his snorts of laughter.

During his first months in the North, John learned much, and learned it swiftly. The Earl gave him into Sir Robert Umfraville's charge; and under that wise guardianship he grew to know the country over which he ruled, and its fierce, dour people. Truces, he discovered, were made to be broken; raids were everyday occurrences until the grip of winter closed on the North; and a burning farm or a Border hold stormed were incidents calling for quick reprisal but no pompous report to the King's Council.

He had the good fortune to be at Wark Castle when he first saw the glow of the warning beacons. It was only a small raid: scarcely worth the attention of the Warden: but Sir Robert, knowing his countrymen, let John put on his harness and join in the skirmish. The Northumbrians, mourning Hotspur, rancorous at the imprisonment of their liege-lord, resentful of the princeling who had usurped his office, were at first startled and then amused to find the princeling in their midst. It was just the kind of scrambling fight and helter-skelter chase to delight a lad thirsting for a chance to win his spurs. The seasoned warriors laughed at John, but liked him the better for his enthusiasm. When they discovered that he was much younger than his large frame had led them to suppose, they liked him better still, and resented him less. If the Earl of Northumberland were to break free from Baginton, and raise his standard, the better part of his people would flock to it; but in the meantime a fearless boy who was neither shy nor boldrumptious could be tolerated. He was found to have an easy way with him, too: easier than my lord of Northumberland, who kept such kingly state that it was hard for common men to approach him. Not for nothing had the Lord John companied with men-at-arms during the years of his childhood! Hopeful applicants laying grievances before him discovered that he had a shrewd head on his shoulders; and more than one grutcher left his presence wagging a discomfited head, and warned his fellows that they would make neither back nor edge of the new Warden.

He was happy in Sir Robert's charge, and deeply respected

him. Sir Robert was witty, and the pattern of chivalry. It was he who taught John, by his example, never publicly to rebuke his servants, never to vent exasperation on a valet, or to lose his temper with lightless villeins who seemed purposely to misunderstand his orders. He was sheriff of the county, and Constable of several castles, and he governed Redesdale for his nephew, who was its lord.

John met this nephew, Gilbert Umfraville, at Harbottle Castle, which loured over the Coquet in a deep valley, and had been the home of the Umfravilles for more than two hundred years. It was a savage spot, surrounded by craggy hills, patched with heather and sweet with the scent of juniper. Gulls screamed incessantly, wheeling round a lonely tarn high up on the moor; and sometimes, in the still of the night, the howl of a wolf could be heard.

Gilbert was a year younger than John. He had been in the wardship of Harry Hotspur, but he was Sir Robert's pupil, and had scarcely known his guardian. He was as courteous as his uncle, and ambitious of knighthood. He hoped that when he had livery of his lands he would be able to lead his levies to war against the French. John thought that he would have enough to do on the Border, but Gilbert shook his head, saying that he would be content to leave his uncle to rule over Redesdale. The two striplings became close friends as soon as John had succeeded in goading Gilbert into forgetfulness of the deference due to a King's son. He spoke despitefully of Gilbert's people, murmuring, 'Redesdale robbers,' and following this up, when he saw Gilbert stiffen, by recalling in a thoughtful tone that he had been told that the devil came out of the north. Such an importable insult could not be stomached; and by the time Gilbert had recollected his duty he was too busily engaged in striving to prevent his much bigger opponent from throwing him to have leisure or, indeed, breath, to waste on apologies. He managed to trip John, and they fell together, and he discovered that John was laughing at him. So he stopped trying to choke him, and gasped, in a stricken voice: 'Pardon, my lord! I—'

'Oh, leave that, a'God's Name!' interrupted John, sitting up, and picking the rushes out of his doublet. 'Gilbert, I heard a

202

wolf howl last night – if it was not the devil! You told me once
that you hold Redesdale by the service of defending it against
wolves!'

'So we do!'

'But how?'

'We take them with nets sometimes, and sometimes we use
haussepieds.'

'You don't hunt them at force?'

'Out of dread! With greyhounds and mastiffs!'

'Then let us do so!' said John. 'I shall be blithe to tell my
cousin Edward of York that I've hunted wolves, because I
don't think he has ever done so!'

4

The King spent Christmas-tide at the monastery of Abingdon,
but John did not leave the North until January, when he
travelled to London with Ralph Neville to attend the opening of
Parliament. He was at Raby for the twelve days of Christmas,
bringing the Umfravilles in his train, and arriving at the dinner-
hour, and to the sound of carols. My lord's own minstrels were
singing '*Of a rose, a lovely rose,*' but when my lord brought the
Warden and his company into the Great Hall they struck up a
fresh tune. The Lord John, recognizing it, chuckled, and trod
up the hall to the dais where the family sat. He kissed his aunt's
hand, and told her that he knew very well who had bade the
minstrels sing '*For now is the time of Christmas.*' He sat down
beside her, and while he dipped his hands in the bowl of water
presented to him by the ewerer, and dried them with the napkin
offered by one of my lord's pages, the minstrels sang the carol of
my lady's mischievous choosing.

'. . . *Let no man come into this hall*
  Groom, page, nor yet marshal,
  But that some sport he bring withal!
    For now is the time of Christmas!
  If that he say he cannot sing,
  Some other sport then let him bring!
  That it may please at this feasting!

> For now is the time of Christmas!
> If he say he can naught do,
> Then for my love ask him no mo',
> But to the stocks then let him go!
> For now is the time of Christmas!'

The Lord John, sending a gold noble spinning into the hands of the chief minstrel, said that he would be set in the stocks without more ado; and when my lady insisted that at least he could sing, proved her wrong by venturing his breaking voice in the refrain of '*All this time this song is best: Verbum caro factum est!*'

It was the merriest Christmas he could remember, the only thing to spoil it being the absence of his brothers. But since he expected to see all three of them as soon as he reached London he wasted no time in repining, but flung himself instead into every offered pastime. There were plenty of these, from outdoor sports to indoor mummeries; and if the Lord John could not sing he was a doughty wrestler, played a lusty game of hand-ball, and rode with zest at the quintain. He generally struck this awry, and received a hearty buffet from the stuffed figure, but this only added to the fun.

When dusk fell, he would run into the castle from the park, hot, and mud-spattered and panting, and clatter up the newel-stair of the tower set aside for his use. He would find his valets waiting with a bowl of hot, herb-scented water. They would strip off his leather jerkin and his sweat-soaked shirt, and peel the muddied hose from his legs; then Steed, the chief amongst them, would rub him with a sponge, dipped in the hot water, till he glowed. After that, and making him shudder deliciously, rose-water was flung over him. Then he was wrapped in towels, and given a dish of spiced cake-bread to eat, or one of pain-puffs, because although he had consumed an enormous dinner at mid-overnoon, and would sit down to a handsome supper during the evening, it was well known that growing lads must be ceaselessly fed. Besides, it kept him quiet while Steed combed his tangled mat of hair. When that was done, a shirt of fine linen was put on him, parti-coloured hose, and a hanseline, or a pourpoint of rich velvet. Lastly, Steed would clip a jewelled belt round his waist, and tie the riband of the Garter about his leg; and off he would go to see what sport had been arranged for the evening.

There was always something. All Ralph's sons and daughters were at Raby that Christmas-tide, and the castle teemed with visitors. Supper for the Earl and Countess, for the Lord John, and for the noblest guests, was served in one of the solars, but the mumming and the minstrelsy took place in the Great Hall. This was warmed by an immense fire of logs, and lit by so many rushlights and candles that it was as light as day. There was certainly no chinchery about the entertainment offered to the King's third son. Every day a new diversion was presented to him. There were mimings, and tumblers; a troupe of sword and rope dancers; and a tregetour who snatched objects out of the air, and even caused a grimly lion to appear suddenly in the Hall. This made all the ladies shriek with fright, and shattered the stolidity of my lord's eldest son by his second marriage, a three-year-old bachelor who shamed his manhood by casting himself upon his nurse's bosom, and bawling much louder than any of the ladies. But just as the entertainment seemed to be fated to end in disaster the lion vanished, and where it had stood a vine shot up from amongst the rushes, and was seen to bear bunches of red and white grapes. Everyone agreed that the tregetour was the most cunning one ever to visit Raby; and my lord's confessor, a very holy, sely man, misdoubted him that he used sorcery. He tried to discuss the matter with Friar Matthew, but the more worldly Dominican was applauding the dexterity of a joculator balancing timbrels, and paid him scant heed. His demeanour quite shocked Father Peter, and he could not, when dancing began, forbear the thought that Father Matthew would have been glad to have taken a place in the ring of the traditional carole. He certainly hummed the tune which the dancers sang, and pointed out to his disapproving brother in Christ the nimblest dancers in the round.

The Lord John was not amongst these. His aunt told him that he reminded her of a bear she had once seen, performing a dance with a female tumbler. Panting from his exertions, he grinned at her, and cast himself down at her feet. He would by no means yield to persuasions to dance the pavone, saying that they only wanted him to make a bobbing-block of himself.

My lady laughed; but she did not think him at all like a bobbing-block. Her quick eyes saw in him a budding force to be presently reckoned with. When he had arrived at Raby from the far north, she had perceived at once that the months he had spent on the Border had done more than tan his cheeks and add to his formidable stature. It seemed to her that the boy was hardening fast into a man. If he talked in company, it was usually of hawks and hounds, or of some japeworthy misadventure which had befallen him; but when he was alone with Ralph Neville his conversation took another turn. Very little, Ralph told his lady, had escaped those heavy-lidded eyes; and what they had seen, or his ears had heard, was not allowed to die unpondered, but was carried to his brain for unboylike consideration.

He had seen and heard things which he believed were not dreamed of in London. He knew that many whom he had counted amongst the supporters of his house followed Percy, not Lancaster, and would most of them swing with the old Earl's changing policies. Some of them still held important castles, nominally in the King's name, but by virtue of Letters Patent issued under Northumberland's seal; and it needed no rede from Aunt Joan Beaufort to inform John that such men as the Captain of Berwick Castle were quiescent only because Northumberland still awaited trial, and sent no word or sign to his vassals. My lady said that Hotspur's death had stunned the North, and she said it with satisfaction, her eyes intent upon the future. While Hotspur lived not all Ralph Neville's alliances would suffice to lift Westmoreland above Northumberland on the Border; but with Hotspur dead, leaving a son in his nonage, and a father with more than sixty years in his dish, she could believe the Neville star to be in the ascendant.

John kept his counsel, but in his breast a conviction grew that not until the Fox was at his last end could the King think his northern Marches securely held. In London they were too often roused to rage by small raids committed by individual Scots, but these, John knew, were of little importance, and by no means one-sided. March-days were appointed, and twenty-four-hour truces declared, during which time the Wardens from both sides of the Border met, and exchanged their rolls and bills. Six gentlemen of Scotland and six of England were sworn as jurors, and bills were cleaned or fouled: on the whole, John thought, with justice. At the time of the great sheep sales, too, men who, a month earlier, had been plundering across the Border with cheerful savagery, met their sworn foes, if not in amity at least under tacit truce, for upon sheep depended most men's livelihood; and no man, driving a flock across the Tweed, needed any other safe-conduct.

But it was common knowledge on the Border that when Hotspur had marched to Shrewsbury the Duke of Albany had mustered a formidable army in Scotland, and had held it in readiness to cross the Tweed as soon as news reached him of a rebel victory in Wales. The news that reached him was of defeat, and he had quietly disbanded his force.

'Well, it was said that there was an army mustered,' Ralph Neville admitted. 'But, think you, John, the King holds Albany's son fast! I misdoubt me he would not have ventured unless he knew Murdoch of Fife to be safe out of ward.' He remembered, too late, another father's reckless venture, and scolded one of his hounds away from the fire, to cover up the slip.

John was frowning, but not at the memory of his own father's landing at Ravenspur. He said: 'He starved his own nephew to death.'

'Some say he did,' Ralph said cautiously. 'It was given out that Rothesay died of a flux, but one never knows.'

'I have heard that he gnawed away his own fingers, enfamined!'

'Leasings! None would do that but a moonling! Rothesay was a rageous waster, but – a'God's half, John, it's importless to us how he parted his life!'

'Faithly, but you think Albany would not put his son in peril, and it seems to me he is a kindless man who might do so lightly enough.'

'Well, he might have done so, if Shrewsbury fight had gone against the King,' conceded Ralph. 'But the event was otherwise, so Albany is importless too!'

'Not so importless!' retorted John. 'Not for boot nor for bale would he venture upon open war unless he were trothplight to that nest of adders! Yea, I mean the Percies, Christ give them sorrow!'

'Now, John!' expostulated the Earl.

'Up there, on the Marches,' said John, with a jerk of his thumb, 'I have learnt some few things! Do you recall the raid Hotspur made on Cocklaw, before he turned south to join hands with Glendower?'

'Out of dread! A sleeveless errand!'

'So it seemed! But there are those who say that Hotspur turned away from Cocklaw as a signal to Albany that the time was ripe.'

'I too have companied with tale-wise people,' said the Earl. 'They say also that Northumberland offered Berwick to the Scots if they would lend him aid.'

'They say sooth!'

'Nay, how can we know, John?'

'I know that there's no hold in a Percy, nor any end to their covetise! Here in the North Percy is a king, but two kings in England, Ralph, shall not serve!'

3 Fox of the North

I

When he reached London, John found Harry and Thomas there before him. They welcomed him joyfully, admitting him to their fellowship. They hailed him as Lord High Constable, and begged him to adjudicate between them on points in dispute, all of which he took in good part, grinning lovingly upon them both, and apostrophizing them as lurdans and cumberworlds. 'Or, as we say in the North,' he added, 'codsheads!'

' "As we say in the North!" ' echoed Harry admiringly. 'Do but pay heed to the worshipful Warden, Thomas! A full five months he has been in office! What's your northern word for malapert, little John?'

John had not met Harry for so many months that for a day or two he was shy of him. Harry, with the scar of his wound still angry on his cheek, was now a man; and if, in holiday mood, he could indulge in madder pranks than any that had shocked his tutors, he seemed to John to have grown ten years beyond Thomas. Thomas had not greatly changed. In his sixteenth year he was fulfilling his early promise to be the best looking member of a handsome family. He was tall, and well-knit; tawny-haired, like his father, and with the straight nose of the Lancasters, and the full, curved lips which gave him a pronounced resemblance both to Harry and to his uncle John Beaufort. All three princes were much of a height, but the two elder ones were built on slighter lines than John. John had big limbs; and the aquiline trend of his nose was becoming more marked, so that Thomas asserted it was hard to tell him and his goshawk apart.

Thomas had enjoyed his service in Wales; and he did not seem to have quarrelled with Harry. He told John that Harry was a great captain, but very stark. 'The men love him, but I can't tell why, for he keeps a stricter discipline than anyone. Do you know, if the Welsh complain of any one of them, and he finds it to be just, he gives the poor wretch only time to be shriven before he sends him to the long-going!'

John asked Harry how he paid his men; and Harry answered: 'Out of my livelihood – and still they are not paid! And you?'

'Well, I have done that too,' admitted John. 'But I own no great livelihood, and the wages are more than three thousand pounds in arrears. Unbosom, Harry! What must I do? What do you do?'

'Oh, I lead my men out to ravage Glendower's lands, and plunder supplies that Father will not!' Harry said.

'I can't do that. I may not break the Border.'

'You may be glad! Plunder and rapine spoil the men, and breed up hatred against us. When I am King I will put an end to such usage!'

'Yes, and in the meantime?'

'Petition the King's grace! He may send you fifty pounds!'

One week in the palace of Westminster had been enough to make John uncomfortably aware of the antagonism which too often sprang up between the King and his heir. He said: 'I think there is very little in his coffers, Harry.'

'Little or much, I see none of it, and nor will you! You will be told, as Harry Percy was, that with better government you will need no money! Holy Saint Cross, does he think soldiers feed on air? We do as we may, but it is not enough, and it is ill policy for a King to stand so deep in debt to his captains. I pawned my jewels long since; now Edward of York is forced into the same straits, and if he grutches, who shall blame him?'

'Not you, at all events,' remarked John. 'You never blame Edward!'

Harry laughed. 'I know him too well! I must not lose him on the Marches: *he* doesn't mishandle the Welsh! But no one will ever make Father understand how to use them. Hotspur tried, but what thanks had he for the work he did? When he and I came to terms with them, the King said the terms were dishonourable to us, and called the Welsh barefooted scrubs! I tell you, John, I have to fight for the life of every Welshman I win to me! The war drags on, and so it will, until I can wrench from the King the means to wage it in *my* way, and the power to treat in *my* way! I shall not make perdurable foes of a brave people, but that is what Father is doing!' He paused, the corners of his mouth curling up in a bitter smile. 'Grey of Ruthin is the man I have to thank for this policy. The longer that makebait remains a prisoner the better pleased I shall be. He hates the Welsh, but knows no more than Father does upon what perilous ground we stand on the Marches.'

'Still – after Shrewsbury?' John asked.

'Glendower bore no part in that battle; his power is unbroken.' Harry's eyes began to smoulder. 'In your northern wilds, John, did any noise come to you out of France? Did you hear that Orleans insulted the King with challenges?'

'Oh, yes, and also that St Pol hung Edward up by the heels in effigy!'

That won the flicker of a smile, but Harry replied: 'They landed to help Glendower, the French. They departed in most hasty wise after Shrewsbury fight, but they are becoming too stomachy, brother!'

'Father calls Orleans a gadling; and as for St Pol, Father had the better of that exchange, if he really did tell him he would give him enough to do in looking after his own domains.'

'I have no liking for empty words,' Harry said grimly.

'Well, Bowet made them extend the truce, so what more would you?'

'Or for empty truces!' Harry snapped, the flash of the lion in his eyes. 'They are still raiding our coasts, and I think Glendower is looking towards them. If I were King—'

He stopped; and John said: 'That way still? Not, I think, while Father lives. He sees no profit in war with France. Nor I, to speak sooth.'

'I shall show you! Or will you oppose me when I am King?'

'Nay, I know my duty! I shall follow you, lief or loth.'

'Loth?' Harry gripped his shoulders. 'Loth, John?'

Humfrey had said once that Harry was a warlock, casting his spells at will. It was a knavish thing to have said, but John

211

remembered the idle speech. He looked into Harry's compelling eyes, and answered: 'Loth, and yet lief. God give you strength to prosper in your beginnings, my liege!'

Harry laughed, and let him go. 'Gramercy! Keep the North quiet for me, my Lord Warden!'

'I shall do my power. But while Northumberland is on life that is little! Father should make an end.'

'Sturdy words! I remember now that Bishop Henry told me you were very stark!'

'Well, Thomas says the like of you!' retorted John.

'Does he? But I would not be so blithe to head my old friends, brother!'

'When were the Hollands and the Despensers friends to Lancaster? Traitorous thatchgallows, every one, and Father enlarged them, as he will Northumberland!'

'What happened when Father seized this throne you may not call treachery. King Richard was then on life,' Harry said.

'He was not on life when Percy, who had betrayed him, betrayed Father!' John said. 'I say that I would make an end! You fear that the French may lend aid to Glendower. Well, I fear, and I have some reason, that the Scots may lend aid to Percy!'

'So!' Harry gave a low whistle. 'Was that in the wind, when Hotspur turned against us?'

'Albany had an army mustered. Do you think the Fox did not know it? No man more surely! He called up his levies, but not to keep the Border! But for Ralph Neville he would have joined Hotspur, while the Scots crossed the Tweed in force – and had Berwick from him for their hire!'

'Do you think that for very truth, John?'

'No, I think it not provable, but by the faith of my knighthood I do believe it!'

Harry was silent for a moment. Then he said: 'I think we shall not see him headed. And if I stood in Father's place— Think, John! Hotspur, that was the last of his sons, is dead; his high offices have been taken from him; he is stricken in years— It is enough!'

'It is too much, or not enough!' John said.

Northumberland was not brought to his assize until February 1404; and in the meantime the princes made merry. Harry, flinging off the cares of his lieutenancy, linked arms with Thomas and John, and went roistering with them along West Cheap, or dropped down the river from Westminster Stairs to land at Southwark, and sup at the Tabard or the Falcon. All the chief hostelries and the cook-shops enjoyed their patronage; many of the great merchants entertained them at their inns within the City; the masons at work on the new Guildhall knew them well; and so did the fair frail ones on Bankside. London adored them, from the sheriff's officers, who often turned blind eyes to their exploits, to the jack-rakers who swept the garbage from the streets. Led by Harry, they indulged in the most shocking pranks; but only Archbishop Arundel frowned, hinting to the King that his heir should demean himself more decorously. Arundel had a stiff-necked pride which made the very thought of Prince Harry asprawl in a tavern with a wench on his knee, and a dozen rude fellows cracking bawdy jokes with him, offensive; but the King only laughed, and took no order to his graceless sons. They were at the bottom of more than one of the hurlings which disturbed the peace of the City, when the sudden shout of 'Staves!' brought apprentices tumbling out of every alley, lusty for a fight. In the cold dawn-light neither Thomas nor John could have told why they had ended an adventurous night in clamorous debate, and a slipping, dodging flight down malodorous lanes, lanterns discarded and the hue and cry sounding in their wake: wine-fumes clouded memory, but never the memory of Harry's eyes, wide open and ablaze with elvish mischief; nor the smile on his lips which mocked and challenged, and lured them to follow him.

'A warlock! Didn't I tell you so?' Humfrey said, cross because Harry would not let him company with him. Harry said he was too young to go a-whoring: Humfrey never knew how narrowly John escaped being excluded also from these heady delights. That was the worst of Harry: you never knew when his discomfortable conscience would smite him. John read prohibition in his glance, and boasted dreadfully of

northern gigelots tumbled in the hay. Harry laughed and
laughed. He may not have believed the tales, but he let John go
with him and Thomas; and John embarked boldly on some
fumbling adventures. The doxies with whom he trafficked
helped him to overcome his shyness; he played his part manfully; and secretly preferred the evenings spent in less perilous
company.

He enjoyed many of these: jolly supper-parties in Master
Askham's inn, that was Mayor of London that year and had the
wit to bid his bouncing children to his board rather than the
staid and bearded aldermen; and quite informal visits to Master
Whittington, in Vintry Ward, where he owned an inn so
crammed with costly treasures that it almost put Westminster
Palace to shame. Master Whittington was an old friend: a warm
man, and a mercer who had supplied the Lancaster children with
silks and velvets for as long as any of them could remember. He
had furnished Blanche with cloths for her wedding attire, and
would supply Philippa too, if ever the lagging plans for her
spousal came to fruition. He was not at all chary of mentioning
his trade, unlike some of his fellow aldermen, who seemed to
wish it to be forgotten that they dealt in merchandize, and
amused the princes by aping lords' fashions. Master Whittington never fell into such unwit, though he might have done so,
since he was well-born: the third son of a knight of Gloucester,
and of a considerable heiress. Both his parents were of the West
Country, and he had married a Dorset damsel, but you would
never have taken him for anyone but a Londoner. He had made
his fortune there, he had been its Mayor, and it held his heart.
He was a spare man, with a clean-shaven face, and shrewd,
twinkling eyes. He had no children; and a considerable part of
his livelihood was spent in enriching the City he loved so well.
The princes, finding themselves in the vicinity of his inn, never
hesitated to hammer on his gate, and never lacked a welcome.
He and Dame Alice would entertain them in an upper room,
smelling of juniper and rosemary, and hung with tapestries
from the hand of Dourdin; and they would drink their wine out
of goblets of blue glass from Murano, or slim, enamelled Dam-

ascus cups; sit upon cushions of fringed red velvet; sup up the dish-meats with silver spoons; turn over the leaves of his Book of Hours by the light of waxen candles set in candlesticks of Limoges enamel; absently take an apple from a green-glazed Persian bowl; or play chess on a tabler cut out of rock-crystal. Humfrey, who was sometimes permitted to go with them on these visits, used to handle these things with a lover's touch, and was avid to know whence they came. Master Whittington was a little vague: that oaken coffer, encased in metal scroll-work, was Flemish, he thought; as he recalled, he had had those ivory-handled knives out of Almaine; that cup of silver-gilt was of Italian craftsmanship, brought him by the master of a Genoese galley, if his memory served him. Humfrey, delicately turning the pages of his Book of Hours, told him of the Psalter which had been made for Father. Master Whittington heard him courteously, and said: 'That is a book for a King, my lord. This of mine is a poor thing.'

'No,' Humfrey said, flashing a crooked smile at him. 'Books are lovely things, Master Whittington.'

Thomas, eyeing him with dubious indulgence, explained: 'He is a scholar, you know.'

'Why, so are you all, sir!' said Whittington. 'I remember, when I brought eight ells of red satin to Tutbury, to make you gowns, that you were busy with your grammar books.'

'That's a long time ago,' said Thomas.

'Witterly. The King's majesty was then my lord of Derby. He bespoke red and white satin for the giton to his lance.'

That awakened memory; it seemed strangely remote. Not satin for gitons did Father now require of Master Whittington, but money for his sore needs. It was common knowledge that he had borrowed largely from Richard Whittington. Harry, who was nursing one ankle on his knee, the long, dagged sleeves of his pourpoint touching the floor, must have been thinking of this, for he said: 'I wish you would lend money to me!'

Master Whittington said, with a twinkle: 'Why, so I will, sir, if I like the security!'

That made them laugh, for they all knew that Harry had been

forced to sell his plate to pay his soldiers.

'You will lend me some one day!' Harry said, with the flash of a confident smile.

'Affirmably, my lord,' Whittington said, bowing. He was watching Harry, as though he tried to read his mind, but Harry met his look softly, betraying nothing.

'Wars!' said Humfrey. 'When I borrow money it will be to buy me such books as this of yours.'

Harry picked up Dame Alice's gitern, and began to play a Welsh air. He neither looked at Humfrey nor spoke to him; it was John who said: 'The Welsh troubles will be ended before Master Whittington will lend livelihood to Harry.'

He and Thomas, and perhaps Whittington too, knew that Humfrey had not had the Welsh rebellion in mind when he uttered his careless speech. Humfrey raised his eyes from the book on his knee, in a wide look, half of innocence, half of contrition. It would be useless, John knew, to rebuke him presently. He was incapable of perceiving his errors; and although he was always sorry to have offended anyone you could place no reliance on his refraining in future. He would commit the most astonishing treacheries, sometimes to gain a private end, sometimes from lightness of mind, when it seemed to him impossible that anyone should be angry with him for doing so understandable a thing. The odd part of it was that no one, not even hottempered Thomas, ever was angry with him for more than a few exasperated minutes. He was so bewildered, if set upon the hone, so contrite, and so unhappy to find himself in disgrace, that he always won forgiveness. His brothers knew that he would lightly betray a confidence, but their old love for him endured. Their love was protective: he was such a young and beautiful creature, graceful and immature, and with the most engaging manners. Women adored him, and said that his oddly crooked eye would crack many poor hearts. Harry thought he was overly fond of being petted in bowers, and told him that he was growing too old to cling to petticoats; but Thomas said in John's ear that Harry was out for once: it was Thomas's belief that Humfrey was more precocious than Harry guessed.

He glanced deprecatingly at Harry now, but read no message in his face, either of blame or of pardon. Harry had become suddenly remote, enclosed within his mysterious citadel. Humfrey's sensitive mouth quivered, and drooped. It was Whittington who intervened, giving all their thoughts a lighter turn by asking demurely if the noble princes had had any more poems written in their honour since the ballad composed by their old tutor, Master Scogan, and presented to them at a supper at Lewis John's house. That drew a laugh from Harry, for the ballad had been a gentle exhortation to the princes to conduct themselves in sadder wise. Humfrey looked relieved, and hoped that his lapse would be forgotten, and that Harry would perhaps let him join his night revels. Harry always said that he would do so in time coming, not choosing to tell him that at thirteen he was far too young to company with his eldest brother's friends.

These, the men who came with Harry from Wales, were nearly all older than he, but they were very ready to play with him. He surprised those, like Gilbert Talbot, who knew him hitherto only as a stern young commander, but he enchanted them too, so that they did the craziest things at his bidding, and thought afterwards that they must have been cup-shotten, or bewitched. Only the Earl of Warwick held aloof from the night junketings. Richard Beauchamp was as little lief as the Archbishop to rub shoulders with common folk. He had, besides, a young wife, and a reputation to maintain. The usual Christmas jousts were being held at Smithfield, and more than one foreign knight was coming to England under safe-conduct to break a lance with him. Richard seemed to be determined to make his name as famous in the lists as ever the King's had been, and nothing, he austerely informed Harry, could more surely impair judgment of eye than night roistering.

Another whose attendance on Harry was fitful was Jack Oldcastle, a strange, intemperate man, swinging between heights of riotous hilarity and depths of troubled soul-searching. Harry held him in great affection, laughed him out of his moods of gloomy thought, soothed him when his passionate beliefs made him ready to come to blows with any who argued too shrewdly against him, and respected him always as the bravest of his companions in arms.

But Harry's closest friend was a man of a different kidney, ten years his senior, easy with his fellow-men, full of laughter, and subtle in his ways. He was Henry Scrope of Masham, a nephew of the Archbishop of York. Harry gave more of his confidence to Henry Scrope than to any man other than John. He had shared his bed with him during their hard campaigning; he would often thrust a hand in his arm; and he never stiffened against his touch. This was a rare thing in Harry, aloof even when most approachable. Women – even the doxies whom he took for his fleeting pleasure – found this elusiveness more alluring than his fine, taut body, or his handsome face. He was a tantalizing lover: urgent and tender, fierce and unexpectedly gentle, impossible to know or to hold. No one would ever know Harry, John thought, a little jealously, watching Henry Scrope coax him out of an elfin humour. Harry leaned his head back on Scrope's shoulder, mischief in his eyes, outrageous schemes for the night's entertainment dropping from a honey-tongue. 'My dearworth, you are quite drunk, you know,' Scrope said caressingly.

'Oh, no, do you think so?' Harry murmured.

'Drunk or brainsick,' Scrope said, not believing it, for Harry was no love-pot. 'You will end in the Clink this gait, my lord, and your poor servants with you. Grace!'

'Very well. I am very treatable,' Harry sighed, meek as a nun's hen.

John wondered if this was something Scrope did believe. He had a little influence over Harry; cajoled him often enough in small matters to think, perhaps, that he would one day cajole him in greater ones.

3

Early in February the Queen received a visit from her second son, Arthur. He came to England to do homage for the Earldom of Richmond, relinquished to him by his brother, the Duke of Brittany, whose scruples forbade him to swear fealty to an

English monarch. Arthur was not yet eleven years of age, but he seemed an intelligent boy, quick to learn, and well grown for his years. The Queen hung upon him with doting tenderness, but he was always escaping from her bower to run after his step-brothers. They were quite kind to him, but they did not encourage him to follow them, because he was too young, and spoke very little English. All the princes could speak Norman-French, but they never did so from choice, using the language only for such official letters as they were obliged to write. The three elders were agreed that Humfrey was the one to entertain Arthur; but since Humfrey repulsed the suggestion with indignation, and Arthur thought him a tame substitute for Harry, nothing came of it.

Parliament had assembled in January, but Northumberland was not brought before his peers until the following month. Henry Beaufort was still Chancellor; and the faithful Commons for the second time chose Sir Arnold Savage to be their Speaker. It was generally thought that this election showed that the session was not going to be pleasing to the King. Savage was one of his sternest critics; a witty man, and an indefatigable orator.

It was, in fact, the most displeasant Parliament which had yet troubled King Henry's peace. The King wanted money, and the three estates were at one in withstanding his demands. Bishop Beaufort was a wittier man than Savage, but although the Welsh were in revolt, the Bretons plundering the southern shore, and the French hovering on the brink of open war, the Commons would lend no ear to his warnings of foreign perils. What they wished to discuss, and did discuss, most apertly, was domestic mismanagement. They grutched at the lavish grants the King had made to his supporters; at the enormous costage of his court; at the abuse of liveries; and most of all they grutched at the continued presence in England of the Queen's Breton servants. As for foreign perils, the King had been granted the Customs, and the wardships of the nobles, and he had the revenues of the house of Lancaster at his command. King Henry replied acidly that he did not mean to leave his house impoverished; but he refrained from reminding the Commons that the Queen whom they so bitterly disliked had not yet received from England her full dowry. She was, of course, very wealthy, which they would no doubt have pointed out to him; and she was drawing a thousand pounds a year from the Lancaster revenues, besides the income from the many manors, castles, parks, and estates which he had bestowed upon her. The Queen's beauty was unfortunately equalled by her rapacity, and she was very beautiful. She was also tantalizing. Not even the King's sister Bess could deny her virtue; but Bess declared that she kept poor Henry lusting after her by the arts of a common ramp. Bess said that she should be called the Bitch Queen. Her horrified lord told her that such talk would place them both in jeopardy, but Bess only laughed, and said that the redeless Commons spoke of the Queen more despitefully still.

.This was not strictly true, for the redeless Commons knew nothing of what went on within the King's palaces. They could see that the King was asotted of his consort, and they called her the Witch Queen; but their real objection to her was that she was an expensive encumbrance. Before they could be brought to consider other matters, they would have all the followers of the Anti-Pope, saving only the Queen and her two daughters, and two attendants, banished from the realm. King Henry, who had tried often to persuade the Queen to dismiss her Breton court, was never more glad to be enforced. He returned an answer so gracious that the Commons were surprised into modifying their demands. If the King would consent to the reform of his household, the Queen might retain ten of her foreign servants.

In the middle of all this, the Earl of Northumberland was brought to his assize. He made an impressive appearance, stately, venerable, and nobly sorrowful. He answered his accusers mildly, and with such cunning that by the time he had finished his defence no one could be sure whether he had been betrayed into treason by his son; driven into it by the unworthy suspicions of the King's Council, which had made him believe that he stood in peril of life and livelihood; forced into it by the need to succour his unhappy son; or even whether he had been marching to join the King, not Hotspur, and had been foiled by the malice of Westmoreland. He spoke so movingly of his loyalty to the house of Lancaster, and of the immense sums he had expended on its support, that several of his bemused peers began to think that it was he and not the King who was the injured party. He said that the King was much deceived in thinking that sixty thousand pounds had been paid to him, for no such sum had ever reached him. He was unable to recall how much money he had received, but he was sure that twenty thousand pounds were still owed to him, besides the ransoms of the Scottish earls taken prisoners at the Red Rigs. He was an old and childless man, full of bale and weariness; and he was being pursued during his last years on middle earth, he said, weeping, by the spite of Ralph Neville.

After a great deal of argument, his peers decided that he had been guilty only of trespass, and should be fined, not headed. The manifesto to which he had set his name was forgotten; and the mustering of his levies was treated as the outcome of a private quarrel with Westmoreland. The two Earls were prayed to be reconciled; Northumberland begged to be allowed to swear an oath of fealty to King Henry on the Cross of the Blessed St Thomas; he was restored to his possessions, if not to all his dignities; and the King forgave him the fine.

Those who were best acquainted with the Lord John expected from him an explosion of wrath. It did not come. He had understood the message of this Parliament; and had seen, for the first time, the price his father paid, and would always pay, for the Crown.

Harry too was aware of it, and in the silent meeting of eyes these two shared the understanding, and put it aside. John knew that it was a thing Harry could not bear to discuss; and Harry knew himself safe in John's hands.

Thomas was not aware of it, but only angry. He had never doubted that Northumberland would lose his head. He saw in the barons' leniency woodhead, but not hostility; and in the demand for the reform of the Royal Household a punishable insolence. 'And the King returned them a fair answer!' he raged to John. 'Why, it is a thing unprecedented! God's Heart, Sir Thomas Erpingham has been telling me that when some fellow dared to propose it to King Richard he would have been hanged only that he was a clerk, and saved by Holy Church! No other Parliament ever demanded such a thing of Cousin Richard!'

'No,' John answered. 'But no Parliament set Cousin Richard upon this throne, brother!'

4 Heavy Cheer

'God have you in His keeping!' Harry said, at parting, holding John's hands in his strong clasp. 'I wish Percy were in ward – or you otherwise – or that I might go with you!'

'Gramercy, brother! I had as lief do my own endeavour!'

'Oh, I cry the Lord Warden's pardon!' Harry said, smiling. 'I took you for a nurseling!'

'Neither a nurseling nor a recreant.'

'No. But I think they may make you heavy cheer in the North.'

'Well I know it,' said John. 'What cheer will they make you in the West?'

'Very hot cheer, but I shan't find privy malice there, as you may. Go charily – and, for my love's sake, John, keep only those about you whom you know you may trust!'

Harry told Thomas that with Percy at large his task was too dangerful for such a youngling as John, but Thomas said cheerfully: 'Oh, I don't fear for John!' He thought he read reproof in Harry's eye, and the jealousy which ran like a discordant thread through his nature made him add with hostility flickering in his voice: 'You need not look as if I had said a sturdy thing! I love John as much as you do!'

'Dreadless,' Harry said gently.

Thomas was as quickly smoothed as he was angered. 'Well, I only meant that he's no rash-head. I think he has more wit than any of us too, even Humfrey. He won't tread overthwart the Fox: I warned him to take keep of that.'

'No, he won't do that. But he is in the same case as I am, and has no remedy. The King must send him money!'

But all the money the King could find to send to John was

sixty pounds, because although he had persuaded Parliament to vote a new land-tax for the defence of the realm, its enactment had been postponed until the meeting of the next Parliament.

For John there was no help but in his own endeavour. With the return of Northumberland to his domains a new spirit was awake on the Border. Where John had before encountered tolerance he found hostility, which grew more overt as the long-overdue wages of his lieutenants and his men mounted. Northumberland was living in seclusion at Warkworth, but his presence in the district hung over John like a menace. His own presence was felt by Neville and Umfraville to be a heavy charge: from the teeth outward Northumberland was benign and mannerly, and Neville, who had exchanged the kiss of peace with him at Westminster, believed him to be at his most perilous in such a mood. He would not apertly instigate rebellion, but his adherents were many of them savage men, and what they might take it into their lawless heads to do to avenge his wrongs Neville thought he would not hinder. Neville would have been glad to have kept the Lord Warden at Raby, but he did not find the Lord Warden as treatable as he had hoped. There was work for John in his own territory, and thither he went, in spite of all Ralph's objections. 'I will not be Warden only in name!' he said.

'Yes, but the times are very sickly,' argued Ralph. 'There are those who would be blithe to do you some mischief: I dare not say how many! You know, you stand in my charge. I am your borrow, as it were – and you haven't fifteen years yet in your dish!'

'Then the King my father had best find him a new Warden!' said John, with a flash of Harry in his eye.

He rode north to Berwick. Ralph Neville could do no more than strengthen his escort with men who wore the Bull of Raby on their sleeves, and send a warning to Sir Robert Umfraville.

Sir Robert met John in Berwick. He knew that John had passed through a hostile country, but John said nothing of this. He did not seem to be nervous, but there was a watchful look in his eyes, and a stiffening in his bearing. The boy, thought Sir Robert, would soon be left behind. Already he had a man's inches, and it was plain that he meant to play a man's part. He smiled at Sir Robert, as he gripped his hands, and said: 'My heart's welcome to you, Robin! Did Ralph send you to bear me in hand?'

'To do your will, my lord,' replied Sir Robert.

'To give me good rede, I hope,' John said, embracing Gilbert. 'I promise you, I'm not so indurate as he says I am! But he has got to thinking himself my serf-borrow, and no man is that, nor shall ever be!'

Ralph Neville had indeed told Sir Robert that the Lord John was both indurate and rash, but Sir Robert found him neither. It was certainly hard to turn him from his will, but he did not form this impetuously; and while he faced unflinchingly any necessary danger he took no needless risks, or ever forgot that it behoved him to tread warily.

There was great need to be ware. On the one hand he had disaffected troops; on the other the Scots were ravaging the Border. With no money to pay his men or to provision them for war there was little he could do to check Scotch bobance. To make his position the more uneasy he knew that upon his departure for London, two of Northumberland's kinsmen, and Clifford, Constable of Berwick Castle, had called together a host of men, arraying them in the livery of the Percy Crescent, and swearing to hold Berwick, Warkworth, and Alnwick in King Henry's teeth. Upon their liege-lord's enlargement they had disbanded this force: John knew not how many of the sullen men under his command had lately put off the Crescent.

While he remained on the Eastern Marches Gilbert Umfraville was never absent from his side. Sir Robert, holding the Middle March against invasion, left his nephew with John. If Percy was a name beloved in the North so too was Umfraville. 'Look you, Gib!' he said, laying a hand on Gilbert's shoulder. 'If I could stay beside the Lord John I would not, for he has a high stomach, and he would not thole it! But you may stay for fellowship, and be some small shield to him, as I think.'

'With all my heart!' Gilbert responded. 'But how may I shield him? He will go where he lists, and I can't stop him.'

'You can go with him,' Sir Robert said. 'These peope of ours will be masterless indeed when they do mischief tlo an

Umfraville!' He smiled at the flush of pride which rushed to Gilbert's cheeks, and pulled his ear. 'They reck little of the King's vengeance, for they don't know him; but me they do know, Master Greenhead, and so you may both be safe!'

2

John accepted Gilbert's companionship gladly, and gave no sign that he recognized it to be a safeguard. Gilbert brought with him a small company of his retainers, and in some ways they served John better than his own retinue, too many of whom bristled with mistrust of the northerners who gave their lord such bleak looks. His meiny was a small one, no regular household having been appointed; but besides his confessor, his steward, his grooms and clerks, a few squires were attached to his train, and a dozen men-at-arms. Several garboils sprang up between these and the Percy adherents; and once John heard a man snarl: 'Thousands for a Percy!' and swung round to see the flash of steel, and a squire of his at death-grips with a man in russet livery. At his furious command his own man released his hold, and fell back. The other sprang after, and was sent hurtling to the ground by a wrathful prince who was not used to have his orders disregarded. 'No cries in my presence but *St George*, and *Forth to the Field*, bratchet!' John said fiercely.

There was a red light in the eyes that stared up at him, but it faded. He had used a north-country word of contempt, and he had spoken the war-cry of all the Border lords, and such simple things pleased rude men. An Ogle confided to a Grey that all would be well for the Lord John if he could but pay his men their dues.

He could not, and all was ill for him, and made worse by loneliness. He came to an impossible task straight from the governance of his tutors, handicapped by youth and inexperience, and obliged to dwell in his own strength. He could seek counsel of his elders, but not even to Ralph Neville might the King's son give his whole confidence. No one knew what he suffered during that time: the anxiety to prove himself worthy of his trust; the greater anxiety for the safety of his house; the doubts of himself, and of his lieutenants; the anguish of impo-

226

tence; and the bitterness of humiliation. These were things of which he never spoke; and so rigid a guard did he set on his face and his demeanour that only Robin Umfraville, more perceivant than Ralph Neville, guessed some part of what he endured. He was a child sent to rule a turbulent land without the means to enforce his decreees, or even to repel the enemy who ravaged his Border. His troops were mutinous; he met with threatening looks when he went amongst them; and knew that one false step would be enough to bring discontent to a flaming head. More than once he stood in danger of his life; and for every confessed foe to his house amongst the lesser Border lords there might, for anything he knew, be three who hid hostility under civil fronts. His servants begged him not to expose his person, and tried, whenever he rode out, to bunch themselves about him. One of his squires had been wounded by an arrow, loosed from what ambush only the devil knew, which had missed its true mark. So narrow an escape might well have broken a stripling's hardihood; it stiffened the Lord John's resolve never to betray a sign of fear or of weakening. He repelled his servants, and went about his business with an unmoved countenance, sometimes with no other companion than Gilbert, who would not be repelled. He did not know how much reluctant respect he won: he only knew that he was a King's son, and must not flinch.

Matters were not improved by the rumours that were flying about the country that springtide. Men said that King Richard was alive, sheltering at the Court of Scotland. Spies reported that this pretender was none other than the Court fool, who bore a resemblance to the dead King; but the rumour had brought to Scotland from France, whither he had fled upon King Henry's accession, one of the grooms of Richard's chamber, who saw a profit in the imposture, and upheld it. The groom was that William Serle who was believed to have been implicated in Thomas of Gloucester's murder. He sent a secret messenger to Richard's old friends, and had actually counterfeited Richard's privy seal. John forwarded to the Council such reports as he was able to collect, and learned presently that the messenger, caught in Essex, had been constrained to give up the names of the people he had visited in England. All over the North the rumour was being whispered. It was just the sort of thing rude men liked to talk about, not troubling their heads over probabilities, but accepting any ferly tale for the truth. An air of expectancy hung over the land: King Richard was going to reappear amongst his loving lieges, and down would tumble the whole house of Lancaster. It seemed as though it had always been King Richard whom the people had loved, and never Henry of Bolingbroke; but Sir Robert Umfraville told a troubled Warden that so it was ever with borel-folk. 'They are never apaid, and they bear nothing in mind above a hand-while,' he said. 'No, not even that King Richard promised the villeins they should go free, and was mainsworn the instant he was delivered from the peril that dragged that vow from his lips!'

'But did they love King Richard?' John asked.

'Nay, how should they love him, or any other great one?' replied Sir Robert. 'Sely men love their bellies, John.'

'Your villeins love you,' John said.

'Sickerly! An Umfraville has always kept their bellies filled!'

John knew that this was something his father was finding it impossible to do, and was not cheered.

But in June he was gladdened by the arrival of a letter from Harry. One of his squires brought it all the way from Wales; its tidings were not comfortable; but the sight of that angular writing seemed to bring him before John; and the thought that in the middle of his crowding dangers Harry had remembered his promise to send a letter north warmed his heart.

Harry was at Worcester; and in worse straits than ever. He knew not where to turn for money, and had told the Council that unless provision was made for his troops on the Welsh Marches they would be forced to retire, and leave the country to be destroyed. Edward of York had pledged his estates in Yorkshire; the rebels were laying the better part of Hereford-shire waste; and Warwick's uncle, the Lord of Bergavenny, must be shent if not speedily relieved. Without the means to maintain more than a tiny force, Henry had sent to summon Richard of Warwick to him, and Richard had responded to the call, joining him at Worcester with a large retinue, at his own costage. He was sending Richard to check the rebels in Herefordshire; the Archdeacon of Worcester, a person well liked by the King, was writing to him in stringent terms, urging the need of support; he had himself written yet again to the Council.

There was nothing in all this to raise the spirits, but John found it invigorating. Harry might tell the Council that he expected to be destroyed, but every line of his letter to John breathed confidence. The letter reached him at Norham, strongest of all the royal holds along the Border, and was brought to him on the northern ramparts, where he had been standing staring across the Tweed, his fingers drumming on the parapet, his mind abstracted. Behind him the great red sandstone keep reared its bulk; and far below, at the foot of the rock on which the castle had been built, the river ran sapphire blue in the sunlight. The day was hot, and there was barely enough breeze to stir the leaves of the trees which grew thickly on the farther bank. Somewhere a laverock was trilling in a cloudless sky, and about the battlements flitted two butterflies. It was a smiling scene, but John had come to it to inspect the repairs to the defences, and the thought uppermost in his head was that it would be a fine night for raiding. He was looking grim; but when he saw what had been brought to him his expression changed. He sat down in one of the embrasures, and as he read the letter a smile began to play round the corners of his mouth. From the scrawled pages Harry spoke to him: he could almost hear his voice, and feel his confidence. John knew that he had no intention of abandoning a seemingly hopeless task. He was grappling it, hammering the Council with his letters, sending for Richard Beauchamp to lend him aid. Of course Richard had responded: men would always respond to Harry's call, always gain heart from his strength, always follow where he led. His magic even reached out to a young brother at his wits' end, and made the world seem suddenly not so bleak.

John put the letter up, thinking deeply. Harry, neglected by the King and the Council, was taking his own measures, and it behoved his brother to follow his example. *I wish there were a*

Warwick for me to call on, he thought. *No, I don't: men are not my need, but only money. Well, then—*!

He began to cast round in his mind for some means of raising four thousand pounds. It seemed rather hopeless. Edward might pledge his Yorkshire estates, but the only estates John had for his maintenance were Hotspur's manors in Cumberland, and those, he was well aware, would be returned to Hotspur's heir when he came of full age, if not before. Besides, it would not improve his position in the North if it were known that he was raising a loan on Percy possessions. It was rather the King's credit he must pledge; and since this was not high he must look for his rescuer amongst the Marcher barons to whom the strength of the Lord Warden's force was a matter of paramount importance. That seemed rather hopeless too. It was sleeveless to think of borrowing from Ralph Neville, for he was already bearing the greater part of the costage of his own wardenship; and although many of the landowners of Northumberland were warm men it was not likely that they would be willing to lend money to Percy's supplanter.

He left the curtain wall that overhung the river, and crossed the inner ward to the keep. This was one of the largest in the country, and contained four floors, built over the basement. An outer stair led to the first floor, where the guardroom was situated, and above this was the Great Hall. Here, while he stayed at Norham, John conducted all his business, and here he interviewed Harry's messenger. The man could not tell him much: only that the Welsh were very strong, and ravaging the Marches, but that everyone about the Prince was in good heart. The Prince was attacking the rebels whenever and wherever he could; no one doubted that as soon as he received reinforcements he would subdue the whole country.

John left him presently, and went away to find Gilbert.

The Constable of the castle thought that he had seen him by the lower gatehouse, and offered to send to fetch him; but John shook his head, and went away to the outer bailey. This was very large, since it was needed not only to house horses and cattle, but also to provide shelter for the villagers whenever the Scots raided the district. The gatehouse was at the south-west corner, with a deep ditch beyond it; and near it the masons engaged in repairing the castle walls had built one of their lodges. Gilbert was standing outside this, talking to the chief setter, who was explaining the diagram sketched on one of the master mason's Eastland boards, but when he saw John coming across the ward he went at once to meet him. He thought, from the frown on John's brow, that he must have had ill-tidings from Worcester; but when he asked if all was well with the Prince, John answered so abstractedly that it was plain he was thinking of something else. Gilbert waited, saying after a few moments: 'Did you come to seek me? I've been talking to that fellow over there. He says the walls need repairing almost everywhere. I daresay they do, but there's Wark to be considered, besides this place, and—'

'I will have Norham made as impregnable as it was when the Bishops of Durham held it, and so keep it!' said John. 'I think it of more worth than Wark, though that too must be restored, of course. But Norham first! You can't take it by storm, and I find that it has else-when withstood a siege of twelve months. Moreover, Wark is in ruinous case. God and the devil know why it has never been put into a state of defence again in all these years! Do you know that it is now nearly twenty years since the Scots dismantled it?' He gave a crack of scornful laughter. 'Northumberland and the enormous sums he spent on his wardenship! Corpus bones! Let him not tell that geste to me!'

'Well, I don't suppose he will,' Gilbert said. 'But I wonder that you should think Norham more important than Wark! It was at Wark, surely, that—'

'If you mean to tell me that I ought to restore Wark because it was there that my thirdfather created the Order of the Garter, stint before I make you!' threatened John, the frown lifting from his brow. 'A'twenty devils! If I've heard that once, I've heard it fifty times! When I put that hold in order it will be because I need all the strong castles I can get me here, and for no other cause!'

'And there's no money to put either of them in order,' sighed Gilbert.

'There shall be. Gib, tell me about the Lord Furnivall!'

'Why, he's brother to my lord of Westmoreland, and—'

'I know that, heavyhead! He was at Raby, at Christmas-tide. Does he own great livelihood? Didn't he marry a rich heiress?'

'Witterly! That's how he became Lord of Furnivall. Her estates are in other parts of the country, though.'

'No charge! They may be anywhere you list!' said John, a light in his eye.

'Gramercy! Also, she was his *first* wife!'

'And of that no charge!' said John briskly. 'God send he may be at Carlisle still! Gib, find me a sure messenger to carry a letter to him. I must ask him to come to me at Newcastle as soon as he may.'

'Come to you at Newcastle?' repeated Gilbert. 'Yea, but – but *why*?'

'I think he may be the one man who would lend me money for my needs!' John said.

3

At Newcastle, word came to John from the Constable of Berwick Castle that he had entrapped Serle, and was carrying him straightway to the King, at Pontefract. This was unexpectedly good news, and did seem to show that Northumberland was not amongst those willing to pretend belief in a mawmet set up to counterfeit King Richard. John began to feel more cheerful.

Lord Furnivall did not keep him waiting long for an answer to his letter, but the time lagged badly for a boy who was half wishing he had never written it. Thomas Neville was a man of King Henry's age, thirty-seven at least: he might think a summons from one who had just passed his fifteenth birthday an impertinence; and there were moments when John, trying to decide just how he should broach the business, felt that it was an impertinence, even though he was the King's son, and Lord High Constable of England. The Lord Furnivall had been Warden of Annandale for years; he was a person of worship and considerable military prowess. John had liked him, when they had met at Raby, but there had then been no question of a loan in either head. John had written him a mannerly letter, taking care to address him as his very dear cousin, and begging him, for the sake of the good will he had shown the King to come to Newcastle, so that he could not – it was to be hoped – mistake the request for a command. Or could he? Harry had requested Richard Beauchamp to go to him at Worcester, but that had certainly been a command. It would be a fell thing if the Lord Furnivall read a command into that painstakingly polite letter, because John had no right to command him in anything. He began to think that Furnivall might not come to Newcastle, or, if he did come, would arrive in dudgeon. It would then be impossible to ask him for any support at all. Already it seemed a difficult thing to do.

The Lord Furnivall answered the letter in person. He sent up word from Neville's Inn that he would be with Sir John as soon as he had washed the travel stains from his person. That gave John time to put off his plain doublet and his buskins, and to array himself in a gown. He very nearly did it. He had a fine gown of blue checklatoun, with a band of ermine round the throat, and sleeves so deep that they reached his feet. It was made very full, and swept the floor behind him, which made him seem taller and older than he was. Then, with a surer instinct, he thought that it would be folly to wear it, because Furnivall knew that he was just fifteen, and because a rich robe ill became a penniless prince.

When Furnivall was ushered into his presence, he rose to meet him, a little pale, and stammering a greeting. Furnivall said: 'You sent for me, my lord, and I have come with my best speed.'

'I thank you!' John said. 'But I did not – at least, I didn't mean it so! I *requested* you to meet me, if it should not be displeasant to you.'

Furnivall's eyes began to twinkle; he said kindly: 'What is it, lording? Why did you *request* me to come to you?'

John answered him bluntly, rejecting all his rehearsed speeches: 'Sir, because of my sore needs!'

'Then you have done me much honour. Tell me!' Furnivall invited, smiling at him.

So after all there was no difficulty. It was not even necessary to explain why he wanted the loan. Lord Furnivall knew; and he said that saving only the reverence he bore the King he had thought for many months that an importable burden had been laid on John's shoulders. When John, flushing painfully, spoke of sureties, he said that his money would be well expended, and he needed no other surety than Sir John's promise to repay. The business which had threatened to be so chargeous was accomplished in a matter of minutes, so that when they sat down to dine nothing remained to be done except to sign the bond which was even then being inscribed by a clerk.

Lord Furnivall had quite lately visited the King, at Doncaster, and could give John the latest news of him. This was not very good. He had thought the King was not in health: perhaps he was forwearied. He had been on progress since the beginning of May, first in the Midlands and now in Yorkshire, and he had had much troublesome business to discharge, besides many cares to drive sleep from his pillow.

'I shall see him next month, at Pontefract,' John said. 'He is there now; and the F—' He remembered that he was not talking to Ralph, and cut the word off short. 'And my very dear cousin of Northumberland,' he amended himself, 'has gone there with William Clifford, which – which is a matter in which we take great pleasure!'

'Certes, it is a thing which must delight all who wish well to the King's grace,' agreed Furnivall.

Everyone seemed to augur well from this event, even Harry, who had mentioned it in his letter. What Ralph Neville thought about it John could only guess, for he had not seen Ralph for some months.

His guess was right: Ralph told his brother that when Percy made large gestures of friendship towards his foes it was time to beware. To Furnivall's objection that the King had not shown himself to be Percy's foe, he replied: 'All are Percy's foes who stand between him and his orgulous desires! Well, the King may be cozened, but I can tell you of one who won't be, Thomas, and that's young John of Lancaster!'

Ralph saw John as his pupil; he was both fond and proud of him, but he thought it unthrifty of Thomas to have lent him a large sum of money. 'You will find yourself all-a-bits!' he said.

'God shield you, I thought you had more kind-wit! You will never see your marks again!'

'I have kind-wit enough!' retorted Furnivall. 'If this house of Lancaster should fall, brother, we shall fall with it! If I don't see my marks again they will have been well expended.'

Ralph was glad to know that John was eased of his worst burden, and glad that John had not turned to him for aid, but he was also a little affronted. He reflected that Thomas had only two daughters to inherit his wealth, thought of his own swarming brood with pride, and said: 'Well, you may be able to afford it! It is otherwise with me! Since my lady was delivered of her fourth knave-child last sennight I have six sons to my name.'

'Yea, and two-so-many daughters besides!' said Furnivall. 'It is no wonder you should be narrow-souled, brother!'

Ralph allowed this insult to pass. He was occupied in mentally enumerating his daughters, for he strongly suspected Thomas of exaggeration.

4

John rode into Pontefract at the end of July, and was startled to be greeted with shouts of 'Noël'. So accustomed had he become to being watched in lowering silence, even to hear the growl of a hostile crowd, that when his meiny approached the town he stiffened a little, bracing himself. A stern-faced prince the townsfolk thought him, but when the cries of 'Noël' broke on his ears he recollected that he was no longer in an unfriendly country, and doffed his cap, and waved it, just as a well-loved Earl of Derby had been wont to do.

Sir Robert Waterton did not think him stern-faced, for he was flushed and smiling when he voided his horse within the castle walls, but he suffered quite a shock at sight of him. It was less than a year since he had visited Pontefract, but he was older, Sir Robert thought, by many years. It was not merely a matter of physical growth, though that was remarkable; the boy had hardened into a man, and had acquired an assurance that was implicit in his look, and in the very tone of his voice. Sir Robert stood staring, found that he was being asked how his cousin did, and made haste to answer that Sir Hugh was well: he had not seen him lately, since he was at Windsor, in charge of the Mortimer boys. He then said bluntly: 'Pardon, Sir John! Dreadless, you wonder what makes me stare! But—'

'Yes, I've grown,' interrupted John. 'They have been telling me so at Raby – all of them! For God's bane, do not you! How is my father?'

Sir Robert shook his head. 'Not in as good point as one would wish, lording. This summer he has lost all lustihood. But I warrant he will be blithe to see you!'

'I will go to him, but first I must put off this gear,' John said. 'And the Queen's grace?' he added punctiliously.

Yes, the Queen had accompanied King Henry on his northern progress, and was even now walking in the herber with some of the ladies and gentlemen of the Court.

She was still disporting herself in the herber half an hour later, when John was ushered into his father's presence.

The King was in one of the solars, dictating to a secretary. The day was sultry, the castle, which John had remembered as a sour yellow hold, was turned to gold in the sunshine, but a fire had been kindled in the solar. The King was sitting beside it in a chair filled with cushions, his gown drawn close about his knees, and a traverse set up behind his chair to protect him from draught. A table-dormant, covered with documents, was at his elbow; he was turning the pages over when John came into the room, but as soon as the groom of the chamber spoke John's name he pushed the papers aside, and held out his hand, saying: 'Welcome, my son!'

John knelt to kiss his hand. It felt hot and dry; and when he looked up into his father's face he saw that his colour was sickly, and his eyes bloodshot. 'You are not well at ease, sir!' he said, concern in his voice.

'I shall soon be amended. Let it sleep!' the King answered. 'How is it with you, my child?'

'Well, sir.'

'You are burnt as brown as a nut!' the King said, smiling. He nodded dismissal to the secretary, saying: 'Come to me again presently! Sit, John! What have you to tell me?'

'I think you know it all, sir.'

The King looked both amused and impatient. 'Are you afraid to trouble me? Well, many things trouble me, but I am not at my last end, and you need not fear to throw me into an accesse. Come, now, unbosom! You borrowed money from Furnivall, and you know that you had my sanction for it. Is it well with you now?'

'No, not well, sir, but it is better.'

The King's eyes searched his face. 'I have seen Ralph, and Robin too,' he said significantly. 'You have been in some peril, my son, have you not?'

'Now and now!' John admitted.

'A smock-faced boy!' the King muttered.

'Oh, well!' said John tolerantly, 'they would like to unfeather me, out of dread, but if it were not for that wily pie at Wark-worth—'

'Learn lip-wisdom, John!' said the King sharply. 'God's death, is it thus that you speak of one that was your elder-father's companion in arms?'

'No – oh, no!' John said, blushing fierily. 'But – but, under favour, very revered Father, the Eastern Marches are not space-ful enough to contain both a Lancaster and a Percy! Late or soon Northumberland will try to bring us to neck-break.'

An angry gesture silenced him. The King said: 'Leave that! Northumberland has sworn fealty to me, and by his own desire, upspring! He has given up the royal castles which he held of me, and has rendered me some service beside. If it was Clifford who brought Serle to Pontefract, remember that Clifford is Percy's man!'

'On the Marches,' said John irrepressibly, ' it is thought that Northumberland is too subtle to uphold the claims of a maw-met. All men of worth know this is none other than Ward, that was the Court fool!'

'And is the world peopled, by your reckoning, with men of worth?' demanded the King, with that acid note in his voice his sons knew well.

'No, sir,' said John meekly.

After a moment, the King said, on the ghost of a sigh: 'Well, you are a child still!'

John swallowed this with as good a grace as he might, and ventured to ask what had become of Serle.

'Oh, he stood to his assize here, and will be hanged and drawn in London!' replied the King. 'That is one broil happily ended! The Countess of Oxford meddled in the plot, but we have placed her where she will work no more mischief. A daffish old woman! She distributed gold and silver hearts over Essex, which was the undoing of the whole. Oh, you don't know, do you? Richard used to give such hearts to his friends to wear as cognizances.' He added, with a quick, lizard-look at John: 'He's dead, you know.' John nodded. The King laughed harshly. 'Some believe him to be on life, and some say I slew him – yea, Orleans apertly appealed me of that! I sent him a round answer. I told him he lied most foully, and offered to make it good upon his person. There ended his hardihood!' For an instant the flash in the King's eyes recalled to his son's memory the gay Earl of Derby, never unhorsed in the lists. It faded; the King moved restlessly, his hand chafing the leather-covered arm of his chair. 'He will do us a mischief if he can. A pity Burgundy has parted his life! He was more ware than Louis of Orleans, and would by no means venture on open war with us. I know little of his son: an ugly fellow, and, I think, orgulous. They call him the Fearless.'

'Because he fought at Nicopolis,' said John, remembering something Thomas had once told him. 'I expect my uncle of Somerset must know him.'

'Very likely!' responded the King with a snap. 'But the less I see of John Beaufort the better pleased I shall be!' He saw a look of surprise on his son's face, and laughed reluctantly. 'Nay, I love him well! But he is just such another as your brother. Money, money, is their ceaseless cry! Somerset never comes into my presence but to tell me that the defences at Calais are ruinous; and as for Harry—' He broke off, scuffling amongst the papers on the table. 'Yes, here we have it! He tells me that the expenses of this Welsh war are unsupportable to him. God's death, does he think I would not send him aid if I could? He has taken to writing now to the Council. He will be demanding aid of Parliament next! Well, so he may! The Commons seem to like him better than they like me.'

There was something more than the peevishness of a sick man in the King's voice. It occurred to John that his father was jealous of Harry; and the thought threw him into discomfort, and a vague dismay. To divert the King's mind, he said: 'I hear that Edward is trying to borrow money from the Abbot of Glastonbury!'

It ought to have made the King laugh, because they all of them laughed at big, stupid Edward: he had been the bobbing-block of the family ever since John could remember. But the King only frowned, and said: 'Edward may think himself fortunate that he was not headed four years ago!'

So the King was angry with Edward too. John wondered what his burly cousin could have done, but dared not ask. He waited, watching a fly that had alighted on the table. It was uncomfortably hot in this small, close room. He had been sweating for some minutes, and could feel a drop running down his cheek. He wiped it away with the back of his hand, and moved his stool farther from the brazier.

The King said abruptly: 'I know what your needs are, and Harry's too. They shall be filled. I am summoning a Parliament in October, at Coventry – without lawyers!' Suddenly his frown vanished; he jerked up his chin, in his old way, laughing. 'There is a sovereign precedent for this! Your thirdfather, King Edward, once issued an ordinance debarring from one of his Parliaments *sheriffs, lawyers, and maintainers of quarrels*!'

His enjoyment of this jest seemed to banish his fretful humour. He began to talk about John's own concerns, asking him questions, not only about his duties, but about his progress in knightly exercises, and his health, and even his hawks. In this mood the King was lost for a little time, and the father who had always dearly loved the nurselings of his family found again. John had plenty to tell him about his hawks; what sport he had had, rivering with his saker; what birds he had flying at hack; how many hawks at fist, and how many at lure. Of knightly exercises he had less to say: amongst the King's sons it was only Thomas who showed any aptitude for jousting, and it did not seem likely that even he would ever rival his father in the lists. Father was always holding Richard Beauchamp up to them for admiration, but perhaps he would not have liked it had one of them surpassed him. Certainly not if that one had been Harry, John thought.

King Henry told John that his uncle, Bishop Beaufort, would shortly be translated to Winchester. That, at least, was what he hoped, but one had begun to think the present bishop, William of Wykeham, immortal. He had been living in retirement for years now, and must be fourscore years if he was a day. It was some time since it was reported of him that he was sinking to the grave, but he seemed to be quite sound in mind, and was taking a keen interest in his school, and his college, and in the rebuilding of the nave of his cathedral. 'He was said to have lost ten thousand marks by his trial – that was long before you were born: I was scarce breeched myself,' the King remarked. 'Enough to have ruined him, one would have thought! But your elderfather always said that no man knew better how to feather his nest!'

'That was why Bel sire hated him, wasn't it?' asked John, remembering scraps of talk overheard in his childhood. 'Because he thought it not right he should hold so many livings and prebends, and live so princely?'

'Oh, well, there was more to it than that!' the King said. 'It was a great abusion, of course: he had a foison of prebends before ever he was ordained! But your elderfather always believed it was he who spread that daffish story that Bel sire was not King Edward's son, but a changeling. Men said it at the time, but myself I don't think Wykeham did so.' He saw that he had startled his son, and added impatiently: 'Idle leasings! Bel sire was not liked of the people: they cleaved to Sir Edward, the Prince of Wales; and when he died it was believed by the redeless that with your thirdfather in his dotage Bel sire would contrive to set Richard aside, and mount the throne in his stead. It was noised that Queen Philippa, that was my granddam, gave birth to a daughter in Ghent, and, overlaying the child, feared to confess the same to the King, but adopted instead the

240

son of some low Fleming. Yes, yes, a gabbing tale, but redeless men will believe any losengery! It was even said that the Queen confessed it to Wykeham upon her bed-mortal. Bel sire believed that Wykeham noised it to do him scathe, and he never forgave him.'

'But – but it *could* not be true!' gasped John. 'That Bel sire—!'

'Of course it was not true!' said the King testily. 'Such gestes are very common, as you will find, but no man of worth lends ear to them.'

It occurred to John that his father had not scrupled to make use of just such a geste when he had challenged his cousin's throne. It had come as a great surprise to his sons when they had heard that Edmund, the founder of their house, had been King Henry III's eldest son, but set aside because he was misshapen. It had sounded most improbable: so much so that not even Thomas had dared to ask Father any questions about it. John withdrew his gaze from the King's face, feeling suddenly uncomfortable, and fixed it instead on one of the nine Amazons portrayed in gold of Cyprus and Arras thread in the magnificent set of tapestries with which the solar was hung. He hoped his father had not read the thought in his mind, but of course he had: he was very quick to read men's minds.

'Yes, that was a leasing too,' the King said gently. 'Or so I believe. No one can know for very sooth. It served my turn.'

John turned his head, shyly smiling. The King's words smutched the vision of his father which was a legacy of his worshipful childhood, but not, he discovered, the affection he bore him. He said, to cover an awkward moment: 'And when William of Wykeham dies my uncle will be Bishop of Winchester, sir?'

'Yes, I have already made known my wishes to the Pope,' replied the King. 'He will nominate him to oblige me. Winchester is the richest See in the kingdom, and I had rather Henry had it than one not bound to me.' He added, fretfully again: 'Not but what this business of providing is meddled beyond any man's wit! The Holy Father may not provide, but if the Chapter's choice should fall on one displeasant to him he may refuse his consent to the translation, which leaves us all at odds. However, in this unhappy state of schism it can't be gainsaid that our dealings with Rome run more smoothly than of yore. It would be a fell thing for the Holy Father if we were to transfer our allegiance to Avignon!'

5

They called King Henry's fifth Parliament Lack-Learning but from it he wrung a more generous grant than from any before it; and the only thing that occurred to mar the harmony of the session was a proposal, put forward by an overbold knight of the shire, that the King should take into his possession for one year all the rich lands belonging to the Church. This suggestion met with a considerable amount of sympathy, for the exactions of the Church were burdens felt by all. Not the most grasping baron demanded of his tenants a moiety of what Holy Church claimed as a right. Besides the Great Tithes, which laid upon every parishioner a tax of a tenth of his gross income, there were lesser tithes which left nothing untaxed that a man might produce to his profit. He paid under threat of excommunication, and it did not increase his love for the priesthood.

The attempt to wrest from the Church a part of her wealth failed, the shire-knight being quelled by the Bishop of Rochester, who stated terribly that anyone upholding such a proposition was a transgressor of the Great Charter, and subject to excommunication.

In Wales, Harry's most desperate needs had been relieved by a limited supply, and the despatch of a number of men-at-arms. Neither the money nor the men were enough to enable him to take the offensive; but he had at least compelled the Council to listen to him; and in November he and Thomas succeeded in relieving Coyty Castle. But he did not join the rest of his family at Eltham that Yule-tide. His scouts were bringing him disturbing tidings; he warned the King that Glendower was mustering a larger force than any he had yet commanded. It was beyond doubt, Harry said, that Owen had formed an alliance with the King of France.

'Which means with that spouse-breaker of Orleans. The King

is quite wood, by all accounts,' said Thomas, cheerfully ampli-
fying this report. 'Lousy, too: he won't suffer them to wash him
now. At all events, Harry must have more men, and the means
to keep them in the field.'

Thomas was not returning to the Welsh Marches, and was in
high fettle. He had not disliked serving under Harry, but he was
shortly to be given a command of his own, which, to one of his
imperious temper, was infinitely preferable. He was to be
Admiral of England, with the Northern and Eastern Fleets
joined under him, as they had been under the Earl of Worcester.
When it was suggested to him by Humfrey that he knew nothing
of ships or how to sail them, he replied that he knew as much as
Thomas Beaufort, who was at present Admiral of the Northern
Fleet. Besides, said Thomas, the Admiral was not expected to
sail his ship: that was the master's business. As Admiral he
was going to execute a special commission. He promised his
brothers he would execute it roundly.

'I expect he will, too,' remarked Humfrey, lying on a banker,
with his head propped on his hand, and his big, dark eyes smiling at John. 'And he will enjoy it. Thomas is *very* vengeable, I
think.'

Thomas was going to harry the Flemings and the Easterlings,
who had taken a leaf out of the French book, and had been
engaged for some time in acts of piracy. He was looking forward to the task, only sorry that it must be several months
before he could put to sea. One did not engage in operations in
the Channel until the danger of spring storms was over. Only
the cogs were at all manageable when the sea was at its roughest.
The big carracks were helpless in the teeth of a contrary gale;
and the balingers, the barges, and the galleys had sometimes to
wait for days in harbour before they could put to sea at all.

Humfrey prophesied that Thomas, thirsting for action, would
be an ill companion throughout the early spring. While the
Christmas plays lasted he was amused; but as soon as they were
done he grew restless, always wanting someone to play tennis or
hand-ball with him; or riding off in search of some sport, even
if it were only a bear-baiting. The princes coursed hares and
foxes, and once the King, who seemed to have recovered his

243

health, joined them, not with any pomp or preparation, but like any other father in holiday humour. It was nearly always his voice which called: 'Up, puss, up!' for he found more hares than they did, and coursed them with as much zest. He was skilled in forms of the chase, almost as knowledgeable as Edward, John thought. But when he said so the King made him no reply; and Humfrey later told him that he would do better not to bring Edward to Father's mind. Edward, Humfrey said, had been trying to have ado with the Queen. John uttered an incredulous exclamation, and Humfrey admitted that it was not quite as bad as that, though bad enough, because his gallantries – he had actually written some limping verses in her praise – caused her great distress, and angered Father.

Thomas shouted with mirth at the thought of Edward in amorous mood, but John said: 'First the Earl of Worcester, and now Edward! I don't believe it!'

'Well, it's true!' Humfrey said. 'And no wonder! She is so beautiful that men can't but love her, do what she will! And she is so shamefast that she never misdoubts her that when she only means to be gracious—'

'Oh, stint! She told *me* that too, full-yore! She's a breedbait!'

'That's a knavish thing to say!'

'Both of you stint!' commanded Thomas. 'Humfrey, if you say one word of this to Father I'll make it the worse for you!'

'Of course I shan't tell Father!' said Humfrey, in an injured voice. 'But it's true about Edward, whatever John may believe; and if he has the least kind-wit he'll take care not to do anything to put himself out of Father's grace!'

'Oh, don't be such a buzzard!' Thomas said impatiently. 'Why should Edward put himself out of Father's grace?'

6

But that was just what Edward did. While the Court, still pleasuring at Eltham, was celebrating the marriage of one of the Queen's Breton ladies-in-waiting, he arrived unexpectedly from the West Marches, to warn the King that there was a plot afoot to assassinate him. How he came by this knowledge did not immediately appear; he was rather vague about the authorship of the plot, and seemed to know nothing of its details; but he said enough to put the King on the alert. The royal family removed at once to Westminster; and hardly had the Council been informed of this new menace than Sir Hugh Waterton arrived at the palace, demanding instant audience of the King.

Never had the princes seen their late guardian so distraught! He did not cast himself at the King's feet, for he was too rugged a man for such arts, but standing squarely before him he announced that he was a jobbard and a nithing, worthy only of a shames-death. He had allowed the young Earl of March, and his brother Roger Mortimer, to escape from Windsor Castle! He seemed to think that to be drawn and quartered was the kindest fate he deserved. The King said: 'Nay, Hugh! Nay, old friend!' in soothing accents; but Sir Hugh smote his brow with his fist, and groaned: 'A suckfist! A bladder-headed stockfish, fit only to show out my visage in the pillory! I should be sewn in a sack, and cast into the Thames!'

It was several minutes before the King could allay his rage; and when he did succeed in convincing his stricken adherent that his trust in him was unbroken Sir Hugh wept, and said that so gracious a master was deserving of a better servant. After that he grew calmer, and was presently able to tell the King the whole.

Edward of York's sister, Constance, the Lady Despenser, was the author of the plot. She had been spending Yule-tide at Windsor; and she had, in nature, companied with her young cousins of March. Unfortunately she had done more than company with them. She had bribed a blacksmith to make a set of keys to certain doors in the castle; and with the assistance of their valet had contrived to steal the boys away one night, none discovering their absence until the following morning. Where they were now hidden, said Sir Hugh, God and the devil knew.

But the King, remembering Edward's mysterious hints, knew too. Questionless, the boys were being hurried westward to the Lady Despenser's estates on the Welsh border. Since her tenants were already numbered amongst the King's rebels, no more secure refuge could have been found for them. King Henry set in motion a number of measures for their swift apprehension, and wished that it were possible for him to dispose of his cousin Constance in just the way Sir Hugh thought his own desert. She ought to have been stitched into a sack and drowned years ago, he said, in an exasperated outburst which won him the whole-hearted approval of his sister Bess. Constance, said Bess, had been born to bring them all to shame and abusion. A wench of the game was what Bess called her cousin, forgetting the circum-stances of her own first marriage. Her loving brother recalled these to her mind; but Bess said that when she had fallen a victim to Sir John Holland she had been betrayed by youth and innocence, and at all events no one had ever accused her of being the leman of a wretched boy young enough to have been her son. No one, what was more, was going to accuse her of not having warned Henry months ago what would come of it if he didn't put a stop to that most unnatural connection, which he should have done, since her nephew poor Edmund Holland, until he came of age last month, had been his own ward. In what way this scandalous affair bore on the abduction of the Mortimers she did not explain, and Henry did not ask.

It was an exaggeration, of course, to say that Constance was old enough to have been Edmund of Kent's mother, but she was certainly too old to have become his mistress. She was the widow of King Richard's favourite, who had been headed at Bristol, and her conduct since that unhappy date had been anything but shamefast. Of Edmund de Langley's three children she was the one who most favoured her Spanish mother, inheriting from her a bold, southern beauty, and a gamesome disposition. King Henry, forgetting that Richard of Coningsburgh had done nothing to incur his wrath, said that his uncle of York had sired a brood of adders, and offered to wager his kingdom against the chance that Edward was not deeply implicated in his sister's plot.

And of course Edward had been implicated in it. The Morti-mers, caught in a forest in Gloucestershire, were brought to London a few days later. They were frightened, and Roger had contracted a bad cold, which was just what Sir Hugh had said would happen. He was a sickly boy, always in need of leech-craft. Edmund was not very hearty either. He was fourteen years of age, well grown, but backward. The King thought he did not look at all the sort of boy to embark on an adventure, and Sir Hugh said, No, he would swear to it he had never had such a notion in his head. He was a quiet lad, rather studious, never giving his guardian any trouble: nothing like the King's spirited sons!

It was plain that neither boy could give the King any information about the plot. So, as Roger was sobbing bitterly, and March looked as if he might swoon at any minute, King Henry brought the interview to an end. He told them that he was not angry with them, but since traitorous persons had tried to use them for their own wicked ends he should send them to a secure place. No, not a dungeon, so there was nothing to weep about!

He consigned them, with a fairly liberal allowance for their maintenance, to Sir John Pelham, who was Governor of Pevensey Castle, saying to those who considered the situation of this ancient hold a trifle bleak that perhaps the sea-winds would amend Roger's cough: he had heard that such breezes were beneficial.

The Lady Despenser was brought before the Council on the seventeenth day of February, and King Henry won his wager.

She made an impressive entry, sweeping into the Chamber in a robe of crimson bawdekin oversewn with gold flowers, a mantle bordered and lined with miniver worn over it, and on her luxuriant black locks a headdress like a decrescent moon which it would have wrung Bess's heart to have seen. She betrayed no sign of penitence, but boldly confronted the King and his Council. She said that her brother of York had been the hub of the plot; and when Edward heaved himself on to his feet to deny with passion such a charge she behaved in a very dramatic way, calling for a champion to avenge her wrongs, and offering to be burnt at the stake if he should be worsted in her cause.

To those dubiously eyeing the Duke of York's bulk the offer did not seem as handsome as might have been supposed. Everyone looked towards the King, but before he could intervene one of the lady's squires had flung his gauntlet in Edward's face, and Edward, purple with rage and effort, had picked it up.

The King did intervene then. Bishop Henry Beaufort told John that for a full minute he had thought that the King was going to burst out laughing, which would have been the best possible outcome. He had not, however; and in the ensuing enquiry the wildest accusations had been flung across the Council table. So serious did the plot seem to be that the ports were closed, and no less a person than the Archbishop of Canterbury had felt obliged to declare his innocence.

There was little doubt that Thomas Mowbray, the Earl of Nottingham and son of King Henry's old enemy, had been implicated. As for Edward, his defence, when he was brought before the new Parliament, ranged from denial to self-justification; and included (to the joy of his young cousins) an assurance that he had not properly understood what he was doing. He said that it had been through his good offices that the plot against the King's life had been disclosed; and went on to enumerate, with gathering passion, the various ways in which the King stood in his debt. His expenses while governing Guyenne were unpaid; he had pawned his plate and his jewels in the King's cause, and had even pledged his estates; in fact, the only payment he had received from the King were his wages as Master of the Running Hounds, which were twelve pence a day.

The proceedings ended inconclusively, the only person to be placed under arrest being the Lady Despenser. The King sent her to confinement in Kenilworth (far too comfortable a prison for such a bawdy-basket, said incorrigible Bess), and the Council set about the task of interrogating all those incriminated either by her or by Edward.

The Mortimers' valet, and the henchman employed by Lady Despenser, the King, never vindictive, pardoned. The Abbots of Colchester and Byleigh came next on the list, but suffered only confiscation of their goods. Queen Joanna had interceded for them, kneeling at the King's feet, and imploring him for the love he bore her to spare the lives of those saintly men. So the King did spare their lives; and bestowed on his consort the Abbot of Colchester's confiscated goods, which she accepted, because although it was not what she wanted, or even dreamed of, she could not find it in her heart to wound the King by refusing the grant.

Towards the young Earl of Nottingham King Henry behaved

with real nobility. Thomas Mowbray was now nineteen years old, and had lately married Bess's daughter, Constance Holland. He was so like his father, the dead Duke of Norfolk, that nobody expected King Henry to treat him leniently. He admitted his guilt, but even though he begged for mercy he did so with resentment in his voice, and a glowering look in his sulky eyes. The Countess of Hereford, in whose care he had spent his boy-hood, had warned King Henry that the boy laboured under a sense of ill-usage. He was Earl of Nottingham, but he had not succeeded to his father's Dukedom. Looking down at him, as he knelt before him, King Henry saw his enemy in that sour young face; and felt an old hatred stir in his breast. A weak, peevish face, it was: frightened, too. He drew a difficult breath, and said: 'Since you are not of full age, Thomas, and have been, as I believe, misled, I give you grace.'

In doubt and suspicion Mowbray remained on his knees, staring up at the King. Henry unclenched his hand from the arm of his chair, and made a gesture of dismissal. Mowbray stumbled to his feet, hardly knowing what he was doing, and was called sharply to order by Bishop Beaufort. 'You have had great mercy shown you, my lord of Nottingham, and can find no word of gratitude?'

Mowbray began to stammer his thanks, but the King said, 'Give me no words! Go, now!'

The Bishop told John of this, and John said hopefully: 'If Father could pardon a Mowbray, he must surely pardon Edward!'

'That,' said the Bishop dryly, 'is another matter! This is not Edward's first venture in treason.'

'Oh, I know!' John answered. 'But Harry wants him back on the Marches, and what he told me once was sooth! One *can't* be angry with Edward above a paternoster-while! Harry has written to beg Father to pardon him, and to Thomas and me, to use our endeavours—'

'Also to me,' interposed the Bishop. 'I have advised him, as I advise you, John to let it sleep! You will only anger the King if you take Edward's part against him.'

'What does he mean to do with him?' demanded John.

'That has not yet been decided,' replied the Bishop. 'The King is very much araged, but he was within ames-ace of laughing when that fat buffard stood before him!'

If King Henry meant to head his cousin, it was Thomas who saved Edward from this fate. Thomas was Steward of England, and it fell to his lot to arrest Edward. Both his brothers advised him to counterfeit sickness, for it seemed to them unthinkable that he should not shrink from such a task.

'Tell Father you're crapsick!' recommended Humfrey. 'If he saw how many lamb tarts you ate at dinner he won't wonder at it!'

Thomas cuffed him, but goodnaturedly. 'Why should I?'

'Thomas, you *can't* force your way into Cousin Edward's inn, and carry him off to the Tower! Why, he must be nearly as old as Father!' said John. 'You've served under him, too. You can't do it!'

'Oh, yes I can!' said Thomas cheerfully. 'Edward will take no force of that!'

In this hopeful view he was mistaken, but nothing could have served Edward's turn better than the scene that was enacted within the walls of his inn, for Thomas faithfully reported it to the King: and the King, after a struggle to keep his countenance, nearly laughed himself into an accesse.

Only Thomas could have executed his commission with such an entire absence of ceremony. Ushered into Edward's presence, he had greeted him with his engaging smile, and had said: 'Cry you mercy, cousin! I arrest you, in the King's name!'

'A malapert jape!' said Edward severely. 'What do you want of me, mam's foot?'

'But I've told you!' said Thomas. 'I'm not bejaping you – faith of my knighthood!'

'What?' gasped Edward. 'Why, you airling, you upspring, you popinjay—! If I do not swinge you for this!'

'You can't do that,' objected Thomas. 'I'm the Lord High Steward!'

'Lord High Gadling, Lord High son of Perdition!' choked Edward, his face alarmingly red.

'Le douce, mon amy, le douce!' said Thomas. 'That *must* be treason!'

'A puling brat I've jounced on my knee!' Edward raged.

'Never!' declared Thomas. 'When I was a puling brat you paid me not the least heed!'

'And I pay you none now, nor ever shall!' retorted Edward.

'But you must heed me!' Thomas pointed out. 'If you won't, I shall call in my escort, and carry you bound to the Tower. The prentices will think it as good as a Corpus Christi procession!'

Edward sat staring stockishly at him. 'Thomas!' he said. 'If I didn't jounce you on my knee, at least I taught you how to speak of venery! Why, the first time you went hunting with me you saw the steps of one of the stinking beasts and called them *traces*, as though you had been talking of a hart! God's dignity, it's importable that you should be sent to arrest me!' His feelings almost overcame him; but after a fulminating pause he said bitterly: 'After all the services I've rendered the King! And I knew nothing about my sister's plot, nothing at all!'

'Edward, you've confessed already that you were a party to it!' said Thomas reproachfully.

'Well, if I was, I repented me, didn't I? If I hadn't dropped a hint in your father's ear, he would have been keycold now, and you too, I daresay! And what is my guerdon? Unthank! And in all belikelihood my head set up on the bridge for the crows to peck at!'

'But I hope you won't head him, sir,' said Thomas, concluding his story. 'For bonchief or mischief we must keep fat Edward on life!'

5 Shipton Moor

The King spared Edward's life, but he deprived him of his estates and his offices, and sent him to safe keeping at Pevensey. Those who knew this hold prophesied that he would fall into a melancholy there. A large part of it was in a ruinous state; there was nothing to be seen from its slit windows but water, the sea on one hand, and swamps on the other; and nothing to be heard but the crash of the waves, and the screams of the gulls which wheeled and soared day-long above the battlements.

The Despenser plot might be scotched, but the King had little other cause for satisfaction. Parliament had been summoned to assemble at Westminster, at the beginning of March, but whether Northumberland would sit amongst his peers was doubtful. He had already excused himself from attending the Council. In an affectionate letter to the King, he pleaded age and infirmity, which made it impossible for him to undertake the winter journey to London. He signed himself 'Your Mattathias,' for it was his favourite conceit that he and his son might have been likened to the Maccabean heroes who led the revolt against Antiochus Epiphanes; but the King read the letter with an unmoved countenance, and acquiesced in Ralph Neville's determination to return to his post immediately.

The mercy King Henry had shown Mowbray bore only sour fruit. The young Earl of Nottingham would never be appeased until his father's Dukedom had been restored to him; and his first act on emerging scatheless from the Despenser plot was to pick a quarrel with Warwick on precedence. The King was forced to adjudicate between them, for Richard Beauchamp's haughty temper took fire, and he brought the matter before the Council. The question was never in doubt: the Earldom of

Nottingham had been created by King Richard II, but Warwick could produce a writ of summons to Parliament issued to his great forefather, Guy, as far back as the reign of the first Edward. Nottingham left the Council Chamber with a black scowl on his face, and at once withdrew from the Court.

Richard Beauchamp was now twenty-three. John would not reach his sixteenth birthday until June, but the gap of age between them seemed to have shrunk. John, who had always looked up to him as his elder, and a most worshipful knight, found that he no longer looked up. Richard was still the model of chivalry, but John's brain had outstripped his. He remembered that Richard had never been quickwitted; discussing with him Harry's difficulties in Wales, he now thought him sometimes a little stupid, and never very farsighted. He was of so autocratic and intolerant a disposition that he could not like Harry's policy of conciliation; but he had so deep a respect for Harry's genius that he never criticized him. He told John that no one on life had ever seen Harry's equal in the field. Give Harry opportunity and a handful of men, and he would put to rout five times his number, Richard said. Before John left for the North his words were proved: Harry, with a force which he described as a small body of his household, had vanquished more than eight hundred rebels at Grosmont.

This was good news for John to carry north with him. He had further cause for satisfaction in the power granted to him to negotiate short truces with the Scots. If he could get ransoms paid and prisoners released, he knew that one cause at least of dissatisfaction would be removed.

Northumberland, to the relief of the anxious, had answered the summons to Parliament; Bishop Beaufort had been translated to the See of Winchester, and had relinquished the Great Seal into the hands of one of the King's most devoted adherents, Thomas Langley, Dean of York. Langley was not as witty a man as Beaufort, but he was more agreeable to the King. His eyes were not always turned towards Harry; nor did he live at loggerheads with Archbishop Arundel.

The Bishop had not been nominated to Winchester by Pope Boniface, but by his successor, Innocent VII, whom the countries in obedience to Rome had recognized. Boniface, or, as the irreverent had called him for the fifteen years of his rule, Maleface, had died of the stone; and his successor was a well-meaning, unwitty Neapolitan, fond of singing and of books, and subject to apoplectic fits.

His election followed a scene of the greatest disorder. No sooner was the death of Boniface made known than riots broke out in Rome, rival factions carrying on a sanguinary warfare in the streets, and the envoys whom Pope Benedict had sent from Avignon to discuss the question of union being cast into the Castle of St Angelo.

It seemed unlikely that Innocent, a slightly feeble old man, would be capable of handling the situation in which he found himself. What with the republicans in Rome, the highhanded behaviour of the Emperor Sigismund in Germany, and the duplicity of Pope Benedict in Avignon, who, while making bland suggestions for a conference, was quite openly preparing to make war on him, it was generally felt that he would be fortunate if he was still in the Chair of St Peter at the date he had appointed for a meeting of the archbishops under his control.

Only very devout Englishmen felt any particular interest in Rome's troubles; and quite a number of the younger men looked upon the Schism as an established thing. It had lasted for twenty-three years; and for seventy years before that Holy Church had been falling into disrepute. From the moment that Clement VII removed his court to Avignon, papal influence, never as strong in England as might have been desired, waned. The Pope had become a vassal of France: the Babylonian Captivity was the mocking title given to those years of luxurious enslavement. There was a rival Pope in Rome, and matters had gone from bad to worse. The whole of Europe was shocked by the behaviour of Urban VI in Rome and Clement in Avignon, for they never ceased to revile one another. Anathemas, excommunications, and the foulest accusations hurtled from one to the other, until not the strictest Churchman thought it blasphemous of John Wycliffe to liken the Popes to two dogs snarling over a bone.

'I remember,' said Ralph Neville, 'that your elderfather, John of Gaunt, whom God assoil, once said that both Popes ought to be deposed. Well, how should sely men forbear to make garboils when the Holy Father demeans himself like any jack-eater? This Innocent sounds to me like a niddicock; and as for old Maledict, he's a snudge-snout, and there's an end to it!'

2

On the surface, things were quiet in the North. John met with fewer black looks, and even, sometimes, with signs of approval. The Scots had so devastated the Border that he had recommended to the Council an entire redemption from taxation for the three northernmost counties; and once this became known the Borderers began to look upon him with friendlier eyes. He received one or two presents, offered by men half-sheepish, half-surly: a tawny spaniel whelp; a cast of eyas hawks; a prickeared alaunt of volatile disposition and evil understanding which harried sheep, bit his horse, and laid unsavoury trophies at his feet. He remembered that Edward condemned all alaunts, saying that they were giddy in their natures, sturdier and more foolish than any other hound. However, John liked the hound, and kept him. He called him Butcher, not so much because he belonged to that branch of the breed known as butcher-alaunts, but for other and quite obvious reasons. His groom, binding a clout round his hand, took what comfort he could from the reflection that Butcher was prepared to defend his master against any peril, real or imaginary.

John thought that if only Northumberland had parted his life he could have been happy on the Border that springtide. But Northumberland was not yet at his last end; and over the whole countryside hung an air of unrest. He had returned from Westminster at the beginning of April, and a disquieting rumour that messengers from Wales had met him at Warkworth came to John's ears. Nottingham was also in the North; he owned estates by Thirsk, so perhaps there was no need to see danger in that. John reported his arrival to the Council in a letter that told also of the many signs of insurrection which he found wherever he went. These tallied so exactly with every other report received in London that on April 15th the King sent the Chief Justice,

Sir William Gascoigne, and Sir Henry FitzHugh into the North to make strict enquiry.

The King was at St Albans, mustering his forces for an expedition into Wales. Since autumn of the preceding year the French had been making great preparations for an invasion. There could be little doubt that Harry was right when he said that a treaty had been signed between Glendower and Orleans, but owing to the pleasure-loving habits of the Count de la Marche, who had been appointed to lead the expedition, the ships were kept for so long at Brest and the men-at-arms (unpaid) at St Pol de Léon that the formidable host soon began to dwindle. Ribalds said that the Count saw the sea and fled; but in November he had actually embarked, in command of twenty vessels, reached Falmouth after eight unhappy days at sea, burned the town, and retired again. Now, in the spring of 1405, it was reported in England that the Lord of Hugueville was taking matters in hand, and was engaged in raising men for a voyage to Wales.

With the King committed to the Welsh venture, Northumberland judged it to be time to strike his blow. The arrival of his friend the Lord Bardolph in the North was the signal for the uprising. Sir Robert Waterton, sent to Warkworth with a message from the King, was cast into prison; and in York the saintly Archbishop Scrope put himself in arms against the King he had helped to crown. His manifesto was couched in pious language, but no one with the least kind-wit could doubt that the mainspring of his conduct was the late threat to the wealth of the Church. With him was joined the Earl of Nottingham; and the pair of them rode about York, the Archbishop with the crozier in his hand, exhorting the citizens to enlist under his banner.

The Lord John, in Berwick, sent off a last message to the Council, informing them that he was now cut off; and prepared to force his way south, to effect a junction with Ralph Neville. The town of Berwick was friendly enough, but the castle was still held by Clifford, and he had lately strengthened it. John had been granted the power to call up all men between the ages of sixteen and sixty, and he put this into execution, and enrolled

256

more than he had expected. He and Robert Umfraville led this force south, evading opposition, and joined the Earl of Westmoreland south of the Tyne.

Ralph Neville was in a towering rage. He had narrowly escaped being taken prisoner at Witton-le-Wear, where he had been the guest of Sir Ralph Eure, an old friend. Four hundred men, wearing the Percy cognizance, had surrounded the castle, but they came too late: the Earl, warned of his peril, was away with his host, and speeding north to the rescue of his royal pupil.

He was extremely glad to find that John was neither dead nor a prisoner; but when he discovered the strength of their combined forces he said that they would all be dead or prisoned soon enough. He thrust a crumpled document into John's hands, saying grimly: 'You may read that, lording! Fine matter for an Archbishop to be scattering all over the town! The fellow that brought it to me out of York might have had a dozen copies or more!'

John rapidly scanned the manifesto. It made no mention either of King Richard or of the Earl of March, but complained of misgovernment, and the need for reform. Particularly did it complain of the burden of taxation, and the injustice with which the clergy were being treated. John passed it to Umfraville, saying contemptuously: 'Pope-holy! What else?'

'Enough matter to make your blood boil!' Ralph said. 'Percy, and Glendower, and Mortimer – no, not young March! His precious uncle, that was taken prisoner by Glendower, and married his daughter! – are all entered into a bond to portion the realm between them, and are calling on the people to rise up against the King's grace! Wait, I have it writ down here, and you shall see for yourself! Such a piece of knavery I never beheld!'

Deciphering the Earl's angry scrawl, John found it almost as bewildering as it was knavish, for it was couched in strange language. A Dragon, a Lion, and a Wolf were to divide the realm between them, according to an ancient prophecy. 'What prophecy?' demanded John, his brow creased.

'That damned Book of Brut, no force!' growled Ralph Neville. 'Did you never hear of a warlock called Merlin? There hasn't been a prophecy yet that didn't issue from his mouth – or so those Welsh scrubs say! How is an honest Englishman to know? Such harlotry!'

'Merlin!' John looked up, as memory stirred. There had been a Hainaulter who told wonderful stories: a clerk, speaking English as one long unaccustomed, who had talked to Bel sire of a prophecy that concerned the house of Lancaster. He snatched at a name, and pronounced: 'Froissart!' He saw that Ralph was staring at him, and said quickly: 'Nay, no charge!' He saw that it would never do to tell these puzzled lords that it had been prophesied by Merlin that the crown of England should fall to the house of Lancaster. He bent his gaze to the paper again, and said: 'What, a'God's half, do all these frothing words mean? *After Richard shall come a Mouldwarp, cursed of God.* My father?'

'I told you it was a knavish piece of work!' said Ralph.

'Japeworthy too!' said John, in a voice brittle as glass, 'for I perceive that this Mouldwarp is called a caitiff and a coward! *How* many men did my father slay with his own hand at Shrewsbury? *An eldritch skin, as a goat* – He was in good complexion when last I saw him! Oh, a Dragon is to come out of the North, and war with this Mouldwarp upon a stone!'

'Percy, of course!' said Ralph.

'I have heard that dragons are akin to snakes. Who is this Wolf from the West? Edmund Mortimer? If he means to *bind his tail* with Percy's he *must* be a jobbard! *To rule all England from Severn to Trent*! Ah, but not before the Thames is choked with corpses, and my father fled! That will be long enough! Who, devil-way, is the Lion out of Ireland who shall be linked with this precious pair?'

'God knows! But the Red Lion who is to conquer all is Glendower!'

'The Red Lion, then, had best learn to face Harry in the field!' flashed John. He crushed the paper, and flung it down. 'Now, and at last, we may make an end! On the Cross of St Thomas did that mainsworn dog Northumberland swear fealty to my father! My father forgave him the fine; *I* have been forced to give back to him his holds, and to watch his men strengthening them! Not four months past he was calling himself the King's humble Mattathias! Christ give me strength to bring him to neckbreak!'

Ralph was startled by the leaping rage in John's voice, for he had thought him an even-tempered boy. He looked all at once like his grandsire: stark and dangerful. Ralph grunted, and said: 'We have need of strength. If the King is embroiled already with the Welsh—' He left the sentence unfinished, and tugged at his moustache.

Umfraville asked: 'Has the King crossed the Severn, Sir John?'

'He reached Worcester on the third day of May,' John replied. 'By now he must be at Hereford, or beyond.'

There was a heavy silence. It was broken by Sir Henry Fitz-Hugh, whom King Henry had sent into the North to make enquiry. He was lord of Ravenswath, in Yorkshire, and a nephew on the distaff side of Archbishop Scrope. He said: 'Under favour, Sir John, it is to our own strength we must look, and speedily. My uncle will bring in many who would not stir to aid a Percy.'

John saw that they were all of them watching him, waiting for something.

'In the matter of leadership,' said Sir Henry bluntly, 'we await your word, my lord!'

John realized suddenly that he could claim the leadership. Only for an instant did he entertain the vision of winning worship by a glorious campaign: matters were too desperate for such dreams. He said: 'With your good will, my lords, let our captain be my uncle of Westmoreland.'

They looked relieved; and Ralph said: 'Well, I think it will be best, John, for I am more seasoned in war than you. You will be captain in name, of course.'

'I care nothing for that, but only for sending these traitors hellward!' John replied. 'What is your rede, Ralph?'

3
Ralph's plan was simple, and his movements swift. As he saw it, the only hope was to get between the two rebel armies before

they had time to coalesce. He hurried his force south, gleaning tidings all the way from his scouts, from pedlars, and even from friars and palmers. The Archbishop, donning a warlike jack, and accompanied by Nottingham, had raised a banner displaying the Five Sacred Wounds, and was calling on all men to rally to him. He was said to have collected as many as eight thousand malcontents, while a band of some seven or eight hundred rebels, under the leadership of four Yorkshire knights, was moving from Cleveland to join him. It was a polyglot band, and badly disciplined, and it scarcely endeared itself to the country people by plundering and slaughtering, and leaving in its wake a trail of burning dwellings. Reaching Topcliffe, on the Swale, it halted to await the arrival of Northumberland. But its leisurely progress had allowed Ralph Neville to slip past, and to reach the Forest of Galtres, which was under his jurisdiction. Here he received some sorely needed reinforcements, sent from his castle at Sheriff Hutton; and here he took up his position, on the slope of a hill called Shipton Moor. It was some six miles north-west of York, on the edge of what remained of the ancient forest. But forest was already a misnomer: the ground was quite open, the only traces of the forest which remained being the stovens that were being stubbed up and carried away by the colliers.

Learning that the marauders had reached Topcliffe, in his rear, Ralph thought it prudent to send off a detachment to disperse them. Hardly had this small band of seasoned warriors left the camp than the Archbishop's force appeared in his front, and halted with banners displayed.

'Well,' said Ralph doggedly, 'we have the worst of the numbers, but the best position, and, God helping us, we will withstand attack.'

The attack, however, was not launched. Either from indecision, or as the result of counsel, the rebel host remained confronting the royal force. Sir Henry FitzHugh thought this was probably his cousin Sir William Plumpton's rede, who was known to have thrown in his lot with their uncle the Archbishop. Sir Henry, who was of an impatient nature, urged Ralph Neville to fall upon the rebels, trusting in superior generalship, but Ralph was too ware to risk so much against such odds.

He was supported by Umfraville and Sir Ralph Eure; and if John shared Sir Henry's wish to come to grips with the rebels he had enough self-control to hold his peace.

It became increasingly hard to do so as the time crept by. For three days the armies eyed one another, neither moving from its position. Someone in the Archbishop's council had certainly perceived the danger of attacking Westmoreland on ground of his own choosing. Had Westmoreland been awaiting the arrival of reinforcements this hesitation would have stood him in good stead; but the only expected reinforcements – and they would be overwhelming – were coming from the north, under the standard of the Luces and the rampant Blue Lion of Percy. All his being in a torment of anxiety, John was more taciturn than ever, for he dared not trust himself to speak. He had given the command to Neville, and by Neville's decrees he must be ruled; but it sometimes seemed to him that Ralph had no understanding of the perils that menaced them, or of how much depended on their ability to crush the northern rising. If they failed, and Northumberland swept south, Glendower would strike in full force, and the King, and Harry too, must be crushed between the two armies. Across the Tweed the Scots were probably preparing to invade England, either for their own ends, or as Percy's allies. From Calais, from Guyenne, from France, the news was all bad. The Count of St Pol was besieging Marck, in the Pale of Calais, and whether John Beaufort, with the slender resources at his command, could succeed in relieving this fortress no one yet knew. Thomas was at sea, harrying the Easterlings; but at Brest the French fleet was reported by spies to be ready to set sail.

It was torture to John to remain in impotent inactivity; almost an impossibility to deny himself the relief of railing against Ralph's caution. He absented himself as much as he could from the councils, spending his time in going about the camp, and watching the enemy's lines. There was never any change in the disposition of the Archbishop's troops; never a hope of making a surprise night-attack: scouts always brought back the same tale of double guards, and sentinels on the alert.

He was beside one of the standing-watches very late one night, watching the glow of the camp-fires on the lower ground, when Ralph Neville came to join him. John heard the rustle of his hauberk, a sleeveless jacket of linked mail which he had not put off since he pitched his camp, and turned his head. The moonlight was too dim for recognition, but he knew who it must be by the hirpling stride, and spoke his name.

'I've been seeking you all over,' said Ralph.

'Well?'

Ralph jerked his head significantly towards the sentry, and led John out of tongue-shot, walking slowly, and apparently chewing the cud of some deep thought.

'Well?' said John again, hearing his own voice gritty with impatience.

'Robin, and FitzHugh, and old Eure have been with me,' Ralph said. 'You went away after supper, so— Well, perhaps it was as well you did.'

'I can't endure it!' John said, at the end of forbearance. 'Must we wait here to be cracked between Percy's men, and this rabble before us? For God's sake, let us strike before it is too late! This gait we must be shent! Ralph, every minute that we lose is a betrayal of Harry – of my father!'

'Swef, mon amy, swef!' Ralph said. He laid his hand on John's mailed shoulder. 'Never cry *sa cy avaunt*! when your hounds are on a stint! I too am pledged to keep the North. Well, God helping me, I will do it, but I can tell you this, boy: only a rash-head would fling this little force of ours at that host down there! Nay, it's not the numbers I dread, but the leadership. I misdoubt me that only the hardiest of our men would have stomachs for a battle against the Church.'

'Then what?' demanded John. 'Will you turn north to meet Percy? You cannot!'

'You say sooth!' returned Ralph, with a bark of mirth. 'Witterly I don't want Scrope and Mowbray at my heels! The matter is this, John, and it's what I came to break to you: there is only one way for us in this pass. What we may not do by force we must do by subtlety.'

'How?'

Ralph took a moment to answer. 'If we had the leaders in our hands, that rabble, as you call it, would be easily dispersed,' he remarked.

'Affirmably! And if we had a cloud-ship at our command to snatch them up on the flukes of its anchor, and so bring them to us, we should speed well!'

'Now, now, not so overthwart of your tongue, John!' Ralph said. 'There are more ways than cloud-ships to bring it about.'

John stared at him, trying to read his face in the dim light. 'What ways?'

'Well—' Ralph seemed to hesitate for words, 'it has been decided between us – under favour, lording – that we must seek a parley with the Archbishop.'

'Yea, and to what end?' John asked. 'Will you bid him to dinner with us?'

'Him, and young Mowbray, and as many of their captains as I can lure into the net,' replied Ralph.

John jumped under his hand. '*Treachery*?'

'Need knows no law,' said Ralph grimly. He waited for a moment, but John did not speak. 'I daresay you'll say the loth word, and so you may. That's why I didn't bid you to our council tonight. It shall be my doing, not yours.'

John shook off his hand. 'No, for my death! What has Um-fraville to say?'

'Well, it is not what Robin would choose, nor any of us,' said Ralph. 'But he and I, John, are pledged to serve the King, and it seems to us that if we keep our hands overly clean all will come to cand-pie, and the whole realm be over-set. For my part, between the King and Scrope I'll betray Scrope, be he ten times Archbishop! One of them I must betray in this pass, choose how! But as for you —'

'Leave that!' John said.

Ralph was obediently silent, nor did he follow when John took a few hasty steps away from him. He had known that John would be shocked, and would have been glad to have been able to have kept all knowledge of what was intended away from him. That was not possible, of course. He wondered how the lad was going to take it. It would make no difference; still, none of them wanted to offend him, and he was at the age when his knighthood was a shining honour not lightly to be smutched. Perhaps it would have been better to have sent Robin to break the matter to him. Robin might have been able to explain that soon or late it must come to a man to choose between evils, not between evil and good, as lads were taught. Ralph thought that he would have to try to do this himself, but he was not apt of his tongue, and knew that it would probably be tied in knots if he sought to put into words all that was so clear in his mind.

It was unnecessary for him to explain anything. Even in that moment of revulsion, when he strode away from Ralph, John knew, somewhere at the back of his protesting brain, that he would make no push to stop the betrayal. He thought of the oath he had taken when he received his knighthood; of the great oath he had sworn in St George's Chapel, when he had been invested with the habit of the Order of the Garter. Not to vilify the Law of Arms; not to proceed in anything further than Faith or Compact or the Bond of Friendship would admit: well, there was no bond of friendship in question, but what of faith and compact, he wondered? What did Ralph, who wore the Garter too, think about that? One of the lurking thoughts in his mind leaped to the fore: what would Harry think of it? Well, he knew what Harry would think, and realized that in this extremity the knowledge did not weigh with him.

His mind steadied, and grew cold. Faith was not owed to traitors. No extenuating loyalty to King Richard lay behind the insurrection. Percy had greed for his motive; Mowbray ill-will; Scrope – God and the Saints knew what had prevailed on him to raise that banner! Anger stirred in John's breast. No hint of the Archbishop's purpose had been allowed to appear at Westminster; he had borne himself towards the King smiling and gracious while he must have been laying his secret plans; and not until he knew the King to be across the Severn did he move into the open. Protected by his habit too, John thought bitterly. Whoever ended this adventure on the scaffold, it would not be the Archbishop, and well he must know it! As for Mowbray, whom any other than King Henry would have headed for his share in the Despenser plot, John would send him to his death without a shade of compunction.

He turned, and went back to where Ralph was standing. 'Yea, let it be done!' he said.

4

A messenger was sent to the rebel camp on the following day, to discover from the Archbishop what was the meaning of his warlike array. For answer he sent back to my lord of Westmoreland a copy of his manifesto. It was the same Englished version which had been distributed in York. It protested against the holding of parliaments in places under royal influence, and against interference with free election; it demanded economy, less taxation, and better treatment for the clergy and nobles. Clearly the Archbishop had been spurred to action by the suggestion of that unwitty shire-knight at Coventry that the Church's huge revenues should be appropriated.

'Well,' said Neville, 'I shall tell him that I think his proposals reasonable, and will do my power to see them adopted. Under favour, Sir John, it *would* be well if there were more strait-keeping in the regiment of the country.'

'It is true that what the Archbishop urges is reasonable,' Umfraville said. 'But the complaints which he issued privately, the manner in which he has written of the King's grace, and his urging of the sely folk to rise up in rebellion—'

'What need of all these words?' demanded FitzHugh. 'If ever I clapped eyes on a traitor, that one is this pope-holy uncle of mind! Make an end!'

The messenger was sent back to the rebel camp with the suggestion that the leaders of both armies should meet for conference. This was rather surprisingly agreed to, and a place between the opposing lines appointed. Umfraville told John that he could find it in his heart to wish that the Archbishop were not so ready to walk into the trap; but John would have none of this. 'If he will be fool as well as traitor, so much the better!' he said.

'He is a man of saintly life,' Robert said gently.

'Yea, and forsooth? But it was not until he saw his purse threatened that he bethought him of this crusade!' John flung back. 'Moreover, Robin, in my sight he does very ill to complain of the burden of taxation! Will Holy Church remit one penny of the tithes she wrings from the neediest in the land? Let this saintly Archbishop take a lesson from my father's book! My father, not Holy Church, has remitted the taxation of the wretches whom the Scots have despoiled! God's death, have we not seen the parish priests spying out what man has sold a cabbage, or a handful of eggs? As for Scrope's folly, I like no man the better for being a daw! Jesu defend! Was ever a trap laid more apertly? Does that papelard think me a nithing? He sends his manifesto, farced with insults to my father, into this camp, and believes *I* will stomach it in all lowlihead? He shall know me better!'

Umfraville said no more. He had caught a glimpse of something stark and implacable in the Lord John's heavy-lidded eyes. He wondered if they would all of them learn to know the Lord John better, or whether the boy did not yet know himself, and would shrink from Neville's ruthlessness at the last.

The leaders met at the appointed hour, on the one side the Earl of Westmoreland, with the Lord John of Lancaster, and Sir Ralph Eure; on the other, the Archbishop and the Earl of Nottingham, attended by the Archbishop's nephew, Sir William Plumpton, Sir William Lamplugh, and Sir Henry Percy of Ryton, a kinsman of Northumberland. After some ceremonious civilities, the articles presented by the Archbishop were read aloud. While this was being done, Westmoreland's face betrayed nothing but thoughtful interest; but it was to be seen that the upward tilt to the corners of John's mouth was more marked than usual. He seemed to smile; but Mowbray, meeting his eyes for a revealing instant, saw no smile in them, and tried to convey an unspoken warning to the Archbishop. But Scrope paid no more heed to this than he had paid to earlier and spoken warnings. Nottingham had begged him not to meet Ralph Neville without a strong guard at his back; but the Archbishop, who combined with scholarship a certain simplicity, had only reproved him for wantrust. Mowbray's eyes shifted uneasily from John's face to Westmoreland's. The sun, shining on burnished breastplates, dazzled him with pinpoints of light like stabbing needles; his own breastplate seemed too small, constricting his chest uncomfortably; and the quilted jupon he wore from neck to mid-thigh was making him sweat.

The reading came to an end; Westmoreland said the Archbishop's demands were pious and saintly; he was telling the Archbishop he would do what lay in his power to carry them out; he was holding out his hand; and the Archbishop was taking it in his, benignly smiling. More handshaking followed; Mowbray himself placed his hand in John's. He was three years older than John, but he had to look up to meet his eyes, and he could not read the expression in them, and was afraid.

Westmoreland was saying that they must all of them drink to the pact, and pointing to where he had had a pavilion pitched. The Archbishop acceded graciously to this suggestion, and Mowbray's stretched nerves made him stammer an entreaty that they should rather retire again to their own camp.

'Nay, this is churlish, my lord!' Scrope said.

Westmoreland laid a hand on Mowbray's arm, saying jovially that he should not allow him to be a let-game; and because he was too young and too unsure of himself to stand against all these older men he went with them, his steps unwilling, doubt in his sick mind, and fear. The Archbishop, he thought, had small cause for dread, but could he not perceive the peril into which he was leading his companion in rebellion? Mowbray had tried to make him understand that if he fell now into King Henry's hands he could not hope for grace, but the Archbishop had told him to fear nothing. As he walked towards the pavilion, he thought that he must have been wood to have joined Scrope. He wanted to fly from this company, and when he answered something that was said to him his voice was so husky that he had to clear his throat.

There seemed to be a foison of people in the pavilion, and the sensation of being entrapped grew upon him. He cast the look of a cornered beast about him, but the scene was peaceful enough. Servants in sanguine livery were setting cups on the board; the Archbishop was extending his hand for his other nephew, FitzHugh, to kiss.

Mowbray paid little attention to what was being said, but he understood presently that the King's lieutenants had agreed to

267

the Archbishop's articles, and that everyone was drinking to the happy issue. But how could the King's son agree to the articles, or Scrope believe it possible that he would? He uttered an inarticulate protest, but when Scrope looked enquiringly at him he could only shake his head, trying to convey a warning with his eyes. He failed, of course. Probably he would have failed had he found the courage to put his suspicion into words. The Archbishop was asotted; he should have known better than to have trusted him.

He tried to take comfort from the reflection that FitzHugh was Scrope's nephew, but he could see that FitzHugh's cousin of Plumpton was watching him narrowly, and his heart sank lower. Besides, it was not FitzHugh who was in command of the King's force, but Westmoreland. A passion of hatred made him dig his nails into the palms of his hands. The King had created this hip-halt, upspring northerner Marshal of England for the term of his life, and that was a title that belonged of right to the Mowbrays. Rancour welled up in him; he saw that the Lord John was looking at him, and, staring into those eyes, glittering under their sleepy lids, he flinched. Just so did cats look when they played with their victims.

Westmoreland had bidden them all to dine with him, and FitzHugh was going to the rebel army to announce the agreement of the leaders. 'Tell them not to await my coming!' said the Archbishop. 'They will be blithe, poor sely souls, to return to their homes!'

Buffard and bladderhead! You are ten-so-wood! Look at the King's son! Look at Neville, smiling under his moustache!

He thought he must have shouted these words, but he had not spoken: they sounded only in his head. They were moving off now, to dine at Westmoreland's board; he found himself between the Lord John and a stranger knight; a quick look over his shoulder showed him more of Neville's meiny following close behind.

The huge kitchen at Raby could scarcely have furnished forth a more elaborate banquet than was set before them. There were no birds served in their plumage, or subtleties which had taken days to prepare; but there was a roe broth, eels in brewet, a caudle of salmon, double-roasts, capon pasties, coffins, and crustards, pain-puffs, and cheeses. The food stuck in Mowbray's throat, but he drank deeply of the red wine of Gascony, wishing all the time that this age-long meal would end, wondering why FitzHugh had not returned from his errand.

Then, suddenly, FitzHugh was with them again, nodding at Westmoreland. The fear that wine had dulled leaped up again; Mowbray stumbled to his feet, knocking over his cup. Someone gripped his arm, too tightly for mere support. He tried to break away, and saw Westmoreland lay his hand on the Archbishop's shoulder.

'My lord Archbishop,' said Ralph Neville, in a conversational tone, 'you are my prisoner!'

The Archbishop sat like a stone, incredulity and outrage in his countenance. Mowbray screamed at him: 'I told you, I told you, and you would not heed! God forgive it you, you have led me to my death!'

The Archbishop looked gravely at him, but said only: 'My son!' Mowbray gave a sob; and the Archbishop turned to Ralph Neville. 'Take your impious hand from my shoulder!' he commanded. 'You have placed your soul in peril by this deed! You are mainsworn and recreant! I came, and these lords with me, trusting to your knightly faith!'

'So went the King, my father, into Wales!' said John.

'Take heed what you do, my son!' Scrope warned him. 'As you have sown, so shall you reap!'

'So be it!' John said. 'I am content.'

6 Scrope's Bane

I

They sent the rebel leaders to Pontefract, in FitzHugh's charge. No attempt was made to rescue them, for the Archbishop had rightly judged the humour of his followers: they were blithe to be dispersed, since there was work to be done on the farms, and most men knew that those who rebelled against the King rarely prospered. FitzHugh had done his work well, and as fast as the Archbishop's force diminished Neville's men seemed to spring from the soil. By nightfall only a remnant of the insurgent army remained, and when these few knew what had befallen they melted away, until only the King's men were left on the ground.

Before FitzHugh had left the camp with his prisoners, Lancaster Herald arrived with letters from the King. No sooner had he received the news of the northern rising than King Henry had left Worcester, and had led his own small army to Derby, by forced marches. He had been there when he wrote to John, in energetic language. He had sent orders to the Council to meet him at Pontefract, with array; he expected to be at Nottingham by the end of the month; and would reach Pontefract by June 3rd at latest.

These were heartening tidings; and there was nothing in the King's letter, or in his rapid movements, to suggest that he was enjoying anything but excellent health. Lancaster Herald told the Lord John that he was in good point, but much araged; and the Lord John, knowing his father's temper, was glad that his duty led him not to Pontefract, but to Durham, there to await Northumberland's onset.

But my lord of Northumberland had not found it as easy to raise the North as he had expected. The very men who had grutched most at John's rule hung back. Not only were the

Scots ravaging the Border, but the Northumbrians, turning the matter over in their slow minds, had seen long labour and little winning in their liege-lord's demands. It was one thing to behave churlishly to the Lord John: quite another to rise in open rebellion against the King's grace. Many men discovered virtues in the Lord John which they had not previously perceived. He was a jolly princeling, and full of hardiment; not stomachy, like my lord of Northumberland, nor yet one with whom you could take liberties. Moreover, it was he, not Percy, who had advised remittance of taxation, and that was an argument so cogent that the better part of Northumberland's force was composed of men who came reluctantly to the muster. By the time he was ready to cross the Tyne it was too late: Ralph Neville had wrenched the linch-pin out of the wheel of revolt at Shipton Moor. Northumberland turned north, and sought refuge, with the Lord Bardolph, in Berwick, whence he sent urgent messages to the Scots. He sent also to Scotland his young grandson, Henry Percy, for safety; and had anything been needed to convince his lieges that his cause was lost this action supplied it. A contingent of Scots sent by King Robert's brother, the Duke of Albany, joined him in Berwick, to the dismay of the Mayor and the citizens; and all along the Border beacons flickered, and fierce fighting broke out wherever other and larger contingents crossed it to plunder, and burn, and slay.

Left to himself, the Lord John would have marched north, but Ralph Neville's hand was on his bridle, and Ralph said: 'Wait!'

He was right, of course: until the King's powerful levies stood squarely behind them it would be fatal to expose their small force to the allied menace of Percy and Albany. 'Look you, John!' Ralph Neville said roughly. 'This is *my* country, and no man on life hates the Scots more than I do, but I do not budge until I have the King's command! And I will tell you this, boy! There shall come good out of this garboil! The Scots in Berwick, and from there to Solway there's not a man that doesn't know it was Percy who called them in! Never again will they be so blithe to serve him!'

So they waited in Durham, but not for many days. Sir Thomas

Swynford came from Pontefract, bearing the King's commands. He brought also an order for John to seize all Northumberland's castles; and reading this John said a little dryly: 'I shall do my power!' This, he thought, would be small enough: he had received such orders before, and had suffered the humiliation of being unable to enforce them. He was better pleased with the authority conferred upon him to pardon where he saw fit. That was good: there was no profit in hanging redeless men who had done no more than obey their liege-lord. He put the order aside, and demanded news of Sir Thomas.

It was so startling that it brought his brows snapping together above the bridge of his arched nose. The King, said Sir Thomas, quite matter-of-factly, was carrying Scrope and Mowbray to Bishopsthorpe, where they would both be headed.

Ralph Neville gasped like a man ducked in cold water. He said, in a stupefied voice: 'Head the *Archbishop*?'

'The King is much araged,' explained Sir Thomas, draining his cup. 'He has sworn to wipe York from the face of the earth if the citizens resist him more.'

Ralph signed himself involuntarily; but John said: 'Yea, so he says in his rage. But who is to try the Archbishop?'

'There is a commission set up to try all the rebels, my lord. My brother Beaufort – Thomas – heads it, and has with him my lord of Arundel, Lord Grey of Codnor, Sir John Stanley, and others.'

'Gascoigne?' John asked shrewdly.

'Well, yes!' Swynford said. 'You may say he stands on the commission, but these lawyers – ! He has told the King's grace that he has no jurisdiction over spiritual persons, and may not try the Archbishop. That casts a little rub in the way, but it will be amended: with Thomas Beaufort in command you may count the Archbishop dead already.'

'God assoil him! He is a traitor, but – but he is Archbishop of York!' Ralph Neville said.

'For my part,' said Swynford, 'I think the King does well to send him to the deathward.'

'It is a fearful thing!' Neville muttered.

'Dreadless! And for that reason men will fear the King's

wrath the more! It will do more good to head the Archbishop than to send a score of lesser men to the long-going.'

He said this not despitously, but in a thoughtful tone. John saw the great keep of Pontefract, as it had first appeared to him, a sour yellow pile, massive with doom. Within its walls King Richard had died, by what means perhaps only three men knew. One of them was before him now: a blunt man, but passing honest. Kindly too, like Dame Katherine, his mother. When they had been children, he and Harry and Thomas had liked him more than their Beaufort uncles, her sons by Bel sire, because he was good-natured, and had often played with them. Once he had picked Humfrey up after a tumble, and stuffed his mouth with sugar-plums to check a howl of dismay, coaxing away his fright. It seemed impossible that he could now be saying, in that cool voice, that it would do good to head the Archbishop; almost as impossible as that his square, capable hands had been stained once with a King's blood. But perhaps they had not been: that was something one would never know.

Ralph Neville was asking Swynford for the story of what had happened at Pontefract. Swynford said that the Archbishop had gone to meet the King at his entry to the castle grounds, taking his crozier in his hand, no one liking to prevent him. That, said Swynford, had been too much for Thomas Beaufort, tired from a long day in the saddle under a sweltering sun. At sight of the Archbishop advancing in such saintly wise, his wrath boiled up within him, and a rather distressing scene had been the outcome. Sir Thomas voided his horse, and shouting at the Archbishop that he was a traitor, unworthy to bear the crozier, wrenched it out of his hands. There had been a most unseemly struggle, but the younger man had won. Then the Archbishop had knelt on the ground as the King rode up, and cried aloud for pardon; but the King ordered him back, giving him only bitter words, and commanding his warders to take him away, and confine him straitly.

'And the King bade me tell you, Sir John, and you too, my lord, that he is well content with the service you have rendered him, and will tell you so with his own lips when he comes to chastise these northern rebels.'

'Well,' Ralph said heavily, refilling the cups, 'if he is content I am apaid, though I did not think, when I set my hand on Scrope's shoulder, that it would end thus.'

'By my head, you did well!' Swynford said. 'Myself, I thought we had come to neck-break when we learned in Worcester what was abrewing here. If you had let Percy join Scrope and Mowbray, Glendower and Mortimer would have been over Severn at this hour, set on realm-rape! Jesu! No man can say what might have been the issue, but I can tell you that we thought ourselves as good as shent!'

'And now?' John interrupted. 'What does Glendower do in this pass? What of Marck?'

'Marck was relieved last month, lording, and that bretheling Count of St Pol given such a buffet as he will not speedily forget. As for Glendower, you know his use! When things go awry, he bolts for the mountains.' He lifted his cup, and nodded to John over its rim. 'The Scots shall know Prince Hal before they are much older!' he said, with a smile.

John jumped, and exclaimed: 'Harry? Coming here?'

'I promise you!' Swynford said, toasting the event.

2

The Archbishop, the Earl of Nottingham, and Sir William Plumpton were all headed on the eighth day of June. The accounts received by John, north of the Tyne, were conflicting, but he gathered from them that not even the King's dearest friend, Archbishop Arundel, had been able to save his brother in Christ from the axe. The King had reached Bishopsthorpe on the eve of Whit Sunday, and from out the town of York the citizens had streamed to meet him, clad in rags, and with halters about their necks, imploring mercy. He had railed at them, and sent them back to their homes, threatening them with dire punishments. John did not think that anything much would come of that: it would be unlike his father to wreak vengeance on redeless folk. He would not have been surprised to have heard that the King had pardoned Scrope, when his rage had cooled, but this did not happen. From all John could glean from the lips of those messengers who passed between Bishopsthorpe and Newcastle, he could only be glad that his father had laid upon his shoulders a task which made it necessary for him to remain on the northern side of the Tyne. He and Ralph Neville, as Constable and Marshal, should both have been at Bishopsthorpe to receive the condemned traitors from the hands of the commission, but the King appointed the Earl of Arundel and Sir Thomas Beaufort to be their deputies. Ralph Neville had had the ordering of more than one execution, but he confided to John that he would as lief have nothing to do with this one. John had held the office of Constable for nearly two years, but he had not yet been called upon to perform that one of its duties. Ralph, knowing this, said, 'And I am right glad you are not to mell yourself in the business, John. Yes, yes, I know you would have done it, but it would have been a displeasant task, and to be conducting an anointed priest to the scaffold is not what I would choose for you. Not with the cradle-straws scarce out of your breech!'

The Archbishop made a good end, hustled to it, it was whispered, after the briefest of trials. The Lord Chief Justice had passed sentences on Mowbray and on Sir William Plumpton; but after that he had left the hall, and a mere knight, commissioned by the King, had taken his place. The doom had been pronounced while the King sat at breakfast with Archbishop Arundel, and the condemned were taken straightway to York, and headed while Arundel was still urging the King to leave Scrope to the judgment of Rome. He had reached Bishopsthorpe very early, before the King had risen from his bed, and had sought instant audience with him. He had not rested for as much as an hour on his ride from London. He was almost forspent, his face grey with fatigue, his legs unsteady, and his throat choked with dust; and the King, distressed to see him in such a plight, coaxed him to rest, soothing him with fair words, promising to listen to him presently.

'And so he did,' Thomas Beaufort later told John, 'but we had made an end by then, and well for us we did! The things Arundel said to your father! But he bore all with patience. As God sees me, John, I know not why your father loves that man so dearly!'

'No. But did Arundel— Are they estranged?'

'Nay, the love between them is too great. Arundel cried out that the deed would be the King's bane, and fell to weeping that he was aweary of his life, and so the King comforted him, and they embraced, and the King promised that Scrope should be honourably interred. Which was done,' Sir Thomas added. 'That eased Arundel's mind, but we always meant to give Scrope decent burial. I don't grudge it to him: he made a good end. He went to his death as merry as you please – too merry, Stanley thought, for a priest, for he jested with the King's physician, telling him he should need no physic from him again. He bade him come to watch how he should die, too, but it's my belief he was only merry to put some heart into young Mowbray. He kept on telling him to be of good cheer, but he might as well have saved his breath for his prayers. Corpus bones! If ever I met such a malten-hearted sprig of treachery! You'll see his head on Bootham Bar what's like to be left of it by the time you come to York again.'

'Gramercy! The only head I want to see there is Percy's!' said John tartly.

Sir Thomas roared with laughter, and bade him be patient a while yet.

He had need of patience. All he could do until the King came in force to Northumberland was to take possession of such of the Percy castles as offered little or no resistance. Prudhoe, lying a few leagues to the west of Newcastle, surrendered to him, but against the great holds of Alnwick and Warkworth he was prohibited from venturing. He knew it would have been sleeveless to have done so without an army at his back and siege-engines at his disposal. Meanwhile, Berwick was held by the Scots, and however ruinous its defences might be it could not be taken by the handful of men John had with him.

King Henry had sent him word that he would march north immediately, and so indeed he did, taking the road to Borough-bridge. The next tidings John received came from Ripon, and were brought to him by a scared groom of the chamber, who seemed to think that some danger lurked behind his shoulder. He shivered a good deal, and kept on looking round, and signing himself when he thought John was not watching him.

No, he said, the King's grace had not reached Boroughbridge. They had encountered wild weather: a buffeting wind, and rain driven in their faces till they were blinded by it: a ferly thing to happen at this season!

'William Thorpe, a sudden storm is not a ferly thing, even at midsummer,' John said. 'If you are trying to tell me that the King caught cold upon his ride, do so, and leave signing yourself!'

The man coloured, and looked away, but said in an uncertain tone: 'It was not that, my lord. They say – they say the King is sick of the Great Malady!'

'The Great Malady! Liar, and son of a liar!'

'My lord, my lord!' Thorpe stammered, cringing from the very real menace that loomed suddenly before him. 'The white-leprey – the serpent-leprey – they say!'

'Who says?'

Thorpe winced, as though the words had been hammer-blows, and shook his head, quaking.

'Scullions' talk!' John said. 'Get up off your knees and tell me the whole!'

'Someone struck the King!' Thorpe said, his tongue stumbling. 'Riding across the moor, in the rain – a great blow, he said!'

'Someone struck the King?' John repeated, frowning down into the pallid face. 'Who dared do such a thing? Do you mean that he was wounded?'

'Nay, lord, nay! How might that be? There was only Sir Peter Buckton riding beside him. But the King cried out that someone had dealt him a buffet!'

'For Christ's sweet Tree, will you stop shaking and maffling like the nithing you are?' John said wrathfully. 'A squall of wind, and the King thought he had been buffeted! Yea, I too have ridden the moors in stormy weather! What then? Did the King fall into an accesse – like you?'

'No, lord,' Thorpe muttered. 'But the storm not abating we drew rein at Green Hammerton, and there rested for the night.' He paused, but upon being told sharply to continue, said in a voice which he tried to make matter-of-fact: 'At nightertale, at

277

two of the bell, the King awoke, crying that he was being consumed by fire.'

'A wan-dream!' John said, himself rather pale.

Thorpe passed his tongue between his lips. 'So we thought, my lord, but could not soothe him. My lord, my lord, the King writhed in great anguish, crying all the time, "I burn, I burn!" Wilkin, who slept that night at his door, fetched Master Grisby to him, and he gave him to drink of some dwale, and presently he slept again. In the morning it was seen that he was sore-stricken, but he would mount him, and press on. We led him to Ripon, lord, and there he lies, sick unto death!' He covered his face with his hands, and broke into weeping, squatting on his haunches, and rocking himself to and fro, uttering disjointedly: 'Botches and whelks! On his cheeks! Such grisly sores as— Ah, Jesu, mercy! My most dear master! They are saying – they are saying the Archbishop's bane has fallen upon him!'

There was a creeping horror in the room. John's hand went to his breast, as though he too would have signed himself to avert the evil, but it clenched suddenly, and fell again to his side. It was a moment or two before he could trust his voice, but when at last he spoke it was calmly, even coldly. 'Up!' he commanded. 'The King has suffered this ill once and twice before. When you reach Ripon again you will find him amended. Look on my face! Do you see a whelk or a push there? Answer!'

'No, lord, no!'

'You will see none on my lord of Westmoreland's face either! If any should speak to you of the Archbishop's bane, tell them that we, on whom his death lies heaviest, are clean of flesh and hale of body! Go now! Eat and rest! I will give you letters presently to take to the King's grace. But I think I shall kiss his hand ere many days.'

3

He spoke the words boldly, but with doubt in his heart, yet they proved true words. For seven days the King lay at Ripon, while his physicans wrought and quarrelled over his suffering body, but it was seen that he was not so ill that he could not manage his affairs. Commands reached the Sheriff of Yorkshire to

278

assemble his levies, and to await the King at Newcastle; and hardly had they been quartered in and about the town than a thousand Kentish archers were reported to be within a day's march of the Tyne. These picked men, despising everything and everyone encountered north of Thames, grinned cheerfully upon the Lord John's officers, grutched unstintingly at their rations, their quarters, and the officers who had brought them by forced marches the length of the country; and squared up like gamecocks at every northerner hardy enough to approach them. They were full of japes and bobance, quarrelsome, impudent, and wholly to be trusted. They had orders for Berwick, and the sooner they seized that town, wherever it might be, the sooner they would return to their civilized south country. They were quite unimpressed by the Archbishop's bane. The only Archbishop they cared about was Arundel, and no one had headed him. As for the King's sickness, who could wonder that he should fall ill in this meedless land of dennocks and drammocks? Anyone knew what all this nasty oatmeal would do to a man: without guess the King was sick of a ventosity, or even, perhaps, the flux. Let them give him wholesome food, and he would soon be amended!

Whatever had been the cause of the King's illness, his recovery was rapid. By the 19th of June he was at Durham; and two days later he rode into Newcastle. He received a great welcome there, for one of his first acts as King had been to raise the town to the level of London, and York, and Bristol, and his citizens had not swerved in their loyalty to him. He looked worn, and there were a few lingering scabs to be seen on his face, but he seemed to be in good spirits, and full of his old energy.

He told John that his physicans believed that the eruptions which had broken out over his body were due to a thickening of the blood. He was being careful not to eat any of the things which were known to thicken the blood, particularly cabbage, a melancholy vegetable. Of his terrible dream he spoke not at all, nor did John question him. It was thrust aside, with that strange visitation. 'I have no time to cosset myself,' the King said.

He thought that the Welsh danger was averted, but not ended. They would not move in force against him until their

French allies came to join them, but he believed that the French fleet must set sail before the summer waned. A rapid campaign in the North was all that he could allow himself before returning to the West. 'The chief holds I will reduce, and the rest I must leave to you, John,' he said.

'With what troops, and with what provisions, sir?'

'I will do what I may. If it is not much you must contrive! Percy's lands, and Bardolph's too, I have confiscated, and I shall bestow the grants on you, for your maintenance. It is of no avail to ask me for money! This garboil has plunged me deep in debt already, and there is still the Welsh campaign to be paid for.'

'And the Scots?' asked John. 'Are they to be permitted to make Berwick their own, and to lay waste all the country within its reach?'

'No, no, why ask such a witless question?' the King said testily. 'They must be driven out, and taught a lesson they will remember! Harry shall attend to that: it is the sort of work he likes. He does it very well. Of course, he has had experience of such warfare.'

4

It was not until July that Harry reached Northumberland, and by that time John was engaged on the first of the tasks at which, all his life, he was to excel: the pacification and the government of a troubled land. Perceiving in his third son this talent for administration, King Henry had bestowed wide powers on him, leaving it to him to seize recalcitrant peles, punish transgressors, pardon penitents, appoint new officers, and negotiate truces. John would have preferred to have gone with the royal army to besiege Berwick, but he knew that he was of more worth to his father in another capacity than that of a soldier in the field. Someone must bring order to this disturbed country, and no one was so fit to do this as himself. He accepted the commission without demur, installed himself at Prudhoe, and from that base swept up the southern and western parts of Northumberland. He demanded Gilbert Umfraville for his lieutenant, picked up a steward for his household in one place, a marshal in another; stuffed the castle with clerks and secretaries to deal with the mass of documents which began to accumulate, and grappled with labour that might well have appalled him. North-eastward, Warkworth, which had capitulated after the seventh shot from King Henry's great gun, was under his general juris-diction, but had been given into the particular care of Sir Robert Umfraville, who had installed as his lieutenant one of his most devoted servants. The choice was a happy one. John Hardyng was not only a witty, lettered man: he had been bred up in Hotspur's household, and was wise in the Percy way of govern-ment. He could be counted on to tread on no man's corns unwarely. He had already discovered much treasonable matter hidden away in the castle, and had sent it off to the King, encamped before Berwick. He told John that there was enough in the bundle to send Northumberland to the long-going, but it seemed as unlikely as ever that Northumberland would so end his days. At the King's approach, he and Bardolph had fled into Scotland. He left to the King's mercy, besides his lieges, a host of remote kinsmen, and a grandson, the sole offspring of his dead son Thomas. This hapless young man was under orders to hold Alnwick against the King, but whether he would make the attempt was as yet unknown, and might depend, John thought, on the conduct of Sir William Clifford, under similar orders in Berwick Castle. It seemed unlikely that Clifford would make more than a token resistance, for the Scots, before follow-ing Northumberland across the Border, had fired the town, and the feeling of the citizens would not give the Captain of the castle encouragement to uphold Percy's cause.

Meanwhile, at Prudhoe, John was making steady, unspecta-cular progress in the work which Gilbert, hankering after deeds of glory, thought importably tedious. He was winning worship too, for it was soon seen that although he was determined to bring a rugged people under rule his disposition was not ven-geable. Those who sued for pardon received it; and the penalties he imposed were seldom heavy ones. The hard apprenticeship he had served had given him strength and authority; there was no mistaking him for other than he was: a King's son, and a ruler; but he had an endearing way of seeming to know who quite insignificant persons were, where they came from, and to whom they were related. Often he did know, for he never forgot a name or a face; and more than one country squire, meeting him for the first time, was surprised and gratified to hear his name repeated, and the Lord John say: 'I should know that name! You wore my elder-father's livery, I think.'

More and more persons, coming to swear renewed fealty, or to transact business, climbed the long paved passage from the outer gate to the main gatehouse of little Prudhoe, perched like an eagle's eyrie on a steep promontory. Everyone told John that the castle was not large enough for his growing needs, but he liked it, and would not willingly leave it for the more modern and far more commodious castle of Warkworth. To the north it looked across the Tyne, sixty feet below the escarpment, to the arable lands on the farther bank; to the south and east it was separated from woodland by a deep ravine; and within its walls there was a turreted keep, one or two smaller towers, and an orchard. There was a tiny chapel, approached by an outer stair which gave access also to the rooms John appropriated to his own use. Father Matthew was much pleased with this. It had a small oriel window – quite the oldest in the country, he thought – projecting on corbels. He was for ever asking Gilbert questions about the castle, because, until it passed through marriage into Percy hands, it had been an important Umfraville hold. But all Gilbert knew about it was that in older and rougher times they used to incarcerate prisoners in its dungeon, because it was a stronger place than Harbottle.

'And you are right welcome to it!' he told John. 'I would live at Warkworth, if I were you. Every time it rains here you have to void your horse at the outer gate for fear he should come down with you on those slippery stones in the passage! Besides, it's too small, and old-fashioned: you couldn't entertain persons of worship in it!'

But within a day of this pronouncement John was entertaining a person of great worship, who arrived unexpectedly, clattered up the paved and embattled slope to the main gatehouse at the head of a small escort, and threw the household into a flutter of excitement.

John was dictating a letter to one of his secretaries in the solar.

He heard the sounds of an arrival, but paid no heed to it until the noise of some unusual bustle below in the bailey made him break off in the middle of a sentence, and say angrily: 'A'God's half, why all this garboil?'

'The Fierce Fenwicks are upon us, no charge!' Gilbert said, sprawling amongst the rushes with the dog Butcher, whom he was lazily teasing.

Then there was a springing step on the stair, and Gilbert turned his head to see on the threshold a young man in a stained leather jerkin, and dusty buskins. John gave a great shout, and strode forward. 'Harry!'

'I might have known you would choose an eyrie to live in!' Harry said, gripping John's shoulders, and kissing his cheek.

Butcher, unused to such a sight, lunged to his master's rescue. Gilbert had scrambled to his feet, and caught him, but pandemonium at once broke out, for although the dog could be held he could not for several moments be cuffed and cursed into silence.

'Well, of all the churlish hounds!' said Harry, when the furious barking had subsided into blood-curdling growls. 'What creatures you do cosset, brother! The last time I saw you you had a half-manned hawk that bated whenever I came near you.' He glanced at the table, with its litter of papers. 'What are you doing here, John?'

'Jack-raking!' John replied, signing to the secretary to take his hound away.

'Ah!' Harry said thoughtfully. 'Yes, that has to be done, of course.' His eyes rested enquiringly on Gilbert, and when John presented his friend he smiled, and said: 'Are you my brother's lieutenant? He has spoken to me of you.'

'My pledge-borrow,' said John, betraying his knowledge of Gilbert's appointed task. 'But he would liefer go with you to win his spurs.'

'Yea? How many years have you in your dish?' Harry asked.

'Fifteen, my lord!' Gilbert said, a wild hope in his breast. He saw the quizzical gleam in John's eye, and reddened, adding: 'In two weeks – only two weeks, my lord!'

But Harry laughed, and shook his head. 'Nay, what would Sir

Robert say? Stay with my brother until you have your uncle's leave to join me.'

There was disappointment in Gilbert's face, but his eyes, as he raised them to Harry's, glowed shyly. John saw that Harry, with one friendly smile, had cast his spell over him. He nodded him away, looking kindly after him, a little amused.

'Oof!' said Harry, throwing himself on to the banker and stretching his limbs with a sigh of relief. 'I've been in the saddle for days!'

'Will you rest here?'

'No, I must push on. I've set my men on the road to Berwick. I wanted to have speech with you.'

'Well?' John said.

'John, how came it about that Scrope and Mowbray were taken without one blow struck?'

'They were taken under a flag of truce,' John replied.

It was like the flicker of lightning, that look of Harry's. John's eyelids quivered, but he kept his gaze on Harry's face.

'So they told me! But I would not believe!' John said nothing. 'John, how could you do so black a thing?'

'There was a blacker thing I could not do.'

'You have stained your knighthood!'

John was very pale, but he answered steadily: 'It is well-worth, since you are here to tell me so.'

He words fell heavily, and were not immediately answered. Harry's fierce eyes stared up at him; he said, after a moment: 'For my sake, this deed? For *my* sake?'

'For your sake, and all our sakes.'

Harry flung out a hand, as though to thrust the thought away. 'No! Not unfaith!'

'Content you, never to you! You bade me hold the North for you, and it is held.'

'Holy Rood, did I bid you use such arts as those?'

'You didn't know, Harry, nor I, indeed, that it would come to this: that I must betray you or our enemies.'

'Not betrayal of me, to keep your knightly faith!'

'Not betrayal, to have the means to save you from neck-break, and to put them from me? God shield you, Harry, do you rate

284

my love so low? There was no other way – or if there was I did not see it.'

There was a strange, haggard look in Harry's face. He sprang up, and lunged away to the window, muttering: 'This throne, this throne! Jesu defend!'

John was silent. Presently Harry said, in a cold voice: 'Was it your stratagem?'

'No, but I might have said the nayword, and did not. I think I should have hurled our little force against the rebels. We should have been shent, and you too, but you would have had time to mourn me, perhaps – a stainless knight!'

Harry's face softened, but he said: 'Did you know, when you suffered it to be done, that you were sending them to a shames-death?'

'Mowbray, yes. Not the Archbishop. But if I had known I should not have said the nayword. Saving only your anger, Harry, I've no gainbite at my heart – and your anger I knew I should win me!'

'Sturdy words, brother!'

'Yea, I will utter no leasings to you.'

Harry passed a hand across his brow. 'It was Neville's rede, I suppose. You couldn't have prevented him.'

'No, I think I could not,' John agreed, a smile in his eyes. He did not add that he had not made the attempt, because he saw that Harry was going to believe what he must, for the easement of his unquiet soul. So it had been when King Richard had died; so it would be many times again. The world might see only Harry's strength, but John knew his weakness, and loved him the more.

'What task are you set, Harry?' he asked after a pause, and in a lighter voice.

Harry glanced at him, still frowning. 'Chastisement. To give the Scots to drink of their own medicine. I don't like rapine, but I shall be blithe to carry fire across the Border: I hate the Scots!'

'Out and alas! They will say you have broken the truce!'

Harry stared at him. '*I* break the truce? God's dignity, what did the Scots, then, when they seized Berwick, and laid waste this country of yours?'

'But they will still call you a truce-breaker,' John said.

'They may hang in hell! What I shall do will be for right and justice!'

'Witterly!' John said, laughing at him. 'What you shall do will always be for right and justice, Harry.'

'Do you doubt me?' demanded Harry, strongly grasping his hands.

'No, not I! Don't set me out of your grace! Will you dine now?'

The grip tightened on his hands. 'John, are you shriven?'

'Yea, I am assoiled.'

'Yet you could say to me that you feel no gainbite? Was it so small a thing to do? So easy a thing?'

'No,' John answered, meeting his look. 'I thought there was only one thing more evil that I could do.'

'Yes. I see,' Harry said, quite gently. 'There's no more to say. The evil lies at Ralph's door. At his, and at—' He stopped, and then said, 'Let it sleep! Take me to dinner: I mustn't linger. Can it be done speedily, my task? I don't know this country, and I must be back on my own Marches before the month is out.'

They went out together on to the stair, and stood for a moment, dazzled by the hot sunlight. 'Do you think the French will come, then?' John asked.

'Yes, and I must be there to welcome them! If I had Edward —' He looked back over his shoulder, as he went down the stairs, his face suddenly softened in laughter. 'John, Edward is writing a book!'

'*Edward* writing a book? Harry, you losel!'

'No, by the faith of my body! I've had word from Pevensey now and now. He fell into great dis-ease, poor Edward, when the King would not answer his petition, but he has a kind gaoler, and is now amended. He must be, if he has taken on him such a task!'

'For God's bane, not more poems to the Queen's grace?' John said.

'No! He's not so wood!'

'Harry, Edward *could* not write a book!' John protested. 'It's all leasings! What could he write of?'

'Lurdan!' Harry tossed at him. 'Of the chase, no force!'

That made John laugh so much that he nearly missed his footing on the stair. 'Oh, does Father know?'

'Nay, it would be daffish to speak of Edward to him at this present. Trust me, I'll have him back on the Marches before Allhallowmas!'

'Will you?' John said doubtfully.

'I must! He sends me word it is for *me*, his great book!'

5

By July 12th Berwick had fallen; and two days later Sir Henry Percy surrendered Alnwick to the King. On July 16th the King was at Newcastle again, transacting business with John with the same nervous energy which had carried him through his campaign. He wore a sterner expression than John had ever seen on his face, but it seemed that with the death of Scrope his rage had burnt itself out. In the one day he spent at Newcastle he signed pardons flock-meal. Very few executions were ordered; and when, three days later at Raby, he signed some death warrants, provision was made for the dependants of the condemned. Confiscations were decided upon at Pontefract, whither he carried John, and kept him for four days crammed to overflowing with business. Following Westminster Law, he was able to reward the faithful out of the confiscated estates, and to make provision for his younger sons. But several manors had to be apportioned to the Queen; and one, from Mowbray's estates near Baldock, he granted to Sir John Cornwall. Something, he told John, must be done to ease his sister Bess of her displeasure: she had not ceased to bewail her son-in-law Mowbray's death since the news of it had reached her.

John did not see Harry again until they met at Eltham Palace at Yule-tide. At the head of the King's force, he swept like a flame through Lauderdale, and Teviotdale, and Ettrick Forest, plundering and burning, until on either side of the Border the land was smouldering. He was gone again before the fires were quenched; and was back on the Welsh Marches when, early in August, the Lord of Hugueville reached Milford Haven with a

287

hundred and twenty vessels, battered by storms, but carrying a formidable host. They were met by Glendower, with a large force; and the two armies moved on Haverfordwest. Failing to reduce the castle, which was held by a little Flemish colony, staunch for the King, they descended on Tenby, leaving a trail of rapine in their wake. But here they were met by ill tidings. The Lord Berkeley, detached by Thomas with the Western Fleet, had sailed into the harbour and destroyed fifteen of their ships. The Welsh drew off immediately; the French, lacking the horses which had perished on the voyage, mistrustful alike of their allies and of a land strange to them, were only with difficulty held from following the retreat. The force was got together again, and besieged Carmarthen; and by the time the King arrived from the North with the reinforcements Harry so urgently needed, all Glamorganshire was over-run, and the invaders were within ten miles of Worcester.

Far to the north, in his own troubled country, John got scant news of the fighting which drove the French out of Wales, and had little leisure to attend to it. All along his own Border a destructive warfare raged. Truces were ignored; on both sides of the Tweed no man dared pasture his cattle, or put off his harness to work in the fields; and the Scots, the stronger at sea as they were on land, patrolled the coast from Tweed to Tyne. Disaffection was rife in Berwick, where the pay of the garrison was six months in arrears; no provisions could reach Fastcastle, and the castles of Scarborough, Whitby, and Hartlepool defied the royal mandate. John was too weak to enforce the mandate; though he pledged his plate and his jewels he could not make good the deficiences in pay and stores; and letter after letter sent by him to the Council, telling of the desperate need of siege-guns and ammunition, urging that the levies of York-shire and Lancashire should be sent to his aid, met with little or no response. He wanted to be granted the means to wage a winter war across the Border, but this was a revolutionary scheme that found no favour at Westminster.

He was before Scarborough when the news was brought to him from York that great crowds were assembling day after day to worship at Scrope's tomb. He sent an order for the dispersal of such false fools, and decreed that stones should be piled up between the pillars of the parclose, to shut the tomb from sight. He heard next that there had been brawling in the cathedral, and that the dead Archbishop had appeared in a vision to an old man, who had straightway removed all the stones in a single night. There was talk of miracles; the See stood vacant; and every day John expected to hear that the crowning disaster of excommunication had befallen them.

It was prepared, and the document even sent to England, but it was never published. Archbishop Arundel, shaken and sick in heart and body, was still the King's friend.

Winter brought an uneasy peace to the North. When the snow covered the Cheviots, the truce was remembered. The Lord John rode south through a landscape shivering under bitter winds, leaving behind him a country torn and blackened by the raids that had swept over it, many of its people ruined, all of them exhausted. His mood was as bleak as the moors which loomed against a grey sky, for it seemed as though nothing had been accomplished, as though nothing would ever be accomplished, even though he was pushing south to confront the Council in person, and to fling before them not entreaties but demands.

It was quite a little thing that gave his thoughts a turn, nothing more than a knot of men gaping unrecognizingly at him as he rode through a Midland village. He had raised his hand instinctively to acknowledge a greeting, but they did not know him, they gave no sign. He rode on, his heart suddenly lighter. They would have had a greeting for him in the dour North. He had been too preoccupied to notice the change in his people, too conscious of his own impotence to drive out the enemy who preyed on them; but it came to him all at once that he needed no pledge-borrow now when he went amongst them. There were rebel castles which still held against him; there were underpaid garrisons which threatened to leave their posts; but he no longer met ill-will. In a hundred little ways, often rude, often grutching, his people had been showing him that they did not blame him for the disasters that had befallen them, or even for the failures which lay like a load on his mind. They would rally to him when he called upon them; they believed that he would win help for them in London; next year, they said, all would be amended.

His controller, riding beside him, pointed to a rift in the clouds, and said: 'Better weather ahead, my lord!'

'Yes,' he answered, lifting his chin. 'God willing!'

Part Four
Prince Excellent
1410–1413

Of his stature he was of evene lengthe,
And wonderly deliver, and greet of strength.

Chaucer

1 Looking Back

1

The Lord John was riding down Ludgate Hill, on his way back
to Westminster from the Elms, at Smithfield, attended only by a
squire, who rode at a discreet distance behind him, wondering
what he was thinking of the events of the day. It wasn't the sort
of question one could ask him; and one couldn't read the answer
in his face. He was looking stern; but he often did so, until
something happened to bring his mind away from whatever
problem had been occupying it. He had paused by St Nicholas's
shambles, where the bladesmiths had stalls; and he had spent
some time inspecting pike-heads, and blades for pole-axes, and
talking to one of the master-bladesmiths about the harm that
had been done to the craft by the malpractices of the foreigners,
who until quite recently had been allowed to flood the market
with swords and points not hard enough to bear the assay. The
squire had held his hackney, fidgeting a little, while this dull
talk continued. He wanted to get back to Westminster Palace,
not only because he had made his own arrangements for the rest
of the day, but because he was almost bursting with the story he
had to tell his friends there. He couldn't understand how the
Lord John found it possible, after what he had been doing, to
become absorbed in such humdrum matters as pike-heads; or,
indeed, why he should choose to dismount to buy himself a
dagger at a street-stall, as though he had been a common person.
It didn't occur to him that the Lord John had done this because
he needed, at that moment, some ordinary, everyday occupation
to bring his life back to normal.

John rode with a slack rein, allowing his horse to walk. The
street was crowded, but way would have been made for him,
had he wished to press forward. Everyone knew him, and at a
glance, no matter how simply dressed he might be, or how

sparsely attended. He was nearly twenty now, and had attained his full height, which was much above the average. He had big, powerful limbs, too, and a hawk-nose there was no mistaking. All the way from Smithfield there had been a doffing of hoods, and an occasional shout of 'Noël!' from an apprentice, or a streethawker. He acknowledged these salutes with a nod, or a lifted hand, but his thoughts were otherwhere.

It had been an unpleasant day. He hadn't expected to enjoy it, but he hadn't expected to be pitchforked into so grim a scene. There had been the chance that the heretic would recant when he was confronted with the stake: all the other Lollards with whom, as High Constable, he had been concerned, had done so: this had been the first actual burning over which he had presided. He had been warned that Badby was likely to prove obdurate, but he had not foreseen that Harry would turn the whole business into a nightmare. When Harry had told him that he had been asked to be present, he had thought very little about it. He knew that Harry could watch with an unmoved countenance the struggles of a soldier he had himself condemned to be hanged; he had supposed that Harry would not be much affected by the burning of a Lollard. He hadn't remembered that a man with a halter choking the life out of him made very little noise. It was otherwise with men burning to death. Probably that was what had upset Harry, though he himself denied it, saying, with his head sunk in his hands, and his fingers writhing amongst his thick locks: 'How could so brave a man be damned in heresy? How *could* he?'

Strange that Harry, a stricter churchman than any of his brothers, should not have realized that that bravery came not from God but from the devil! Perhaps Dean Courtenay, who loved him, would be able to show him the truth, and bring ease to his troubled soul. John had left him with Courtenay, thankful for only one circumstance; that it had been Courtenay, not one of Archbishop Arundel's adherents, who had been at the Elms this day. Not but what Arundel would be araged when he learned what Harry had done. One couldn't blame him, either. Harry had not meant it so, but it must seem to Arundel importable presumption, to have imagined that he could succeed,

294

where Holy Church, wrestling for more than a year for the soul of John Badby, had failed. Arundel would never understand that Harry had acted on the impulse of his heart: the rift between them was too wide; neither would ever perceive the good in the other. They were at open variance at the moment, too, which made it the more unfortunate. Since he had rendered up the Great Seal, at the end of last year, when they had all feared that the King would part his life, Arundel had not once attended a meeting of the Council. That was not solely because he was the enemy of the Beauforts, and Thomas Beaufort was now Chancellor. Arundel would attend no Council presided over by Harry. They had never liked one another; since Harry had ranged himself on the side of the University of Oxford, in its fight against the Archbishop's determination to appoint delegates there to suppress all who were infected by Wycliffe's doctrines, the dislike between them had flamed into open enmity. John hoped that today's affair would not lead Arundel to suppose that Harry himself sympathized with heresy. No: he could not think that, any more than he could think Courtenay, Chancellor of the University, a heretic. Courtenay was withstanding him because he saw in his Thirteen Constitutions a threat to the liberty of the University; and Harry supported Courtenay because Courtenay was his friend, and one of the men whose judgment he most respected.

But the rift would widen, whatever Arundel believed. What could have possessed Harry to have behaved so outrageously?

John passed under the great arch of Ludgate, waiting for a minute or two for a cart, mounted on sleds, that was being dragged in to the city from the west. His hackney shied at it, and the gateward cursed its driver, threatening him with awful penalties if he did not get out of the way of the noble prince. John saw the wagoner staring at him, with a scared look on his face, and gave him a friendly nod. The fellow was not really frightened; only startled; but for an instant his expression had reminded John of something he wanted to forget. He rode on, out of the city. The air seemed cleaner almost immediately. One was always encountering noisome stenches within the city, of course; particularly in the vicinity of the butchers' quarter, when they were burning offal. One's nostrils still quivered at the reek of burning flesh.

Ralph Neville had told him that more hardened men than he had been known to vomit when first they saw an execution, so, in a way, he had been forewarned. He hadn't vomited, though his stomach had seemed to turn over within him. Ralph hadn't so much as changed colour; he had been much more concerned with the consequences of Harry's rash act than with the sufferings of a Lollard. He had told Harry afterwards that he would outgrow his squeamishness, adding reminiscently that when he had first seen a man hanged and drawn he had nearly disgraced himself by falling down in a swoon. 'But I was only a lad then,' he explained.

Harry had thrown him a strange glance, his lips close-gripped.

'Look you, my lord!' Ralph had said roughly. 'There are things more worth your ruth than a damned heretic!'

That was true; and if one did feel ruth one had to remember that it was better to suffer a short agony here on middle earth than to be cast into flames to all eternity. If Harry's confessor had not explained that to him, Courtenay would surely do so. But Harry knew it; what he had done had been of impulse, unthinkingly.

It had been a disturbing affair. He himself, when Badby had been delivered up to him, had been aware of some quality in the fellow he had not before seen in a condemned person. He had seemed to be a decent man; bore himself with a courage one wouldn't have expected in one of humble birth. He came from Evesham: a tailor, someone had said, not even a man bred to arms. He had been quite quiet; very haggard, with a sick pallor betraying the terror that must have possessed him, yet with shining eyes that had met his for a moment in a steady look that held neither entreaty nor resentment, but an expression almost of exaltation.

Nobody had wanted him to die, not even Archbishop Arundel, who was merciless towards heretics. He had been granted a year's grace for reflection, and even when he was brought before the Convocation in London, and still maintained his blasphemy, every effort was made to bring him to a state of grace. The most learned of the churchmen explained his errors to him with meticulous care, but it was to no avail. After hours of argument, he was still asserting that a toad or a spider was more fit to be worshipped than the Host, since they at least had life, and the Host had none. There was nothing to be done after that, of course, but to condemn him, and to hand him over to the secular arm.

No one had had to persuade Harry to be present at the execution. He had consented willingly, shocked by such blasphemies as Badby had uttered. The change had come quite suddenly. Harry had watched the Constable's men place Badby in a barrel, chained to the stake, his face rigid and austere. The Prior of St Bartholomew's had exhorted Badby to recant; the Host was displayed; Courtenay, whose golden voice would have moved a stone to tears, begged him to save his soul from perdition and his body from the fire. Badby only shook his head, and there had been nothing in Harry's face but cold anger, as torches were laid to the kindling under the faggots.

It had been a long time before the first groan had burst from Badby. It was his courage that had made it so unendurable a spectacle. John had set his teeth, and hoped that the wretched man would speedily lose consciousness. And all at once Harry was on his feet, shouting: 'No! Quench the fire! *Quench* it!'

They had all of them been so much astonished that they hadn't known what to do. John still didn't know what could have been done, when Harry so imperiously took command. He ordered the men to pull away the faggots; with his own hands he helped to tear away the flaming staves of the barrel; and when they laid the pitiable wreck at his feet, he fell on his knees, beseeching the scorched wretch to recant. It was seen then that Badby was no longer conscious. But he came to himself again. Harry offered him life, freedom, a pension, and he made a gesture of refusal.

'Recant, recant!' Harry had implored him. 'You are too brave a man to die thus! You shall live your days in peace – in comfort! I swear it – I, Harry of Lancaster, by the faith of my knighthood!'

And again Badby had made that gesture of refusal.

It had stunned Harry. He had risen slowly to his feet, looking white and shaken. John had made an imperative sign to the executioner, saying under his breath: 'Deliverly!'

He had been obeyed; probably the executioner was as anxious as anyone to end the affair quickly. Harry hadn't spoken again, or betrayed by so much as a quiver of his taut muscles the turmoil in his breast. John knew, and Courtenay too, he thought, that under that frozen calm Harry was realizing, too late, the dreadful outcome of his interference; but none of all those in the crowd of citizens who watched him could have guessed it.

Once the faggots had been rekindled, it hadn't taken long. Or not long before Badby had passed beyond feeling. Ralph Neville thought that no harm had been done, though he had been afraid, at one moment, that the borel-folk might make trouble. The Archbishop's statute against heretics had never been liked by the people, and there had been a good deal of sympathy felt for Badby. However, it seemed that his refusal to recant at the Prince's entreaty had changed the people's pity to disgust. 'One of my squires has been telling me that they're saying now that the rogue deserved to be thrust into the fire again, for behaving so churlishly to so tender and gracious a prince,' Ralph had said, meaning to reassure Harry.

But Harry had turned away his face.

2

Well, it was of no use to dwell upon it; far worse to be beguiled into thinking every Lollard a Badby. John knew that in general there was not a more abandoned or disruptive set of people in the realm. For every one of them who was tormented by religious doubt there were five who used Lollardy as a cloak to hide sedition. Father Matthew said that John Wycliffe would have repudiated all who were now calling themselves his disciples; no doubt Dean Courtenay would show this to Harry, if it was needful. But probably it wasn't. When he had tried to save Badby from the fire, Harry had seen in him, not a miscreature, not even a man with his soul in peril, but a decent little tradesman: just such an one as would bring lengths of fine cloth to his lodging, and, while he measured him for a new pourpoint, would chat to him, with the respectful familiarity of the privileged, of the latest jet of fashion or the advantages of the new joined-hose.

For himself, he was going to put the whole thing out of his mind. There had been a moment, when that charred body had been chained again to the stake, and by his order, when he had thought that he would never again visit Smithfield without seeing this picture. That was folly. He would remember instead watching Thomas joust there, or the jugglers that haunted the great Fair, or the palfrey he had bought there last year. Ralph was right: there were things more worth one's ruth than an obdurate misbeliever. There were also things of greater importance to trouble one's mind. There was the King's increasing ill-health; and, more immediately pressing, there was the imminent prospect of having to hurry north, to meet a Scottish invasion. His and Ralph's officers were sending to London reports that told the same tale. It might mean calling out the levies of the northern counties, but it was unlikely, he thought, to amount to much. Providence had thrust a painful bit into the Regent Albany's mouth, and had placed the reins in English hands.

It had been the most amazing stroke of good fortune. In the spring of the year following Scrope's execution, the heir to the Scottish throne had dropped – you could call it nothing else – into King Henry's hands. No one had dreamed of such a thing's coming to pass; affairs had rarely been in worse shape on the Border. But poor, doting King Robert, in dread of his brother, feeling his little strength to be ebbing from him, remembering the fate that had befallen his elder son at Albany's hands, had sent young James out of Scotland, to be educated in France. That, at least, had been his intention, but the vessel that carried this precious freight had been intercepted off Flamborough Head by an English ship out of Cley, and its cargo had been carried straight to King Henry.

Young James had then been in his twelfth year, a red-headed, stocky boy, with freckles, and fearless brown eyes that stared sturdily into King Henry's. He was not frightened; he was in a passion of rage; and very pugnacious. But if you had been taught to be mannerly towards your elders it was a feat beyond your power to treat with rudeness a man of King Henry's years and exalted position. Besides, King Henry had four sons of his own, and he knew how to handle spirited imps. Young James, who hated Englishmen, found himself telling the King all about his life at St Andrews, what his studies had been, what disports he liked best, and how much he wanted to become skilled in feats of arms. 'You shall be,' King Henry promised, liking the eager boy.

He told the infuriated Scots that if education was what they wanted for the Prince he was better qualified to supply this than King Charles of France, which was unanswerable, because Charles the Well-Beloved was seldom in possession of his wits, and he himself was the most lettered king in Christendom. He said that James should receive careful instruction, and he kept his word. The boy was allowed to retain the young squire who had accompanied him to England; he was placed in the custody of a governor, supplied with tutors, as well in knightly exercises as in book-learning, and given every opportunity to disport himself with hawks and hounds.

The news of his capture had dealt King Robert his death-stroke. Before three months were out, the Prince had become the King of Scotland, and a doubly potent weapon in King Henry's hand. Beyond a certain point, Albany, now Regent, dared not go, for fear of having a most unwanted King sent back into Scotland. This dread weighed far more with him than did the continued detention of his own son Murdoch of Fife in England since his capture by Harry Hotspur at Homildon Hill eight years before; and it was a threat held always over his head. Not, John thought, that King Henry had the smallest intention of sending James back to Scotland. He was neither so witless nor so conscienceless. James was useful only as a potential danger to his uncle; and once across the Border the life of such an untried stripling would not have been worth a day's purchase.

John hardly knew him, but Humfrey had met him once or twice, and said that he was a boy of decided parts, quickwitted, fond of books, and bidding fair to become an accomplished jouster. John had had a glimpse of him three years ago, when he had been taken to watch a wager by battle in the lists at Nottingham. John had not himself been sitting in the royal gallery, but below it, in the Constable's siege, but Harry had told him afterwards that James had hugely enjoyed the entertainment – to the extent of having to be reproved for laughing so loudly. No one had blamed him for laughing, of course, because it had been quite the most japeworthy combat ever seen in the lists. It had been between two elderly men of Bordeaux, one of whom had accused the other of having incited him, seven years earlier, to treason. Each was bursting with rage against the other; nothing would do for either of them but to fight it out in the lists; and very doughtily they had fought, if a trifle stiffly, first riding several courses against each other, and then waging the battle on foot. From the moment that John cried: 'Lasseir les aler!' and the two old men charged furiously against each other, the crowd took them to their hearts, and broke the strict rule of silence at a tournament, cheering both of them impartially. When treason was the cause at issue, the vanquished was dragged by the heels from the lists by the Constable's officers, and hanged, but the King had not allowed the entertainment to end so unhappily. When it was plain that the combatants were tottering on their thin shanks, he had shouted Ho! and had announced them both to be leal men and true, which pleased everyone but the King of Scots, who was young enough to think this a tame ending to the affair. 'Will not the Lord John drag one of them away to be hanged?' he demanded.

'It's not a thing he does himself,' said Harry gravely. 'We only let him drag people out of the lists by their heels on his birthday.'

'No, but his officers!' James cried, knowing that Harry was laughing at him.

'You know,' remarked Thomas, 'such a kill-cow as you would have had splendid disport in France! What a pity you didn't go there after all!'

It was, in fact, extremely fortunate for James. With the death of Duke Philip of Burgundy, and the accession of his son John to his power, all semblance of order had vanished from the land. The Burgundians and the Orleanists, each striving to become supreme, grew daily stronger and more outrageous. The King was diswitted; his gross German Queen was said to live in open concubinage with his brother of Orleans; and all over the land a state of anarchy flourished. Those who visited the country brought back the most hair-raising accounts. There had been nothing comparable to it in England since the time of King Stephen, when, if the chronicles were to be believed, the barons threw up strongholds without licence, pursued private quarrels with every circumstance of ferocity, and behaved towards their tenantry like so many Paynims. English ambassadors told of unheard-of luxury and magnificence amongst the nobly born in France, and of such poverty amongst the humble as had shocked them beyond description. Only the nobly-born had any rights, they said. The poor had not even the right to hold their own half-acres inviolable. No French lord would think twice about invading the dwellings of his tenants, or of throwing the wretched creatures out to starve, if he happened to want the land on which their hovels stood. He was never confronted by a slow-thinking, obstinate country-fellow, who proved, in a long, rambling tale, stuffed with irrelevant details, that his fathers had enjoyed some tiresome right or other since time immemorial. He never had to decipher interminable letters from a harassed steward, informing him of what John Daw deposeth, and what witnesses he bringeth to support his contention, and how Margery Nokes remembers the day, because it was the very day on which she delivered her neighbour Brown of her fifth son, that lost a leg in the French wars; and he certainly never had to own himself baffled in an encounter with one of his hinds.

As for the Dukes of Orleans and Burgundy, upon the accession of the Fearless to his father's ducal cap, Louis of Orleans took for his device a knotted stick, with the motto *Je l'envy*, which was an expression used in dicing, and signified, *I defy you*; and the Fearless promptly countered with a carpenter's plane (for the shaving off of the knots on Orleans' stick) with a motto of two Flemish words, also culled from the dice-table: *Hic houd*, which meant, *I hold it*.

Thoughtful Parisians, perceiving these portents, lost no time in providing themselves with weapons of defence; no person of kind-wit ventured into the streets after dusk; and the more timorous barred their doors and shuttered their windows as soon as the shadows began to lengthen.

No one was really surprised when, on a chill November night, in 1407, one of the rival dukes gruesomely met his end in the Rue Barbette.

Louis of Orleans had gone to pay a ceremonial visit to Queen Isabeau, lately brought to bed of a child in her hotel in the Rue du Temple, fast-by the Porte Barbette. In spite of the fact that the infant (which, it was freely asserted, was of the Duke's own begetting) had survived for only one day, the meeting was a merry one, the royal lady and her brother-in-law sitting down to supper in the best of spirits. But a false message had been brought to Orleans, telling him that his presence at the Hotel St Pol, where the King lay, was instantly desired. Still in merry mood, he set forth, scantly attended, his oiled locks bare to the winter sky, a song on his lips. He was set upon by masked men, who erupted from an empty house, smote down his followers, dragged him from the saddle, and literally hacked him to death, even going so far as to cleave his skull to the teeth. They ran away after that, dropping caltraps in their wake to discourage pursuers, and for several days no one knew who was the instigator of this brutal murder.

'And they would hardly imagine that it could be Burgundy, would they?' said Humfrey, listening in wide-eyed innocence to this tale.

It was Burgundy, of course, and within a very few days he had fled from Paris to his own province of Artois. According to the accounts received in England, he boasted dreadfully of the deed, once within his own domains, so that anyone might have supposed him to have struck Orleans down with his own hand. But he was popular with the Parisians, and by Shrovetide in the following year, back he came to the capital, at the head of a thousand men-at-arms – a circumstance which perhaps accounted for the pardon he received a month later. However, he apparently felt none too sure of his safety, for he instantly began to erect a fortress in the heart of the city.

The new Duke of Orleans was a youth of sixteen years. Report said of him that he was an accomplished boy, with gentle manners, a strong leaning towards the poetic, and a melancholy disposition. This did not sound as though his cousin of Burgundy, a ruthless and a seasoned schemer, eighteen years his senior, would find in him a formidable opponent. He seemed, moreover, to have been born under an unlucky star. A year before his father's murder, he had been married to a most unwilling bride, a lady older than himself, and a widow, still, and while life lasted, mourning her first husband. Madame Isabelle, daughter of Charles the Well-Beloved, and Queen Dowager of England, wept during the marriage ceremony, and continued to weep throughout the jollifications which followed it. It was an unnerving experience for the youthful bridegroom; and hardly had he succeeded in reconciling Madame to her lot than he was plunged into all the turmoil of his father's abrupt taking-off. Not only did he fail to obtain vengeance on the murderer: he saw him pardoned for the crime; and he found himself with two women on his hands who extracted from the tragedy the last ounce of drama. Madame Isabelle, who really seemed to enjoy an excess of grief, was driven, with her mother-in-law to demand justice of the King, through the streets of Paris, in an open chariot, both ladies draped in sable weeds, and weeping without stint, to the admiration of all beholders. After this, the Dowager Duchess draped her hotel as well as her person in black cloths, and, in superb disregard of the fact that she had enjoyed little of her murdered husband's society for several years, devoted the rest of her life to extolling his virtues, mourning her loss, and exhorting her children never to rest until they had avenged his death. A year later the young Duke himself was mourning the loss of his spouse: Madame Isabelle was brought to bed of a maid-child, and parted her life within the hour. Decidedly, it did not seem as though Charles of Orleans was destined to be fortunate.

However, in this year of grace, 1410, he had found a second wife, and his prospects seemed to be rosier. His father-in-law, the Count of Armagnac, was a forceful person, and soon appropriated to himself the leadership of the Orleanist party. He was so forceful that it was not long before the country was plunged in civil war, a state of affairs perfectly agreeable to the English, but quite ruinous to the wretched people who suffered its depredations.

No: France was not at all the sort of place to which a father would wish to send his son for safety. King James had been more fortunate than he knew.

3

Thinking of Madame Isabelle brought his sister Blanche to John's mind. Blanche too was dead, and in childbed. When this tragic news had reached the King, nearly a year ago now, he had let a dreadful cry, and had fallen into bitter weeping, saying over and over again: 'Both my little maids! both, both!' Those about him had reminded him that Philippa was on life, but he would not be comforted. He had never felt happy in Philippa's marriage to Eric, King of Denmark, Sweden and Norway, and often he spoke of her as though she were dead. If she had shown only the smallest dislike of the contract, he would have broken it, for the reports his servants had brought him from Denmark were of a rude court, and of a bridegroom of uncertain character. But Philippa was not afraid. She wanted to be a queen; and the tears she had shed at parting from her father, and her brothers, at Bishop's Lynn, four years ago, had been quickly dried. The scanty tidings that had from time to time been received from her made her brothers say that it was well for her she was of a hardier temper than her sister. Her husband proved to be a man of few morals, but an inordinate liking for liquor.

They bade King Henry take comfort from the knowledge that Blanche had had no such trials to bear. If her life had been short, it had been happy; and rarely had a princess found in marriage so much love as Bavarian Louis had lavished upon her.

The Queen bade him consider how much more blessed was his state than hers. His four sons were around him, but all seven of her fair children had become as good as dead to her, since she never now set eyes on them. Heaven knew how hard it was for her to appear cheerful under such circumstances, but she did it, because it was her duty, and her dear lord must follow her example.

But King Henry would not be comforted. His doctors said that his grief was responsible for the growth of his malady. No one was in a position to dispute this, and certainly the King's health had seemed to be worse during the past year; but, looking back over the years which had elapsed since Scrope's execution, John thought that he had never been in good point in all that time. But he recalled, also, that the first signs of the mysterious disease had shown themselves a full year before that date, and he continued to turn a stony face upon any man unwise enough to speak within his hearing of the Archbishop's bane.

For a year after his recovery from that strange seizure at Green Hammerton, the King had continued in fairly good health. It had not been until the end of the following year that he had become so ill that he had thought himself upon his bed-mortal, and had drawn up his Will. His condition was then so alarming that Thomas had been recalled from Ireland, where he had resumed his lieutenancy; and Harry had received special permission from the Council to remain at his father's side. A meeting of the Council had been cancelled; the King, who had been carried from Eltham Palace to his manor at Greenwich, was rumoured to be at his last end. It was here that he dictated his Will; and it was here that King Richard's ghost haunted him.

Very few people knew how grievously the King had been tormented. John had as little liking for Archbishop Arundel as Harry, but he would always be grateful to him for having arrogated to himself the command of the King's household at this time. He had permitted none but the King's doctors, and his most trusted attendants, to enter the sickroom while the King lay raving in delirium. What King Henry had betrayed in his madness his sons might guess, but could not know.

He had recovered, perhaps because he had recalled an old vow to build a chapel on the site of Shrewsbury Field, and at last began to erect it. By May, he was at Windsor, hunting with his harthounds; and in August he was well enough to sit for eight days in a specially built gallery at Smithfield, watching the jousting there between English knights and Hainaulters. But even though he had seemed to enjoy the sport he had not been in such very good surety of his person, John knew. He had lodged throughout the tournament at the priory of St Bartholomew, because the daily journey to Smithfield and back again to his palace of Westminster would have taxed his strength beyond what it could bear. Since then he had scarcely been seen in public, and he had become increasingly incapable of attending to business. Indeed, after the close of the parliament he had summoned to assemble at Gloucester in the autumn of 1407, no writs had been issued until this present spring of 1410, when it was Harry, and not the King, who presided at the Council table.

No one, not the cleverest of the foreign physicians summoned by Master Malvern to King Henry's aid, could give a name to the evil which was making his life hideous. The redeless whispered that God had smitten him with the Great Malady, but that was untrue. Unlearned persons were prone to speak of every ill that bore the smallest resemblance to this dread sickness as leprosy; but the doctors knew that it was not that. They had assured those who questioned them privily that there was no danger to anyone who came near the King; this sickness was not infective; and in several respects, plain to their trained eyes, it differed from the Great Malady. But what it was that was causing the King's flesh to rot, covering his face from time to time with sores so ugly that he was forced to wear a mask, not one of them had as yet discovered. Dr Nigarelli, a witty Jew from Lucca, believed it to be a sickness common in the eastern parts of Europe. He suspected that it had its roots in the rye which was used there for breadmaking, and that the King must have contracted it years ago, when he had fought in Poland for the Prussian Knights; but for all his profound talk he did not seem to be able to cure the King.

It was fortunate that Harry was free to take his father's place at the head of the Council. John knew how little the King liked relinquishing it to him, but he also knew – none better – that matters had been allowed to drift for too long. A little grim smile tilted the corners of his mouth as he remembered that he had believed his own troubles nearly ended at the close of the year of the Archbishop's heading. It was true that never again had the safety of his house been seriously threatened, but he would not, for anything that could be offered him, relive those next disheartening years, when no plea of his won him stores, or pay for his garrisons; and the only thing that saved Berwick from capture by the Scots was the rising of the Tweed, and the flooding of the land all about it. He had been powerless to protect the land in his charge, powerless to help its people; and it still seemed to him a thing past understanding that they remained loyal to him, and even obeyed his exhortations to them to stand firm. He had promised that they should be paid in full, but in his heart he had despaired of seeing that promise fulfilled. It wouldn't have surprised him if they had returned to their old allegiance; he thought that he would scarcely have blamed them; and when they gave him proof of the affection they felt for him he had been as much amazed as he was moved.

Nothing, he reflected, fell out quite as one had hoped it would. It had been his dearest wish to meet Northumberland in the field, and to defeat him. He had dreamed of carrying the aged sinner to London in chains, and of seeing his false head struck from his body; but it hadn't happened like that. Northumberland had been dead for two years now, but he had had no hand in sending him to the deathward.

The Fox of the North had spent many months in fruitless intrigue, flitting from Scotland to France, to Flanders, to Brittany, and to Wales, all the time trying to gather to him allies. He had threatened an attack in 1407, but his plans had been foiled; and when at last he crossed the Border, early in the following year, accompanied by the Lord Bardolph and those of his lieges who had remained faithful to him throughout his exile, and at the head of a force of Scots, neither John nor Ralph Neville had been in the North.

He came at the end of the Big Winter, the hardest winter that ever was known in Europe. All over the continent the rivers were frozen for months, and when the thaw came, after Christmas-tide, ships in the Danube were crushed by the moving ice-floes. The Garonne was frozen even at Bordeaux; in Paris, not only the wooden bridge of St Michel fell in, but also the Petit Pont, which was built of stone; and in England the whole country was snowbound from December to March, and littered with the corpses of small birds. No man could remember so bitter a winter; yet it was in such weather as this that Percy chose to launch his attack against King Henry's power.

He crossed the Border in January. He must have expected that his Northumbrian lieges would flock to his standard, but hardly a man joined him. The Northumbrians thought him wood to seek a battle in such a season, and worse than wood to bring the Scots into England. He had been trafficking with foreigners, too: a disgusting crime. You wouldn't find young John of Lancaster doing that; no, nor living snug amongst the enemies who ravaged his people! Give the lad his due, no matter how bad things became, he didn't desert his post.

'That was what they said, on all sides, my lord,' Robert Umfraville told John. 'And I remembered me that I foretold, when first you came amongst us, that you would win worship in the North.'

Undeterred by his failure on his own Marches, Northumberland had pushed south to his Yorkshire estates. Displaying his banner at Thirsk, he announced himself to be England's consolation, and called upon all who loved liberty to join him. No one of note responded, and no one of note withstood him. It was the sheriff of Yorkshire who gathered a force together, and defeated my lord of Northumberland on Sunday, the nineteenth day of February, on a site of my lord's own choosing, at Bramham Moor, with the snow lying deep on the ground. Northumberland was slain on the field of battle; the Lord Bardolph died a few hours later of his wounds; and King Henry was rid of his worst enemy.

4

Looking back, one could not feel that Scrope's curse had been effective. In the turmoil of events as they occurred, it had often seemed as though a blight lay over the whole land; but in retrospect it could be seen that by insensible degrees the throne had been rendered secure to the house of Lancaster. Though the King's health was broken, no one now threatened his power; and none of the evils which had been prophesied had ever befallen him.

All that talk of excommunication, for instance: well, John reflected, as he crossed Ivy Bridge, leaving the paved part of the Strand behind him, they had to thank Archbishop Arundel for the way in which he had handled that business. Nothing had ever come of Pope Innocent's threat, beyond a lame retort to one of King Henry's more caustic messages. Irritated by the Pope's reproaches to him for having slain Scrope, his son in Christ, King Henry had despatched to Rome the Archbishop's mailed jack with the sardonic enquiry: 'Is this your son's shirt?' All that Pope Innocent could think of by way of reply was: 'A beast has mauled it,' which was considered in England to be no answer at all. His third fit of apoplexy carried him off at the end of 1406, and he was succeeded by an aged Venetian, of severe piety, who was elected to the Chair of St Peter under the name of Gregory XII and instantly announced his willingness to resign, if Benedict, at Avignon, would do so too. It was not difficult to see why, in all the hotch-potch of duplicity which followed Benedict's cordial reception of this suggestion, the affairs of England came to be set aside. In fact, the only revenge Rome took on King Henry was to refuse to nominate to the vacant See the man of his choice. The King had wished his old friend, Thomas Langley, to be elevated to the archiepiscopal throne. Pope Innocent had at once nominated to the See the then Chancellor of Oxford University, Robert Hallam; and since neither he nor the King would recognize the other's choice, the See stood vacant for two and a half years, during which time miracles continued to be performed at Scrope's tomb, creating a great deal of unrest and alarm in York, and considerably adding to the Lord John's load of care. A way, agreeable both to King and Pope, was at last found out of the dilemma, when Gregory XII translated to York the Bishop of Bath and Wells. Since Langley had been provided for a year earlier, and had become Bishop of Durham, no candidate for the See of York could have been found who was more welcome to the King. The Bishop of Bath and Wells was quite as devoted a friend to Lancaster as Thomas Langley, for he was that Henry Bowet whom King Richard had condemned for having dared to act as proxy for banished Bolingbroke. Scarcely had he returned from escorting the Lady Philippa to Denmark than his translation took place. He went to York, and from that date the miracles ceased.

John could smile without impiety at this recollection. He had never believed in the miracles, nor had his spiritual advisers encouraged him to do so. No odour of sanctity hung about Archbishop Scrope: he reflected that very little odour of sanctity today hung about anything to do with Holy Church. Perhaps it wasn't surprising that so many men had lost their faith. Really, nothing could be more scandalous than the behaviour of the rival popes! All over Europe, people were cracking the lewdest jests about them; no one could decide which of the two was the most japeworthy; a French knight had declared, three years ago, that both ought to be pitched on the fire: a pronouncement felt to be so just that nobody rebuked him. At that time, it had still been hoped that they would meet, each having declared himself willing; but as each went about armed to the teeth, and neither would move a step beyond his own jurisdiction, nothing came of this attempt to end the Schism. Envoys found Benedict exuding sweetness and mendacity; and, travelling on to Rome, discovered in Gregory an emaciated and parsimonious old man, whom they soon suspected of being slightly wood. His intellect was certainly not powerful, and in spite of being wholly ignorant of the law he insisted on managing all papal business himself.

As far as anyone in England knew, the two popes spent several months each declaring his earnest wish to meet the other in friendly conference, taking every precaution to prevent such a meeting's coming to pass, and flitting from place to place. Benedict accused Gregory of duplicity; Gregory, living luxuriously in Siena, described himself as a fugitive in a foreign land. It became apparent that no meeting between them would ever take place, since Benedict refused to go beyond reach of his galleys which had brought him to Nice, and Gregory would not venture near the sea, for fear of being kidnapped. By this time, Louis of Orleans, Benedict's most powerful supporter in France, was dead. King Charles, prompted by the University of Paris, sent a message to both popes that if they had not reached agreement by Ascension Day, France would make shift to dispense with them both. It might have been supposed that Benedict would have recognized that this was not the moment for a display of autocracy. Unfortunately, the threat of contumacy fired his Aragonese blood, and he sent off two messengers with a Bull of excommunication, which they presented to the King when he was at Mass, taking to their heels as soon as they had done it. They were wise, but they did not run fast enough: they were caught, and set in the pillory, while the Bull was publicly rent into pieces and burnt.

After this, matters went from bad to worse. France declared her neutrality, and issued orders to Marshal Boucicault to arrest Benedict, who immediately fled, and, after some vicissitudes, reached Perpignan, where he created several new cardinals to fill the places of those lost to him through his quarrel with France. Since Gregory was doing exactly the same thing, the bewildered world found it hard to keep pace with the new elections. In this atmosphere of hatred and mistrust, the Council of Pisa took place. It was supported by all Christian monarchs, and inaugurated by the revolted cardinals, and it opened on the 25th day of March, 1409. Galaxies of bishops, priests, monks, and learned doctors, attended it; and after two months Christendom was ordered to abjure both popes, who were declared, in an impartial spirit, to be devils from Hell. In June, the Patriarch of Alexandria excommunicated them as schismatics, heretics, and enemies of God. A month later, a Franciscan of humble birth but cheerful disposition was crowned as Alexander V, and to celebrate the occasion both the other popes were burnt in effigy. Alexander was a merry-hearted person, desirous of pleasing everyone, but scarcely the man to fill a position so fraught with difficulty. He had as his chief adviser the Legate of Bologna, Cardinal Baldassare Cossa, an astute Neapolitan of considerable ability, and the most unsavoury reputation.

So now there were three popes, for although England and France might recognize the decision of Pisa, naturally the deposed popes did no such thing, but vied with one another instead in hurling anathemas at Alexander, and apostrophizing the Council of Pisa as the filth and scum of iniquity.

No: the growth of heresy was not altogether surprising,

perhaps. If the Holy Father made himself contemptible, one could dimly perceive that a little tailor from Evesham whose soul was troubled by doubt might find it impossible to repose his trust in the teaching of his appointed priests.

5

John jerked his thoughts away. He was not going to think about that little tailor from Evesham. It was to be hoped Harry wouldn't think of him either. Probably he wouldn't: when that first revulsion had passed he would realize, as all men must, that courage was no excuse for heresy. John thought it unlikely that he would return that day to Westminster Palace. Harry had several rooms there, but the King's manor at Byfleet had lately been put in order for his use, and he much preferred it. At present, he rarely spent a night at Westminster, but rode up from Byfleet, or Kennington, to attend Council meetings. If the King's health showed no amendment, and all the business of the realm fell on Harry's shoulders, he really ought, John thought, to be given an inn of his own in London. Even though the King kept to his own chambers, and was rarely seen by his sons, Harry would never feel at ease while he lived under the same roof with him. Between them there seemed to be some deep antagonism which time only strengthened. In the King, this arose from jealousy; in Harry, from several causes, one at least of which he kept locked in his soul.

The King's jealousy was understandable. John, who felt both affection and compassion for his father, knew how bitter a thing it must be for a man, once the darling of the borel-folk, to see his son preferred to himself, not only by the borel-folk, but by the members of his Council, and certainly by the sturdy Commons. The handsome Duke of Hereford, whose knightly prowess all other knights had striven to emulate, had become an ailing monarch, old before his time, his strength too little to support him through a day in the saddle, his beauty ravaged by the foul malady that was consuming him. He had won a throne, and he had held it against every attempt to wrest it from him; but he had won no worship from the people who had once hailed him as the shield and comfort of the commonwealth.

They grutched at his most reasonable demands; to wring from them the grants he needed he was forced to use all the arts and wiles at his command, even to submit to humiliating restrictions; but Harry, who had had nothing to do with the winning of the throne, might have what he needed for the mere asking.

An unwitty courtier, thinking to please him, told the King that when Harry rode through the streets, the apprentices ran at his stirrup, and sober aldermen doffed their hats to him. 'Yea, he is young and debonair!' the King answered.

But that was not just. Of course the citizens were disposed to look kindly upon a handsome young prince; no force but he cast over them his magic; but he was not loved only for his comeliness and charm. The King might demand of his other sons what Harry had done to deserve such worship as was lavished upon him, but the truth was that Harry had done much, and the redeless commons knew it. His expedition into Wales in the year of Scrope's death had been King Henry's last. From then on Harry had held untrammelled command on the Marches, and just as he had told John he would, he had conquered and was pacifying an unruly people. Aberystwyth, the last of Owen Glendower's fortresses, had fallen nearly two years ago, but before this Harry had been thanked by Parliament for his great services.

John smiled, recalling this episode. Harry, kneeling before the King, had prayed that thanks might be rendered to his very dear cousin of York, whose good counsel (he said) had saved them all from ruin.

Edward burst into tears whenever he spoke of this. 'I shall never forget it, never!' he said, mopping his blubbered cheeks with his sleeve.

John really believed that he would not. Edward had a yearning affection for Harry, as though he saw in him not only his liegelord, but the son he might have fathered. There were seventeen years between them, but Edward's formidable bulk made him seem older than his thirty-seven years. He was still childless, and all the doting fondness he would have lavished on a son was Harry's. As well it might be, John reflected. It was certainly to Harry's good offices that he owed his release from his dungeon at Pevensey and his restoration to all his possessions. It hadn't been a dungeon, of course, but that was how Edward saw it in retrospect. Not even ribald Thomas was unkind enough to ask him how he had contrived to write his great book in a lightless dungeon.

Harry had been right about Edward's book: it was all about the Chase. He had not managed to finish it at Pevensey, but he had done so a year later, and had had it written on vellum sheets at great costage. It was in Harry's library now, and he had told Edward, when Edward had said, a little wistfully, that other and finer books would one day be presented to him, that he would never care a leek for them beside this one that was the first ever to be inscribed with his name.

'Well,' said Edward, puffing out his cheeks with pleasure, 'I took more pains over my Prologue than all the rest together!' He added, with the anxiety of an author: 'Do you like the lines I have set down in your honour, Harry?'

'Witterly! But you have said in the Prologue that you submit the book to my noble and wise correction, and you know very well, Edward, you would not brook one word from me about the Chase!'

'Well, well!' said Edward, almost bursting with pride in his work, 'it is the custom with us scriveners to flatter princes!'

It was Humfrey who pointed out that the most part of Edward's *Master of Game* was nothing but a translation of the French book, called *La Chasse*, which had been written by Gaston de Foix. However, he was chastened for this display of scholarship. Harry told him that Edward made no secret of it; and Thomas, more forthright, said: 'Well, *you* haven't made a translation of anything, for all your learning, so you may as well be silent!'

Thomas: the reminiscent smile faded from John's face, as thoughts of this not least dear but certainly most difficult of his brothers entered his mind. Sir Thomas Beaufort had said to him only two days ago, bluntly, that it was time a wife was found for Thomas. John might have retorted that it was no business of his to find a wife for Thomas, but he hadn't. He had grown accustomed to receiving this kind of confidence. Anyone with a complaint to make against Harry, or Thomas, or Humfrey, seemed to think his was the most fit ear to receive it. Why any man should think this was a matter passing his comprehension. Sometimes, of course, he was able to smooth away a misunderstanding, but more often he could do nothing but listen, and hope that in the recital of his grievances the injured person would find relief. He knew that this frequently happened. Ralph Neville had once said to him, after an outburst of exasperation: 'You know, John, it eases my heart to talk to you!'

But Beaufort hearts would not be eased by talking to John, if heedless Thomas went too far along the course he seemed now to be treading. Already eyebrows were being raised; and when the charitable pointed out that the Lady Somerset was his aunt – by marriage, if not by blood – the more worldly-wise winked knowing eyelids, and snickered. Margaret Holland, who was married to Uncle John Beaufort, was the mother of five hopeful children, the eldest of whom was nine years old, but she still had the face and the figure of a girl, and was, in fact, much nearer in age to Thomas than to her grave husband.

According to Humfrey, the affair had started a year ago, when Thomas, recalled from Ireland, had been idle and restless, missing his new Irish friend, the young Earl of Ormonde, and ripe for any mischief. He had dined at the Cold Harbour one day, and had apparently looked upon his aunt-by-marriage with new eyes. She was a comely woman, John supposed, but by no means a beauty. She had a trim figure, very little chin, but a pair of large, roguish eyes, and a gurgling laugh, which was roused by quite simple japes, or even, John and Harry thought, by nothing at all. You couldn't help liking her, because she was as artless as a child, and as confiding, but after an hour in her company you were heartily bored by her prattle, and could willingly have choked her when that pretty, foolish laugh broke from her. She was very like her younger sister, Sir John Neville's wife; less like her eldest sister, once Duchess of York, and now married to Sir William Willoughby. Joan Holland was wittier by far than Meg, or Bessy, or quiet Eleanor, who was married to the young Earl of Salisbury; but, on the other hand, she was not as good-natured. All four sisters had lately become substantial landowners, through the untimely death of their only surviving brother, Edmund of Kent, Margaret getting for her share his rich Lincolnshire manors; and as they had been handsomely dowered at the time of their marriages, their husbands were generally considered to have done extremely well for themselves.

Whether John Beaufort thought this no one knew. He was just as taciturn as he had always been; and if his countenance was rather worn, with two clefts dug between his brows, this might well be due to the cares of his office, which must have weighed with increasing heaviness on his shoulders as the years went by. It was no enviable post, that of Captain of Calais. The defences and the harbour were in almost as ruinous a state as those of Berwick, and little money was forthcoming for their repair, or for the wages of the garrison. Like Harry, like John, like Edward, John Beaufort had been forced to pledge his own goods to pay for the bare necessities of his command. A great deal of money had been owing to him for years, both for Calais, and for his expenses when he had been on the Welsh Marches, but it was going to be paid at last. A month ago, Harry had had a meeting with him, at Cold Harbour, to discuss the matter. Harry had gone to Cold Harbour because the Earl was in poor health – very ill indeed, Harry thought, though he made no complaint. His youngest brother, Thomas Beaufort, the new Chancellor, had gone with Harry, and the Treasurer, too, who was Harry's close friend, Scrope of Masham, and all the details of repayment had been settled as speedily as everything else was settled that Harry set his hand to. The Earl had received them in a small solar. He had not been in bed, but Harry had felt as though he was in a sickroom, and the sound of a harp's being played somewhere near at hand, and the faint echo of a sweet, high voice singing a gay air had struck discordantly on his ears. An unpleasant suspicion that the Countess was entertaining his brother Thomas had crossed his mind, and it was soon confirmed. He was still at Cold Harbour, standing in the great hall while a servant put his fur-lined cloak round his shoulders, when Thomas – so like him, thought John – came lightly down the stairs, humming the refrain of that gay song. He had been momentarily disconcerted, but quite impenitent.

'Did you set him on the hone?' John asked.

'Not then. Later, a little. He gave me nothing but sturdy words, and since I don't choose to quarrel with Thomas – yet – I let it sleep.'

'For God's love, Harry, don't you too be a jack-eater!' John begged him. 'You know Thomas doesn't mean the sturdy things he says!'

'I know he doesn't mean to do as I bid him! But he will have to!'

'Yea, so shall we all, and all of us know it. Ease your heart, brother! Thomas won't put himself in your danger. As for this love-sickness of his, Father takes no force of it: he says it is Lenten-love, and he will soon be mended.'

'Oh, Thomas cannot sin in Father's eyes!' Harry said bitterly.

Thomas, in his turn, told John that Harry seemed to fancy himself King already. 'Pope-holy, too! Does he think me a spouse-breaker, just because I chanced to be at Cold Harbour when he was visiting Somerset?'

'No, but he doesn't wish to see you stumble into abusion,' John answered.

'God give him thanks! I wonder what he would say if I were to read him a preachment about the way *he* plays the brothel with any wench of the game that takes his fancy!'

'Less no more – but give you a swinging box on the ear, if I know Harry!'

Thomas was betrayed into a chuckle, but flung away, still smouldering. However, John had lured him and Harry both to supper a day or two later, and after a few stiff minutes they had become reconciled.

6

The squire heaved a sigh of relief, for they had at last reached the palace at Westminster, and provided that the Lord John did not take it into his head to keep him kicking his heels at the great gate, while he went into the new tower which had been granted to him for the transaction of all the business which fell to the lot of one who was both Constable of England and Warden of the Eastern March, he might expect to be released from attendance

318

in a very few minutes. He saw John glance towards the tower, and held his breath, but apparently John decided that he had transacted enough business for one day, for he rode on, past the fountain, whose waters glittered crystal clear in the pale March sunlight, and into the farther court, where, amongst the heterogeneous collection of buildings which constituted the royal lodgings, he had his own apartments.

His squire was wrong: he had every intention of transacting more business; but he meant first to change the official robe he was wearing for a more workaday and comfortable houpelande. However, he found one of his secretaries waiting for him, with letters from Berwick, which it was thought should be shown to him immediately, so he sat down to read these. He was still frowning over a vile scrawl, which his lieutenant in the castle had chosen to write with his own hand, when Thomas lounged in.

Thomas seemed to be in holiday mood – or perhaps he had dressed himself in a new hanseline of over-gilt sendal for a visit to Cold Harbour. It was just such a slop as was always being reprobated by decent persons, made insolently short, and furnished with huge padded sleeves. He had sheathed his shapely legs in hose divided blue and white, and his corn-coloured locks had been freshly curled and scented. Anyone else, tricked out in such a fashion, would have looked a milksop, reflected John. Thomas didn't: he looked what he was, a lusty young knight, decked in the trappings of a courtier.

'Airling!' John remarked, after a glance at his brother's magnificence.

Thomas laughed, but only said: 'Where have you been? I came to find you hours ago! Have you been hearing more of the Hastings case? If you give it in favour of Reginald Grey, Harry will never love you more!'

'Alas-at-ever! But I've been at the Elms.'

'At the Elms! What, was it today that you burned your Lollard?' Thomas exclaimed. 'A mending take you! You might have told me: I meant to see it!'

'Did you? Cry you mercy, then! There was nothing you would have cared for.'

'Well, I've seen a-many men hanged, but none burned. Was Harry there? Did he like it?'

'No.'

'I should have thought he would have: he hates heretics! Oh, well! I suppose there was a frape of borel-men there, stinking enough to make you choke. I've had better company here. Who do you think has come riding into London today?'

John looked up. 'Not Richard?'

'No force! He lay at Rochester last night, and came here to do his duty to Father.'

'Richard is so mannerly!' John quoted, laughing. 'Did Father see him?'

'No. He's not in good point today. *I* saw him, though. He looks just the same. He wanted to find Harry, but I told him if he wasn't shut up with the Council in the Painted Chamber he was probably out at Byfleet; so we dined, and he went off to Warwick Inn, to greet his lady, I suppose.'

This piece of news seemed to make a dark day brighter. 'Oh, I shall be blithe to see Richard again!' John exclaimed impulsively.

2 Supper at Westminster

1

Richard Beauchamp, Earl of Warwick, had been absent from England for two years. Like many of his generation, he had been seized by a desire to travel in foreign lands. A licence had been granted to him to go on pilgrimage. The Holy Land had indeed been his determinate end, but he had extended his pilgrimage to all the most remote parts of the continent, even reaching Muscovy on what he called, perfectly gravely, his journey home.

King Henry had also granted him a licence to commune with the heathen people, which he had been anxious to do, because he had wanted to discover if anything not set down in the English chronicles about his great ancestor Guy of Warwick was perhaps known to the Saracens.

As might have been expected, the Lancaster princes had shown him no quarter when they had heard of this. 'Going to visit the Soldan?' had exclaimed Harry. 'Richard, for my love, don't venture yourself amongst the Saracens! Out and alas! You will certainly be shent!'

Surprised, Richard had explained that pilgrims from all over Europe went to the Holy Land in perfect safety.

'Yes, but not pilgrims whose ancestors slew a Saracen every day for disport!' objected Thomas. 'If the Soldan winds you, Richard, he'll use you as a prick-wand for his archers! Don't you go!'

'Sir Guy of Warwick,' said Richard, always a little stiff when anyone jested about his great ancestor, 'did not slay Saracens for disport. And—'

'Well, it won't matter to the Soldan what he slew them for: he will certainly slay you!'

'He will have to go in a disguise,' said Harry.

'I don't think we shall ever see him again, even if he does,' John said, shaking his head. 'You know what Father told us about the Holy Land! Richard will offend the Turks, no charge, and they will massacre him. He will run over their graves, and laugh in the streets –'

'And let them see him when he's cup-shotten!' added Harry, with zest. 'No, no, Richard, you shall not go!'

'Lurdans all!' Richard had apostrophized them, with his wry grin.

And now he was home again after his extensive journey, and Harry was giving a supper party in his honour.

Harry's supper parties were famous amongst his intimates. They were always gay, and seldom decorous, and very little formality was observed at them. Harry disliked the tedium of dinner parties, for he ate sparingly himself, never touching the richer dishes that other people partook of in large quantities. To sit for several hours, watching a host of guests and retainers stuffing themselves with food and drink, while his minstrels played airs he knew by heart, and his fool amused the company with the pranks and quips used by every other household fool in the kingdom, was a penance to Harry. He had spent so much of his life in camp that he had developed a habit of dining alone, or with one or two only of his officers. His master-cook was permitted to display his talents in the messes that were set before the guests at his table, but he knew better than to send up the triumphs of his art for his lord's platter. Conies in clear broth, a roasted capon, perhaps a fish jelly (if not too pungently flavoured), a caudle of almond milk, or a flawn, were the sort of meats Harry ate; and he had been known to dine with apparent relish off a hunk of hard cheese and some apples.

So a supper party, when his table was spread with such light dishes as mortrews of fish, blank-manges made of chickens and almonds, small tartlets of veal, pain-puffs, and doucets, exactly suited Harry. Anyone who liked might sit down at the board, and make a hearty meal; most of his friends preferred to lounge on a banker, as he did, helping themselves at random from the dishes which his servants carried round the chamber.

2

Edmund Mortimer, the young Earl of March, the first to arrive at Harry's lodgings because he had feared to be the last, found a place for himself in a secluded corner when the other guests began to come in. In his shy way, he was enjoying the party. He was gratified to have been included amongst Harry's friends, but he found it difficult to talk to them. That was what being a state prisoner did to one. It set upon one a seal of loneliness, so that always, perhaps, one would feel a little apart from other men.

Probably he had been treated more kindly than many a boy born into happier circumstances; he had certainly been as carefully instructed as the King's own sons; and when he listened to the stories they told, recalling the outrageous pranks of their boyhood, he realized that no tutor had ever flogged him and Roger, his brother, or sent them supperless to bed for getting into mischief. But Roger had always been too sickly to want to flout authority; and when one was virtually alone there wasn't much temptation to do the sort of things the princes seemed to have spent their youth doing. There had never been any opportunity, either: state prisoners were strictly guarded, rarely allowed to stray beyond the vision of tutors or servants. No bars had confined them, no key had been turned in the lock of their chamber door; they could go where they chose in the castles that had housed them; and if they wanted to ride abroad ponies were at once saddled for them. Only they were never alone, and all the mannerly people who waited on them had been placed there by the King, and had orders to keep them under observation. Sometimes, too, the little liberty they had was curtailed. Excuses were made to them to explain their sudden confinement to the castle grounds, but they soon learned that these restrictions meant that there was unrest in the land.

When they had lived at Windsor, they had sometimes had visitors, but at Pevensey no visitors had been allowed. They had not even been permitted to see their cousin Edward of York, when he too had been confined there.

They had been long and empty, those years at Pevensey, each

day following the pattern of the one that had gone before. Edmund hadn't been unhappy, except when Roger was ill, and the fear that Roger would die and leave him quite alone had haunted his mind. Looking back, he thought that neither of them had been happy or unhappy, but perhaps just resigned.

A year ago, Roger had died, but Edmund had known for some months that he would not recover from his lingering sickness, so that when the end came he was prepared for it. He had missed him, of course, but not so poignantly as he had feared. Roger had been too feeble in health to afford him any companionship for many months. He had grown to depend on his books, of which he had a great number, for he was studious, and King Henry generous in supplying him with any volume he asked for.

It had seemed to him as though he would live all his days at Pevensey, but shortly after Roger's death he was told that he was to have a new guardian: King Henry had granted his wardship to the Prince of Wales.

Edmund could scarcely remember his cousin Harry: but he thought it was unlikely that Harry would trouble himself about the comfort of his ward. It probably meant only that Harry, and not the King, would enjoy the revenues of his estates. He was surprised when he learned that he was to leave Pevensey; and incredulous when he was told that he was to go to Worcester. Yes, the Prince's Highness had sent for him, and he was to set forth on the journey immediately.

He was escorted to Worcester, but by the time he reached that town, the Prince was in the field. Those who had him in charge supposed that they were to await, in Worcester, the Prince's return from his campaign, and were quite as staggered as the young Earl when they received instructions to join the Prince.

They found him encamped before some town whose name Edmund was ashamed to be unable to pronounce. This was the country of his birth and his inheritance, but he had been reared far from it, and the Welsh lilt struck strangely on his ears. It was the first time, too, that he had ever seen a military camp. It was a town of pavilions, some large, some small, some with banners and pennons floating from their bell-shaped tops, some blazoned all over with their owners' arms. Edmund and his party had clearly been expected; they were conducted down an avenue of pavilions, and when they halted before one, Edmund, lifting his eyes, saw the gold and azure bars of his own standard. They swam in a sudden mist; he felt as though he were choking, and dismounted clumsily, his eyes lowered.

He had been taken to the Prince's pavilion by the two squires who attended him, and had found it bewilderingly full of people, all, it seemed to him, talking in loud, confident voices, with bursts of laughter, as if they knew one another very well. He had wanted more than anything to run away, and had stayed just within the pavilion, miserably self-conscious, almost wishing himself back at lonely Pevensey. Then a lithe, tanned young man, with tawny hair flattened by the helmet he had been wearing all day, detached himself from the group gathered round the board set up on trestles at one side of the big pavilion, and came to him, holding out his hands, and saying: 'Cousin, you are right welcome!'

He had put his hands into Harry's, and raised his eyes to Harry's and had seen them smiling. He had stammered something, not the speech he had rehearsed, but that hadn't seemed to matter. Harry had led him forward, saying, in his low-toned yet authoritative way: 'Leave disputing, you cumberworlds, and give my cousin of March a welcome! Cousin, love the Lord Talbot, for my sake, if you can't for his own; and also his brother John, who is not such a fierce fellow as he looks! Also Roger Leche, my steward, and – ah, never mind the rest! Here is a kinsman of your own to welcome you! Hugh, come and do your devoir to my lord of March!'

There had been a great deal of bowing, and many polite things uttered; and then, perhaps in obedience to a sign from Harry, all the stranger lords and knights had gone away, and he, and Harry, and the two squires who guarded him, were left alone in the pavilion. It was then that Harry had spoken the words that had changed his life: quite simple words, but they had brought the tears welling to his eyes, and spilling over to run down his cheeks 'Send your people away!' Harry had said. 'I want to talk to you!'

The surveillance under which he had lived had ended at that moment – or, if it had not, it had become so imperceptible that it never irked him. He could go where he liked, and disport himself as he liked. Indeed, if he chose, at the end of this supper party, to visit the stews, the servants who attended upon him would not so much as remonstrate with him – at least, the ones who had been with him at Pevensey would not. Remonstrance, and scolding, would come from the Mortimer retainer, who had served his father, and had joined his household when he had revisited his own domains. Not that he had the smallest intention of visiting the stews, for he was of a sober disposition, and rather young for his nineteen years; still, it was comfortable to know that he could: almost as comfortable as the knowledge that if he told the servants they might go back to his inn, not waiting for him, they would go, and without demur.

Now he was learning a soldier's trade on the Marches; already he had a small command of his own. He had not been granted livery of his lands yet, but he hoped that when he came of full age the King would allow him to take possession of them. In the meantime, it was easy to feel that he was in the same position as other royal wards who were also under age, but not prisoners. He had money for his needs; he was living, not apart from his peers, but as one of them; Harry's officers managed his estates for him, and would render account to him, Harry said, when the time came; and, to crown his feeling of well-being, Harry had invited him to this party of his particular friends.

The chamber was rapidly filling. The Talbots, Gilbert and John, had arrived soon after he had, and the Prince of Wales's brother the Lord Thomas had followed them, with Harry's close friend, the Lord of Masham. Henry Scrope was the Treasurer now, a witty man with a soft, caressing voice, and a smile that seemed to mock himself as well as other men. He and Edward of York were the oldest by far of Harry's guests. Edward had rolled in, with his younger brother in his wake, and wholly obscured by his bulk. He had greeted Edmund genially, but Edmund stood in considerable awe of him. He was so very large and magnificent, and for all his geniality he had a rather commanding air. It seemed fitting that he should occupy the chair of estate into which Harry thrust him. His brother, Richard of Coningsburgh, emerging from behind his massive form, looked to be many years his junior. He was quite slim, and rather effeminate, wearing his hair in long curls, and adopting every freak of fashion. He was always very pleasant in company, but his face was not, like his brother's, a kindly one. He too had fought with Harry in Wales. He was married to Edmund's sister, and Edmund was well acquainted with him, but never quite at ease in his presence. It so often seemed that Sir Richard was sneering when he uttered his smiling compliments.

The Lord Humfrey had just come in, a shimmer of blue samite interwoven with silver threads, with a peacock's feather in his high-crowned hat, and a pair of silken crackows, with upward curving toes, upon his feet. He and Edmund were just of an age, but had little in common beside their love of learning. Edmund was shy of Humfrey, who knew so many things that had nothing to do with books, and who was so quick-witted that he made his cousin feel clumsy and stupid. Like Thomas, he was wearing a very short hanseline, but the sleeves of it, instead of being made tight to the wrists, were so long that they trailed on the floor when he let his hands fall to his sides. Edward called out, in his rumbling voice: 'God amend the Pope, gadling, what a gazing-stock you make of yourself!'

'Of force, Edward, of force!' Humfrey tossed at him. 'Since it did not please God to do it for me!'

A graceful gesture described his cousin's bulk; there was a roar of laughter; Edward's visage became empurpled, as he struggled for words with which to abash his impertinent young relative. Harry was watching Humfrey with indulgent amusement in his eyes, but he said, as he pulled him down on to the banker on which he himself was lounging: 'Keep a meek tongue in your head, malapert, or you shall be sent to your bed!' He looked up, and smiled across the chamber at the large figure on

the threshold. 'John shall carry you there under his arm!' Then
he broke off, and sprang to his feet, as John stood aside to let
another man come into the room. 'Richard!' he cried, and flung
out his hands.

3

It was at moments such as these that Edmund felt the gulf
between himself and his fellows yawn widest. They were all
crowding round my lord of Warwick, embracing him, clapping
him on the back, laughing, and jesting in the manner of old
friends. He only stood aloof from the circle, because to him
Warwick was not Richard Beauchamp, whom he had known
from his cradle, but a remote and splendid figure whom he had
never until now set eyes on. He did not quite wish himself
otherwise, because to meet Warwick was every stripling's
ambition; but he wished from the depths of his soul that every
circumstance of his life had been different. Presently, he knew,
Harry, who was standing with an arm thrown across Warwick's
shoulders, would remember him, and make him known to my
lord, drawing him into that circle of warmth and friendship.
But he, Edmund Mortimer, sprung, like Harry, from a line of
kings, ought, all the years of his life, to have been at the heart
of it.

He heard his name spoken, and turned to find Sir Gilbert
Umfraville at his elbow. Gilbert had slipped unnoticed into the
chamber; he whispered: 'Do you know him? I don't! Of course,
he went away before we joined the Prince, didn't he?'

The feeling of isolation receded; he and Gilbert were just two
squires – only Gilbert had won his knighthood – too young to
be acquainted with the great Earl of Warwick, that was all.

John saw them standing together, watching the hero, and
came over to them. He had thought that Edmund was looking
forlorn, and felt sorry for him. Thomas complained that
Edmund was too good and too dull, but Thomas was always
incapable of understanding the difficulties of other men's lives,
and never suspected that under a stolid front a man might be
concealing grief or bitterness. 'Come and let me make Richard
known to you before Edward begins to ask him what beasts he

found to hunt on his travels! You know Edward's way!' he said, slipping a hand in Edmund's arm.

Edmund's rather heavy face lit up. He decided that John, whom he scarcely knew, was, after Harry, the most likeable of his cousins. Later, when supper was served he wished that he could have sat beside him at table, instead of beside Humfrey, who was engaged in a lively conversation with Henry Scrope, and paid no heed to him.

It was foolish of Edmund to have chosen that place, John thought, seeing him with his attention concentrated on his platter. Humfrey never exerted himself to talk to people he didn't think amusing; he became unaware of their existence, unless he disliked them, when the chances were that he would be rude to them. Watching him, John thought that they had all of them indulged Humfrey too much. He was still the darling of the family. Even forthright Thomas found excuses for his way-wardness; and Father, though Humfrey visited him infrequently, and always had some reason for flitting away again as soon as decency permitted, regarded him with the fondest of eyes, and bestowed more benefits upon him than he bestowed on Thomas, his favourite child. He had made him the custodian of Hadleigh Castle, in Essex, when the sickly Earl of Oxford had parted his life; and Humfrey spent much of his time there. It was con-veniently near to London, without being so near as to make it possible for any of them to know just how he occupied himself there. Thomas knew, but he would not tell tales of Humfrey. Once, in an unguarded moment, he had called Humfrey a John-among-the-maids, but when questioned he had laughed, and said: 'Oh, well! We are none of us monks, after all!'

They were not, of course. They were lusty young bachelors who took what sport was offered to them. As for the pleasures of love, they must have been ascetics to have withstood the lures thrown out to them wherever they went. Four young princes, all well-visaged, and brimming over with spirits, all with the beckoning look in their bright eyes, were beset on every side with temptation; but only Humfrey, John believed, was in danger of falling into excess. Harry's confessor might reprove him for being overly fond of the pursuit of Venus, but for months together Harry led a life of the strictest abstinence. It was only in holidaytime that he thrust the rigid young commander out of sight, cast his cares from off his shoulders, and gave himself to wild rule. Thomas and John took their pleasures lightheartedly in leisure moments; but all Humfrey's moments were leisure ones, and already, at nineteen, his face was beginning to show betraying lines. Did Harry know? John thought that he must guess. Probably Harry knew that he was powerless to curb Humfrey's appetite. He had less influence over Humfrey than over any of them, because Humfrey, who seemed the most affectionate, was in reality the least. He was fond of many people, but loved only himself, which made it strange that he should have won so much love from his brothers. Perhaps it was because they had always regarded him as a young and tender creature whom it was their duty to protect; or perhaps it was his endearing charm which held them. He had the most engaging smile too, mischievous, rueful, and wholly disarming, so that wrath melted under it, and however naughtily he might have demeaned himself one felt that he had done so innocently, and must not be too harshly judged.

Thomas and Humfrey both had that gift of charm: it was not Harry's magic, but something akin to it that won them many friends. John would have been amazed to learn that he was endowed with it also; and would have written Edward down as cup-shotten had he overheard what Edward was at that instant saying to Warwick.

'John?' said Edward, chewing grains of paradise taken from the dish at his elbow. 'Yes, he is a man grown. Grown to be as huge a fellow as the giant Colbrand, whom your ancestor slew! A good lad: plenty of kind-wit, too. I tell Harry John is the most evenheaded of them all. You can always trust John!'

But John was unaware even that Edward's and Richard's eyes were turned towards him. He was listening, with a crease between his brows, to Sir John Oldcastle – or, rather, as he reminded himself, to Lord Cobham. It was difficult to remember this, because that title had belonged for as far back as any man could remember to a Kentish gentleman of unquenchable spirit and incredible length of days. He had died in extreme old age, leaving as his heiress his grand-daughter, a much-married lady, who was then mourning her third husband. Jack Oldcastle, himself twice a widower, had married her a year ago, and had this year received a writ of summons to Parliament under the title of baron of Cobham. He was still one of Harry's dearest friends, though eight years his senior: a big, burly man, with the strength of a bull, and enthusiasms which were childlike, or even as John suspected, a little mad. He was a competent commander, and a very brave man, but John could not forbear the thought that Harry would have done better not to have invited him to this supper. Harry had seen to it that there should be no fair frail ones present tonight, for that was not at all the kind of thing Richard liked; but it seemed to John that if Richard, a rigidly orthodox man in his religious beliefs, heard the things Oldcastle was saying he would be far more shocked than by the sight of a Felice or two in Harry's lodging.

Really, Oldcastle was the strangest man! Was he perhaps drunk? No, not drunk, but slightly enflamed by the wine he kept on gulping, whenever he paused in his discourse. It might as well, or better, have been water, for it was plain that he drank unthinkingly, to wet a dry throat, and could not have told whether the liquid he tossed down it were Rhenish, or Romoney. It was being served in large cups of blue Murano glass, and Oldcastle never noticed when the servants refilled these. He had started out by impressing upon John the excellences of the poet who enjoyed his enthusiastic patronage; but from quotations from the works of Master Hoccleve he rapidly passed to bible texts, which he recited to illustrate some nebulous doctrine that seemed to be irritating his mind. What it was John did not know: the subject was unsuited to a supper party, and smacked a little of heresy. John Wycliffe's name kept on cropping up, too. Well, there was no harm in that, since Wycliffe had never been convicted of heresy. Moreover, the reform of clerical abuses was desired by the strictest churchmen, and frequently discussed. But Oldcastle seemed to have been exchanging letters with the rector of Prague University, who had been forbidden to continue preaching in his diocese. John knew nothing about this John Hus, but it all sounded rather perilous. He caught the eye of his cousin Thomas Fitzalan, the Earl of Arundel, and saw it brimful of amusement. Arundel was looking at Oldcastle as a man might watch a bear performing japeworthy antics. Well, if Oldcastle's friends only laughed at his utterances, John supposed that there could be no real harm in them. He had a wide circle of friends, and not all of them young men. One of them was the King's old crony, Sir Thomas Erpingham, a most respectable person.

The Lord Talbot had been sitting on John's left hand, but he had joined the group at the other end of the board. Arundel, with a wink at John, slid along the bench into his vacated place, and said across the table: 'Jack, you're jugbitten! You'll be put out of the Prince's grace!'

'I was never jugbitten in my life!' declared Oldcastle. 'Must a man be drunk before he can perceive the corruption by which all Christendom is beset? I tell you, unless these ills are re-formed—'

'Reform my uncle the Archbishop!' said Arundel, who was slightly drunk himself. 'Start a crusade! Let us march against Lambeth, Jack! I'll join you, and Harry too, I'll swear!'

'Cousin, an egg and to bed, I think!' John interposed, good-humouredly, but with an unmistakable note of command in his voice.

Arundel stared at him, his colour rising. It was never easy for him to brook reproof, and John was nearly ten years his junior. He felt, moreover, in his rather fuddled state, that he had a good right to say what he chose about his uncle, even if he was the Archbishop of Canterbury. Everyone knew that they had been on bad terms since Scrope's taking-off. Then, under the un-wavering gaze that held his eyes, he recollected that John was the King's son, and he swallowed the hasty words that had risen to his lips. Since he had served under Harry's command he had become very friendly with him, but he was no fool, and he knew whose part Harry would take in a quarrel between his cousin and his favourite brother. So he forced himself to laugh, and to say: 'Very dread lord, I cry you mercy!'

John smiled, and Arundel, mollified, said confidentially: 'Words swim when the wine sinks! It's this damned ozey.'

John got up, nodding. Oldcastle, he could see, was going to continue to argue about the corruption of the clergy, and he had not come to this party to discuss theological questions. He moved across the chamber to where a merrier group had gathered round Harry. He, and Henry Scrope, and John Talbot were mocking Humfrey for the extravagance of his raiment.

'The horrible, disordinate scantiness of your slop, brother,' Harry was saying, with an expression of great piety, 'is an offence against all shamefastness.'

'But his sleeves atone for that!' said Scrope. 'Tell us, Humfrey! Is it true that they were designed by thieves for the better concealment of the trifles they steal from honest men?'

'I will tell you something else,' replied Humfrey, not in the least ruffled. 'You will never prosper if you don't learn lip-wisdom! Only lurdans speak of sleeves within John's hearing!'

This made them all laugh. For nearly two years the Court of Chivalry, over which the Constable and the Marshal presided, had been engaged on a suit which hung upon a sleeve. The sleeve was a red one set upon a field of gold; it constituted the arms of the Hastings family; and the right to bear it was being bitterly contested by the heirs of John Hastings, that unfortunate Earl of Pembroke who had met his death by an accident in the joustinglists when less than twenty years of age. He had died childless, and the right to bear his arms was being claimed by Reginald Grey of Ruthin, as heir-general, and by Sir Edward Hastings, as heir-male. It was an issue of extraordinary complexity, and of considerable importance to all who had the right to bear arms. When other topics for conversation failed, there was always the Hastings case to be discussed, generally with mounting acrimony, since only the officers of the Court of Chivalry found any difficulty in reaching a decision in the matter. The rest of the world, though sharply divided into opposite camps, knew just what the judgment should be, each side maintaining its finding with passionate conviction.

For the Court of Chivalry, it was not so easy. The claim had to be traced back through several generations, to the first John Hastings, who had lived a hundred years ago, and had had (as John of Lancaster despairingly said to Ralph Neville) the unkindness to take two wives to himself. From the first of these had sprung the Earls of Pembroke, and Reginald Grey of Ruthin, directly descended from John Hastings' daughter, Elizabeth. There lay the rub: could the right to bear the coveted arms be transmitted through the female line? On the other hand, Sir Edward Hastings, impeccably descended through males, sprang from that fatal second marriage, and claimed the honours only through the half-blood. Witnesses had been called; and out of the main issue had arisen a number of questions of vital importance, such as whether livery of lands could, or could not, transfer the right of bearing arms. John and Ralph Neville had been heartily sick of the case for months; the contestants were understandably impatient (since the costs were already enormous) to have it decided; and the only persons who would be sorry to see it ended were the officers of the Court, who found it of absorbing interest, exhaustively examined all the witnesses, argued the evidence amongst themselves, and kept on digging into musty archives to discover with triumph some nice point of legal or chivalric precedent.

As was inevitable, Humfrey's words started the usual discussion amongst all who heard them. Edward of York caught the name Hastings, and called across the chamber: 'What's that you are saying? Are you speaking of the Hastings case? Now, I'll tell you what I think, John!'

'Gramercy, Edward, you have told me a score of times already!'

'Which of them do you mean to give it to, Sir John?' asked Gilbert Talbot.

'A'God's half, Gib, you may not ask him that!' expostulated Thomas.

Then Richard Beauchamp's voice made itself heard, demanding enlightenment, and at least six people began to explain it to him.

It was not Harry's practice to allow business to spoil his private parties, but when he saw his guests happily engaged in argument he sent John an unspoken signal, and John went to where he was sitting, and set his hand on the high, carved back of his chair, his brows lifting.

'I have read the letters you sent me,' Harry said. 'It seems to me that you will have to truss up your baggage, brother.'

'So does it seem to me,' agreed John.

'These damned Scots! What of this Hastings case? Must you continue to preside over it?'

'No, but I must read the judgment.'

Harry smiled. 'When will that be? On Jeffrey's Day?'

'I have often thought so, but we hope now to finish this month. I can go north then, but I tell you to your head, Harry, Fastcastle cannot be held unless I have money and supplies to send to the governor Holden. Perhaps not Berwick, even.'

Harry thought for a moment. He said presently: 'Hold Berwick. I shall send you money, but not in time, perhaps, to save Fastcastle. A truce – till Michaelmas, if no longer – would best serve us at this hour.' He tilted his head back to look up at John. 'If you go into the North, can you prevail upon the garrison to hold Berwick?'

'Perhaps. But I must pledge my word that the wages shall be paid. I have been told before that I should have money for my needs, Harry.'

'Not by me!'

'No.' John smiled at him. 'Are you so sure that you can prevail?'

'Trust me!' Harry said, with a challenging look. 'This parliament shall grant money for your needs as well as mine!'

3 Discord

1

A few days later, the Court of Chivalry decided the Hastings claim in favour of the Lord of Ruthin, and John read the judgment in the White Chamber at Westminster. Sir Edward Hastings was ordered to pay the costs of the suit, but as he immediately entered an appeal against the judgment, Reginald Grey was unable to enforce this decree, and was consequently very much the poorer for his triumph.

John had not left for the North when they learned at Westminster that the Earl of Somerset had parted his life. Sir Thomas Beaufort brought the tidings to Harry. John was with his brother, and they were both shocked, not so much by their uncle's death, which they had expected, as by the manner of it. They had not known that when he had felt his ending-day to be near he had had himself carried from Cold Harbour to the Hospital of St Katherine-by-the-Tower.

Harry exclaimed; and Sir Thomas said gruffly: 'No, well – he told none of us. Not even brother Henry was there when he uncorsed him. You'd have thought he would have wished at least for him. I know I'd liefer have Henry to shrive me on my bed-mortal than any other. And I'd liefer by far it was my own bed, too, not a wretched pallet in a hospital where they house needful old dotards! However, he was always the pious one of us: we used to say it was he who should have been made a priest, not Henry. He has been a confrater of Holy Trinity at Canterbury for years, you know. If it was soul-heal he was seeking, I wonder he shouldn't have— But all talk now is more and no more! God assoil him, he died in a happy hour! Yes, yesterday it was, on Palm Sunday. I wish I had seen him –

though we never had much to say to one another. Well, he was no tongue-pad, was he? Still, he was my brother, and I wouldn't have had him go to his last end alone – for I take no force of a parcel of poor brethren.'

'But his lady – his children?' Harry said, staring at his uncle.

'No, I tell you: not one of us!' Sir Thomas answered, wiping his eyes on his sleeve. 'Nor any of his people, not even his attorney, to set his Will down aright! It seems he took no thought to earthly business. That's what comes of it, when a man runs into religion! Not but what the brethren, to say sooth, bethought them of the need, and begged him to say whether he would make his testament or no, which he did, and they must presently swear to, for he had no strength left in him to sign it. All goes to brother Henry, as his executor. No bequests, except a little money to his servants, as Henry shall think proper. Eh, when I remember what pains my father, whose soul God pardon, took when he made his Will— A strange man, my brother John! Well, God rest him: he was weary of his life.'

Neither of the princes spoke. Each was oppressed by the thought of that proud withdrawal from a world that must have become importable; each was wondering how much their brother Thomas had to answer for.

'His lady will go to her manor in Lincolnshire, after the burying-day,' Sir Thomas said, making Harry start, and redden. He continued, averting his eyes: 'Henry is taking order to that. She may not remain at Cold Harbour: it was granted to my brother only for the term of his life. Besides – it will be best for her to leave London.' He paused, but still neither of the princes spoke. 'Well, I must go to the King,' he said. 'He was still abed when I came to you, and I would not rouse him with such ill-tidings. He always loved John the best of us Beauforts.'

It was unfortunate that Thomas should have entered the chamber hard upon his uncle's departure. He came in with his carefree grace, saying: 'Has Thomas Beaufort been with you, Harry? I saw one of his fellows below, and he told me that Somerset has been clay-cold these many hours.'

Harry looked at him with hard eyes. 'God forgive it you, Thomas, I do not!' he said.

Thomas flushed, and answered furiously: 'Commend you to the devil: what had I to do with his death?'

'You best know!'

'Yea, marry, so I do! Did I send him to St Katherine's? Did I bid him turn monk at the end?'

'Would he have done so but for you – spouse-breaker?'

'Harry!' John said sharply.

'Now, by my head, you whore's bird!' Thomas shouted furiously, closing with Harry.

There was a short, violent struggle before John got between them. 'Stint! Buzzards and makefrays, both of you! Do you wish every scullion to hear you fliting?'

'I care not a rush! Harry shall unsay that!'

'If it was false, it is unsaid,' Harry responded, breathing a little hard. 'But I was at Cold Harbour when you disported yourself in the bower there! If I lie when I call you spouse-breaker, do I so when I say you have played the spill-love between Somerset and his lady?'

'You may go hang in hell!' Thomas said. 'I am not answerable to you for what I do!'

'Well for you!' Harry said swiftly. 'Look to yourself, brother, when that day comes!'

'Yea, God pity all of us when you wear the crown! It is not yet!'

'Avoid, rackrope, avoid!' John said.

'Oh, I know full well you would bear Harry's part!'

'My redoubted lords, saving only my reverence, I would bang both your heads together for a pair of branglesome niddicocks!'

Harry's face relaxed a little, but Thomas flung out of the chamber in anger. 'Unless I take order to Thomas, it will be God pity me when I come to the throne!' Harry said.

'For my love, Harry, no more unthrift!' John begged. 'That garboil was of your making! Why should you dub Thomas spouse-breaker when Somerset did not?'

'Would any man dare to appeal the King's alder-liefest son?'

'Phrrt!' uttered John, jerking up his thumb in lewd contempt.

'*John*, you scapegallows!' Harry expostulated, breaking into scandalized laughter.

2

At Neville's Inn John found, to his relief, that his aunt regarded the whole affair in a more robust spirit than did either of her Beaufort brothers. She was childing again, but the prospect of adding yet another infant to her teeming nurseries had not prevented her from accompanying her lord to London, and was not going to prevent her from returning with him to Raby. She would go mounted on her palfrey, too: none of your bone-shaking whirlicotes for my Lady Westmoreland! She had no wish to drop the child before her time, whatever might be my lord's desires. Besides, how was she to be expected to keep a watchful eye on the carts and wagons, and the hirelings, if she travelled cooped up in a whirlicote, or a horse-litter? Ralph Neville, having enjoyed his lady's companionship for thirteen years, refrained from telling her that he had no such expectation. His household boasted almost as many officers as the King's, but well he knew that my lady would trust none of them to arrange the details of the journey. She would not readily forget, she told him, the occasion when two wagonloads of gear wanted on the road had been sent, through the wanwittedness of his controller, by sea.

John found her in the midst of a scene of activity and disorder, ushers and grooms and pages scurrying about amongst bales and barrels. From the appearance of the Great Hall, my lady had gathered together every one of her earthly possessions, besides those of her lord and all his household, but this was not true: fourteen cartloads of victuals, she told John, had been sent off to the riverside, together with ten of my lord's harness, and seventeen of furnishings and utensils. What he beheld was no more than the gear to be carried by road.

He had come to see Ralph, but my lady took him off to one of the solars, and said briskly: 'Now, I charge you, John, no prating to my lord about all this gainstrife that is sprung up over my brother Somerset's ending, for he is nigh diswitted

339

already by the debate, and he will not for his life mell himself in it! God amend the Pope! I never knew John to do such a tilty thing in all his days! Turning eremite, and setting the family all-to-bits! To use no ambages with you, nephew, Henry and Thomas have pepper in their noses, and lay the business at *young* Thomas's door, which is witaldry, and so I have told them! If young Thomas has been at Cold Harbour oft and lome, Somerset should have taken order to it. God rest his soul, it is full-yore since he entertained his lady as a husband should! If he was not in a broil in Wales, he was in Calais, which must be the most chargeous, displeasant place in Christendom from all I ever heard tell of it! I'd as lief live in Berwick! And, when he did come home to his lady, demeaning himself like a monk since ferne-ago! Well, how long is it since she was brought to bed? Thirteen years a wife, and no more than five brats in her nursery! I promise you, I pity her! Yes, and if that doesn't show that there was nothing so much amiss between her and young Thomas, I know not what may! No, no, John, my brother was forspent, and no wonder, with all the travail and teen he had had in life!'

'Madam, it eases my heart that you should say so, and indeed I think it is very sooth. Thomas is *not* a spouse-breaker!'

'As to that,' said my lady trenchantly, 'you may say so, since he won no bolding! My good-sister is *not* a bed swerver! Alas-at-ever! She's a pretty, sely soul, with no more kind-wit than you may truss up in a eggshell! And there she is, widowed before she's thirty, with five brats to rear, and the eldest of them with more than ten years to endure before he has livery of his lands! Well, the King must give him a seemly allowance for his support, and so I shall tell him!'

In the event, it was not needful for anyone to persuade the King to deal generously with the orphans. He had been greatly distressed by his half-brother's death; and when the widow came to Westminster to petition his grace on her son's behalf, bringing the boy, and his next eldest brother, with her, he was much affected. John Beaufort had never allied himself, like his brothers, to the Prince of Wales's party; he had remained King Henry's friend; and the sight of his fair young widow, with her two lovely imps escorting her, caused the King to shed tears. Margaret wept too, as she had been doing, in a gentle way, since her lord's death. Her grief might not be profound, but it was quite sincere. She had been fond of her grave husband; his hence-going made her sad, for she had no one now to protect her. If he had been on life, she thought, he would not have allowed his brothers to speak unkindly to her, or to pack her off to Lincolnshire, as though she had misdeameaned herself, which, as she had told Bishop Henry new and new *indeed* she had not.

The two boys at her side made a touching picture of orphanhood, both of them clad from head to foot in black weeds, and looking rather frightened. The elder was the King's godson, and his namesake; he favoured his mother; but little Jack, a sturdy six-year-old, was the very spit of what John Beaufort had been when the King had first seen him. The King embraced them both, and promised to stand to them in the place of the father they had lost. He made Margaret sit down beside him, and patted her hand while he talked kindly to her; and the little boys, overawed by their surroundings, oppressed by so much weeping, sniffed dolefully, wiping their noses on the backs of their hands, instead of on the clean clouts with which they had been provided. However, one of the resplendent persons who stood behind the King's siege detached himself from the group, and came to them, whispering: 'Slutty little snudge-snouts! Here!'

They perceived that he was Thomas, and accepted gratefully the sugar-plums he slid into their hands. He made a face at them, and went back to his place at the King's elbow. They smiled shyly at him, surreptitiously munching his largesse. He was quite the most exciting person of their acquaintance. You never knew what he would do, though you could be sure that it would always be splendid, even if it was on one of the days when he didn't notice you. He was quite likely to pay no heed to you as to toss you a rare gift, or encourage you in the sort of rough play frowned on by your attendants; and at no time was he at all like any other adult person.

King Henry made Lady Somerset an allowance of a thousand

marks for the support of his namesake. She had also her dower, and a third of John Beaufort's lands: a fortune which would make her the most sought-after widow in the kingdom, said her sister-in-law.

3

Before John left Westminster, the quarrel between his brothers was patched up, through his unwitting agency. It was Thomas who rescued Harry's little spaniel from the jaws of John's alaunt, getting bitten almost to the bone for his pains; and Harry, learning of this, sought him out to render thanks. Thomas was stiff at first, but none of them could resist Harry when his hands were held out to them. Thomas melted; and if the cause of the quarrel was not forgotten it was laid to rest, the contestants becoming as one in abuse of John's savage pet.

But to those who knew them both it was plain that a truce only had been declared. The Countess of Somerset had withdrawn to her Lincolnshire estates, and Thomas was demeaning himself with discretion; but between him and Harry was a barrier that had nothing to do with any woman. Thomas belonged to the Court party, inimical to Harry, but even more to the Beauforts who supported him. Thomas did not dislike Thomas Beaufort, but the Bishop he detested, and the Bishop was Harry's chief adviser. From having been the favourite son of his father, Thomas had always enjoyed more of the King's confidence than his brothers; and he had identified himself with the King's policy; a little, John thought, from jealousy of Harry. He was on good terms with Archbishop Arundel, who was always at loggerheads with Harry. None of his brothers liked their great-uncle Arundel. John, because he was bound to Harry; Humfrey, because he read condemnation of himself in the Archbishop's eyes. Thomas encouraged his father to lean more and more upon Arundel; Harry was nauseated by the King's dependence on him. The Archbishop had taken upon himself the care of his ailing monarch; and Thomas, genuinely attached to his father, was willing to abet him in anything that might afford him solace. The King had begun to call himself the Archbishop's son in Christ; he was never happy when apart from him; and hung upon him with a fondness that drove Harry almost wood with rage, and was, indeed, a little maudlin.

With this uneasy situation at Westminster, which he could do nothing to mend, John was not sorry to turn his face to the North. Not that anything pleasant awaited him there: he knew only too well what he would find, and what he would be obliged to grapple with before Harry could send him the money and the supplies he needed. Harry had begun his administration – if this it could be called, when he gave up his seat at the head of the Council whenever the King was well enough to attend to his affairs – by informing the Council that without money he could do nothing. It was a bold gesture, and one which the King would have hesitated to make; but Harry was not an ailing monarch who had usurped a throne, and found it hard to hold. He was an energetic young prince, with success at his back, a high destiny before him; and the approval of his father's subjects to give him encouragement – if he needed it. John thought he did not. Harry had always been quite sure of himself. He knew, untroubled by misgiving, the thing he wanted, and never doubted his power to obtain it. Perhaps it was this confidence that swept the Council and the redeless Commons along the road of his choosing. They received his message meekly, and quailed under the flash of his eyes when he told them that he would never tolerate an attempt to wrest its wealth from Holy Church.

Parliament, John thought, would give Harry a fairly generous grant; what would be voted to his administration by the two Convocations was dubious. On the one hand, the clergy knew that against the efforts of the estates to seize Church property he was their champion; on the other, he was opposed to Archbishop Arundel's determination to exercise jurisdiction over Oxford University. This meant that he was opposed also to the King. The University was in the diocese of Lincoln, but it had been made independent by papal Bull, which rendered it subject in civil matters to the King, and in spiritual to Rome. But the King had renounced his rights to the Archbishop, and had told Richard Courtenay that he would not support the University's claim. No one could foretell what would be the outcome of the struggle between Arundel and Courtenay, but one result was already plain, in the open rift between the Prince and the Archbishop.

Within a few days of John Beaufort's death, the King bestowed Cold Harbour on the Prince of Wales; and on the same day made him Captain of Calais. He was already Captain of Dover Castle, and Warden of the Cinque Ports; and John knew only too well that Harry would set the needs of Calais high on the roll of expenditure. He was going there in April, to see with his own eyes in what condition its defences stood. It did not seem likely that after Dover and Calais had been served there would be much money left for the defence of the northern Marches.

But it was pleasant to be in the North again, even though winter had scarcely left the uplands, and biting winds swept the moors, and tossed the grey sea into foam. Newcastle gave him a royal welcome, the mayor, the aldermen, gildsmen, in livery suits of murrey, crimson, and green, and a rout of apprentices, streaming out of the town to meet him, and (since his arrival coincided with the feast of Marymas) conducting him to a covered platform from which he could watch the performance of a mystery play. Traverses had been erected on three sides of the platform to protect him from the wind, but in spite of these, and the fur-lined cloak in which one of his valets muffled him, it was a chilly entertainment. However, he knew that his presence was adding zest to the performance of the mummers, so he assumed an expression of interest, laughed at all the farcical interludes, and only chafed his benumbed fingers under the cover of his cloak.

An even warmer welcome awaited him at Warkworth, which had been for some time his chief residence in Northumberland. He retained his fondness for little Prudhoe, but those who had told him it would prove to be too small for his needs were right. Warkworth, except for Alnwick, was the most commodious, and certainly the most comfortable hold in his possession, its private apartments stretching along the whole of the western curtainwall, and comprising a magnificent hall, roomy solars and chambers (all reached by inner stairs), buttery, pantry, huge kitchens, and a chapel. These, with the stables, two towers of defence, the well-house, and the foundations of a collegiate church, were situated in the outer bailey, which was reached through a vaulted arch beyond the drawbridge, and flanked by guardrooms. To the north, and at the extreme end of the inner bailey, the keep stood, a large, octagonal tower, at present in an unfinished state, but already containing ample accommodation for the garrison, and the squires, pages, valets, ushers, clerks, and yeomen who constituted the Lord Warden's household.

John had grown accustomed to the castle, and no longer noticed the Percy lion carved over several of its doorways; but his occupation of it carried with it no feeling of permanence. Although old Northumberland had died under attainder, the day would come when Hotspur's son, young Henry Percy, would be restored to his grandsire's possessions. He was being kept in honourable captivity by the Regent Albany, possibly as a counter-threat to King Henry holding the King of Scots; and must now, John thought, be sixteen years of age. Something that had been said at Raby, where John had spent a night, had made him wonder whether Ralph Neville, that skilful match-maker, was thinking of an alliance between Percy and one of his daughters. It would be just like him, John reflected, with an inward smile. It might be quite a good thing, too. A Percy could not be for ever kept from his inheritance; but a Percy under Neville influence could be a gain to the King instead of a danger.

Meanwhile, John held that inheritance; and he had not been many hours at Warkworth before the steward and the controller were laying their accounts before him; while, awaiting their turns for audience outside the solar, and quarrelling over rights of precedence, were gathered several other officials, including the receiver, the auditor, and the surveyor, all with much business to discuss, and all with formidable rolls in hand. By the following day, Warkworth was full of the Lord Warden's officers, and John was plunged once more into the unrewarding toil which made up the greater part of his life.

None of the news brought to him by his officers was good. He had not expected it to be, or that this year, unless funds were immediately forthcoming, would differ materially from those which had gone before. Last summer, Jedburgh Castle, of which he had been appointed constable, had fallen, because the Council would send him neither men nor supplies for its relief; this summer, Fastcastle would fall, for the same reason. He had managed hitherto to provision it from the sea, but he had had word from Thomas Holden, who held it, that it was now being closely watched on all sides; and he knew from the reports brought in from his officers that the Scottish Earl of Mar was cruising between Berwick and Newcastle to intercept seaborne supplies. Berwick was still protected by the swollen Tweed, but its captain wrote that unless the Lord Warden could send money for wages he feared the garrison would desert. The floods, though they had saved the town from capture, had created great distress: victuals were very dear; on all sides dissatisfaction was rife; and the fortifications were in such a state that they would crumble under assault.

As usual, negotiations for a truce with the Scots ran through all this like a brittle thread. In April a meeting was arranged. Except for a suggestion thrown out by the Scottish envoys that the Lord John should wed one of the Regent's daughters, it was the same as every other meeting he had attended. He reported the proposal to the Council, without comment. If the King thought that such a match would be advantageous, he was perfectly ready to marry the lady, for he had always looked on his marriage, whenever it should be arranged, as a matter of state policy. But he did not think that his father would care for this match; and certainly Harry would not, for Harry disliked the Scots.

Nothing came of the proposal. Fastcastle fell, after its prolonged siege; and in June a truce until November was agreed to.

News from London was scanty, but in September a summons to appear before the Council by Michaelmas reached John. This was so unprecedented that for a moment he stared uncomprehendingly at the document, wondering in what way he could have erred. Then he knew that Harry must be behind the summons, and turned to find that Antelope Herald was proffering a second letter.

Harry's note was brief, and hastily scrawled. *'Trescher,'* Harry wrote, *'if it please your gentleness, come with your best speed to Westminster, and declare unto us what may be your needs. God send you good years and long to live!'*

Within two days John learned that Ralph Neville had also received a summons; and, with him, his son, Sir John, who, since the death of Thomas Neville of Furnivall, had acted as his father's lieutenant in Annandale. The new Lord Furnivall was a stranger to the North: he was Jack Talbot, who had claimed the title in the right of his wife, Thomas Neville's daughter; and his work lay not on the Scottish border, but on the Welsh. He and his brother, Gilbert, were close friends of Harry's. Harry said that of all his lieutenants Jack Talbot showed the fairest promise of becoming a great captain. John was barely acquainted with him: he seemed rather a stark young man, with a fiery eye and an impetuous temper.

'Well-an-ere!' exclaimed Ralph Neville, almost as soon as John had reached Raby Castle. 'I was never so awhape in all my life days! Unbosom, John! In what sort is the wind?'

John dug Harry's letter out of his pouch, and handed it to him. The Earl read it with starting eyes. 'Holy Saint Cross! Well, if I ever thought to see those jobbards at Westminster set the saddle on the right horse, you may call me a Paynim! By my head, John, this brother of yours is a prince apt for a kingdom!'

4 Lusty Bachelor

I

Westminster Palace, at the end of the summer, seemed almost deserted. Only such persons as the clerks of the Exchequer remained there throughout the year. The King had been in the country ever since May, at first at Windsor, or at the Queen's manor of Sonning, but latterly at Woodstock, where he had stayed nearly two months, in great physical dis-ease. He had moved at the beginning of September to Leicester, and was still there, not well enough, it was reported, to transact business, or to enjoy any pastime. The palace servants were not quite sure whether the Lord Thomas was with him or whether he had gone to his manor at Barrow. One of the yeomen ushers told the Lord John this, darting a quick look at him to see how he would receive it. But the Lord John only nodded, and turned away. He seemed not to be interested, which was disappointing, since Barrow was in Lincolnshire, where the bereaved Countess of Somerset was still residing: a circumstance which was giving the royal household much food for conjecture.

Humfrey was not in London either; but when the shadows lengthened across the courts Harry came clattering in from Berkhampsted, hot, and covered with dust, but full of energy, and with his eyes very clear and shining in a lean face tanned as brown as a nut. He caught John in a muscular embrace, exclaiming remorsefully: 'I meant to be here to welcome you! I cry you mercy, tresâme!'

'Where are you from?' John asked, kissing his cheek.

'Berkhampsted. I like it there.'

'Oh, so did not I! Where is Humfrey?'

'At Hadleigh – and in what company I know not!'

'Out and alas! Are you living chaste at Berkhampsted, brother?'

Harry laughed. 'I promise you! But in London—! What will it please you to do this night? Shall we go to Lewis John's for a rear-supper?'

'All the way to the Vintry, only to end in the Clink? No, I have been riding for a senight – at your behest!'

'Oh, not ride! We'll drop down the river to Cold Harbour presently, and then it shall be as you choose. And we shall *not* end in the Clink!'

'The last time I went with you to Lewis John's, I was pitched into a broil in Bridge Street for the devil knows what cause, and at the height of the hurling out came the sheriffs upon us!' retorted John.

'We will be sad and discreet,' promised Harry, with elves of mischief in his eyes. He sat down, looking affectionately up at John. 'Give me thanks for wordfastness! You will come before the Council in three days.'

'I would it might have been before Fastcastle was lost to us,' John said ruefully.

'But, John, I gave you foretokening it could not be! I have done my power! If you knew how much there is to do! The Council met twice last year – *twice*!'

'Jesu mercy!' John exclaimed. 'Because of Father's sickness?'

'Affirmably! But the affairs of this realm must not be neglected because the King is sick! Nor should his Chancellor be content to have it so! Arundel has let my needs sleep, and yours too. I tell you, John, I have had more toil since I took Father's siege at the Council than in all my fighting days!'

'Tell me!' John said, pulling forward a stool.

'Yes, but order your people to carry your gear to Cold Harbour! I sent word my barge was to come to the stairs here. There's no pestilence in the city, and I like it better there.'

John lounged over to the door, and set up a shout for the groom of his chambers. When he turned back into the room, the elvish look had vanished from Harry's eyes, and he was frowning. He said abruptly: 'I have had to weigh our needs, you know. Men and supplies for Wales was the most urgeful of these.'

'Well, you would think so,' John agreed. 'But still?'

'To end the war. We have Glendower's son in ward, but Glendower is still on life. I want peace in Wales, and I shall not get it without a strong force there.'

'I should be blithe to have peace on the Eastern Marches,' remarked John.

Harry smiled. 'Makefray, are you asking me to conquer Scotland? We shall not otherwise have peace on the Border. But the Scots will not dare to venture too much.'

'And the Border is far from Westminster,' John said dryly.

'Indeed, John, I have set your needs high,' Harry answered.

'As high as the needs of Calais?'

'Calais!' Harry's face changed. 'John, if it was accidie or lachesse I know not, but Somerset was Captain of Calais overlong! The debts that were owed to him by the King should have been two-so-many. I have seen with my own eyes what is lacking! It is not the harbour alone, nor the battlements, which have suffered from this lachesse: I could show you the accounts from my victualler there which are *shendful*! All is to get: spikings, faggots, elkhorns, hoists, crows, picks, ropes even!'

'Yea, Harry, but have you found it so easy to get such things?'

'No, but I have not been content to fold my hands while all goes to ruin!'

'I think Somerset was forspent,' John said. 'So my aunt of Westmoreland told me. And I also, by my wit, think that Calais is an importable burden.'

'Not importable!' Harry said. 'I shall show you one day that it is of all our cities the most needful to us.'

John looked thoughtfully down at him. 'Do you know, Harry, what was the costage of our thirdfather King Edward's wars in France – and nothing gained?'

'Nothing gained, because he was so unthrifty a captain,' Harry replied coolly.

'*Unthrifty*? Our thirdfather?' gasped John.

'All-utterly! Those miswrought chevauchées— chance-medleys of rap and rend!' Harry said contemptuously. 'I shall not so order my campaigns!'

'Harry, to say that King Edward was an unthrifty captain is

to go beyond the nock!' John protested.

'Abide for the time!' Harry challenged him, his eyes glinting. 'I shall show you!'

'I had liefer you showed me how to fill the Exchequer's coffers!' retorted John.

'Not so!' Harry said, with his delightful smile. 'That, brother, you shall show me. When my time comes – oh, John, I shall need you as never before!'

'I wish your physician would give you a clyster to drive this way-worm from your head!' said John.

Harry laughed, and jumped up. 'There is no clyster with power enough to do that. Come! If my barge is not waiting for me, it will be the worse for the master!'

But his barge was lying by the King's Stairs, a long, low craft, with thwarts painted Lancaster blue, and Harry's standard hanging limp in the stern. It was splendidly furnished: too splendidly, John told Harry, for a dusty prince in buskins and a cameline pourpoint. Harry, pausing on the steps to find a coin for the inevitable beggar beseeching alms there – this one was a legless veteran of King Edward's unthrifty wars – said: 'Only wait until you see me go up the river on my way to a Council meeting!'

'I warrant ye, I warrant ye!' piped up the vagrant, hopping on his crutch. 'Ah, the sweet prince, in his robe of state! God's blessing on that lovesome visage! At Poitiers, most dread lord: that was where my leg was laid in earth!'

'Gloser and losenger, avoid!' Harry said, tossing a silver penny into the crooked palm. 'It was reft from you in a tavern brawl!'

'That's in all likelihood the true tale,' remarked John, disposing himself amongst the silken cushions with which the barge was provided. 'The last time I gave a largesse he told me he got his hurt with Bel sire, in Spain.'

'No force where, poor knave!' Harry answered, sitting down beside him.

The barge was pushed out from the stairs, and began to glide downstream on the tide, the painted oars dipping and lifting almost lazily. The late autumn afternoon was golden and still, with what little breeze that stirred wafting across the water the country smells from the Surrey bank. Men were reaping the corn in one of the fields; a little farther along the apple trees in an orchard were heavy with ripening fruit. Past the Staple, the river took a deep bend to the north, and the barge, avoiding this, hugged the Surrey bank for a little way. Within the bend, with a garden running down to the water's edge, the Bishop of Durham's inn reared its great round towers to the sky. It was separated from the ruins of the Savoy Palace by the stream that ran under Ivy Bridge; and beyond the Savoy lay the inns of the Bishops of Worcester, and Lichfield, and Llandaff. The barge drew nearer to the northern bank again by the Temple gardens. Past the Whitefriars, the Fleet river was flanked by the old palace of Bridewell, and the monastery of the Blackfriars; above the roofs of the clustering houses to the east, the spire of St Paul's dominated the whole city.

The barge slid on, past Queenhythe. The Steelyard was in sight now, and, beyond it, the Cold Harbour stairs; while ahead the great piles of London Bridge loomed across the river; and on the Surrey side the red roofs of Southwark were warm in the sunlight.

'Do you know, Harry, I think I haven't set foot inside Cold Harbour since all of us lived here?' John said, as he stepped out on to the stathe.

He remembered suddenly that the last time he had lived there was during the uneasy weeks when Harry had been with King Richard in Ireland, and wished that he hadn't recalled this. However, Harry only laughed and said, slipping a hand in his arm: 'Do you remember how angry we were when Johanna wouldn't let us run out to see a fire? And how much we wanted to join in a hue and cry?'

'Witterly! And I don't suppose,' said John, 'that she ever thought there would one day be a hue and cry at *your* heels, brother!'

2

In the end, they were not seen at Lewis John's notorious hostelry that evening. They supped alone at Cold Harbour, and sat talking far into the night, while the thick quarriers in the wall-sconces burned lower and lower, and the candles on the table guttered in their sockets. John sat with his arms folded on the table, occasionally picking a plum from the bowl in front of him, and eating it; and Harry lay stretched upon a banker, in his shirt and hose, his pourpoint cast aside, one hand under his head, the other idly caressing his spaniel. The servants had shuttered the windows to keep out the foul night air, and it was stuffy in the chamber, with the smell of hot wax overpowering the scent of the herbs with which the floor was strewn. The talk was desultory, flitting here and there, with long, intimate silences. Both brothers were taciturn by disposition, but between them there was a deep understanding which often rendered words unnecessary; and a trust that made it possible for Harry to say to John what he would have uttered to no man else.

Harry talked a little of France. There was no member of the French royal family, except, perhaps, the King's cousin of Burgundy, worth a leek, he thought. His uncle, the Duke of Berry, was nearly eighty and wholly given over to ease and luxury; his sons, the Dauphin, Louis, and John, Duke of Touraine, were striplings, bred up in a vicious court; his cousin of Orleans had waited only for his mother's death to become reconciled with his father's murderer – *une paix fourrée*, the Court fool christened it; and Berry's son, the Count of Clermont, who had come to England in the spring with two ship-loads of harness and horses for a joust with Thomas at Smithfield, had impressed no one. 'He hates Burgundy above all men,' Harry remarked. 'Do you remember, John, how Thomas said that Burgundy was called the Fearless because he demeaned himself so worshipfully at Nicopolis?' John nodded. A smile lifted the corners of Harry's mouth. 'It was not so. According to what Clermont told us, he was called the Fearless because he once vanquished the citizens of Othée in a mêlée. It endured a full half-hour, too, maugre the fact that the citizens had no arms – or very few.'

'Harry!' John expostulated, bursting into laughter.

'Well, I should not lightly believe what Clermont said of him, but I have discovered this to be a soothsaw. As for Nicopolis,

353

our uncle Somerset told me full-yore that nothing he did on that day could have won for him that title!'

'Or since,' said John reflectively. 'He slew that bitch-clout of Orleans by the hands of his minions – and boasted later of the deed; and after all his bobance this spring Calais is still ours. What drove him off from that enprise? Did some bandog bark at him?'

'Oh, we bribed a carpenter to cast Greek fire over the siege towers and the stores he had had collected at St Martin, and they were consumed! Also the Abbey, for which I am sorry. What happened to his great gun, I know not. We were told that it took eight horses to drag it. Perhaps he will haul it to Paris – if the Orleanists have not already driven him out of the city. There is a brisk war raging there – too brisk for any of them to think more of troubling our peace.' He paused, and turned his head towards his brother. 'It would be of good liking, I think, if we were to mell ourselves a little in that debate.'

'Of good liking,' John agreed. 'We owe them a blow or two! Besides the scathe they have done to the southern ports, I would have you know, Harry, that the Earl of Mar's ships are afloat on French gold! But I see no winning in a French chevauchée. Show it to me, and I shall be blithe to accord with you!'

'No winning anon-right, but presently – in only a hand-while, perhaps – it would be speedful if I had won me an ally in France.'

John looked frowningly at him. 'Burgundy?'

'Sickerly!' The smile that crept into Harry's eyes warmly embraced him. 'Of my three brothers, only one with in-wit, and that one my alder-dearest!'

Colour rose to John's cheeks, but he replied only: 'I have enough to know you would not join hands with the brood of Orleans: not enough to tell why you should seek alliance with that rushbuckler of Burgundy!'

'A rushbuckler, but a subtle man of great power, and wide domains,' murmured Harry. 'Burgundy and Flanders lie under his hand, and, betide what betide, he cannot hope to climb the steps to the mad king's throne.'

'And so you think he will help you to do so! A'God's half, Harry, let not there be two mad kings in Christendom!'

'My claim is good!' Harry said, challenging him.

'Yea, if they held by the apron-strings in France! But they have their law Salique, so for Christ's sweet Tree, Harry, prate to me not of our fore-elder, King Henry III, that married the heiress of France! *That* way-worm was our thirdfather's bane!'

'The law Salique! Witaldry!' Harry said contemptuously.

'Soothly? Then will you set March upon this throne of ours, when Father comes to his last end?'

'March?' Harry said blankly. '*Edmund Mortimer?*'

'Edmund Mortimer,' repeated John, holding his eyes, 'who had for his granddam, Philippa, that was the daughter of our grand-uncle Lionel, older by two years than Bel sire!'

'But, John— !' Harry's eyes had snapped wide open, an arrested expression in them. 'But - but - King Henry's son, Edmund of Lancaster, that was called the Crouchback—'

'Oh, Harry, Harry!' John choked, dropping his head in his hands.

'Losel, stint laughing! How can we know it was not true, that tale?'

'As true as the tale that Bel sire was the son of a Flemish lavender!'

'*What?*' Harry gasped.

'Did Father never tell you? Oh, I must, then!' John said, and did so.

To both of them the tale seemed so absurd that in laughing at it Harry's large claims to France were for the time forgotten. A chance word brought the Beauforts to mind: Harry said that Sir Thomas was not overly pleased to have been summoned to Westminster to attend another Council meeting. 'I had liefer Henry were Chancellor,' he said. 'Thomas can scantly be made to heed any matter that is not one of admiralty. Nor is he so witty a man as Henry.'

'No, but Father likes him better.'

'Father likes neither, but Henry he hates, because Henry is my friend, and no friend to Arundel. If Father should be amended of his sickness, he will bring Arundel back, and everything I have toiled to accomplish will be overset for very despite.'

'Well, I have no love for the Archbishop myself,' John admitted. 'But is he so much your enemy as that, Harry?'

'Yea, very perfectly my enemy! Who but he contrives that I should have less of the King's confidence than any other in this realm? None but the Archbishop must advise the King! None but he must rule in England! That was why he resigned the Great Seal last year! Well he knew that if *I* sat at the head of the Council I should not fondle him, and extol his wit, and leave all to his judgment! He was always an orgulous man, and always an indurate clodhead – unlettered, too: You should hear what they say in Oxford of his lack-learning! And since the King took him to his bosom he has grown above the moon in his own eyes! Archbishop! The Pope's throne would be scarce high enough for him!' He stopped, and gave a sudden crow of laughter. 'Now, if only he would take it into his head to become Pope! He could be no worse than the man the cardinals elected in May – this John XXIII, who began his worshipful career as Baldassare Cossa, a Barbary corsair, and has more crimes to his credit than you would think could be committed by any one man.'

'Is this one of your merry gestes?' demanded John.

'No, alas!' Harry answered, laughter fading. 'It is a great abusion. It is even noised in Rome that he poisoned the late Pope. That may be: what is sure is that we have a gig for Pope – a beastly fornicator!'

'Certes, Arundel could be no worse!' John said. 'Even you, Harry, cannot charge him with that!'

3

John could not remember that he had enjoyed any period in his life more than the two weeks he spent at Cold Harbour. He was several times required to appear before the Council, but his affairs seemed to be progressing favourably, and when he left these sessions he had nothing to do but to amuse himself. He and Harry snatched two days at Windsor, staying at Birdsnest Lodge, and hunting the roe deer with Edward. Edward had become the King's Master of Game. He was delighted to arrange a royal hunt for the princes, though he thought it a great pity John had not come south in August, when he could have chased the hart. However, he was not one who despised the roebuck: indeed, he told the princes that if it were only as fair a beast as the hart it would be better worth the chasing, since it would run longer, and more cunningly, and had no season. He ordained a splendid gathering, warning over-even the sergeant of the office, the yeomen berners at horse, and the lymerer, and laying strict injunctions on the parkers to attend upon these officials. He showed the princes excellent sport, too; and the only thing that marred his own pleasure was Harry's failure to leave a long enough interval between the blowing of the moots for the first prisc. 'Half an Ave Maria between the first four moots and the second – and the second you must blow a little longer, as I have told you fore-oft, Harry!' he said severely.

'Well, if we take another buck, you shall blow the prise,' said Harry.

'For God's bane, Harry, will you bear in mind what I tell you? It is the chief personage present who must sound the prise! Now, bethink you, dearworth, what will men say of you when you come to be King, and cannot well sound the prise?'

'Pleaseth it your mastership,' Harry meekly replied, 'they will say that I was ill-taught – by my fat cousin of York!'

Edward rumbled a laugh, but he shook his head as well, because it seemed to him a melancholy fault in Harry that he was not out of measure fond of hunting.

At Cold Harbour, John found a way of life far different from the more formal rule kept at Westminster. No one could, when he chose, present to the world a more regal aspect, but there was not in all Christendom a more accessible prince, or one who would more readily put off his royalty than Harry. He had a genius for friendship; and if it was the magnet of his charm which first drew into his net such unlikely persons as Sir Thomas Erpingham, his father's staunch adherent, or a sober city merchant, it was his unaffected cordiality which kept them ensnared. Those who suspected that his interest in their concerns sprang from an easy affability discovered that it was real, and that he neither forgot the troubles that were confided to him, nor spared the pains to alleviate them. Nothing pleased him more than to be able to serve his friends; and nothing could have been more endearing than his manner of granting boons. An embarrassed petitioner, haltingly beseeching his intervention, found his prince eager to help him, but absurdly bashful, blushing to the roots of his hair, stammering a little, and shying away from gratitude. He was prodigal of alms, too: much too prodigal, said John Spenser, the controller of his household, imploring him, for the sake of his mounting debts, to be more sparing of largesse. There was always a throng of suppliants at his gates, and no man displaying a patch over his eye, or the stump of a limb, ever failed to arouse his compassion. As for those who had at some time served him, the gateward knew better than to turn them away. An old groom, fallen on evil days, must be given an allowance from his privy purse, if the King could not be induced to grant him a corrody; while his nurse, whenever she presented herself at Cold Harbour, must be received with all the deference due to ladies of high estate, and on no account be allowed to depart before she had seen her nurseling. No matter how busy he might be, no matter how deeply sunk in one of his morose fits, he would always see Johanna Waring, and submit patiently to her fondling, and her unwelcome anecdotes of his sickly infancy.

After a very few days under his roof, John would scarcely have been surprised to have found himself dining with a jack-raker, so mixed was the company Harry kept. You never knew whom you would find at Cold Harbour. It might be Bishop Henry Beaufort, from Winchester House, in Southwark; or Bishop Langley, his disciple, dropping down the river from Durham Place; or Richard Courtenay; or the learned Dr Patrington, discussing abstruse theology with Robert Mascal, a fellow Carmelite, and Harry's confessor. It might be the Lord FitzHugh, being encouraged by Harry, at his most mischievous, to prove conclusively to Warwick that he, who had been on several pilgrimages, even penetrating to the Grand Cairo, fighting with Saracens and Turks, and erecting a castle on the island of Rhodes, was by far the more experienced traveller.

You might as easily see Harry strolling under the trees in the herber in close conversation with Master Marlowe, who was Mayor of London that year, as walk into the Great Chamber to find him the centre of a merry gathering of his closest friends: the Lords of Masham, and Zouche; Sir John Cornwall, Aunt Bess's husband; his cousin of Arundel; Jack Oldcastle; or the Lord Camoys, who was married to Hotspur's widow, but saw in that alliance no bar to friendship with Harry.

A much more unexpected guest at Cold Harbour was young Mowbray, brother to the ill-fated Earl of Nottingham. He had just attained his full age, but he was still in the King's wardship, unrestored to his brother's honours and estates; and, until quite lately, he had been living with his great-aunt, and the princes' granddam, the Countess of Hereford. He seemed to be still under surveillance, and, like Edmund Mortimer, had been rescued by Harry from loneliness. He was not as shy as Edmund, but he was quite as grateful. John, concealing his surprise at finding him at Cold Harbour, greeted him with easy kindness, and wondered how his overtures would be received. But Jack Mowbray seemed to bear him no ill-will. He was a pleasant youth, eager to prove himself, and bearing little resemblance to his dead brother. Ralph Neville, who met him at Cold Harbour at dinner one day, said that he was a very likely lad, and rapidly passed his unmarried daughters under mental review.

To yet another class of person were Harry's doors open. A middle-aged Benedictine could often be encountered, lovingly inspecting the books in Harry's library, or reading his latest ballad to a select company. This was a very cultured man, who had been a schoolmaster, with his own school, at Bury St Edmunds, which he had founded for the sons of noblemen. Harry introduced him to John as the author of the *London Lackpenny*, so that John, who, like every other lettered young man, had read and hugely enjoyed this popular poem, knew that he just be John Lydgate, and counted it an honour to grasp his hand. He had easy, polished manners, and a humorous face; and he had known and loved Master Chaucer. He knew Master Chaucer's son, too, but he had too much lip-wisdom to talk of Thomas Chaucer at Cold Harbour. If the Lancaster princes were agreed on nothing else, they were at one in their dislike of this thrusting, hard-faced shire-knight, and viewed with hostility his growing wealth and power. From small beginnings, he had become Constable of Wallingford Castle, Chief Butler for life, and had married a Burghersh, daughter and co-heiress of a considerable landowner. The Commons had twice elected him to be their Speaker; and he plainly thought himself a man of worship. But Harry, who cherished a copy of *Troylus and Criseyde*, bound for him in rich velvet, said that Master Chaucer, of dear memory, was a man of greater worship; and Humfrey went so far as to assert that men would revere the father when the son had been for centuries forgotten.

John Lydgate was accustomed to moving amongst the nobly born, and he knew exactly how to demean himself to their liking that even so haughty a lord as the Earl of Warwick accepted him graciously. But not all Harry's mockery or his cajolery could induce Warwick to unbend towards Thomas Hoccleve, another of the poets who enjoyed Harry's favour. He said that Hoccleve was a despisable clap-dish; a mere cockney clerk, with a knack of stringing lewd verses together, and one whom it was quite beneath Harry's dignity to notice. 'A brothel-ing, and a haunter of taverns and stews,' said Warwick disdainfully. 'I love not such wastegoods!'

'Richard, Richard, love you not *me*?' demanded Harry.

But Warwick would not be beguiled. 'To the roots of my heart, Harry, but I wish you might learn to be more sad!' he said.

'I will – in time coming!' promised Harry.

Meanwhile, he continued to encourage his disreputable poet, who was really, John thought, the merriest of spilltimes. He was indeed a haunter of taverns – in fact, he lived, somewhat precariously, in one – and there was not a cookshop in West-minster with which he was not familiar. He admitted unblush-ingly to being a glutton and a wine-bibber, and an incorrigible wencher; but he had a fund of good stories to tell, and he remained cheerful in the face of many adversities. He was employed as a clerk in the office of the Privy Seal, but his wages never seemed to have been paid to him, or the pension the King had granted him either, so that he was always announcing himself to be on the point of trotting into Newgate.

'Dreadless, he treads the slippery ways of life,' said Bishop Beaufort, 'but only our very reverend father in God at Lambeth could suppose that he, or any man, could lead Harry into them.' His penetrating gaze went past John; he demanded, with a touch of asperity: 'Now, what made Cornwall bring that springald to this gathering?'

They were seated in the window-embrasure of the Great Chamber, after one of Harry's supper parties. Harry's musicians had been discoursing music to the company, but Henry Scrope had coaxed him to take up his harp, and to sing a song of his own composing. He had just discarded the harp for a gitern, and was regaling the company with quite a different ditty. It was as well that his confessor, who considered him to be too much addicted to music, was not present to hear such unchaste rhymes; his uncle, when a rusty line reached his ears, merely smiled; and the younger members of the party sang the refrain with gusto, and clamoured for more.

John turned his head, to follow the direction of the Bishop's eyes. Seated on a stool, and hugging his knees, was young Jack Holland, a sturdy stripling, very smart in a new pourpoint, his freckled countenance one large grin, as he watched his fascinating cousin. 'Between you and me, and God before, Henry,' John replied ruefully, '*I* bade him to supper tonight!'

'I thought you had more kind-wit,' said the Bishop. 'He's scarcely out of his swaddling-bands! *Why* did you bid him to supper?'

John had bidden his cousin to supper because his Aunt Bess had told him that if he wished to please her he would bring poor little Jack to Harry's notice. Sir John Cornwall was indurate in refusing to take Jack to Cold Harbour. He said that Jack was too young for Harry's parties, but that, Bess assured her nephew, was a very unthrifty way to talk, since Jack was fifteen, and well grown for his years. Besides, if no one made a push to help him, what was to become of him? It was plain that Bess, despairing of bullying her brother into restoring Jack to his father's dignities, had turned her still brilliant eyes towards the rising sun. That was what came of paying mannerly visits to one's aunts, John realized, particularly on Aunt Bess, who was not a whit less redoubtable than she had been in her tempestuous youth. She had a fiery temper, too: there had been nothing for it but to bid Jack to Cold Harbour, and to cry Harry mercy for having done it. Harry said he cared not a rush whom John bade to his inn, but he would dearly have loved to have seen his large brother put to rout by Aunt Bess. 'But as for bringing Jack to my notice, I've seen him full-oft: he's been squiring John Cornwall this year past. I don't know much about him, though. Let him come! If we don't like him, we can give him the bells and let him fly!'

John knew his astute uncle well enough to be sure that there was no need for him to explain all this. He merely said: 'Well, I went to visit my aunt, you see.'

The Bishop saw exactly, as his lively eyes betrayed. 'Bess!' he uttered, conveying in this scathingly delivered monosyllable his unflattering opinion of his half-sister. He brooded over her for a minute, looking, John thought irreverently, very like a falcon, with his predatory beak of a nose, and his hard, fixed stare. Then he appeared to dismiss Bess and her son from his mind, and turned his face towards John, looking him over critically. 'Well, John?' he said. 'I have not had as many as two words with you alone since you came to town. You spoke very well before the Council, let me tell you! You should be on it, of course! Have you ever regretted that command in the North, which you so greatly desired?'

John considered the question, remembering humiliations, endless, unrewarded toil, mutinous garrisons, the unforgettable grace of a tern's flight, the swathes of purple heather on the moors, and the sharpness of the wind that swept across them. 'No,' he said. 'Grant me only the means to pay my men, and repair my holds, and I shall be content.'

'Well,' said the Bishop, with a gleam of amusement in his eyes, 'Harry says he will not rest – or let us rest – until you have them, so I expect you will! Harry's fell energy! He has attended every meeting of the Council that has been held this year – and so many of them have there been that some of our number were driven to protest! He allows us no leisure.'

'Or himself,' John said, smiling. 'I know Harry!'

'Or himself,' agreed the Bishop. 'No force but that he has achieved what no other could, but young cocks love no coops, and he is impatient still, and would turn the world up-so-down, if he could. Green wood! But ripening fast, I promise you.' He regarded through half-closed eyes a great ring he wore upon his finger, and said: 'If the King should mishappily be unable to take upon himself again the government of this realm, he will find that in Harry he has a passing excellent successor.'

'Successor?'

There was a note in John's voice which the Bishop recognized, and dispassionately approved. He was glad to know that he had not been mistaken six years ago when he had perceived in the King's third son the seeds of mastery. Just like Harry, he thought: thus far, and not an inch farther would he let you go with him. 'Deputy,' he amended, with a faint smile.

4

John went back to Northumberland having at last achieved, he felt, something he had set out to win. After much questioning, and much haggling, the Council had promised to Berwick the sum of two thousand six hundred and sixty-six pounds for the pay of the garrison. It was not the half of the sum for which he had petitioned, nor could it be sent to him outright, but it was more than he had succeeded in wringing from the Council for many a day. In spite of forced loans, money was woefully scarce; but Henry Scrope was confident that the sum could be raised within a few months by making diligent enquiry throughout the land into the annual incomes of all persons of worship, and of imposing a fine of three pounds on any gentleman possessed of an income of forty pounds a year who refused to take the order of knighthood. This was an ancient practice, invariably adopted in times of financial distress, and always productive of considerable revenue. Anyone who had the right to coat-armour, and who was possessed of lands to the value of a knight's fee, was technically compelled to take the order; but as the honour carried with it many chargeous obligations the majority of the squirearchy, unambitious to excel in feats of arms, was glad to compound for a relatively small fine.

By November the first substantial instalment of the sum promised him was sent to John in Berwick; and before he travelled south again, to spend Christmas-tide at Kenilworth, he had had word from Harry that the second would be forthcoming early in the New Year.

It had been hoped that the King would have been well enough to have returned to London before the winter, but December found him still in the Midlands, fluctuating in health, sometimes fretting to resume the charge of his affairs, but more often, to the grief of those who loved him, listless, and disinclined to exert himself. His closest friends, visiting him in his seclusion, came away heavy-hearted to see him so unlike himself; and none who had seen the ravages of his disease was surprised when at the last he chose to travel no farther south than to Kenilworth.

It seemed strange to be spending Christmas-tide otherwhere than at Eltham Palace. As he rode into the outer bailey, it occurred to John that he had never revisited Kenilworth since a golden summer, many years past, when Father had returned from his pilgrimage. Dimly he could remember Father playing at handball with Sir Peter Buckton, teaching Harry and Thomas their knightly exercises, playing at chess with Mother. There had been dogs, too: little spaniels, like the one Harry possessed; and masons at work on an enormous hall. The memory of a rose-pink castle, perpetually sun-soaked, came to him, and he raised his eyes to look at the great Norman keep. No, he didn't remember it. Had it always been that rather ugly red? Perhaps, when the sun shone, the stones took on a softer hue. No building looked its best on a grey winter's day, after all.

Within the inner bailey he dismounted, and stood for a moment, looking about him. His first feeling was of disappointment to find the castle much smaller than he had remembered. It had seemed to him, as a child, immense; but he now saw that it was considerably smaller than his own castle of Warkworth.

The Great Hall was certainly a magnificent erection; but the buildings on the south side of the bailey looked scarcely large enough to contain the family. As for the keep, if that was where the grooms and the valets were to be housed, there would be a great deal of grutching from them. Some of the old, slit windows had been enlarged, and glazed, but there were very few of them, and the grim mass of masonry held out no promise of interior comfort. He began to think that they were all of them going to spend a discomfortable twelve days at Kenilworth, huddled so close together that tempers would be rubbed, and quarrels break out.

But in the end it passed off much better than might have been expected. The King, though he looked very ill, and moved as if even to put one foot before the other cost him an effort, was pathetically glad to have gathered his sons round him again. When he asked them if they remembered living at Kenilworth many years ago, the dreadful change in him was brought home to them, and for a moment none of them could answer him. Then Harry said, in a gentle voice: 'Verily, sir.'

It made Harry's gorge rise to look upon his father's face, disfigured as it was with evil eruptions; and his eyes flinched from the sight of his gloved hand. One of the King's fingers was missing: rotted away. If his malady was not leprosy, it was hideously akin to that awful scourge; but his physicians still maintained that it was not. The Queen – one could hardly blame her – had made them swear to her on a very holy relic that there was no danger to anyone touching the King.

The Queen was at Kenilworth, not complaining about anything, but unable to forbear the wish that it had pleased the King to be carried to Eltham, or to Westminster, where he would have been very much more comfortable. For herself, it was well known that she could be content to live in a hovel, but it grieved her to be unable to house the princes as befitted their estates. Harry, in particular, should have had the Sainteowe tower, adjoining the Great Hall, and linking this with the King's Great Chamber, allotted to him; but although she had lain awake all night, trying to think how this might be achieved, it was quite impossible, and she had been obliged to agree to the Groom of the Chambers' suggestion that dear John should share the tower with him.

As soon as he set foot inside the Sainteowe tower, memory came flooding back to John. He exclaimed: 'This was our nursery! And there is a great lake outside!'

He strode over to the window, and thrust it open, leaning out. The Mere could be seen beyond the curtain wall, a huge sheet of water, protected, on the eastern side, by a large outwork, known as the Brays. John was delighted to find that memory had not cheated him, but he was obliged to admit that the prospect, on a winter's day, was not very cheerful. Kenilworth was certainly not a winter palace.

It was a quiet Christmas, but if it was enlivened by few sports and mummings it was also undisturbed by quarrels. The King and his eldest son seemed to be more in accord than they had been for a long time. The Queen said that Harry's visit was doing her dear lord a great deal of good. It had roused him from his accidie. All the year, he had hardly seemed to care in what case his affairs stood, but now that Harry was here he had begun to take an interest again.

It was quite true. The King had many talks with Harry, not saying much himself, but listening, and interpolating now and then comments or questions which showed his mind to be still shrewd and alert. Harry must have used great lip-wisdom during these sessions, John thought, for the King's jealousy slept throughout the twelve days. He gave the Queen a little credit for this: there was no doubt that she really did try to smooth Harry's path, assuring him always that she would use her best endeavours to further his desires. It had hitherto been supposed that Humfrey was her favourite amongst her stepsons, but it now appeared that it was Harry for whom she felt the tenderest affection, and the greatest admiration. In her weak, woman's way, she said, she had new and new tried to persuade the King to give Harry more of his confidence, believing, as she did, that no one knew better than he just what should be done at every turn.

Harry himself said rather grimly that the happier relations with his father were due to the absence of the Archbishop.

366

'That breedbait,' was what Harry called his grand-uncle Arundel. 'When he is not at hand to whisper in Father's ear that I am a rash-head striving to overset him, I can bring Father round my thumb. But he is not as witty as once he was, John. For a little, he can see as clearly as ever he did, but that does not long endure. He forgets, too. I have said the same things three and four times within an hour – and he used to have the keenest remembrance of any I ever knew – even you!'

Harry had talked to the King of the civil war in France, feeling his way cautiously at first, but soon finding that in this his father took a shrewd interest. The King was at one with him in thinking that if England lent support to either of the factions it should be to Burgundy; and in considering the possibilities inherent in English intervention he became so much like his old, energetic self that Harry feared he had excited him too much. He seemed to think that if an expedition set forth for France he would himself lead it: a suggestion that would seriously have alarmed Harry, who had the poorest opinion of his generalship, had it not been so obviously absurd.

Perhaps he had indeed said too much: on the following day, the King kept his bed; and the princes, released from attendance on him, conceived the happy idea of riding to Warwick Castle, and taking Richard Beauchamp by surprise. Off they went, all four of them, with a tail of grooms and squires. The cavalcade clattered into the bailey at Warwick just as my lord and his lady were sitting down to dinner in the Great Hall, but there was never any real hope, as Harry had prophesied, of startling Richard out of his calm. It had been their intention to demean themselves like humble persons, giving up their basilards to the porter at the gate, walking unheralded into the Hall, pulling off their hoods and gloves there, and, after bowing to the company, standing meekly before the screen until it should either please an usher to lead them to table, or Richard should catch sight of them.

But Richard, who lived in princely state, kept servants far too well trained to make this jape possible. Minutes before Harry could tell him to forbear, the porter had recognized royal liveries approaching, and had sent a page flying with the news. The page panted it to an usher, and the usher nipped across to the Marshal of the Hall with it, and by the time the princes were half-way across the inner bailey my lord himself had reached the door, and was coming to meet them, with a cloud of men in his livery at his heels. He was not in the least discomposed; nor were the officials of his household. Within the Hall, the Marshal cast a competent eye over the new dispositions at the high table which the grooms and ushers were swiftly making under the direction of the butler; and the only person to be flustered was my lord's Countess, who was shy of company. She was inclined to be sickly, too; and, so far, the only living outcome of her union with Warwick was a brace of maid-children, which made her feel herself to be despisable. However, if she must entertain unbidden guests, she had liefer by far that these should be the King's sons than certain of the noble ladies of her acquaintance. The princes were unlikely to look at her with eyes of galling pity; and she hoped they wouldn't notice that she was wearing her second-best robe.

Misgivings about her attire soon vanished: the princes were wearing leather jerkins and buskins, for which Harry, raising her from a deep curtsy, and kissing her hand, begged her pardon. They were all plainly in holiday humour; and she could see, by the wry smile on my lord's face, that as usual, he was the victim of their unsparing tongues. The Lord John, it seemed, was complaining that when he appeared before the Council, Richard had scantly deigned to recognize him; and the Lord Thomas was explaining, in an audible aside, that ever since he had become a member of the Council Richard had grown too stomachy to recognize any of them but Harry. The Countess's eyes went apprehensively to her lord's face, for although he was a kind husband, she stood in some awe of him, and was always afraid, when the princes made him their bobbing-block, that he might take displeasure. Heaven grant that my lord's new fool, catching the infection of the princes' merriness, should not be emboldened to utter any perilous japes!

But my lord's fool was far too ware to run the risk of a whipping, or worse, by saying one word that could be thought to bear on the King's infirmity, or the Archbishop's quarrel with Dean Courtenay. His predecessor had been sent packing for making quite a mild sally about young cockerels and old cocks, and was now reduced to a wayfaring life, travelling about the country from fair to fair with a tumbling girl. Fortunately, the garboils in France provided plenty of good stuff for japes, which were certain to please. You might even venture so far as to mime the antics of a mad king without seeing the countenances of the royal guests stiffen ominously. Heartened by the Lord Thomas's first shout of laughter, the fool excelled himself, won largesse from the princes, and an approving nod from his lord, and retired triumphant. It had been his first attempt, in my lord's household, to amuse guests of high rank, and he felt that he was now reasonably assured of permanent employment.

5

It was on their ride home from Warwick that Harry, ranging alongside John's stout hackney, told John that he wanted a lasting truce with Scotland.

'How lasting?' demanded John.

'At the least, two years, and for as many more as you and Ralph can contrive. Could you bring it about?'

'Perhaps – at a price. It wouldn't give us peace on the Border. There would be raiding still, and Albany would declare he had had no tokening of such outlawry.'

'That, possibly, but it would take from us the threat of invasion in force.'

'It might do that,' John agreed.

'A settled truce would be speedful,' Harry said. 'I've talked with Father about the French business, and I found him apt. If Burgundy makes us offers, I – we – must have peace on the Border – or what passes for peace there. He will do that, I think. The mettle of Orleans has grown apace since Armagnac took on himself the charge of his affairs, and all the tidings we've received out of France show the Fearless to be hard bestad. Armagnac has Germans and Gascons in his pay now. Burgundy must soon look about him for allies, and what other way should he look but this?'

So when John journeyed north again, in the spring, it was

with instructions to negotiate a long truce. But before he left London, Sir Robert Umfraville, acting as lieutenant for the Admiral of the North, and taking advantage of the expiration of the truce, had put to sea with six vessels, which carried, besides their crews, a small force of men-at-arms and archers, and had sailed boldly up the Forth, doing great scathe. The Scots were taken unawares, for it was by no means the season for expeditions by sea, and before a sufficient number of ships of war could be sent to engage his tiny fleet, he was away, with thirteen captured vessels crammed with every sort of merchandize, from wheat to wines and spices. He brought this rich booty home to his enfamined countrymen, winning great worship. He had seen a good deal of fighting, for the Scots had put out in cogs and barges to try to drive him off almost every day, and he had sustained some losses; but he had cruised in the Forth for no fewer than fourteen days. It seemed incredible that he could have done it, and returned with such prizes, but no one who knew him doubted the tale. He was always ready to lead what other men thought foolhardy ventures, and he was amazingly fortunate. Four years earlier, he had swept across the Border in a retaliatory raid, and had burnt the town of Peebles. That had been in revenge for Berwick, and it had earned him a new name. He had descended on the town on market-day, and the Scots had called him ever since Robin Mendmarket.

Harry feared that his latest exploit might prejudice the chances of negotiating a lasting truce, but John believed it would rather facilitate his work: it would certainly take from the Scots some of their bobance.

So it proved. John was busy throughout April and May, arranging, with Ralph Neville, the preliminaries, and by the end of May matters were far enough advanced for a Commission to be appointed to treat with the Scottish Earls of March and Douglas at Handenstank.

It was headed by Warwick, Westmoreland, and Bishop Langley of Durham; and if nothing very definite was agreed to, at least the Scots showed themselves willing to treat. Warwick, instructed by Harry, wanted to push matters on to a conclusion, but Westmoreland, wiser in Border customs, prophesied that the—

[*Here Georgette Heyer's manuscript breaks off. For those interested in the subsequent careers of her characters a historical note is appended*]

Historical Note

Henry IV died in March 1413, and for the remaining months of his father's reign, John remained in the North, keeping peace in the East Marches and fortifying Berwick.

Shortly after the accession of Harry, who thus became Henry V, John was created Duke of Bedford, and in September 1414 he resigned his wardenship. He had a seat on his brother's Council, where he supported Henry's policy of an alliance with Burgundy – as opposed to Humfrey and Thomas (now Dukes of Gloucester and Clarence) who favoured the Orleanist faction in France.

When Henry invaded France in 1415, claiming the French crown for himself, Bedford remained in England as lieutenant of the kingdom. After the success of Henry's Agincourt campaign (where Edward of York died, smothered in his own armour), Bedford led a successful naval expedition to relieve Harfleur, and in 1417, when he was again lieutenant of England in his brother's absence, he and Sir Thomas Beaufort (now Duke of Exeter) successfully repelled a Scots invasion.

Thomas of Clarence had fought in France with his brother, where he had gained the reputation of a brave but rash captain. In March 1421, when he led a small English contingent against a much larger French force at Baugé, he and most of his men were killed.

Henry V had married Catherine, the daughter of the mad King Charles VI of France, and Bedford stood as godfather to their son, also named Henry. He escorted the Queen to France in 1422 to join her husband, and when Henry V fell ill, he took command of the English army there. Henry died on August 31st, naming Bedford guardian of England and the young king,

Henry VI, and he also became Regent of France when Philip of Burgundy, son of John the Fearless, declined that office.

Bedford's responsibilities were now enormous. He was faced with prosecuting the war in France, where he proved himself an able and prudent general, and in his administration of the British possessions there – Normandy, Maine and Guienne – he tried to give good government and to restore prosperity and order. The key to his policy was the Burgundian alliance, and he found this endangered when Humfrey of Gloucester, who filled his place in England during his absence, married a kinswoman of Burgundy, Jacqueline of Hainault, and claimed her lands – lands which Philip of Burgundy had hoped to gain for himself.

Humfrey of Gloucester proved himself a selfish and faithless character in public life, constantly intriguing for his own ends and stirring up faction whenever Bedford was not there. His title 'The Good Duke' depends only on his literary interests. His irresponsible behaviour contributed greatly to Bedford's difficulties.

However, the alliance with Burgundy was strengthened by Bedford's marriage in 1423 to the Duke's eighteen-year-old sister, Anne, described by a chronicler of the time as 'bonne et belle'. The Duke and Duchess of Bedford held their court at Paris in considerable state, and Anne also accompanied her husband on his journeys and campaigns, returning with him to England in 1426, where he acted as peacemaker in a quarrel between Humfrey of Gloucester and Bishop Henry Beaufort.

Meanwhile, King Charles VI of France had died, his son, Charles VII, was as yet uncrowned, and French fortunes were at a low ebb. In 1424 Bedford had won a great victory at Verneuil over a far larger French army supported by a Scottish contingent. The enemy losses were enormous. The Armagnac army was completely routed and their Scottish allies, led by the Earl of Douglas, were annihilated. The French called it a second Agincourt. In 1429 the English were besieging Orleans, but then the tide turned. Jeanne d'Arc persuaded the Dauphin that under divine guidance she could lead French troops to victory, and in April 1429 she relieved Orleans, and in July Charles was crowned at Rheims. Jeanne d'Arc then advanced on Paris, but turned away from battle with Bedford, who had gathered together troops to bar her way. Normandy wavered in its allegiance to the English and Philip of Burgundy made a truce with Charles at Compiègne. Bedford reacted swiftly: he resigned the regency in Paris to Burgundy, and thus regained his support, and set off to campaign in Normandy.

Jeanne d'Arc had failed to storm Paris in September and in May 1430 she was captured by John of Luxembourg, an ally of Burgundy's. He sold her to the English through Pierre Cauchon, the Bishop of Beauvais, who claimed her as a heretic caught in his diocese. The Church, rather than Bedford himself, directed her trial as a sorceress and heretic, and she was burnt at Rouen in May 1431.

In 1432 the English lost Chartres, and later that year Bedford's duchess, Anne, died, to the grief of her husband and his Burgundian allies. The following year, whem campaigning in the region of Calais, Bedford allied himself to the powerful Count of St Pol by marrying his daughter Jacqueline of Luxembourg. However, he had done this without consulting the Count's overlord, Burgundy, and the rift between Philip and himself, weakened already by Anne's death, widened.

Bedford returned to England to justify his conduct of the war before Parliament, and to help the finances of the realm he offered to take only £1,000 as his salary as Chief Counsellor – in the same position Humfrey of Gloucester had taken £5,000. In June 1434 he returned to France for the last time. His vigorous prosecution of the war helped the English and Burgundians to gain much ground, but he was forced to agree to Burgundy's request to send ambassadors to a council held at Arras the following year to discuss peace. Unable to agree to the French terms, the English ambassadors finally quitted the council, leaving Burgundy to ally himself to Charles VII.

The cause for which Bedford had laboured so long was ruined, and he himself died a few days later, on 14th September 1435, at Rouen. His death removed from English politics a restraining and conciliatory influence, and from now on, under the weak rule of the young Henry VI, party strife amongst the great nobles sharpened, order in the country began to decline, and so did trust in the King's government. The conditions that were eventually to lead to the Wars of the Roses were already evident. In France, the English were never again to regain the commanding position and great territories they had briefly won and held under Henry V and Bedford.

John was buried in the cathedral of Notre Dame at Rouen. Some years later King Louis XI of France, being counselled to deface his tomb, replied:

'What honour shall it be, either to us or to you, to break the monument, and to rake out of the earth the bones of one, who, in his lifetime, neither my father, nor any of your progenitors, with all their puissance were ever once able to make fly one foot backwards; that by his strength or policy, kept them all out of the principal dominions of France, and out of this noble duchy of Normandy?

Wherefore, I say, first, God save his soul, and let his body rest in quiet; which, when he was living, would have disquieted the proudest of us all; and, as for the tomb, which, I assure you, is not so worthy as his acts deserve, I account it an honour to have him remain in my dominions.'

The House of
Plantagenet and its Branches

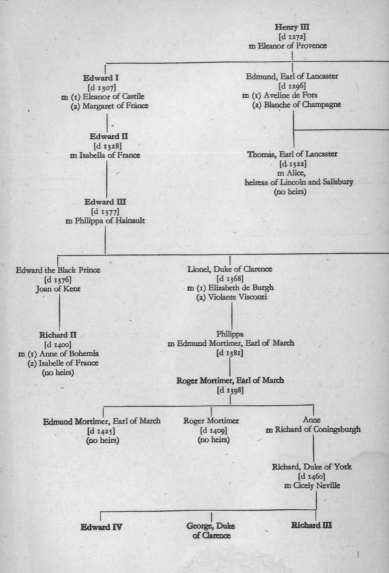

Henry III
[d 1272]
m Eleanor of Provence

Edward I
[d 1307]
m (1) Eleanor of Castile
   (2) Margaret of France

Edmund, Earl of Lancaster
[d 1296]
m (1) Aveline de Fors
   (2) Blanche of Champagne

Edward II
[d 1328]
m Isabella of France

Thomas, Earl of Lancaster
[d 1322]
m Alice,
heiress of Lincoln and Salisbury
(no heirs)

Edward III
[d 1377]
m Philippa of Hainault

Edward the Black Prince
[d 1376]
Joan of Kent

Lionel, Duke of Clarence
[d 1368]
m (1) Elizabeth de Burgh
   (2) Violante Visconti

Richard II
[d 1400]
m (1) Anne of Bohemia
   (2) Isabelle of France
(no heirs)

Philippa
m Edmund Mortimer, Earl of March
[d 1381]

Roger Mortimer, Earl of March
[d 1398]

Edmund Mortimer, Earl of March
[d 1425]
(no heirs)

Roger Mortimer
[d 1409]
(no heirs)

Anne
m Richard of Coningsburgh

Richard, Duke of York
[d 1460]
m Cicely Neville

Edward IV

George, Duke
of Clarence

Richard III

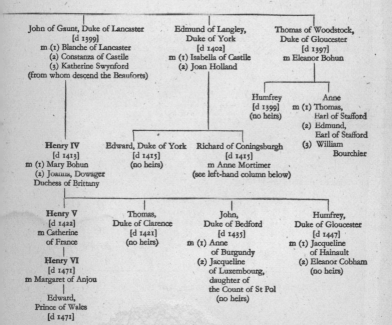

Beatrice
m John, Duke of Brittany
[d 1305]

and heirs following

Henry, Earl of Lancaster
[d 1345]

Henry, Duke of Lancaster
[d 1361]

Blanche
m John of Gaunt
(see below)

John of Gaunt, Duke of Lancaster
[d 1399]
m (1) Blanche of Lancaster
(2) Constanza of Castile
(3) Katherine Swynford
(from whom descend the Beauforts)

Edmund of Langley,
Duke of York
[d 1402]
m (1) Isabella of Castile
(2) Joan Holland

Thomas of Woodstock,
Duke of Gloucester
[d 1397]
m Eleanor Bohun

Humfrey
[d 1399]
(no heirs)

Anne
m (1) Thomas,
Earl of Stafford
(2) Edmund,
Earl of Stafford
(3) William
Bourchier

Henry IV
[d 1413]
m (1) Mary Bohun
(2) Joanna, Dowager
Duchess of Brittany

Edward, Duke of York
[d 1415]
(no heirs)

Richard of Coningsburgh
[d 1415]
m Anne Mortimer
(see left-hand column below)

Henry V
[d 1422]
m Catherine
of France

Thomas,
Duke of Clarence
[d 1421]
(no heirs)

John,
Duke of Bedford
[d 1435]
m (1) Anne
of Burgundy
(2) Jacqueline
of Luxembourg,
daughter of
the Count of St Pol
(no heirs)

Humfrey,
Duke of Gloucester
[d 1447]
m (1) Jacqueline
of Hainault
(2) Eleanor Cobham
(no heirs)

Henry VI
[d 1471]
m Margaret of Anjou

Edward,
Prince of Wales
[d 1471]

Glossary

accesse fever, illness

accidie noon-day sickness, sloth, torpor

advowson right of presentation to a church or spiritual living

airling coxcomb, sycophant

alaunt large, usually fierce hound with a short broad head

alder-first first of all

alder-liefest dearest (alder=most)

ambage ambiguity, circumlocution

apertly openly

assoil absolve (from sin)

asotted besotted

astringer keeper of goshawks

awhape amazed

baggingly squint-eyed

banker bench with a tapestry covering

bardings horse armour

barful ominous, dangerous

barmekin battlement of a castle's outer fortification, with stables on the inside

bascinet light steel head-piece

bastlard dagger

bate (falcony) to beat the wings impatiently and flutter away from fist or perch

bawdekin silk, brocade

becks beckonings

berner huntsman in charge of a pack of hounds

bestad circumstanced

blanch-powder white powder sprinkled over apples, pears or sweets

blazing star comet

bobance pride, pomp, boasting

bolding encouragement

borel-folk rough, unlettered people

bowes (1) provisions of a benefice granted by the Pope
(2) postern gate

brassart upper arm armour

bratchet worthless wretch (northern)

bretheling coxcomb, sycophant

brose broth, spoonmeats

buxom obedient

caltraps iron balls with spikes so placed that one is always pointing up. Used to discourage pursuit

camail piece of chain mail attached to the helmet to protect the neck

cameline stuff, supposedly of camel's hair

cand-pie disappointment, loss (northern)

cautelous artful, deceitful

chacechien attendant on hounds

chalons bed coverings, blankets

chamberer chambermaid, or intriguer

chapman merchant

checklatoun costly silk from which gowns were made

chevauchée raid, expedition

chinchery stinginess, niggardly

clapping chattering, idle talk

clyster injection

cog broadly-built boat

corrody prebend or allowance

coudière armour protecting the elbow

covetise avarice

crackows shoes with six-inch long turned-up toes stuffed with moss

curtilage court or yard attached to a castle or dwelling-house

dagged edges of a garment having been cut into long pointed jags

dauberer plasterer

dennocks oatcakes

despitously contemptuously, scornfully

destrier war-horse

devoir duty

dirige original form of "dirge"

dorser ornamental cloth

doucet custard or pasty

dragés sweets

drammocks oatmeal and water (northern)

dreadless without doubt

dwale opiate

escheat reversion of a fief to a superior in default of a lawful heir or upon attainder

even-Christians fellow men

favel flattering

Felice Quean, harlot

ferly strange, a wonder

ferne-ago long ago

fetching crafty scheme

fewterer keeper of greyhounds

file harlot

flawn custard, pancake

fleer mock, laugh at scornfully

fliting strife, contending

foison plenty

forlogne (hunting) to leave behind at a distance, or note of recall on a horn

forstraught distracted

franchise privilege or exceptional right

frape crowd, pack

fripperer old clothes man

gainbite remorse

gaingiving misgiving

garboil brawl, tumult

garderobe latrine

gateward porter, guard

genouillière piece of armour protecting the knee

geste deed or tale

gigelot wencher, adulterer, strumpet

gitern guitar

giton pennon

glosery falsehood, flattery

goky foolish

grutching grumbling

guerdon reward

hallings tapestries

handfast troth-plighted, betrothed

hanseline slop, short jacket

hauberk mail shirt

haussepieds (1) tight-fitting stockings (2) traps

herber garden, arbour

hip-halt halting, lame

houpelande loose tunic, slit at the side

hurling strife, tumult

hutch chest, cabin at sea

importable unbearable, insufferable

indulgence remission of sin, relaxation of ecclesiastical law or obligation

indurable not lasting or enduring

indurate obstinate

jack (1) loose coat or tunic of leather, could have mail sewn on, tunic of war (2) common fellow

jack-eater braggart, swashbuckler

jack-raking drudgery, garbage-collecting

janglery jesting

Jeffrey's Day never

jobbard fool

joculator juggler

jongleur harpist, itinerant minstrel, or juggler

jupon a sleeveless surcoat worn outside the armour and emblazoned with arms

kennels gutters alongside a street

kill-cow terrible fellow, braggart (northern)

kind-wit common-sense

lachesse negligence

Langue d' Oil speech of northern France. cf Languedoc

'Lasseir les aler!' 'Let them go!' Signal for the commencement of a tournament

lavender washerwoman

leasings lies

leman mistress

let-game spoil-sport

lewd vulgar or immoral

lickerish amorous

lome often (oft and lome=time and again)

losel worthless creature

lout bow (in salute)

losengery flattery

lurdan fool

lymerer man who tended bloodhounds and other large dogs on the chase

maffling stammering (northern)

malapert presumptuous or impudent person

malten-hearted cowardly, poor-spirited

marchpane marzipan

mawmet, mammet idol or puppet

meiny armed following

mell meddle

mess group of persons feeding together

mimbudget, mumbudget silent

moot blast on a hunting horn

mortrews pounded meat

mouldwarp mole (northern)

mumpish sullenly angry, depressed in spirit

murrey reddish-purple colour

nightertale night-time

nithing cowardly fellow

no force beyond doubt, or no heed

orgulous over-proud

orle narrow band, half the width of the bordure, following the outline of the shield but not extending beyond it

orpiment arsenical ointment

ozey sweet French or Alsatian wine

paindemain fine white bread

papelard hypocrite, pope-holy

Paynim heathen, Saracen

pele, peel small tower without other defences

perdurable permanent, lasting

placebo vespers for the dead

pourpoint stuffed and quilted doublet

prise, pryse blow on a horn to signal that a stag is taken

pursuivant minor herald

quarrier very thick candle

rede advice

redeless lacking good advice, ignorant, unwise

roil rove about

rushbuckler braggart

ruth pity, mercy

'Sa, sa, cy avaunt!' 'Forward, sir, forward!', hunting term when the quarry is in full view

sand-blind half-blind, dim-sighted

scathe hurt, injury

sconce oil lamp

scope-law start (in a race)

sely happy, carefree, innocent, simple

sendal thin, rich silken material or garment

serf-borrow, pledge-borrow pledge, surety

shakebuckler swashbuckler

shamefast modest

shapster female cutter (of cloth or garments)

shendful disgraceful

shent ruined

sickerly assuredly

sieges seats, especially those used by persons of rank

sleeveless useless, unprofitable, leading to nothing

solar parlour

soothsaw true saying

stathe quay, wharf

steerless rudderless

stew slum, brothel

stewpond pond in which fish are kept till wanted for the table

stint cease

strait-keeping thrift

suckfist fool, dolt

surcingle saddle-girths

tabler chessboard

table-dormant side table

tallage tax

tartarin rich silk stuff imported from the east

teen harm, mischief or damage, or angry (northern)

tendable attentive, ready to give ear to

terret leather strap for a hawk

tregetour illusionist, magician

traverse curtain

treatable tractable

trental set of thirty requiem masses or the payment for them

tresâme dear one

trescher 'my most dear'

two-so-much twice

vaward van

ventosity colic

viand royal name of a dish fit for a king or other great guests – usually venison in broth or roasted

villein serf, peasant

void dismount

voider plate for bones and other inedibles to be placed on

wainsman waggoner

warder baton carried as a symbol of office, especially used to give the signal to begin or to halt hostilities in a tournament

whirlicote horse-drawn vehicle

witaldry folly

witterly assuredly, truly

wood mad, distraught

yellowbeak youth, youngster